Arch Wizard

Arch Wizard

ED GREENWOOD

SOLARIS

First published 2009 by Solaris
an imprint of Rebellion Publishing Ltd,
Riverside House, Osney Mead,
Oxford, OX1 0ES, UK

www.solarisbooks.com

ISBN: 978 1 844167 64 7

10 9 8 7 6 5 4 3 2 1

A CIP catalogue record for this book is available from the
British Library.

Designed & typeset by Rebellion Publishing
Printed in the US

The Story Thus Far

ROD EVERLAR, A successful author of Cold War action thrillers and fantasy novels set in his imagined world of Falconfar, is astonished one night when Taeauna—one of a race of good winged warrior women he created for his fantasy books—literally falls out of his dreams, onto his bed.

Badly wounded and beset by sinister black-armored warriors known as Dark Helms (created by a computer game manufacturer who purchased the rights to his world), Taeauna pleads with Rod to aid her—and Falconfar.

Rod discovers that the world he thought was created only in his imagination is all too real—and that its people believe he, Rod Everlar, is its Lord Archwizard or Dark Lord, the most powerful of the "Dooms," powerful wizards who can literally change Falconfar with their magic.

Plunged bewilderingly into a Falconfar that is familiar but also dangerously different from his imaginings, Rod finds himself swept into an ongoing civil war in the kingdom of Galath, where one of the Dooms, the wizard Arlaghaun, is goading the King of Galath into establishing absolute tyranny over the Galathan nobles.

For years, the three Dooms—the wizards Arlaghaun, Malraun, and Narmarkoun—have fought each other, in an uneasily balanced struggle wherein none of them could achieve supremacy. Rod's arrival shatters that balance, just as Arlaghaun is on the verge of seizing control over Galath.

There are signs that a long-dead wizard of matchless might, Lorontar—the only Lord Archwizard ever known in Falconfar before Rod—is stirring, somehow still alive (or perhaps not), and seeking to control the living.

At the end of *Dark Lord*, the first novel of Falconfar, the wizard Arlaghaun is slain in the fortress of Ult Tower. The wizard Malraun appears, snatches Taeauna, and magically whisks her away as his captive, leaving Rod Everlar (laden with magical items from Ult Tower he's snatched up but doesn't understand) raging helplessly, wanting to rescue her but not knowing how.

For what happens next, read on…

Chapter One

THE DARK HELMS laughed.

They stood at ease, forming a ring in the dark, torchlit stone chamber, hands on hips, not a blade drawn. In their midst, emerald eyes blazing in fury, clad only in manacles attached to a few rattling links of chain, Taeauna of the Aumrarr swung a sword at them.

A sword that skirled and shrieked as it struck—nothing. Empty air as hard as stone, in front of every Dark Helm. Spells shielded them all from her steel, striking it ringingly aside amid sparks as she slashed and swung and panted, sobbing in frustration.

Rod Everlar snarled out his own frustration, standing in front of the magic mirror with the gauntlet that held the orb raised in front of him, fumbling with Klammert's notes.

"Take me there!" he spat, glaring at Taeauna and the Dark Helms, in the mirror before him. She was in a dungeon or a fortress somewhere—a large, bare, stone-lined chamber with iron torch-sconces in the walls, but that room could be anywhere…

"Take me to Taeauna!"

His shout made the orb against his palm quiver, as if it was an egg trying to hatch, and the gauntlet covering it grew a sudden glow. A glow that washed away again in a handful of instants, leaving the gauntlet as dark as ever.

In the mirror, the Dark Helms were advancing, crowding together, their ring tightening around Taeauna, and they were raising their own gauntleted hands.

"Take... me... to... Taeauna," Rod snapped, spacing the words out slowly in fierce determination as he glared hard at the image of the bare, wingless Aumrarr.

They were starting to slap her now, or rather, swinging their hands at her and letting that stone-hard air bludgeon her, driving her back and reeling, the sword clanging out of her grasp. She fell to her knees, crying out in pain—and Rod, trembling with the head-pounding effort of trying to *will* himself to her, roared out his own wordless rage.

And Ult Tower, around him, flickered and turned golden. The walls, the air...

Everything had a golden hue, as if he was peering through gilded goggles. "Taeauna!" he shouted. "Tay, *I'm coming!*"

In the mirror, Taeauna's head jerked up, and she stared around, wide-eyed in hope, for all Falconfar as if she could hear him.

Against his palm, the orb suddenly started to burn. Around him, the golden hue blazed up brightly, until he could no longer see the walls, the mirror, the very floor under his feet...

There was nothing under his boots, nothing at all! Though the orb was painfully hot and getting hotter, the air around had acquired a chill and was

moving, the faintest of whistles rising past his ears…
Was he falling? Hurtling down to his death, smashed
on unseen rocks below? It didn't *seem* as if he was
descending…

"Taeauna," Rod snarled, clinging to his last image
of her, head lifted in hope, looking around for her.
It didn't feel as if he was falling at all. Around him
there were no walls now—nothing but a fading
golden glow, a radiance as thick as mist that hid
his surroundings from him, yet showed him space,
empty air, further away from him than the walls of
Ult Tower around the magic mirror…

He was rushing along through a great nothingness,
as the golden glow around him ebbed into silver; a
strained and thinning hue that he could see through
now, could see a golden, roiling cloud ahead, a cloud
he was rushing to meet at a speed that made him
blink and swallow.

He was still swallowing when he raced into the
depths of that cloud, surging golden flows of energy
that slowed him and thrust against his arrow-swift
flight, shoving him and buffeting him… as if in a
dream, he became aware that some of the enspelled
armor he was wearing had flared into angry radiances
of its own, and was melting.

Not a fiery death he could feel—there was no heat
at all—but it was shrinking and being clawed away
by the golden mists around him, silently leaving
his limbs in great spreading holes and gaps as he
plunged on. Ahead he could see the torches of the
chamber again, hear the faint laughter of the Dark
Helms as they clustered closely around Taeauna,
chuckles rising in a crescendo as a gasp of pain burst
out of her.

9

"Taeauna!" he cried again, willing himself on. The orb had lost its heat against his skin, and he was slowing... slowing...

Glossy black armor loomed up in front of him, almost close enough to touch. He reached forward, stretching out his arm, straining—and Taeauna's slender, long-fingered hand thrust out between two dark-armored legs, reaching for him, trying to—

The golden radiance surged up in front of him with an audible snarl of power, hiding Taeauna and the Dark Helms and the torches all at once, smashing at his stretching hand... driving it back.

Wincing at the sting in his fingers, Rod shook his bruised hand and thrust it forth again—but the silver mist around him was gone, drowned in angry gold, and he was tumbling, heels snatched above his head and flung back, thrust along in wild and sprawling helplessness, slammed back across uncharted emptiness amid a chaos of angrily-roiling golden fire.

Tumbling crazily over and over, glimpsing momentary rifts and rents in the thundering golden surges, rifts that held silver-shimmering air, tall castles on great fists of rock that floated in midair, bat-winged and hulking beasts with long claws and no heads that waited with arms spread hungrily, and armies galloping with lowered lances through the billowing smoke of dozens of fires... unfamiliar scenes all, faster and faster until Rod was almost weeping in confusion, his head spinning, and—

It ended as swiftly as it had begun, leaving him standing silently in the damp green depths of what looked to be a trackless, seemingly endless forest. Rod Everlar didn't have to look all around to know he'd never seen it before.

"The eternal lost one," he murmured aloud, "who knows not where he is."

Most of his armor had melted away, leaving the various belts and baldrics bristling with pouches and scabbards of hopefully magical stuff sagging loosely around him, but he still had his gauntlets.

With a sigh, Rod tugged off the one covering his left hand, and peered at the small, unblemished orb in his unscarred, unseared palm.

"Take me back," he hissed at it.

Nothing happened.

"Take me to Taeauna," he growled, glaring at it, bending his will upon it as he'd just been doing.

His head started to pound, and the orb quietly cracked apart and collapsed into sand-like grit in his hand.

THE SECOND TIME the great chamber shook, the blue-skinned man sighed and rose from among the dead women who were caressing him.

"They're going to a lot of trouble over this," he murmured, as he plucked his greatcloak off the spire of sculpted rock where he was wont to leave it, shrugged it on over his blue scales, and took up a long, thin black staff from where it leaned against the wall. "I suppose I should be flattered."

The tall man strolled down the great room unhurriedly, his every movement smooth and elegant, spell-glows awakening around the staff in his hand and chasing each other up and down its length.

He was barefoot on the old, smooth stones, and made almost no sound at all as he walked. More noise arose from the dead wenches—rotted away to bared bone in many places—who clung to him and caressed him as he passed. He patted them and smiled upon them, but slowed not at all, as he headed for a rail-less ribbon of stone steps that climbed one curving end wall of the chamber, heading up to the battlements.

The room behind him was dank and cold, but as he ascended the air grew colder, mountain breezes blowing in the open windows ahead.

Those winds brought shouts, and the occasional ringing clangs of swords striking upon metal. Sornspire was besieged.

Built centuries ago by a man long dead, it was neither a pleasant nor a comfortable home. Wizards never seemed to crave comfort as much as one might think they would—or perhaps they spun comfort out of their spells, and needed only privacy and great masses of stone around them to shield them from rivals and stray spell-blasts.

The man with the staff had never given it any thought, for he was not what he seemed to be. The tall stature of Narmarkoun, Doom of Galath, was not the body he'd worn a season ago. From his bald blue head to his long, blue scaly limbs, bared to the icy winds at every stride as the cloak swirled back from his shoulders, his shape was new.

Not that anyone else in Galath—or all wider Falconfar—cared what Malagusk Sorn's tastes in architecture had been. Least of all these knights of Galath, who'd come all this way up into the most inhospitable peaks of southwestern Galath with their army, to bring death to a wizard in the name of King Melander Brorsavar for the unthinkable crime of ignoring his summons to court.

For years, this remote peaktop keep had been a secure enough hide-hold for Narmarkoun. It overlooked the barony of Chainamund, and fat, blustering, sneering Glusk Chainamund had been terrified of wizards. Not without good reason.

"Lack of good reason," the bald, blue-skinned man murmured now, stopping on the battlements to watch men whose armor was sparkling with frost struggle up between the stone merlons to crash their boots down heavily on the battlement walk, and confront him. "That's what causes all of this unpleasantness."

"Wizard Narmarkoun!" one of the knights called sternly. "You are summoned by the King of Galath! Will you come with us now, so that this violence can be ended?"

The blue man strolled forward, carrying his staff as if he'd forgotten he was holding it. "Sir knight, I very much doubt it's in your power to end any violence, anywhere, regardless of what I might do."

At his approach, the knights all raised their shields nervously. Small metal badges had been crudely hammered onto them, badges that flickered and glowed with magic. Almost certainly they bore spells to ward off anything a wizard might hurl.

"So you defy us?" another knight barked.

The tall blue man regarded him calmly. "Not yet."

"'Not yet' my left *haunch!*" the first knight snarled. "Twelve men we lost to your stone statues on the stair, and another seven fighting the walking dead women who guard your walls!"

"Peaceful inhabitants of my castle," the man with the staff replied, "who would have done nothing to you if you'd been invited, or spoken the right words of greeting to them."

"Oh? What words are those?" The knight's bark

was as loud and sudden as a sword-thrust. Several of the dead women's swords had thrust points deep into his metal armor, and his broken ribs hurt like godsfire.

"I am come peacefully to speak to Narmarkoun, rightful ruler of this part of Galath."

"'Rightful ruler' my *right* haunch!"

The wizard shrugged. "If you lose them both, you'll fall down, you know. 'Rightful' might not be a term familiar to a velduke who made himself king bare days ago, but I have held this castle for longer than the lives of King Brorsavar, his sire before him, and his grandsire before that, and in all that time no one else has ruled these few peaks. Chainamund seemed not even to know they were here."

"Enough clever words," the other knight said grimly. "Will you come with us?"

The tall blue man smiled gently, and shook his head. "No. Tell the King of Galath I am too busy keeping him alive, in the face of what the *other* Dooms of Galath are doing, to have time just now for trading little threats with him at court. When Lorontar has been truly destroyed, perhaps."

"Lorontar? Lorontar's been dead for centuries!"

The man with the staff sighed and regarded the glowering knight rather sadly. "If you believe that, Galath has far greater problems than the absence of one reclusive wizard at court."

He turned and strolled away. Some of the knights traded glances behind his back, reached silent accord, and started after him—only to halt in mid-stride when he turned back to face them and added mildly, "I would have thought the absence of a baron to stand in Chainamund's place at court to be of far greater importance to the throne of Galath than my lack of attendance. Or is Melander proposing to offer the barony to me?"

"You?" one of the knights sneered, only to fall silent at a glare from the first knight who'd called out to the wizard.

That knight turned his gaze back to the tall blue man and said simply, "No." Silence fell, and they stood in the cold, faintly whistling mountain wind like statues for long enough that he felt compelled to add, "Three knights administer the barony now, until it should please the king to name a new baron."

The man with the staff nodded, as if he'd already known how matters stood in the barony below, and said almost gently, "And so it goes. Devaer gives way to Melander, yet the knights and nobles of Galath dance the same dances. Obey the royal dancemaster, or fall from grace... and life. Have men sworn to the sword truly nothing better to do?"

Leaving that question hanging in the air unanswered behind him, the tall blue man turned back to the stair that had brought him up onto the battlements in an unhurried swirl of his cloak, and walked away from them.

"Wizard!" one of the knights barked. "Halt!"

The tall man gave no sign that he'd heard.

"Wizard! Surrender!" the knight roared.

Beside him, the first knight called sternly, "Throw down your staff and turn back to us, unleashing no magics! In the name of Brorsavar, King of all Galath, I charge—"

"Ah, yes," the tall blue man murmured, never hesitating in his graceful walk. "Charge."

That quiet command brought dead women suddenly streaming up the stair before him in a naked, gray-skinned flood, swords and glaives and wicked gutting-knives in their hands. He grounded his staff and stood still as they raced past him, sprinting stiffly along the battlements at a dead, barefoot run, heading for the knights, who swore various oaths and hefted swords and shields, instinctively drawing together to form a shield-wall.

"No! Get away!" the first knight bellowed at his fellows, waving his sword. "Stand not together, to give yon wizard a target for his spells! Knights of Galath, may this day beee*uuurk!*"

The dead women were naked and therefore distracting—alluring here and hideous there, where flesh and all had fallen away to lay bare a staring skull above parted lips, or an empty ribcage on one flank where a shapely breast still adorned the other. They were slender women, besides, not battle-trained knights of the realm, and—

When four of them swarmed over a knight at once, not caring in the slightest what his blade bit into in their quick, unfeeling haste to slay him, he went down.

A few of the knights lasted a few struggling steps backwards, slashing and thrusting for all they were worth, and managed to hack down some of the dead women by hewing away limbs. Yet before the man with the staff could unhurriedly turn around again to gaze down his battlements, all of the score or so armored valiants of Galath who'd clambered through the ramparts to stand on these lofty stones had fallen.

The wizard sighed, watching dead women calmly picking up the bloodless remnants of their felled sisters, and asked the cold blue sky above him, "Now, where *were* my thoughts, before this unpleasant little distraction?"

For the first time ever, it seemed the sky had an answer for such a query. A flight of falcons came pouring down out of it, swooping out from among the line of peaks in the north that had hidden their approach from Sornspire until the proverbial last moment. Gray falcons about thrice the size of the largest falcon Galath had ever seen.

Which meant, of course, they weren't falcons at all.

The tall blue man cursed, spun around, and raced back to the stair, raising his staff in both hands and awakening it to snarl with surging blue tongues of fire.

He hurled his first fire-bolts before he sprang onto the steps—which was about the time the foremost lorn had started to take their real shapes, and come swooping right at him.

Horned, mouthless skull-faces are poorly suited for triumphant laughter or the bellowing of battle cries, but lorn eyes are very good at conveying hunger and glee.

They were doing that now, as he blasted a lorn to ashes and another lorn swerved out and around the tumbling remains to come swooping in, batlike wings folded back, slate-gray head looming, barbed tail cracking as it swerved again at the last instant to rake blue-scaled hands and face with razor-sharp talons.

A second lorn didn't bother to swerve. Even as the blue man silently lost his grip on his staff, mouth open but no cry of pain roaring out, it crashed right into him, plucking the wizard off his feet and dashing him back against the stone steps with spine-shattering force.

Then all the lorn were swooping and tearing, the thin black staff tumbling forgotten down the stair as the slate-gray, struggling cloud tightened around those few steps at the top.

When they drew apart, to wheel back up into the sky and away, all that was left on the steps was a dark stain, a few fragments of bone, and some scraps of dark cloak small enough to have been the hides of tiny scuttling mice.

"And so I die," a calm voice observed, as its owner turned away from his fading scrying. "Overwhelmed and torn apart by lorn. Well, there are worse deaths, I suppose."

Narmarkoun beckoned one of the most decayed of his dead women with a silent look. As she began her slow crawl across the great hall of his cold castle, and his other dead women parted in front of her like a hastening gray sea, he looked down into the dark and empty eyes of the just-as-dead women entwined around his legs, who were stroking ardently as high as they could reach, and murmured, "There is one being in Falconfar I fear: Lorontar. It is merely sensible to fear Lorontar."

Bony fingers reached his inner thigh. He gently captured them in his grasp, and smiled down at their owner. "Lorontar the *true* Archwizard of Falconfar, the real Dark Lord. Who now rides the body of the Aumrarr Taeauna, and has a spell-link sunk, like a great hook, deep in the mind of Malraun."

Chill fingers were climbing his other leg, now. He dispensed another smile down into the face of their owner.

"Wherefore it is only prudent, cold ladies, that your lord and master Narmarkoun for now works only through false Narmarkouns and lesser agents, and remains hidden here with you."

The crawling servitor had almost reached him. He turned to face her, and murmured a word that slapped back all of the dead women entwined around him into shuddering, curling retreat.

He had transformed no less than four of his undead women into semblances of himself, and installed them in as many remote tower lairs, just to see if Lorontar paid any attention.

The "himself" in Galath had just been torn apart by lorn, and those lorn could only have been sent by Lorontar. Wherefore the Lord Archwizard was hunting for him; he'd been right to set forth his duplicates.

Narmarkoun smiled. He could have spun a spell to pluck up the decaying woman—she was barely more than a lolling skull, two arms, and a crumbling pelvis trailing a few ends of bone—to hang upright in the air facing him. Yet it was easier to just reach down, physically embrace her, and hold her against him while he breathed the spell into her pitiful bones.

Besides, nothing thrilled him more than these silent, chill embraces.

Chapter Two

NOTHING BUT DUST and grit. Rod rubbed a pinch of it between his finger and thumb, sighed, and let the rising breeze slowly take the rest out of his hand.

Damn. When his hand was empty, he drew the gauntlet back on, anger flaring again. He was *useless*. As bumbling and fumbling as always... Shaking his head, Rod turned and looked all around.

Trackless forest, in every direction. He looked down carefully at the ground, seeking markings or anything special that would help him find this exact spot again, or show him some evidence that magic had in the past brought more people here than just him.

Nothing. A muck of dead leaves and loose forest loam everywhere, small tree-roots wandering through it all, muddy here and over there... it was the same as everywhere else underfoot that he could see.

Face it, Rod, you're lost.

As bloody usual.

Lost in the heart of some forest he'd never seen before, a *real* forest. Deep and dark, stretching away in gently-rolling hills that he could barely see through all the trees, as gloomy as Hades in all directions. No proper clearings, the sky above a bright milky overcast so he couldn't even try to tell east from west... oh, he was lost, all right.

No roads, no trace of woodcutters' axes... this forest was *old*. And by the looks of things, he was highly likely to become "forest prey" for something, once it got dark.

Rod stepped a few paces away from the spot where he'd appeared and looked back at it. No, nothing special. No kindling magic or little glows or... or anything.

Rod sighed. So, Robinson Crusoe, how to keep from walking in circles and getting scurvy?

The trees looked very much the same in all directions. He wished them a naughty word, declaiming it slowly and pleasantly, as he tried hard to think of *something*, and... chanced upon a thought.

Rivers flow downhill, and eventually to lakes, perhaps the sea, and if he was *very* lucky, a port or fishing village or something of the sort. And if he was always following a stream, he might zig and zag a lot, but he could hardly walk in circles.

Of course, all the dangerous beasties came to streams to drink, didn't they?

Huh. Dangerous beasties including *him*.

Not that he could think of anything better to do, even though he stood and tried for a good long time.

So eventually Rod Everlar shrugged, squared his shoulders, peered at the nearest tiny trickle of water under the trees, strode to it, and started following its flow.

He looked back several times, at first trying to keep in his mind what the spot he'd appeared at looked like, in case he needed to find it again. He doubted he could, though, once he'd walked two dozen steps or so.

Then he looked back for another reason: to see if anything was creeping after him.

Always he saw the same thing. Nothing but trees, endless trees.

He'd already descended a surprising amount, though. When he'd been looking down from where he'd first stood in the forest, the land hadn't seemed to slope so much, but... well, it did.

He trudged on.

Sigh. This tramping along in the muck was going to get wearingly old very soon. Not that he need feel lonely. After all, he had such company in his walk: bumbling fantasy writer, great conquering hero, Lord Archwizard, and Dark Lord of all Falconfar. Quite a crowd.

Rod Everlar muttered his favorite naughty word again, and kept on walking.

THE TONGUE ARDENTLY thrusting into his mouth was cold, so cold. Narmarkoun felt lust stirring in him again as satin-smooth limbs of his own creation tightened around him, breasts brushed against his, the undead woman kissing him started to moan with need...

Well, of *course*. She needed his life. She longed and hungered for his warmth and vitality more than anything else in all the world. Already her thighs were locked around his, and one of her icy hands was fumbling for his loins...

Enough. He could indulge himself with scores of his servitors, whenever he wanted to; he had another purpose for this one. Reaching around behind her to capture her far elbow, Narmarkoun tugged firmly, twisting her about and away from being pressed against him, tearing their joined mouths apart.

All he needed was a brief moment. His freed mouth murmured the spell. Then he embraced her even more fiercely, pressing against her hard as the flesh he'd conjured over her bones started to flow and *creep*.

It was an eerie, eerie feeling. One he never tired of…

All too soon, it was done, and he gently disengaged and stepped back from her. Or rather, "her" no longer.

His refleshed servitor was now an exact duplicate of himself. Tall, bald, and scaled, the skin blue rather than putrifying gray, his own coldly calm eyes gazing back at him. Just a few more spells to augment the decaying mind inside, to transform the undead woman who'd been embracing him into a false Narmarkoun who walked and talked like the real one.

He smiled. Whoever that was.

THE STREAM WOUND on and on, snaking this way and that amid the trees. All around him, the forest was deep, green, and beautiful. In other circumstances, Rod Everlar would have been happy to enjoy the gnarled forest giants soaring all around him, the splashes of dappled light here and there in the rare spots where treefalls had opened gaps in the otherwise unbroken leaves overhead.

Could this be the Raurklor? Oldest and largest of the forests of Falconfar, he'd imagined it so long ago, now, that he could only just remember staring at the large expanse of blank white paper beyond Sardray, and deciding it should be a great woodland, larger than any kingdom...

Or had it been here all along, as the great mossy girths of these trees suggested, and he'd only dreamed of something already there? Something that had somehow—Lorontar's magic?—reached out to him, to whisper in his dreams?

Rod sighed.

Whatever, however... what did it matter?

He was lost, and if this *was* the Raurklor, he'd soon be hunted. Perhaps he was being hunted right now, by something padding along in velvet silence, unseen but watching him. Stalking patiently, and awaiting nightfall to pounce.

The tiny trickle had become a creek some time ago, and was now a stream. He'd instinctively edged a little farther away from its banks, lest it get deep enough to hide something with tentacles that could lunge out at him—

Angrily he banished a mental picture of dozens of little fanged mouths, all on the end of snake-like tentacles, thrusting at him in a hungry cloud...

Damn it! To think of something here might be to make it real!

He had to—had to get *out* of here, and get to Taeauna!

Who was somewhere else in Falconfar, that stretched away in identical green, tree-choked gloom all around him. A world as vast as the real one. A world it seemed he could alter by writing about it.

Pity he didn't have pen, pencil, or paper, only all these pouches full of gewgaws he didn't know how to use.

Thinking of which...

Rod peered down at himself a little ruefully. It wasn't all that heroic a sight. He looked, well, moth-eaten.

His once grandly-sinister armor was now nothing but a web of half-melted patches of metal, shaped something like the black markings on a black-and-white cow, and he could find nothing that seemed magical about his heavy war-gauntlets.

He'd snatched up a lot of stuff from Ult Tower, though, and not all of it had fallen or melted away with his armor.

He wore baldrics slung over both shoulders, to cross on his chest. Sheathed along them were a few daggers and something that looked like a hooked metal claw with a whip attached to it, plus some tools.

Then there were the belts. Three of them, one bearing only a water-skin and an empty scabbard. Sheathed on the second was a sword of some sort, whose pommel glowed from time to time all by itself. The third belt, now sagging low on his hips, was the one he'd threaded six pouches of various sizes onto.

There were four little thong-drawstring soft leather bags full of what had been glowing, sparkling dust, in the end pouch. The next one along held a fine neckchain—almost certainly jewelry that had no magic at all to it—that he'd hastily clasped through seven finger-rings while racing through Ult Tower. At least five of those rings had been glowing various hues at the time he'd snatched them from the hands of sculpted Ult Tower figures. Finely sculpted, life-sized bare women they'd been, their faces carved in the same vacant, disinterested pouts he saw on fashion models strutting down runways in the real world. On television, of course, not in person; Rod Everlar's "real world" wasn't quite that glamorously unreal.

The third pouch was the largest, and it was stuffed full of a chain about a dozen feet long that ended in two ornate bars with rune-like symbols graven all over them. He *thought* he'd seen a similar chain, earlier and somewhere else in Ult Tower, standing stiffly out from a wall like a flagstaff, with garments hanging from it. So perhaps this one could be made to go rigid and defy gravity, too.

The fourth pouch… oh, hell, he couldn't even keep them straight in his mind. Time to find a high spot in the forest, so he could see if anything came creeping up on him—he hoped—and stop for a rest, to go through all this stuff.

He peered around.

Ah. There. The stream curving right around it on three sides, so I can't get lost and I'm safe. Unless there's something in that monster tree right in the middle of it.

He tried to peer up through leafy boughs—and shrugged. There could be an army of Dark Helms up there, perched on every branch, and he'd not know until they started pelting him with things. Drawn daggers, for instance.

He winced, clambered up to the high spot, and sat down, instantly creating a tangle of scabbards, sheaths, and loops of leather belt all around himself.

"Hail, conquering hero," he muttered. "Who'll trip over his own underwear next, to the wild applause of the crowd." Now, what *was* all this stuff?

Well, he rapidly discovered, none of it was labeled. Or particularly obvious.

There was certainly *something* magical about the sword—it glowed, it made no sound even when he clinked it against some of the tools, and it was far too light to be as hard and, well, made of metal, as it was—but he was darned if he could figure out anything on or about it that could unleash jets of flame, or anything else useful.

One of the daggers bore magic, too. If drawn and waved about and then released, it refused to fall to the ground, but hung motionless in the air, right where he'd let go of it, until he grasped it again.

On an impulse he hung a pouch on it, and it served as a rock-solid peg—stuck into nothing—but try as Rod might, he couldn't get it to do anything else. Maybe it *didn't* do anything else.

Likewise the powders in the little bags, and the rings. He could make four of the rings glow and tingle just by putting them on, but tapping and rubbing them did nothing, and none of them—unlike in his books—had helpful little words engraved on their inside curves, that could be read aloud to unleash their powers. He didn't leave any of them on his fingers.

The big rune-chain proved to be the one bright spot. It did have words graven on those morningstar-like spike-studded bars at both ends, and when you said one of them aloud, the chain snapped out to a rigid spear-like length that could take all his weight, even jumping and kicking at it—without bending. The other word made it collapse back into a clinking heap of chain again.

Pouch ye fourthe was the one he'd stuffed full of coins. They all looked a bit odd—weird shapes rather than round, for one thing—and certainly didn't bear the names or kingly faces of anything he'd ever written about, but only one of them had an inscription he could read: "Sarbrik."

When Rod said that aloud, the coin started to glow, and got so hot that he had to drop it or sear his fingers. It set the wet leaves underfoot to smoldering, until he hastily scuffed it all out with his boot and kicked the coin onto a rock. By the time he'd been through the last two pouches, it had lost its glow and its heat again.

So he had a firestarter. If he dared carry it.

He decided he did, and put it all alone in pouch five.

Whatever he'd put in that pouch—he had a vague memory of a cluster of gruesome-looking eyeballs, enclosed in a gold-encaged spherical glass or rock crystal egg; eyes that turned and focused on him as he'd stretched out his hand to pluck up the egg— had vanished, all by itself, right through the closed fastenings, leaving behind only a spicy smell.

The sixth and last pouch held two metal bracers— nicely-shaped metal armbands—that ought to be magical, but had no powers that he could awaken. Rod donned them anyway, spent some time shifting things around and tightening belts so he didn't feel in quite such a hopeless tangle, stood up, looked around at the endless trees, and sighed.

So whether or not he'd created Falconfar by writing books about it, or he'd just somehow dreamed about a world that had been there all along, here he was, lost somewhere in it.

Lost and helpless... and increasingly angry.

Nor was he the only one who could change it. He'd foolishly sold it to Holdoncorp, and their busy, bright-eyed computer designers—he always pictured fat, pale young men in food-spattered T-shirts, feet up on pizza-box-littered desks with keyboards in their laps, sneering at him through thick glasses as they rubbed self-consciously at tangled, pitiful attempts to grow beards—had given Falconfar Dark Helms and a lot more sinister wizards and super-powerful lorn and—and *dragons*, damn it, and—

—and none of this brooding was getting him one step closer to rescuing Taeauna. To *finding* her first, damn it.

Snatched from him by the wizard Malraun, younger and probably more dangerous than Arlaghaun.

So not only would he have to master all these baubles he was carrying, he'd need several hundred more. And the gods' own luck.

Whatever gods there were right now in Falconfar.

"Cue heavy sigh," Rod told the trees around him, as he tramped along—and then stopped, very suddenly.

Had that been a rustling, off to his right?

He peered and listened. Nothing.

After long moments of straining to hear something, he sighed heavily and strode on.

"So," Narmarkoun asked himself, raising an eyebrow in challenge, "just why is the Raurklor hold of Ironthorn likely to become the most important battleground in all Falconfar, very soon now?"

"*If* true," his newly-fashioned false self replied, "that's a mystery to me. I'm sure all Galath would assume their kingdom is the most important land in Falconfar in any circumstances, just as the Stormar cities are sneeringly certain all Falconfar trembles before them."

"Indeed," Narmarkoun agreed. "So I'd better tell you."

"Why?"

Narmarkoun blinked. Well, now. The wench's undead mind had a little more sharp steel in it than he'd hitherto suspected. He could hardly tell the blunt truth—so you can yield this lore as a lure to Lorontar or anyone else powerful enough to destroy you, to bring them to Ironthorn and within reach of the traps I've prepared—so tactics would have to suffice.

"Because it's something *I* know, that's of importance right now, and it should inform your thinking."

A notion dangerous to the rest of his false selves, yet this one could obviously handle it. And all too much more. He'd best cast a few goading spells at the knights in Chainamund, to make them assault Sornspire again, the moment this one was installed there. Or she just might seek alliances with them, to build herself into a challenge to the *real* Narmarkoun.

She was wearing a little smile right now that he liked no part of. Sun, stars, and Aumrarr, why was everything so *complicated*?

"Very well," she asked, "tell me: why *is* Ironthorn so important? As opposed to any other Raurklor hold, or Galathan castle, or waveswept isle in the Sea of Storms?"

Narmarkoun nodded approvingly. "There are places of magical power in Falconfar. Places that can renew waning magics on swords and wands and the like, or erupt in lightnings and other magical furies if the wrong magic is cast nigh them, or that can awaken magical powers in certain creatures who may not even be aware they possess them."

"Your oh-so-casual tone tells me it's the latter ability of the place that interests you now. So some magical innocents are going to awaken there? Perhaps shifting balances among the Dooms?"

Narmarkoun smiled. "The balances are shattered already."

"Lorontar."

It was not a question. Briefly Narmarkoun considered calling forth all the slumbering magics in his cold castle around them, and utterly destroying this false semblance of himself.

He decided against it. There was danger here, but not failure, yet. A powerful Narmarkoun would last longer against Galath, and do more harm to Lorontar when he at last reached out to slay. If the old Archwizard instead chose to mind-conquer and subvert, Narmarkoun's little trap would be waiting for him, and the harm would be inescapable.

"Indeed," he said again. "Some of those innocents may become Shapers, and thus players in their own right, or—"

"Or the most powerful weapons any Doom could hope to wield against another," his double interrupted.

Narmarkoun made himself nod and smile. "You see it all. Why Ironthorn is so important to the Dooms, and therefore why the strife that matters will soon erupt there."

"Do you know who these innocents are?"

"If I did, would I be just standing here, talking to you?"

"So how—"

Narmarkoun decided it was more than his turn to interrupt. "Aumrarr legends and certain writings of Stormar seers—the sort who had dream-visions, of old, and wrote them down—tell us there are all manner of these innocents. Falconaar—beasts as well as humans, but for the most part they will be human—who are ignorant of their magical powers but who, if ever awakened, may far outstrip any trained wizard in the hurling of magic. Beings who can *feel* the flows and webs of magical force, and wield them through sheer instinct, not painstaking experimentation and following the written spell-processes of others."

"And Ironthorn is one of the places they can easily awaken to mastery of magic, all by themselves."

"It is. Rod Everlar was one innocent. The Dooms all seek to learn who the others are, so we can destroy them before they ever reach Ironthorn. Yet there is a restlessness in Ironthorn right now, that warns me one of them may have wandered there already."

"So why are you sending me to Galath and not Ironthorn?"

Narmarkoun eyed his false self thoughtfully, and calmly enunciated the largest lie he'd uttered in a long time. "Because the magics I used to lend your mind some of my power, so you can cast spells, would burst apart in Ironthorn—rending your wits utterly."

"And you know this how?"

"I've tried it before."

Well, after all, one lie often needs to stand on another.

THE DEEPENING GOLDEN hue of the sunlight told Rod Everlar the day was drawing on.

The sunlight he could see very clearly, ahead, where it came stabbing down through the endless green gloom in a great shaft, to illuminate the first real clearing he'd seen in this great forest.

The stream beside his boots zigged this way and then that, only to plunge right through that clearing; he could see it sparkling in the sunlight. He could also see something moving, up there. No, two somethings.

They were too far away to identify clearly, yet. Two creatures that could fly or at least hop and flutter wings, they looked to be. Creatures that stood upright on two legs when they were on the ground. They were fighting each other, or courting, or—well, facing each other and moving quickly, in some sort of excitement, anyway.

Rod started to run, ignoring the meanderings of the stream for the first time. It was too large to lose now, perhaps a dozen feet wide and knee-deep or more in places. If he ran up its bank, heading for the light, he would have to cross only a few strides of uneven, tree-choked forest before he'd be slithering down its banks again, as its winding brought it back across his path. Clamber along around its curve, then up over the next hump of land, and—

A scream rang out, of rage and pain more than fear. From the clearing, of course. It sounded like a woman.

Rod blinked, dodged around a tree, kicked his way through a rather nasty thornbush—there hadn't been all that many bushes of any sort, in the gloom beneath all these soaring trees, but trust him to find one and blunder right through it—and hastened on.

It hadn't sounded like Taeauna. No, this was someone with a deeper, rougher voice, someone—

Someone who was just a fatal moment too slow with her sword. As Rod came charging up over what proved to be a narrow ridge of land, tripped over a tree-root, and slithered headlong in wet, rotting leaves toward a face-first meeting with the chuckling stream, he saw it all.

The largest lorn he'd ever seen, twice the height of a taller man than Rod Everlar, its barbed tail slashing around to catch the sword of its foe and pluck her off-balance, so she leaned helplessly forward into the reach of its long, thickly-muscled arms. Talons that stabbed into her breast and tightened viciously, forcing out a sob and coughed blood.

That foe was an Aumrarr in dark, well-worn leather armor, her wings slashed and tattered, her face utterly unfamiliar to Rod. He had time to see little more before the lorn pulled the Aumrarr close—and tore out her throat.

Blood fountained, drenching that horned and mouthless skull-face, and the Aumrarr's head flopped over, to dangle at an impossible angle.

Though it had no mouth, the lorn looked like it was chewing.

Then it swallowed.

And then it leaned forward to gnaw her face away.

As Rod Everlar, spewing forth the contents of his heaving stomach, scrambled up from the stream-edge mud and sprinted along the water's edge, around its last curve before the clearing, so he could charge up one more forest slope, crash through more trees, yelling out incoherent fury, and burst out into the bright sunlight to confront it.

The Aumrarr was very dead. There was blood everywhere, and the reek of death was strong.

For the first time Rod realized just how much danger he might be in—and something else, too: he hadn't the faintest idea what he was going to do now.

The lorn lifted its head from the bloody ruin of the Aumrarr's face, and regarded him expressionlessly. Without a mouth, its face a gray skull-like mask, it couldn't do much else, yet somehow Rod felt that it was *sneering* at him.

This close, he could see how the lorn had been able to bite out an Aumrarr throat without a mouth, then devour her face: a lamprey-like, chewing throat tube drew back out of view, under its jaw. Revealing two saw-edged, curving horns—like giant beetle pincers—that were just emerging from under that same jaw.

Horns that thrust forward again, spreading wide, as the lorn took a step closer to Rod, casually throwing the limp corpse of the Aumrarr over one of its arms. And then another step.

Oh, *shit*.

Chapter Three

IRONTHORN HAD LONG been a vale where the cold and careful courtesy of meeting and mingling only in certain neutral places—the market-moots in Irontarl, and at Har's Bridge and Blackstones Hill—kept the three rival lordly families of Hammerhand, Lyrose, and Tesmer from rising to bathe the valley in open red war.

Though vale-folk and traveling traders alike spoke of "the ever-brawling knights of Ironthorn," those frays erupted with fists and daggers in the taverns, between a hot-headed few, not from end to end of the valley with armies that slaughtered, pillaged, and burned.

The abiding hatreds of the lordly families had not quite turned them into nest-despoiling fools. Yet.

By grudgingly-forged agreement, underscored by cold graves on all sides of the dispute, the forest around Ironthorn had been deemed a place for hunting stags and boar, not men. Its trails were open to all, and it was understood that men who walked or rode there would leave their armor and their bows at home, and carry nothing more menacing than their everpresent swords, belt daggers, and boar-spears.

Stags were to be ridden down and speared, or for the most daring, taken with sword and daggers; arrows were for bustards in the sky above, and vermin—four-legged vermin—in the fields below. Not that bows were much use against Ironthar knights and senior armsmen; no armor was worn in the valley that was not treated with the spells that slowed and then turned aside iron. A strong man could bring a sword to bear on an Ironthar-armored foe, fighting through the magic with teeth clenched in effort, but the bow had not been made that could drive even the mightiest war-quarrel home, through the air, to bite.

Yet despite the ban, this day saw two armed and armored warbands out riding the largest forest trail—the only one where two horses could *just* pass without touching, if the riders were careful. The trail that wandered through the Raurklor heights from one end of Ironthorn to the other, and beyond. The two forces were riding right toward each other.

Neither intended to meet the other, or even knew the other was abroad. Both were bound for hostile territory, on violence bent; purposes that inevitably brought them, in time, face to face.

Where mounts were reined in, hard.

The two forces then regarded each other in a stony silence that for many breaths was broken only by the snorting of their head-tossing mounts. One band numbered eight in all; the heir of Hammerhand and seven knights, three of them riding with visors down, as if expecting war.

The other mustered twelve: the Lyrose heir and his two younger brothers, three bowmen whose saddle-slung crossbows were only a few turns shy of full, firing-ready tension, and six knights.

"Well, now," Eldred Lyrose said at last, flashing a brief and mirthless smile, "it seems the forest yields up stranger game at our every hunt. Ready bows."

His eyes never left the Hammerhands as he spoke those last words, so calmly that two of his bowmen did not at first take them as an order, and had to scramble to join the third in cranking windlasses to bring their bows to full, straining tension.

"Do you customarily hunt in full armor, Eldred?" the Hammerhand heir asked coolly, making a casual gesture that brought swords sliding out of scabbards in hissing unison amid the Hammerhands behind him.

"It seems I scour out *vermin* when full-armored, Dravvan," Eldred Lyrose replied softly, and raised his riding whip to point at Dravvan Hammerhand.

"Bowmen, scour me this talkative one," he announced with a smile, then added, "Fire at will."

Three crossbows loosed their quarrels in a triple crash—and Dravvan Hammerhand's head spun bloodily around on his shoulders, neck broken and skull shattered by three heavy war-quarrels bursting into it in eager unison.

There were gasps from the Hammerhands and shouts of glee from the Lyroses—ere the foremost Hammerhand knights spurred forward with furious bellows of "Fell magic! Slay them! *Slay them all!*"

Eldred Lyrose's casual manner vanished in an instant as he spurred his horse off the trail and out of the way, seeking to circle around behind the Lyrose warband as he snatched at the helm bobbing on his saddle.

"Kill me yon Hammerhands!" he shouted as he rode. "Let not a one of them—"

A low-hanging bough swept him out of his saddle into a startled landing among the dead leaves.

The rest of his words would have been drowned out anyway in the loud tumult of snorting horses, shouting men, and ringing clangs of furiously-swung swords clashing with each other and rebounding off armor. Horses reared, lashing out with hooves and crying their displeasure, as men fought to find room enough among the trees to swing their blades.

Dravvan rarely rode anywhere without his bodyguard, three strong and serpent-swift veterans. They led a charge, aghast at Dravvan's death and the impossible manner of it—his armor should have stopped that bowfire!—and it so happened the spot where the Hammerhands had halted upon seeing their rivals afforded them space enough to spur their horses, whereas the riders of Lyrose were hampered by trailside trees.

So it befell that one Lyrose knight, in less than the time it took him to draw breath again after roaring out his mirthful approval of Dravvan Hammerhand's fate, was driven from his saddle by the sheer force of the sword cuts seeking his face. Head ringing, he fetched up against a tree, dazed and stumbling, and was ridden down and trampled ere he could raise his blade with any strength.

The bowman behind him, helmless and in lighter armor bearing weaker iron-warding spells, was promptly rendered faceless by a deep-biting Hammerhand blade. He hadn't even started to topple from his saddle ere swords were slashing out across it, to hew the crossbow held by his nearest fellow into ruin.

Then the Hammerhand bodyguards were in among the Lyrose, hacking and thrusting at wild will, dealing death viciously with no thought for their own safety.

That savagery won them two more kills before a Lyrose blade first drew blood. The wounded Hammerhand bodyguard, reeling in his saddle and beset from all sides, caught sight of the running Eldred Lyrose—and spurred his mount right at the terrified Lyrose heir.

He was dead with three Lyrose swords in him before his snorting, plunging mount reached the oldest son of Lord Magrandar Lyrose. Yet his screaming, pain-seared warhorse, sides slashed by Lyrose blades and the dead man on his back falling hard and heavily down to the left to batter against trees and drag the saddle painfully awry, charged right through Eldred Lyrose, hooves thudding hard. On it galloped, fleeing wildly through the trees deeper into the Raurklor, leaving a trampled, groaning man thrashing feebly in its wake.

Swords were swinging in earnest now, everywhere, as the Hammerhand bodyguards sought vengeance and above all the deaths of the bowmen, and the Lyrose knights eagerly sought to carry out their lordling's orders.

Riding just behind the Lyrose heir were his two brothers: cruel Horondeir, a loud, fair-haired burly giant with a grin on his face and his sword drawn, and sly, quiet Pelmard.

Horondeir had fairly crowed at the sight of the new war-quarrels working so well—downing the Hammerhand heir, too! Now his gleeful bellows had given way to grunts of effort as he fought for his very life, surrounded by thrusting Hammerhand blades. Pelmard was nowhere to be seen.

Save by Eldred, who had time for one glimpse of his younger brother grinning down at him ere the hooves of Pelmard Lyrose's warhorse crashed down on his skull, twice and thrice. Pelmard deftly reined it around to return to the battle, its hooves dancing hard atop his brother.

Only one Lyrose knight saw what had happened, and Pelmard smiled a tight smile and drove his sword right through that man's opening mouth, before it could so much as exclaim a word. He spurred on, and that killing went unseen in the swirling fray.

"Back!" he shouted, pulling his horse wide of the trail, deeper into the trees. "To me, men of Lyrose!"

He was well content. The enspelled war-quarrels gifted to House Lyrose by the wizard Malraun had been everything the wizard had promised them to be, his cruel older brother was dead, and oafish Horondeir was doomed to die, too, if he didn't get clear of the busily-hacking Hammerhands. The Lyrose knights had been hastening to Horondeir's aid, but if his own rallying-cry drew them off just long enough...

"Over here!" he shouted again. "To me, Lyrose!"

He couldn't even see Horondeir, who was somewhere in the heart of a great knot of milling armored men on horseback, all of them plying their swords like madmen at a farm-reaping. Some of those men were screaming. A Lyrose knight fell from his saddle, one uselessly-dangling arm bouncing free as his corpse landed. Then a Hammerhand knight went down, falling on his face without a sound atop the fallen man of Lyrose.

One of the screams ended suddenly, and something wet and heavy flew out of the fray to thump and roll past Pelmard. His horse shied away, almost braining him on a tree, and he had to fight with his reins **before he dared look down at the grisly thing again.**

It had stopped facing him, staring up at him in unseeing horror, its mouth agape. The head of his brother Horondeir.

Then the fray was whirling around, and Pelmard realized in horror that Hammerhand knights were coming for *him*.

Desperately he clawed the head of his horse around and raked its sides with his spurs. "Home!" he shouted. "*Home*, Jhallon!"

A flung dagger bounced off his shoulder to spin tauntingly in the air before him, just for a moment. Then Jhallon, ears laid back, was racing through the trees as swift as any arrow, heading for a brown ribbon in the trees before them. That ribbon was the trail, winding its way through the trees. The trail back to Lyraunt.

Pelmard Lyrose let go of his sword and clung with both hands to the raised, flared front of his saddle, as the thunder of hooves rose behind him.

Either some Lyrose knights had won free, or the Hammerhands were still after him. Just now, with tree after dark tree seeming to leap past him in an endless whirl, he didn't dare try to look back.

"BE CAREFUL, MY son. Oh, be careful. It is *so* easy to put a boot wrong when walking among the Ironthar— and the price may well be your life, there and then. They have been warring with each other for so long that burying blades in folk faster than someone can sink a sword into them is what they *do*."

The young and darkly handsome Stormar managed not to sigh. "I have heard this before, Father, and not forgotten. Trust me."

"No, Amaddar, that I do not. You swallow a sigh

and seek to stride off, lost in your own impatience. *Hear me*."

That tone in his father's voice, even now when it was but an enfeebled, ghostly echo of his lost vigor, brought Amaddar Yelrya to a halt, as still as any statue. He turned around, and looked down into that wasted face with nothing but eager obedience on his own. He had been well taught.

"For years now," that failing, familiar voice told him, "Ironthorn's verdant farms and busy gemadars have been ruled uneasily by three rival lords. Lord Burrim Hammerhand is the strongest. He uses the badge of an iron gauntlet—a left-handed gage, mind, upright and open-fingered, on a scarlet field—and rules from Hammerhold, a castle on a crag just north of Irontarl, the market town of Ironthorn. The town stands on the banks of the Thorn River."

By the greatest of efforts, Amaddar managed to avoid sighing, rolling his eyes, or letting any exasperation at all cross his face. Lions of the morning, he was going to tell it *all*.

"Just south across that river is Lyraunt Castle. There Lord Magrandar Lyrose rules, lording it over three side-valleys to the southwest. His badge is a pinwheel, like a caltrop, of three steel-gray thorns, joined at the base, on a yellow field. They say the wizard Malraun smiles on House Lyrose."

Amaddar nodded, struggling to seem interested, trying to look as if any of this was new.

"In the southeast is the valley of Imrush, where Lord Irrance Tesmer rules from his keep, Imtowers. He's the one who used to have all the gems, and buys slaves from every Stormar who'll sell. His badge is a purple diamond on a gray field."

Amaddar nodded. "So he I should cultivate," he murmured, just to show he'd been heeding. "He'll welcome me."

"No!" His father's eyes blazed like two golden suns for an instant, ere fading again. "Stay far from the Tesmer lands, have naught to do with him, and do *not*, for any reason at all, surrender your real name to any Ironthar!"

Amaddar frowned. "Why?"

"Tesmer's wife was—probably still is—very beautiful. I... she will remember me. So will her lord, and doubtless seek to close claws on the son, when he can't reach the father."

Lion, this *was* new!

Amaddar realized he was gaping, and shut his mouth with an effort.

"*Father!*" he heard himself say reproachfully, a moment later.

His father's eyes flashed again. "The gold that reared you to have such pride I earned in season after season of dealing with Lady Telclara Tesmer. We understood each other very well, and when you're older, you'll see better *why* that leads to... the other."

"But... Mother..."

"Knew all about it, suggested it before ever I rode all that way north, and hooked the cunning Lady Tesmer and played her like a master, with me the straining fishing-line between. Go ask her if you believe me not, and come back to me wiser."

His father lifted one wasted, trembling hand long enough to level one long and accusative finger at Amaddar. "Then perhaps you'll stop fighting down yawns and pretending to listen, and learn enough to keep yourself alive in Ironthorn for a day or two. Perhaps."

Two Hammerhand knights had been everywhere in the battle, hewing and thrusting and whirling to deal death elsewhere before wounded foes could strike back.

One was tall, and fought with his visor raised. The weathered face that stared sternly out of his helm was one even the youngest knights of Lyrose knew: Syregorn, a laconic, scarred man who had long been one of Lord Hammerhand's most trusted veterans.

The other was one of the Hammerhand rearguard, who'd ridden with visors down. This anonymous knight was faster and more reckless than Syregorn in the fray, darting here and there like a hungry falcon. His sword had laid open the throat of Horondeir Lyrose, and he was now swinging it hard and fast at the last few Lyran knights, as the fray dwindled down into a tight knot of snorting, kicking horses in the trees.

Pelmard Lyrose—now heir of his house—was well away and beyond catching, now, if he didn't fall off and his mount avoided breaking a leg.

In the tight fray he'd left behind, a knight of Lyrose suddenly swerved away from a chance to hew a Hammerhand flank, and spurred out of the hacking, ringing heart of the battle to flee after the Lyrose lordling.

The falcon-swift Hammerhand knight pursued the hurrying Lyran, crouching low and urging his mount to greater haste by dealing stout slaps to its withers with the flat of his blade. Like an arrow he raced away from the dwindling knot of bloodied, sword-swinging knights.

He had almost caught up the fleeing Lyran before that knight heard the drumming of pursuing hooves, turned in his saddle, stared in alarm, and swung his sword wildly.

The racing Hammerhand caught the Lyran blade with the tip of his own and swung his sword in an awkward arc to abet rather than dispute its slash. Overbalanced, the knight of Lyrose was swung right around in his saddle, crying out in pain, and—was impaled for a moment on a tree-bough his terrified horse had already ducked past.

A moment was all the Hammerhand knight needed. His own blade sang down under the edge of the Lyran helm and around as he swept past, drawing a deep and bloody smile across the throat beneath.

Almost beheaded, the knight of Lyrose flopped bonelessly in his saddle, sagging back as his sword tumbled from his dying hand. His body followed it—all but one boot, firmly trapped in its stirrup. The horse raced on through the trees, terrified anew by the ringing, clanging carrion it was now towing.

The Hammerhand knight slowed his snorting, bucking mount and let the Lyran horse flee, turning to follow the trail slowly back to where horses snorted, the smell of blood was strong... and the battle was done.

Syregorn was grimly ordering the bodies of the Lyrose brothers be bound to their horses, and the severed head retrieved. He'd had no need to give orders to his four surviving knights regarding the reverent raising of the dead Dravvan Hammerhand.

"Pelmard?" was all he asked the returning knight, who tore off her helm to watch her dead brother gently laid on his snorting horse, his head wrapped in a Lyran cloak someone was too dead to need any longer.

"Escaped me. Taking with him his father's excuse for raising war."

She pointed at one of the knights of her house to get his attention, and snapped, "Find every last Lyran war-quarrel, and the bows! We must discover if they can pass all our iron-wardings, or we'll all be rotting vaugren-meat, and soon!"

"Yes, Lady," the knight murmured, lowering his eyes from the bright ribbons of tears down the cheeks of the woman who was now the next ruler of Hammerhold. If she somehow lived long enough.

Amteira Hammerhand didn't care if all Falconfar saw her tears.

Dravvan was dead. It was all up to her, now.

TRYING TO LOOK menacing, Rod slowly drew his sword. As he did, it flashed with a brief, bright white light—and the bracers on his arms winked back at it.

The lorn stiffened, and stopped striding forward.

He stared at it, hefting the sword, trying to look as if he buried the thing in handily nearby lorn every day.

The lorn regarded him as expressionlessly as only lorn can, that mouthless, unchanging skull-face staring back at Rod. Betraying nothing.

God, it was big. Even without that bone-shattering tail, it could probably tear him apart with casual ease. Studying it, close enough to see the little line of breathing and speaking holes under the line of its jaw—well, the chin of its face, even if it lacked a mouth; it certainly *looked* like the underside of a human jaw—and the two pincers, now slid back inside little sheaths of flesh there, Rod had to fight down a shiver.

Whereupon it sneered at him—he could *tell* it was sneering, as plainly as anything, though its skull-face remained a frozen mask—sat down, and started eating a hearty meal of Aumrarr. Those pincers slashed and sliced, the flesh that sheathed them rippled and flexed like little gripping hands, and the throat tube with little teeth lining its inside thrust forward obscenely to suck in the blood and meat...

Revolted and suddenly furious again, his fear gone, Rod shook off the gauntlet on his free hand and put it into the pouch that held the rings. Fumbling with the chain until he got its clasp open, he started putting on rings, working by feel and never once taking his eyes off the lorn.

It went on eating, affecting unconcern, but it was watching him closely.

Which meant, for one thing, he dared not retreat. And would be dead once night fell, or sooner. Probably sooner.

Ult Tower, don't fail me now...

Two of the rings made his fingers tingle. Rod raised his hand until he could see them. Staring at the one on the left, he tried to will it to do something. *Anything.*

Nothing happened. He tried visualizing flames shooting out of it to scorch the lorn, saw the lorn blazing and blackening, collapsing, slate-gray hide melting and crumpling... nothing.

He gave up, and glared at the ring on the right, bearing down with his will until he was trembling and sweating, his head starting to pound. Suddenly—

Nothing happened. And went right on happening, damn it.

The sword... no, it wasn't reacting to the rings, even though their tingling was growing stronger.

Blazing up like Rod's temper. A God-damned *arsenal* of magic he'd snatched from Ult Tower,

49

things that glowed and hummed and bloody well *buzzed*—and not one of them, not *one* of them, could he make work. The bloody armor had damned well *melted* away!

He—

No. No, none of it was going to work. Not at all. It would tease him, glowing and humming and tingling like fury, but—

Shaking his head, Rod reached down, plucked up his gauntlet, and slid it back on.

It promptly flared into bright life. Some of the metal fingers spat sudden flames into the air.

The lorn stiffened again, lifting its head.

Rod quickly closed his gaping mouth, made himself smile, and pointed at the beast's inscrutable skull-face.

And a thin tongue of flame spat from his fingertip, right at the lorn.

The beast was gone before the fire arrived, dropping its meal in a sudden scramble, great clap of slate-gray wings, and bound into the air.

It was fleeing! Just like that!

Up it climbed, clawing at the air with its wings in seemingly frantic haste, racing up at the hole in the canopy of leaves that was letting the sunlight in, as Rod wagged his finger at it and pointed again, rage and—yes, exultation rising in him.

His jet of flames fell well short of that lashing tail, but the lorn looked back at him fearfully, and flapped all the faster.

Rod sighed. It was getting away.

No, it had *got* away… and was gone.

He looked down at all that was left of the Aumrarr—one severed foot, still encased in its boot—and, exultation gone in an instant, had to fight down a sudden urge to vomit.

Sighing harder, he turned away.

Somewhere overhead, the lorn gave tongue to a strange, ululating call.

Chapter Four

"WHY HERE, ME Viper? Why Stormcrag Castle? Locked in an' with spells to keep us that way? What'd *we* do, that—"

A strange, ululating call echoed across the endless green treetops of the Raurklor, startling Garfist Gulkoun into silence in mid-rumble, and causing the skeletally thin woman in the tattered leathers and once-grand, fur-trimmed cloak to fling up one bony hand in an imperious signal for silence.

Iskarra thrust her head sharply to one side, like a snake seeking to taste the air, and listened hard.

The call came not again, but they sat for a long time in silence ere the stout and growling man who'd been in mid-bluster before the unfamiliar cry dared to rumble, "What was that?"

His longtime companion shook her head slowly, but said nothing.

"Isk?" he growled, a few breaths later.

"It was a strange call," Iskarra said waspishly. "Is your *hearing* going now, too?"

Garfist rolled his eyes in exasperation, belched loudly, and started to pace again. "No, Viper mine, there's nothing wrong with my ears! It's my patience as has broken—again and again, mind—since we got here!"

"Gar," the woman once infamous as the Viper said patiently, uncoiling herself from where she'd been sitting on the room's lone table with her back to the wall, and striding to the window in the thigh-high boots she'd spent three days prying all the hobnails out of, to make them quiet, "I *have* noticed this. Even before you remarked on it. The *first* time."

The bright, acid edge to her voice seemed lost on the burly, pacing-once-more man, who waved his large and hairy hands in the air in wild circles of exasperation and growled, "How can ye take it all so quietly?"

"With all your noise, 'quietly' isn't a term *I'd* apply to these last few days," Iskarra replied, peering intently out over the endless forest in search of anything flying or clambering... or just different about the view. It was a search she knew would end in failure, and so was not disappointed.

Giving up, she swung around to face the striding Garfist, and stepped forward at just the right moment to deftly reach out and clap her cupped hand under his codpiece, dragging him to a painfully startled halt.

"Hoah! What? *Viper!* I—"

"Could start using this on me, you know, while we wait," she said warningly, keeping hold of his rather tender area with one hand and raising her other to the thong-loops of her bodice.

Garfist blinked. His Vipersides was about as buxom as a boar-spear, but she could bend her body as alluringly as any slithering snake—and ply her tongue better than any serpent he'd ever seen. Not that he was in the habit, mind, of entertaining snakes *that* way...

"Old Ox," Iskarra said coldly, "stop blinking at me as if a thought is battering at your thick skull demanding entry with utter lack of success, and *listen*."

By means of the handle she refused to relinquish, she towed him over to the wall, thrust his great shoulders back against it, and tapped his chest with the forefinger of her free hand.

"Now," she said, as severely as any nursemaid teaching a rebellious youngling, "when was the last time we didn't have to scramble for coins? Or think about where we could find a bed that wasn't a-crawl with biting bugs or within easy reach of some thieving night-knife? Or get endless meals for free? Or have our own place to stay, as warm and as roomy as we could want for, with no one hounding us over debts or because of what we'd done to them a few days back? Our own glorking *castle*, mind you?"

"Our own prison, more like."

"You think I don't know that? What I *don't* know is why you can't just accept that it's a prison we can't get out of, and *relax*. Rest a bit. Eat like the utter boar I know you can be, given feastables enough! Find the most comfortable bed, in all these bedchambers *full* of comfortable beds, and get in some snoring!"

"I—I—" Garfist shook his shaggy head, words failing him. "It's just—just... It sticks in my gullet, it does, to be so swindled! *Reward*, they said, not imprisonment! See it or not, there's a wall of magic around the fishpond and garden as hard as rock and as high as I can throw a stone! We're penned in here like beasts! Strange sort of reward, indeed, those four feather-lasses gave us!"

"Reward, my left teat, Gar," Iskarra snapped. "Those four wingbitches wanted us well out of

Galath, too far away to worm our ways back into any of its castles—and all that gold and wine and jewels just lying about for the taking—without them seeing us coming, all the way down open, wind-howling, arrow-filled Sardray."

"Well, why'd they not just kill us, then?" Garfist rumbled. "Why carry us—three days and nights of hard flying, mind!—over half Falconfar, to set us down here, in a deserted castle in the heart of a forest, that just happens to have barrels of flour and apples and a glorking stocked *fishpond?* They wouldn't even have had to fight us, to slay us; just soar high enough and let go!"

"Gar, are you truly that much a fool? Or just playing at being one to nettle me? They brought us here—away from our foes, too, mark you—because they still have a use for us, some task or other too risky to chance their own necks in. When they judge the time right, they'll be back to pluck us up and fly us right back into waiting doom, you'll see! I'll wager they've laid magic on us that tells them just where we are, and lets them watch and listen to us whenever they please!"

"Have they, now? Well, I hope they were listening *last* night, when I was teaching ye a thing or two about—"

"That will be *quite* enough, loosetongued Old Ox! We're not back in last night now, and I've had my fill of certain vices—"

Garfist leered.

"—to last me a season or two. It may take that long for the marks to fade."

Garfist stepped back from his longtime lover—only to come to a painful halt. She hadn't relinquished her hold.

"Strange sort of thinking ye have," he growled, pointing down at her hand. "Had yer fill, have ye? Then why d'ye keep hold of me? And speak of me using it on ye? So, now, which is it? One, or the other?"

"Both," Iskarra said tartly, but let go. "These last few days, have you forgotten *everything* you've learned about women?"

"No, but I thought ye were *better* than all the rest," Garfist said bitterly. "Ye said not a word when I knotted the bedsheets and tried to climb out yon window; most lasses I've met would never have let me forget it."

The bone-thin woman smiled. "And worked their ways around, by now, from astonishment at finding some invisible spell that let in wind and rain but made the air as hard as stone to our passage, to having anticipated and told you about such a barrier beforehand, so they could scold you repeatedly for ignoring their advice and climbing out the window anyway!"

The large and shaggy onetime pirate, sometime trader, and constant swindler she'd spent so many years with frowned at her as he thought her words through, nodded, then grinned.

Iskarra smiled back. The grin hadn't taken long to appear, this time.

"So the Aumrarr have left us here—stowed us in a cupboard—until they need us again," he said, still nodding. "While back in Galath—"

"Back in Galath, Melander Brorsavar is calling himself king, and of course the nobles—sponsored by this greedy merchant of Tauren or that greedy one from some city on the Sea of Storms—are all fighting each other or allying with the royal forces.

Castles burning, veldukes spurring their warhorses this way and that, creeks running red with the blood of the butchered… and we're well out of it all, Gar. No amount of loot is worth losing your head over, or having your belly slit open and being left staked out in a forest to await the hungry little jaws that come scuttling in the night."

"Huh. Only if ye get caught."

"Old Ox, how many wizards do you have to gawp helplessly at before you accept that you're *going* to get caught? Time and again? Galath is no place to be, just now."

"*I* kept hearing the Aumrarr saying all their scrying and prying magic was going awry, and so was everyone else's, too," Garfist responded, a little sullenly. "Blamed it on Arlaghaun's death, they did."

"Yes, detection spells are failing all across Galath, probably farther, upsetting spellhurlers no end. And aren't testy wizards the very sort of folk to be close and cuddling neighbors with, when you want to keep your neck intact? *Think*, Gar—think!"

"But all those battles… all that coin to be made…" Garfist said mournfully.

"You think there's some danger of Falconfar running out of *battles*, for you to make coin from?"

Iskarra's near-shriek of incredulity left her favorite shaggy swindler blinking. Then frowning again. Then, slowly, chuckling and nodding.

"All right, all right," he said at last. "There'll always be others. I'll grant ye that."

"Why, *thank* you, sir!" came her reply, in mocking mimicry of a haughtily scandalized velduchess.

He snorted, then lost his grin again when a memory struck him. Looking thoughtful, he said slowly,

"One of those Aumrarr—the older, tall one, with all that hair—said there was war all across Falconfar."

"Not *all* across, Gar. I heard her, too; she said it was spreading fast enough to soon be 'right across Falconfar.' War that was spreading as a warlord conquered hold after hold in a way no sword-swinger would have been allowed to, in the days when three Dooms glowered at each other and kept any one of their number from rising above the rest."

"The one with scars said it was an 'Army of Liberation' that was marching to 'hurl down thrones.'"

"No, Ox, you must learn to listen harder. She said that's what the warlord—Horgul—*said* his army was. She snorted when she said it, remember?"

"She did," Garfist rumbled slowly, frowning as he fought to drag a hazy memory out into the light and give it a good hard glare. "That mean it isn't?"

Iskarra turned away so he wouldn't see the wild roll of her eyes, and managed to turn the loud sigh she was about to emit into a "Yes" that was as calm and gentle as kindly mother's. She hoped.

"DIE, FLAP-WING *BITCH!*"

The Galathan knight hacked at the swooping Aumrarr so viciously that when he missed, his sword broke on the flagstones with a ringing clang that flung shards into his face, sent others clattering off the wall, and left him numbed and helpless, reeling and groping blindly for that wall, or an Aumrarr wing, or *anything* to hang onto.

"*No*, Juskra," Ambrelle snapped, from across the chamber. "Fly clear. Don't kill him. His velduke may need him, when the time comes to cross swords with Horgul's army."

"Horgul, Horgul, Horgul," the battle-scarred Aumrarr replied, waving hands that held two wickedly-sharp daggers wildly in exasperation. "That's all I hear from you, these days! That and Ironthorn, Ironthorn, Ironthorn!"

"Juskra!" the three other winged women in the room all cried, in swift and angry unison.

"*Not* in front of Galathan ears!" Ambrelle added furiously, waving at the still-blinded knight and his fellows across the room, who stood uncertainly in a doorway with swords out and faces stern with fear.

"All right," Juskra said with a cruel grin, her gliding turn bringing her around to head for that door. "I'll cut some off."

That caused a general fleeing stampede of shouting men, swords ringing off stone walls, and pounding boots. Juskra dived after them as slowly as an Aumrarr with no rising air to ride could without falling on her face, and even swerved considerably aside when the knight who'd lost his sword came sprinting and stumbling along, seeking that same door, his face a mask of streaming blood.

One wild eye regarded her in terror through his gore, and she gave it a kindly smile and cheery little wave.

In reply the running knight shrieked, sprang into the air just high enough to brain himself on the curving edge-stones of the arch overhead, and crashed senseless to the floor beyond. Juskra landed lightly by his spasming, kicking boots, caught hold of the door-pulls, and drew the double doors firmly closed on the Galathans, ignoring the few who'd rallied to await her with swords raised.

As she kicked off from the stones and flew back

to join her sister Aumrarr, they heard the door-bolts being slammed home in terrified haste.

"Mmm," Lorlarra said scornfully. "You'd think they'd never seen a woman with wings before."

"More like they'd never heard the truth about us before," Dauntra countered, from where she sat preening on a fur-draped couch.

"The former rulers of all humankind?" Juskra teased. "Masters of all magic, who chose to be beautiful battlemaids with wings?"

"*Those* truths, yes," Dauntra said quellingly. "Let's not wag our tongues now about your interesting fancies about Aumrarr having a deep, driving need to bed all wingless men who don't flee fast enough, hmm?"

"Agreed," Ambrelle said sternly, tossing her head so her almost-ankle-length hair swirled around her in a flood of purple-black glossiness. "Sisters, it's high time we were gone from Galath's coils. We've tarried here to steer nobles for as much time as we dare spare on men who love fighting too much to stop. Brorsavar's rule and eventual triumph is as secure as anything in this benighted realm can ever be, and more important fights await."

"Horgul's self-styled Liberators, you mean," Lorlarra said quietly.

The eldest of the four Aumrarr nodded and pointed across the room at the open window. "Let's fly. They'll be back through that door as soon as they find courage enough."

"Reinforcements enough," Juskra corrected, taking wing for the window.

Ambrelle merely nodded, as they left that keep behind and soared.

Only two arrows sped after them, and both were woefully late and low.

As usual.

In one of the scryings, a castle suddenly exploded.

Narmarkoun turned and strode over to the floating scene, to watch the great cloud of flames and stone and upflung dust rise to its full height, rocking the land all around... and then, slowly, begin to rain down. Impressive.

The undead women responded to his keen interest, entwining themselves around him and caressing with renewed vigor and purpose.

"I had no idea anyone in Galath had dragged a wizard that powerful into things," he remarked. "I don't think Malraun—or Lorontar, come to that—could have caused that without my knowing... hmmm..."

Watching the wet, torn remnants of several hundred knights and armsmen patter down all over a Galathan valley, he shrugged.

"Well, it happened. In Galath, which for now is just one great brawl among the steel-heads." He turned away.

"I have the Tesmers to see to," he told his caressers, striding toward the distant doorway that led to his favorite spellcasting chamber as fast as his purposeful walk could drag their limp bodies.

Halfway there, he stopped so abruptly that two of the undead women clinging to him fell over. "How long has Lorontar been watching my mind-riding spellwork, I wonder?"

Neither the animated dead nor the walls around offered any reply.

GARFIST STARED OUT the window, across the endless treetops of the Raurklor. "So is this Horgul a Stormar, then? I always wondered when the dusky-faces would stop fighting each other and scheming how to daily do each other out of coins long enough to reach out and conquer us all."

"No, you always wondered why they hadn't already, and what was keeping them from getting around to it," Isk corrected. "Making one of the big mistakes, Gar. Believing everything *you* think is right, and if everyone just came to their senses they'd all end up thinking just like you."

The big man opened his mouth, an eager growl of irritation rising to his lips... but no words came to him.

After standing with his jaws open for a little while, gaping like a fish, Garfist closed them again. Then he coughed, regained his mournful look, and rumbled, "I hate it when you change the whole world for me, Vipersides. You always make it more complicated. Things used to be far more simple. Eat, sleep, rut, kill someone, take his things, get drunk, then do it all over again. I didn't have to *think*, then."

"And there are empires full of men like you," Iskarra said wearily. "Bloody map-filling *empires*."

"IS THIS ANOTHER of your notions, Jusk? Or one of your rants coming on?" Dauntra asked impishly.

Juskra's reply was a wordless, menacing snarl. Dauntra's beauty, set against her own sword-scars, always aroused her ire anyway, and the most alluring of her four sworn sisters loved to tease.

When the veteran warrior did speak, it was to Lorlarra and Ambrelle, her head pointedly turned away from the most beautiful of the four Aumrarr.

"I know this Horgul is now of paramount importance, and Ironthorn, too. Our spells tell us, our dreams tell us… yet I don't know *why*. Is this a Doom using sly spells to lure us, again? Or are there truly gods, or Falconfar itself, speaking to us—to all Falconaar creatures—deciding what will be the latest focus, the trendiest battlefield?"

Ambrelle smiled a little sadly. "Sages, elder Aumrarr, and even kings—"

"Even dimwitted kings," Lorlarra murmured.

"—have pondered what you're now voicing, over and over again, as the unrolling ages have passed."

"That's nice," Juskra replied caustically. "Have any of them *concluded* anything?"

"No," Dauntra put in brightly.

Ambrelle shot her a hard look. "Of course they have. Yet their various conclusions seem of no use to others at all. Nothing we—or anyone—can predict, or influence, or quell."

Far below the four, Sardray unfolded, vast and nigh empty; endless gently rolling rises—ripples in the land too gentle to be called hills—of waving grass.

"I think there *is* a Doom behind this," Dauntra said unexpectedly, waving one slender hand down at the grassland below. "I can't see a greedy warlord—no, I know nothing of this Horgul that the rest of you haven't heard, but *any* greedy warlord—passing up the chance to ride like a storm wind through all this empty country, to plunge into the Raurklor the easy way, along the roads, to conquer this hold and then that hold, instead of struggling up through the trees from the Stormar cities. Unless someone or something is riding his mind, and forcing him to come through the forest." She stared into the thoughtful gazes of her sisters and added, "I just can't see a bold conqueror sort resisting the way of easy haste."

"Unless he fears Sardray for some reason," Juskra said thoughtfully, eyeing her usual rival with something akin to respect. "Otherwise, I'd have to agree with you: some spell or other is guiding him. And the only wizards with power enough to do that are either riding with him—"

"And probably bedding him every night, so as to swamp his reasoning with love or at least burning lust," Lorlarra murmured.

"—or they're Dooms. And we've not heard of Horgul having any such."

"No." Dauntra's headshake was emphatic. "I've heard he hates and fears spellhurlers, and has even hedge-wizards and altar-priests put to death when he finds them. With him it's the sword, the blood-drenched sword, and the ever thirstier sword!"

"Charming," Ambrelle commented. "Another butcher. Why are they *always* butchers?"

"Those who aren't, don't get as far," Juskra told the wind. "And we hear less of them, and don't go flying across half Falconfar to fight them. When he was one Stormar swording others through the farms of the Yulmeads, we cared not. When he first set boot out of the Stormar lands and hewed his way through the Raurklor to take Blacktrees, we lofted eyebrows. When he took Dawnarrows, we started to take interest in him as more than a mere curiosity. Now that he's lording it in Hawksyl, and on, bound for Darswords without delay, we're seeing Dooms and crying great change for Falconfar!"

"Well," Dauntra said impishly, eyeing her sisters, "I *was* getting bored with Galath."

Chapter Five

ROD BLINKED, AND came to a sudden halt.
So sudden that he almost lost his footing, landed on his rear, and started a bruising, bouncing slide down the steep bank.

Almost. Instead, when he started to slip, he launched himself into a frantic gallop to keep from falling—and ended up half-stumbling, half-sprinting down the bank in a wild, undignified race. It ended when he fetched up in a scrabbling-to-stop crouch atop a handy protruding boulder, where he could rise unsteadily to stand half-blinded in the bright late sun of the day, and look all around.

The endless forest he'd been trudging through had ended quite suddenly—if temporarily, for he could see its familiar dark green gloom on the horizon ahead, along the heights that rose on the far side of the vale—in a great open valley that stretched to Rod's left and right as far as he could see.

It was a valley of farms, small and odd-shaped fields bounded by untidy hedgerows. Along its winding slopes snaked many lanes, little woodlots were everywhere, and a river glimmered down at its heart. Far off to his left, where the valley widened, he could see the mouths of what must be side-valleys, carrying sun-sparkling streams down to join the river. That must be a fair-sized bridge, yonder, and—

"*Hold*, outlander! Keep your hands away from your weapons!"

The voice was cold, and close by, and it rang with the iron of authority.

Rod froze, then shivered, swallowed, and managed to turn his head. To look straight down into the hard, unfriendly eyes of a man in chainmail, a helm, and a leather jerkin that had large armor plates sewn onto it.

There was a younger, but just as unfriendly-looking guard off to one side, and that one had a long, slightly curving sword in his hand. Both of them had bright red diamonds painted on their breastplates, and those diamonds bore a painted iron gauntlet, each. Left-handed, vertical, thumb and fingers open and to the top.

Gage on a scarlet field. Hammerhand, in Ironthorn. He'd found Ironthorn.

And Ironthorn had found him.

As THE FLICKERING glows of his spell died away, the darkly handsome man stepped forward to loom over the table. "So," he asked the woman on it gently, "do you know who I am?"

The woman strapped to the table looked up at him with an eager, almost shy smile, the fires of his last spell still flickering across her eyeballs. "M-master," she murmured. "You are my lord and master."

The man smiled down at her. "And my name is?"

"Malraun," she whispered in awe and longing, as if he was a god.

"Yes, Taeauna," he said fondly. "Will you obey me, Taeauna?"

"Obey you and serve you," she said fervently, her eyes dark with longing. "Yield to you."

The handsome man's smile broadened, and he started undoing the straps that bound her ankles and hips.

"We won't be needing these, then."

SARDRAY UNFOLDED BELOW them, vast and empty, dark ripples in the grass marking the passage of hurrying breezes.

Used to such winds but not wanting to feel the colder bite of arrows, the four Aumrarr were flying high, up where the air was chill and thin.

"Now that Horgul's taken Hawksyl, the next hold is Darswords—and it stands in the shadow of Yintaerghast," Lorlarra said quietly. "Castle of the not-nearly-dead-enough Lorontar."

Juskra nodded. "And the hold after that is Harlhoh, and that means Malraun. Are you saying he'll never reach Ironthorn? Or that it can't be Malraun who's goading him?"

Lorlarra shrugged. "We can't tell that until we see what he does after Darswords. If he goes right past Harlhoh, following the eastern edge of the Raurklor around Sardray, he'll—"

"Come to upland Tauren. Where no one goes at all except to reach Ironthorn," Juskra put in. "So do we go back to Ironthorn ourselves, now?"

Dauntra shrugged. "The Dooms know Ironthorn's going to be important just as well as we do. Perhaps better; they might know *why*."

"Well, I'm not flying up to one to ask him," Ambrelle said firmly. "We dare not try to do much of anything in Ironthorn yet—show our faces there, least of all—but must be there and ready to pounce, once the Dooms are busily fighting each other up and down Thorn Vale."

"They will be," Lorlarra agreed.

There was a general sigh of agreement.

"Oh, yes," Juskra murmured, "they will."

They flew on in thoughtful silence for several wingbeats before Dauntra turned to look at her sisters. "Burnt Bones is the first hold west of Ironthorn, on the Long Trail. Should we fly there?"

Ambrelle shrugged. "We penned our two old rabbits up in Stormcrag; we may as well go there ourselves. It's a long way from here to Burnt Bones."

"Not if you use the old spell-gate," Juskra said quietly.

The other three Aumrarr all turned in the air to look hard at her.

"*What* 'old spell-gate'?" Ambrelle asked sharply. "As in Osturr and the Three Maidens? You're not starting to believe fireside tales, now?"

"No," Juskra said calmly. "Falconfar hasn't yet spawned a fighting hero as strong or perfect or unflaggingly virile as bright and smiling Osturr. The tale is pure fire-fancy."

She gave her winged sisters a dark smile. "The gate, however, is quite real. Have you *never* wondered why the Gold Duke—and why does just one coin grasping, Galathan-noble-hating merchant of Tauren style himself 'Duke,' anyway?—guards his family crypt with more coinsworn blades than stand watch over his treasury?"

"I always thought it was because he kept his *real* treasury in the caskets," Dauntra admitted. "You're saying the crypt holds a spell-gate between Tauren and Burnt Bones?"

Juskra's smile never wavered. "I am."

Lorlarra frowned. "And you want us to wing our ways right through all the Gold Duke's guards—and their venom-tipped crossbow bolts—because of this wild hunch of yours?"

"No hunch. I've walked the gate."

Three eyebrows lifted in unison.

"You must tell us about that, some day," Ambrelle said softly. "For now, though, you're suggesting we take this gate from the heart of Tauren to Burnt Bones? With all too many forest outlaws and hedge-wizards mind-thralled by Malraun the Matchless, or serving him out of well-founded fear?"

"Sisters," Lorlarra said quickly, "I don't think we dare try to use it."

Dauntra nodded. "If the Dooms all know about it, we'd be flying to our deaths."

Juskra nodded. "I'd say they can't *not* know about it."

"Then we use it not," Ambrelle decreed. "And we turn north, now, sisters, to reach Taurentar Wood. We can sleep there and go on to Ironthorn on the morrow. Waiting in the Raurklor until dusk, and only then darting straight to Stormcrag."

"Where we'll hope one of the Dooms hasn't installed a garrison before us," Lorlarra said darkly.

"What? Are you tired of fighting lurching dead men in armor, or flying toads?" Juskra teased.

"No," the quietest of the four sisters replied grimly, "but I'm thinking we all soon will be. Very soon."

As ROD STOOD and stared at them, both of the Ironthorn guards started moving, striding well out to either side of his boulder before slowly advancing on him. They both had their swords out now.

Rod glanced at one menacing face, then at the other.

"This is Ironthorn?" he asked the older guard, trying to make his voice sound calm and casual. He backed off the boulder as he spoke, turned, and started up the steep slope again, fumbling with his gauntlets.

Earlier, tramping through the forest, he'd taken them off and threaded the spiral rings adorning their cuffs through some of the metal loops his belt was studded with, to leave them hanging at his thighs. Now, of course, unthreading the rings wasn't going smoothly.

"I gave you an *order*, outlander!" the older guard said harshly, sounding very close.

Rod remembered that the closest part of the man would be his sharp swordtip—and then, thank God, he got that left gauntlet unhooked, pulled it on, and wheeled around.

"So you did," he replied sternly, "and I thought it rather a rude way of greeting someone who has aided the Hammerhands so much, over the years."

The guard was close to him and climbing the hill, sharp sword first. Rod's words made him frown in puzzlement, but not slow his pursuit.

The younger guard was farther down the hill, but keeping wide as he climbed, so as to be able to come at Rod almost from behind if Rod dared to stop to talk to the older one.

Rod started backing up the hill, out of the pincers of their closing trap. He had no idea what sort of fanciful lies he'd try to spin about aiding the Hammerhands, if he was asked.

Yet it didn't look as if he was *going* to be asked. Gods, he missed Taeauna. She always handled the meetings and greetings...

"Stay back!" he ordered, making his voice as stern and heavy as he could—and raised his left hand, gauntlet gleaming, to point at the guard.

The ring tingled, the gage started to tingle, too—and flames spat forth.

Well before the bright stream of fire reached him, the guard sprang back with a startled curse.

And lost his footing, of course, falling heavily and rolling a brief, crashing way back down the hill.

Rod turned to face the younger guard, who had halted, still far away and well below him.

"I'll not warn either of you again," Rod told the man, keeping his voice firm and flat, as he watched that angry face slowly go pale.

He raised his hand again, not sure if he should point at the second guard when the first one was now struggling grimly to his feet and starting to climb again.

Rod retreated a few more steps toward the trees.

"Down him, Urlaun," the older guard commanded, climbing right at Rod with dark, hot anger in his eyes. All trace of coldness had gone from the man; he was angry, and wanted blood.

Rod took one challenging step down the hill to meet him—actually to return to a level spot where he could stand and balance with some confidence—and pointed at the angry guard with his gauntlet-covered hand.

Fire flared from it again, spitting and snarling... and then faded away, exhausted. The gauntlet, and then the ring beneath, lost their tinglings.

Shit. Again.

Rod backed away and spun around, so he could climb the slope back into the trees in real haste.

The two guards were following him grimly, their drawn swords menacing him.

Rod turned his back on them and hurried. He was perhaps two minutes away, if not less, from having to face the fact that he hadn't the faintest idea how to use any of the magic he was carrying. At all.

The price he'd have to pay for that ignorance would be in blood.

A lot of it, and all his own.

"I CAN'T BELIEVE the *Stormar* spat out a 'warlord' who lasted more than one battle doing anything but fleeing," Garfist rumbled, "let alone one who managed to win battle after battle, and take hold after hold! He *must* have help!"

"He must have a Doom's hand in his head or up his backside, you mean," Iskarra agreed calmly, returning to her seat atop the table and lounging back against the wall. "How else could he take the field with monsters fighting for him, as well as hireswords?"

"But they say he butchers wizards whenever he can catch them," the onetime pirate and former panderer rumbled.

"Well, who would want wizards slain more than a Doom desiring all rivals swept away?"

"Oh. Huh." Garfist's wits had been far swifter in his younger days, but years of seeing unsubtle menace defeat deft cleverness had taken their toll. Swindlers shrieked and died just as quickly as fools when you took a sword and slit them open from chin to shivaroons. "So who's back of him, d'ye think? Malraun or Narmarkoun?"

"Or Arlaghaun standing up in his grave, or the new Lord Archwizard—"

"Huh. *That* idiot. Not likely."

"—or Lorontar the Undying?"

Garfist sighed, regarded his nigh-skeletal lover unhappily, and rumbled slowly and bitterly, "As the years pass, I find I like anything to do with magic and wizards less and less. Give me a good sharp knife handy to a foe's throat *any* day. Or better, night."

"I believe, Old Ox, that many a king, knight, and dung-covered drover has expressed those same sentiments before you," Iskarra said wryly. "Some of them quite forcefully, and more than one of them screaming it as his last words."

"Huh," Garfist said again. "Trying to scare me?"

The woman once infamous as the Viper raised a withering eyebrow. "Why should I try that? 'Tisn't as if it's going to work, after all these years."

The large and shaggy former pirate grinned and nodded. "Heh. *That's* true." Then he lost his smile in an instant, and asked in a lower, warier voice, "Viper mine, d'ye think the Aumrarr as brought us here might be working for a Doom? Or living all enspelled by one, and not know they were doing his bidding?"

Iskarra frowned. "It's possible, I suppose," she said slowly, "but I... no, I *can't* believe it. All these years they've fought the Dooms; if one was behind them, he'd have used them on his rival Dooms long since, when he saw a good chance to destroy one."

"But the Lord Archwizard, he's new," Garfist said darkly. "And all that time, none of us knew Lorontar was anything more than a nightscare legend, too. If he was drifting about like a ghost, from one Aumrarr mind to another, all those years..."

Iskarra shuddered. "Do I *want* to hear this?"

"And another thing," Garfist told her, drawing himself up in grim triumph. "All the tavern-talk we heard in Galath, about who the Aumrarr *really* are. Those flying lasses have been keeping secrets from us all for years!"

But his longtime lover shook her head, grinned mirthlessly, and waved a scornfully dismissive hand. "Someone's been spreading stories to try and make us mistrust them, more like. Now *there* I think I see a Doom at work, yes!"

She leaned forward to wag a reproving finger. "Gar, spew it all back out of your head right now, all this about the Aumrarr once ruling us all, starting as the great lords and ladies of some bygone age who shapeshifted themselves all into winged women long, long ago. Did you ever hear talk of it before King Devaer and Arlaghaun were thrown down? Aye? And wouldn't they have hurled such dung into every passing ear, and spread it from end to end of Falconfar, if they'd heard aught of it?"

"Well, aye, uh—"

"You *know* they would have. Think, my Ox. If the Aumrarr really were seeking to become one with Falconfar, as the tavern-tales said, by finding the right physical form, why'd they end up as women with wings? What's so 'right' about that? Wouldn't they've done better to become men taller and brawnier than all the rest, with manhoods a foot long?"

Garfist snorted, but Iskarra's finger stabbed at him.

"Aye, 'tis funny enough, Ox, but I'm serious. Wouldn't that have been a better shape, to conquer

Falconfar? And what better way to 'become one' with the world, than rule it all?"

Garfist started to frown thoughtfully. Then, very slowly, he nodded.

The Viper leaned forward still more. "And have you ever heard of an Aumrarr 'seeking to become one with Falconfar,' *now?*"

"No," he rumbled. "Kill this ruler or that in Falconfar, yes. Teach yon merchant a lesson, or end a blood-feud by slaying the heads of both warring houses, aye, but dwell with all the rest of us and share in our lives and stand forth in every village and trade-moot, no."

"Exactly."

Garfist was still frowning. "But in the taverns they were saying Aumrarr lie with men only to breed enough new Aumrarr that they don't all die off."

"Yes, and they were *also* saying in the taverns—you heard it, too; you were right at my elbow, three tankards gone and slowing on your fourth—that these long-ago rulers of all turned their great mastery of magic into shaping, reshaping, purifying, and healing their bodies. Does that sound like the same sort of folk who'd need to fly to men by night to rut, just to bear little ones?"

"Hmmph. No. But why say all this, if none of it's true?"

"To spread lies enough to make us see the Aumrarr differently. False lore piled atop false lore, until some of it gets believed. As has been said a time or two before, one lie often needs to stand on another."

"And sometimes even raise a third as a shield, and make a spear of a fourth," Garfist rumbled slowly, nodding as he completed the old saying.

"And having swallowed this, we're supposed to believe these great masters of magic lost control over the rest of us when everyone started to learn spells, and we great grunting unwashed, who outnumbered the Aumrarr so greatly, started winning a few battles. Then all the Aumrarr saw we beasts could defeat Aumrarr, and a few of them stood with us to defeat Aumrarr foes and rivals, and... do *you* believe any of that?"

"No," Garfist replied flatly. "Even before that Stormar trader claimed Lorontar was one of these rebel Aumrarr. Nor do I think it glorking *matters* who did what to whom, centuries upon centuries ago. Too many old tales get used as excuses for what ambitious brutes do to others now."

He started to prowl again, restlessly. "I may swindle a man out of a keg here and some coins yonder, but the real villains sit in castles and cry vengeance and rob knights and armsmen and poor steaders just trying to grow enough tharuk to eat of their *lives*."

Iskarra nodded. "Well," she said briskly, "it's good to know we, at least, can see all Falconfar's troubles so clearly. Now, if someone else would see clearly enough to put us on some thrones—in Galath, say—everything could get—"

"No," Garfist growled. "Oh, no. Everything *wouldn't* get fixed. Problems are like dirt, or rocks: dig one away, and there's always another underneath. And for us, it's getting our backsides out of this glorking castle—or keeping our necks intact through whatever those four Aumrarr have planned for us. Just so long as whatever it is happens *soon*. I'm fair going witless, waiting here just talking talking *talking*, when—"

The pleasant, placid view out that high window of Stormcrag Castle was suddenly blotted out by something large and dark, looming up fast with wings spread.

Wings that flapped hard, to slow a racing flight, exertion that came with a sob of pain. As Garfist swore and grabbed for his dagger and the sword he no longer had, and Iskarra sprang from the table like a restless bolt of lightning, the wings snapped back and their sobbing, gasping owner dived headlong into the room.

Landing heavily, running hard and stumbling, to a hard-breathing halt that became a frantic drawing of weapons.

An angry-looking Aumrarr they'd never seen before stood glaring and panting at Iskarra and Garfist, who stared back at her.

The winged woman was bleeding all down her left front, where her leather tunic had been slashed open by what looked to be several sword-blades, to hang down in gory, dripping folds.

"I know not who you are or how you came to be here," she hissed, stalking forward a little unsteadily, "but I know what's going to happen to you *now!*"

"We're going to die?" Iskarra yawned. "Again?"

Chapter Six

M**Y, BUT THE** Gold Duke loved guards. Guards, guards, and more glittering guards, all of them tall and gleaming in their armor... and all of them bored enough to be *really* dangerous.

They strolled to and fro, sighing and preening, whirling often to send hawk-like glares down this or that dark passage. They were spoiling for something—anything—to happen, so they could draw their swords to shout and run and hack.

Sweating so hard that it dripped off his nose almost in a steady stream, Alander Thaetult drew back from the cellar-passage corner he'd been peering round to watch the latest selection of ducal guards, and whispered another shadowcloak spell incantation. The air around him dimmed still more, his magic's dark tendrils drifting and swirling.

He shrugged. So what if he looked like a traveling cloud of smoke? He had no intention of ending up as the "interesting anything" these murderous sword-swingers were seeking.

Malraun's orders had been clear. Reach the Tauren end of the spell-gate as stealthily as possible—no matter how things went, Malraun wanted the Gold Duke to think a lone and perhaps deranged person had passed through his gate, not an invading army or any other sort of threat he had to muster a stronger standing guard to prepare for—traverse it to Burnt Bones if possible, and use the new farspeaking spell Malraun had given him to report everything that happened to the listening Doom.

Gnawing pestilence take him.

Alander didn't want to serve a Doom.

Alander didn't want to skulk through guard-infested cellars.

Heaving himself up out of his chair to answer the bell-pull of "Thaetult's Useful Magics" was adventure enough for him. He had no dreams of greatness, or even of lording it over an apprentice or two. He was a hedge-wizard, and proud of it. A cowardly and placid master of a paltry handful of spells, quite content to make a modest living casting this and mending that mold-banishing for a coin or two, and occasionally—very, very occasionally— spying on this wayward husband or seeking that stolen heirloom for larger handfuls of coins. No "adventures," no travels to far places and skulkings anywhere that had lots of armored men eager to use their swords…

Yes, there'd been shadows drifting through his contentedness. Alander had known his own boredom, vague dissatisfaction with his lot—but when the sleek, darkly handsome little man had appeared so suddenly in the cluttered forechamber that served him as office, spellcasting sanctum, and untidy storage room, and uttered that softly-spoken, calm ultimatum, Alander had discovered that he wanted very much to cling to his comfortable little life.

Which was why he was here in a dank, dark passage deep in the cellars of the Gold Duke's fortress-mansion in Tauren, half a dozen clumsy, spell-hushed murders in his wake, trying to get to the Gold Duke's most closely-guarded secret.

The Yuskel family crypt held not just stone coffins, moldering bones, dust, and forgetfulness… it held the many gold coins and gems popular lore whispered so excitedly of, and guards to watch over them.

It also held the real reason so many armed men were wasting their lives away yawning and sighing down here: the spell-gate.

It was here, all right. He could feel its silent, patient pulse in his blood now, a slow and rhythmic thudding that rolled through him steadily, ever stronger… it was very near.

He fancied he could see its flickering, past this latest group of bored sentinels, a ribbon of gold that split the darkness for an instant here, and an instant there, in time with the deep throbbing that was singing inside him.

Keeping him excited with its song, thrilled despite himself. Alander hated stealth and deceit almost as much as he loathed violence and doing murder. Yet six guards were dead this day by his hand—soon to be discovered and a hue and cry raised at his back, making retreat nigh-impossible. There were eight more guards around that corner, and unless some miracle or other took them away or at a stroke dropped them into blindness or slumber, he was going to have to kill them to get to the spell-gate, and have any hope of escaping the fate Malraun had so calmly promised him.

An especially large droplet of sweat plummeted from his nose and found splattered oblivion on the stones in front of his boots with a "splat" loud enough to echo.

"What's *that*?" a guard snarled from around the corner, and Alander drew in a shudderingly deep breath, and—suddenly found himself very calm. This was it.

Killing time.

He whispered the brief incantation as if it was a prayer, swept his hand up, and let go of the knife.

Then he stepped smoothly back along the wall, retreating from the corner. He'd managed two steps when the first guard sprang around the corner, sword up—and the little silver fang of his knife, that had been hanging motionless in the air just where he'd released it, sprang forward every bit as energetically as the guard, leaping at the man's face in a gleaming blur.

The guards all wore open-faced helms, with gorget-plates dangling from the outthrust chinguards of those helms rather than strapped to the throats they were intended to guard. That fashion choice would earn them swift doom.

The first guard was gargling out his life already, staggering and clutching a throat sliced too deeply for him to utter any warning cry. The knife had flown on, darting around the corner.

Silver no longer, but dark with wet blood, it sought more.

Alander drew his second knife, uttered the same incantation, reached around the corner, and let go of the weapon. It almost bruised his fingertips in its eagerness to leap away.

Which meant the guards he couldn't see must be

rushing toward him right now, as soundlessly as a hurrying mouse, and almost—

Around the corner lurched a struggling, gargling warrior, clutching his slit throat and choking on his own blood as if he was racing to find death before the first guard could. Alander watched him trip over the first guard's feebly-thrashing body, stumble, and fall headlong to the stones, arms flying wide as he bounced, in a great spray of gushing blood.

Alander swallowed, shaking his head to try to avoid seeing and hearing more. There were sounds of dying from around the corner, too, and he'd tarried long enough—sooner or later, this much death would be noticed, and someone would cry the alarm.

Drawing in a deep breath, Alander Thaetult threw his arms wide to make his shadowcloaks billow up in front of him, ducked his head as if running into coldly lashing rain, and sprinted around the corner.

Two guards were staggering around swinging swords frantically, like men trying to beat away wasps, tripping and stumbling over six—no, seven— fallen comrades, armored bodies sprawled amid dark and spreading pools of blood. The throbbing, waiting darkness he sought was straight across the room, short-lived rents of gold beckoning to Alander.

Who ran as fast as he pantingly could, knowing many warriors believed killing a wizard would end his spell in an instant.

He was more than halfway to the spell-gate when one of the guards saw him, roared out a wordless stream of fury, and stumbled to intercept him. Alander saw the flying dagger swoop, spiral around the man's frantic parry, and dart home. Metal clanged, the warrior slapped the knife aside and twisted in the other direction, lost his balance, and—

Alander was past, even before a despairing cry behind him ended in an ugly wet gurgling. Past and not slowing in the slightest, boots pounding on the crypt flagstones, running right into—

Sudden golden radiance, all around, and a deep thudding like a heartbeat, that came from everywhere. His racing feet came down on soundless nothing, there was nothing around him but swirling and streaming golden light, banishing his shadowcloaks in a sighing instant.

He breathed in golden air, and his vision blurred. The sounds of his own panting suddenly boomed in his ears, and a horrible *stirring* arose inside him, as if his innards were rearranging themselves as he ran.

Golden nothingness gave way to wan sunlight, and trees. He stumbled, his legs seeming heavier and somehow *longer*. Even before all the golden hue was gone and he saw men with crossbows stepping forward out of a deep green forest to loose war-quarrels at him, Alander Thaetult knew something had gone horribly, sickeningly wrong.

"There!" the outlaw chief barked, pointing. "It comes! Let it not live to reach us!"

His men were hastening forward, all around, just enough to let their quarrels fly free. Crossbows cracked, one after another—and the running, wild-eyed thing that was half-monster and half-man staggered as it grew a thick new hide of quivering crossbow bolts. Then fell on its face, shuddered, and died.

That face had two large but mismatched eyes, and a shapeless, flaccid snout that flopped aside and left bare gums and teeth, above hands that had slumped into tentacles, fingers grown impossibly long and grotesque. Its head was the shape of a bird's head, and its legs…

Men cried out in disgust and fear as they beheld it.

"Well done!" their leader cried. "We've kept this horror from our midst! No one would've been safe with such as *this* lurking in the forest!"

He smiled, then, the same soft and satisfied smile that was on the face of the blue-skinned Doom who was looking out at Burnt Bones through his eyes.

Narmarkoun was well pleased.

"So the gate twists those—wizards, at least—who step through it, forcibly changing them," he murmured aloud, walking the outlaw leader away from those near enough to hear his dupe echo his words. "And my bowmen can handle all others. Malraun won't get in this way."

* * *

IN ANOTHER CASTLE, another Doom sat up naked in a great bed and smiled a sleek, darkly handsome smile of his own.

"So," Malraun purred aloud, "the ruse works, and the lurker reveals himself. Narmarkoun *is* watching over this route. Ironthorn it must be. And soon."

"Soon," Taeauna echoed, beside him. Her long-fingered hands never stopped hungrily caressing all she could reach of his bare body.

"INTRUDERS!" THE AUMRARR spat as she stalked toward them, hefting her sword and dagger. Blood welled out and down her left side in a quickening stream, spattering the floor in her wake, but her eyes burned with more rage than pain. "How *dare* you enter into Stormcrag! You, you—how many more of you are there?"

"There's only one of me, Lady of the Aumrarr," Garfist told her dryly, retreating toward the door. A quick glance told him that Iskarra was down off her table and backing away down the far wall of the room. "None have complained of that, mind ye, thus far in my life, but I've heard ye winged women have strange tastes, an'—"

With a snarl the Aumrarr charged him, swinging her sword viciously but holding her dagger warily ready behind it. No recklessness nor clumsy fumblings with steel here; she knew how to wield a blade.

So did Garfist, and he ducked easily away from her slash, keeping his balance with casual ease as he retreated another two swift steps, correctly anticipating her follow-up lunge and backslash.

Without a word Iskarra plucked up one of the chairs at the next table she came to, and hurled it, high and hard.

Tremble, woman with wings, she thought angrily. *You face Iskarra, Hurler of Chairs. Whom you'll likely slay, in a breath or three, Dooms take you.*

ROD REACHED THE trees, and more or less level ground, at the same time. Darting three swift strides into the shade, he spun around.

The two guards were trudging patiently after him, keeping well apart, and holding their swords up in front of them. The looks they were giving him were a lot worse than unfriendly.

Rod swallowed. "Sir," he said to the older and closer guard, "please do not misunderstand me. I do not want to fight you, nor am I any threat to Ironthorn. I have given my warning, and wish to pass on my way in peace, to see Lord Hammerhand. Ground your sword, and let us talk."

The warrior gave him a look that was half-glare and half-sneer, said not a word, and kept on coming. Both of the guards had now reached the trees, and more or less level ground.

Rod retreated a few steps more, backing away until he fetched up against the unyielding trunk of a large tree. He looked at the younger guard. "Urlaun? How does anyone get to see Lord Hammerhand, if you kill anyone you see coming out of the forest? Or are you two just robbers and murderers, and don't serve him at all?"

"We serve Lord Hammerhand," Urlaun snapped. Yet said not a word more, as the older guard shot him a darkly furious look.

Rod looked quickly behind himself, in search of a really large tree he could stand against like a wall. He hadn't remembered any such, but—

"*Halt*, outlander!" The older guard wagged his leveled sword at Rod as if it was a disapproving finger. "Who are you, and how do you know Lord Hammerhand? Tell us—and reach for no weapon, or Lord's friend or not, you'll taste steel before you can do aught else!"

Rod halted, managed a smile he hoped didn't look too sickly, and spread his empty hands wide. "I... Burrim Hammerhand is still Lord of Ironthorn, right?"

"He is," the older guard snapped. "And I am Briszyk, yon blade is Urlaun, and you are *who*, I ask again, outlander?"

Rod drew in a deep breath, and replied unhappily, "My name is Rod Everlar. If you have heard of me at all, you probably know me as the Lord Archwizard of Falconfar."

Their eyes blazed, and they lifted their swords grimly, just the way he'd expected.

Rod sighed, and wondered how it would feel to be sliced apart.

DYUNE OF THE Aumrarr turned to see what was coming at her—a wooden chair that fell far short, bouncing and sliding harmlessly—and beheld a second chair, and a third, all slid across the room with all the force the skeletally-thin woman could muster.

Not at her, but to where the shaggy man she was pursuing could easily sidestep and snatch them up.

He hurled the first at her high and hard, and it came crashing down on her swordarm, head, and shoulder from above, bruisingly.

Dyune snarled out her rage and flung it aside, launching herself into a fresh charge that brought her racing, face-first, right into the second chair.

That stung, dazing her and forcing brief weeping, and she hacked empty air blindly and wildly to keep him at bay as she hastily blinked away the tears that were blurring her vision.

Something large and dark came swinging at her, and she got her sword up only just in time. The blade bit deep into the wooden seat of this latest chair, and almost got snatched out of her hand as the man wielding it twisted it away.

"Keep 'em coming, Isk!" he bellowed. "I think she *likes* 'em!"

Off-balance and straining to keep hold of her

sword, Dyune couldn't stop the response: a chair that came hurtling at her from behind, crashing down around her head and dashing her to the floor.

She lost her dagger somewhere in that bouncing, breath-snatching landing, and ended up rolling clumsily, trying grimly to keep hold of her sword as the shaggy man kept planting himself above her and hammering her with his chair, beating her about the head and shoulders, and kicking at her sword to try to knock it out of her hand whenever he dared risk his balance.

In the end, she let it go and instead whirled toward him, ramming herself against his legs. He toppled over her with a great crash, like a stone wall falling over, and she rose groggily to retrieve her sword and put it through him.

Only to hear the thin woman shrieking her way nearer. Fast.

The Aumrarr fought her clambering way over the fallen man—who kicked and punched her with a fine disregard for her sex—to try to pluck up her sword before that deafening banshee reached her. Thinbritches would have a knife or three, she was sure, and—

The man's boots caught her ankle in a scissors-grip. She toppled helplessly, slamming to the floor with force enough to drive all her wind out of her, leaving her unable to even sob in pain as her slashed left side erupted in fresh fire.

So she writhed in silent, gasping agony, insistently forcing herself to roll toward her fallen sword, and expecting the cold kiss of a dagger across her throat at any instant.

Thuddings shaking the floor right behind Dyune told her the man was rolling, too, keeping close behind her.

One of his hands—as large and hairy as a bear's paw—clawed at her hip, slowing and twisting her as she strained her way onward. She wasn't more than the length of her hand away from the hilt of her blade, now—

Thinbritches fell on her, hard, screaming and stabbing wildly, rolling over her and off. The thin woman must have slipped in her sprinting haste, or tripped over the man, to tumble so rather than pouncing, and—

Dyune's fingers closed on her sword.

Spinning around on her hip, she swung it in a great slash, slicing deep into the man crawling behind her, whose great body took it solidly. He grunted, sounding more surprised than pained as his blood sprayed.

The Aumrarr kept right on spinning, cutting thin air—and then the ribs of the lunging, energetically-clambering woman, who was already clawing for her with that dagger.

Thinbritches made a sound that was half-sob and half-shriek, and collapsed, more blood spurting.

The sword had slid along the woman's ribs, glancing off rather than plunging in, so she might not be hurt all that badly, but Dyune didn't plan to give these two intruders time to wallow in pain.

They were going to die, and die *now*, before she collapsed and ran out of time to reach the healing.

Clenching her teeth against the agony tearing at her left side, she struggled to rise from her hip to her knees, to crawl to... to...

She fell back, heavily, a flood of tears blinding her. The fire all down her left side was spreading, and she was melting into it...

She heard her sword clatter on the floor; it sounded as if it was far away, though it must be right beside her. She could no longer feel her fingers, and was somehow on her back and staring up at the ceiling. There was a groaning, that might have been rising from inside her, except that it was deep and rough, and snarled out curses that were new to her.

She turned her head, but instead of her chair-tormentor, saw Thinbritches, lying gasping on the floor beside her in the wet center of a slowly-spreading pool of blood. The woman was staring back at Dyune with a doomed look, like a caged boar that knows its time on the spit will come soon.

That deep groaning came again, and Dyune turned her head the other way.

There was the shaggy man, sprawled on his back on her other flank, in the heart of *his* pool of spreading blood.

So behold, she thought wryly, *the Fallen Three. Our battle done, as we lie together, slowly dying from our wounds, too wounded to fight on. This isn't how things went, in all the ballads.*

Chapter Seven

ROD EVERLAR SHOOK his head. "*No*. Briszyk and Urlaun, *don't* make the mistake of killing me. You'll be dooming yourselves, and all of Ironthorn, too."

Briszyk's eyes narrowed, and he stopped advancing and flung out his free hand in a "stay your blade" signal to the younger guard.

"His death will trigger spells," he said warningly to Urlaun. "We must torture him—breaking fingers is best—and force him to quell them, before we cut off his head and burn it. One can't be too careful, when slaying wizards."

"Perhaps not," Rod snapped, trying not to tremble too much. "But I'm not a wizard. I'm *the* Archwizard. And I haven't blasted either of you, have I?"

Urlaun sneered. "You can't. Your spells are gone. We can see that."

"So I'm no threat. Yet you rush to slay me?"

Briszyk shrugged. "One less wizard to worry about."

Rod sighed, drew in a deep breath, and started to stroll among the trees, clasping his hands behind his back and doing his trembling damnedest to seem unconcerned.

"Sure you can kill me," he told the Hammerhand guards. "But you'll destroy all of Ironthorn—all *Falconfar*—if you do. Not just topple a lord or a castle, but wipe away everything. You, your parents, your friends, children—*everything*. I'm the Lord Archwizard. All life in the world, all magic, is rooted in me and flows through me. If I die, the world dies with me."

He swung around to face them, and managed a smile. "I get sick or angry, bad things happen. Nearby, and right away. So keep me happy. Very happy."

Urlaun had gone pale, and was swallowing and backing away, sword raised to menace Rod as if he could hide behind it.

Briszyk, however, was glowering suspiciously. "If all magic flows through you, why aren't you blasting us with a spell, right now?"

"Because I'm not that stupid," Rod snapped. "Unlike the lesser Dooms, I *know* every single magic unleashed in the world affects everything. Sometimes in little ways none of us notice—and sometimes in great disasters, when mountains shake and slide down to bury entire towns, maddened dragons fly through the skies biting every living thing they see below, and castles collapse, crushing everyone inside. Most wizards don't care how much harm they do, but *I* don't want to do any more damage than I have to."

He took a step toward the older guard and asked quietly, "If every time you drew your sword, a dozen people died—not enemies you could choose, but you'd never know who or where your victims were—how often would you dare to unsheathe it?"

Briszyk shrugged, but his glower was gone, and his weathered face was going pale. He took a step back when Rod added quietly, "How soon would you have to run home and see if it was your wife who died, this latest time your sword came out? Or your son? Your daughter?"

"The Lord of Ironthorn," Urlaun blurted out, "wants nothing to do with wizards. We want nothing to do with wizards. We are sworn to defend Ironthorn, and that means keeping wizards out!"

"Does it? As I recall, Lord Hammerhand claims all Ironthorn, but rival Ironthar lords dispute that. Are you sure neither of them welcomes wizards as allies?"

He fell silent and waited, seeing grim uncertainty on both loyal Hammerhand faces. The moment they shot swift looks at each other, Rod added quietly, "So do you still dare to kill me or turn me away, when I come to Hammerhand in friendship?"

It was Briszyk's turn to sigh heavily. "You seek audience with Lord Burrim Hammerhand?"

"I do. In peace." He spread his hands. "No blades, and no spells."

Urlaun spat in Rod's direction, but lowered his sword. "Wizards need neither, sometimes. They can talk a man to death!"

Rod grinned. "Now that, I'll grant you. I'll try not to, though. All right?"

Briszyk and Urlaun traded glances again. Then the older guard waved his sword in a beckoning command and said curtly, "Well enough. We'll take you to Lord Hammerhand. You walk in front of us, though, and keep your hands away from your belt. Start casting a spell, and—"

He hefted his sword meaningfully.

Rod nodded. "I understand. Which way is the trail?"

"That way," Urlaun said, pointing with his sword.

Rod stumbled forward down the slope obediently. He'd descended perhaps half a dozen strides when the younger guard muttered, "You don't *act* like an Archwizard."

"Oh?" Rod asked over his shoulder, not turning his head. "How many Archwizards have you watched closely, recently?"

Neither guard made any sort of an answer to that.

DYUNE OF THE Aumrarr knew she was dying.

She was drooling blood, but it felt like she was spitting out fire. Fire that slid out of her endlessly, welling up a-fresh inside her to replace all she leaked out. She could feel nothing but searing fire on her left side—even the left side of her *face*, now—and her right side felt weak and sick.

Dyune tried to lift her hand, and the sick feeling surged, raging through her and leaving her gasping. Healing was only two rooms from here, but it might as well have been kingdoms away across Falconfar.

"Dying, all of us," the shaggy man muttered suddenly, close by on her right. "Less ye've got healing up yer sleeve, woman with wings."

"I do," Dyune gasped, or tried to; it came out very much like a whisper.

A handful of moments later she found herself shaken feebly—fresh fire rocked her, forcing out sobs—as a battered face glared into hers nose to nose, and its owner growled, "Where? Where and how—and no tricks, now! Or I'll—I'll—"

"Kill me?" Dyune fought to smile. "I tremble, man."

"Glork ye! Ye're *dying*, Aumrarr! Can't ye leave off sneering at us poor idiot bumbling man-folk for one glorking *moment*?"

"Evidently not," Dyune managed to hiss, but her smile was real this time, and the shaggy man saw that.

"Garfist Gulkoun am I, an' this is my Iskarra, yonder," he told her, blood welling out of his mouth. He spat it out scornfully to one side, and added, "And ye found us here because four Aumrarr *put* us here. After flying us here across Falconfar three days and three nights, too!"

He regarded her for a moment, and then added, "Seeing as we're dying, too, will ye tell us just what enraged ye so, finding us here in Stormcrag Castle? Is it sacred to ye wingbi—er, Aumrarr, hey?"

Dyune hadn't the strength left to laugh or groan, she found; all she managed was a sort of croaking, heaving choking. "And I attacked you," she spat out, when she could form words again.

Garfist merely nodded. "Ye wouldn't happen to be right sorry over it, and have healing magic handy, would ye?"

Dyune tried—and failed—to laugh again, and settled for whispering, "Will you heal me, and make peace between us, if I tell you where healing magic is hidden?"

"I will. Strike me if I lie!"

Dyune smiled at that, and whispered, "Then go out through that door you were trying to get through. The room beyond has three doors in its far wall. Open them—and leave them open. They're weighted to swing shut; use chairs or your boots as wedges, to keep them open. Then close the left-most of the doors, twist its pull-ring to the right, right around a full turn and more. Once you hear a click, wedge the door wide open again, and you'll reveal a stone on its sill, right by its hinge, that's darker than the rest. Push it down. You can then pull out the standing part of the doorframe the door swings closed against. There's a niche full of vials, all the same. Drink two and bring two each back, for your lady and for me. Then I'll say more."

"Heh. Just a little trust, eh?"

"All I can spare, man. All I can spare."

The man let go of her, and Dyune sank back into her pool of gentle fire. Warm and welcome it grew slowly cooler and deeper… deeper…

Abruptly she was shaken awake again, as ungentle fingers thrust her head upright and dug at the corners of her mouth.

"I'm—I'm—" she struggled to say, before her mouth flooded with water. Water that was like minted ice, minted ice that had caught a-flame and was sluicing away the deep, smoldering fire that had claimed her left side and crept through much of the rest of her, too…

Dyune arched and gasped, shuddering, as the pain ebbed. She'd tasted these healing quaffs before; Garfist hadn't played her false. She'd helped fill the vials—many seasons ago, it seemed—from an enspelled healing pool the Aumrarr had found in the castle of the dead wizard Heldohraun, and—

Ah! She could see again, tears blinked away and shudderings done, and beheld the man and the woman sitting on either side of her. Garfist had her sword in his hands, and Thinbritches—Iskarra, that's what he'd called her—held her dagger.

"Peace?" she asked them, with a wry smile.

"Peace," they replied, in perfect unison.

Dyune let her smile sag in relief, drew in a deep breath, and asked, "Do you know why four of my sisters brought you here? And who they were? How did you come to meet them? I—"

Garfist waved the sword. "Hold tongue, there! I'll be forgetting all you ask, in a breath or two!"

"Another thing," Iskarra said crisply. "*We* have the blades, remember. So, a question answered for a question answered."

She leaned forward to fix Dyune with a steady look that wasn't quite a glare, and added, "To your first: no, we know not why we were brought here. We have our suspicions, but they're just that. Our suspicions. Some Aumrarr seem to delight in keeping secrets. I'm going to hope you're not one of them." Wagging the dagger in her hand like a disapproving finger, she asked, "As Gar asked and you avoided answering, O Nameless Aumrarr, what's so special about Stormcrag Castle?"

Dyune stared at her for a moment. "I did, didn't I?" she said slowly. "Iskarra and Garfist, I am called Dyune. This castle once belonged to a wizard-king, long ago, but for centuries has been a hide-hold of the Aumrarr. A refuge, where we hide folk and things and ourselves, when the need arises."

"Falconaar say Stormcrag Castle is haunted, and stands lost in the heart of the Raurklor," Garfist growled, almost accusingly.

The Aumrarr shrugged. "Well, it *is* haunted, and does stand near the center of the Raurklor. It's hardly 'lost,' though. We're right in the heart of embattled Ironthorn, with the Lyrose vales all around us."

"The who?" Iskarra asked sharply.

"Haunted by *what*, exactly?" Garfist asked, just a little more slowly.

"Ghosts of things—headless floating warriors who swing swords, huge four-armed skeletons fused together out of the bones of many smaller dead beasts—we hopefully won't see. They appear to those who try to walk in and out of Stormcrag, or use magic against its wardings. They are bound to thwart such farers, not harm Aumrarr who fly in and out of the castle."

"Someone or something keeps this place clean, and mends its leaks and shutters when storms get in," Iskarra said warningly. "I don't think you're telling us true and full, Aumrarr."

"There are ghostly Aumrarr, too, but they keep themselves hidden from non-Aumrarr," Dyune admitted. "Forgive me; secrets are all the armor most Aumrarr ever wear; sharing them is not something I am in the habit of doing." She managed a faint smile. "Now, I believe you owe me another answer, before I share more."

"The four who brought us here were Ambrelle, Juskra, Dauntra, and… Lorlarra," Iskarra replied. "Now, who or what are 'Lyrose vales,' and why is Ironthorn embattled *this* time?"

Dyune rolled slowly onto her side and sat up. She was pleased to see that neither her sword nor her dagger were raised menacingly against her. "You know Ironthorn has three lords, bitter rivals who make war on each other constantly, yes?"

"Yes," Garfist and Iskarra said together.

"Well, Lord Magrandar Lyrose holds sway over three small valleys that make up southwestern Ironthorn. Those valleys are separated from each other by Harstorm Ridge, a long, steep-sided height that's covered with thick forest and roamed by many monsters—"

"What *sort* of monsters?" Garfist interrupted suspiciously. The sword did come up, this time.

"Any sort we can find, spell-snare, and bring here," Dyune told him wryly. "Prowlcats and sharruk bears, mostly."

"So 'haunted' Stormcrag Castle stands atop this ridge, and your hungry roaming beasts keep Ironthar away from the gates," Iskarra put in.

"Exactly. Only the bravest Lyrose foresters set axe to even the outermost trees of Harstorm. None that I know of have dared climb the slopes of the Stormcrag."

"So we're sitting in the middle of all this right now," Garfist said slowly. "The war between the lords; how fares it now? What's befallen this last season or so?"

Dyune shrugged. "You've time to spare, don't you? Well, now... Ironthorn is mainly farms in the forest, but it has its gemadars, too, so Stormar now know and care about Ironthorn, and—"

"We know about gemadars an' Ironthar swords," Gar interrupted. "An' we know Hammerhand is strongest of the three, but Lyrose an' Tesmer defy his rule, calling themselves 'Lord of Ironthorn,' too. Hammerhand is the gauntlet on blood, Lyrose the caltrop, and Tesmer the diamond. Tesmer has most of the gem-mines, but is the least of the three. If I remember me a-right, Burrim is the Hammerhand lord right now, Melvarl—*there's* a sly, dark sneering villain, if ever I met one!—is Lyrose in Lyraunt Castle, an'... Lance? Rance?... is Tesmer, an' his lands lie along the Imrush."

"Irrance Tesmer," said the Aumrarr, "and Melvarl lords it no longer. He raped and butchered Lady Venyarla Hammerhand, and Burrim caught and killed him for it. Wherefore Burrim now has no wife, and Magrandar son of Melvarl is Lord Lyrose. A cruel echo of his father; less brains, backbone, and subtlety, though he knows it not."

"You're telling us," Iskarra said dryly, "That it's much safer inside this castle—even with Aumrarr bursting in trying to kill us—than out there in Ironthorn, where the warring never ends."

Dyune nodded. "And every visitor becomes another sword in the hand of someone, to use on someone else. Until that sword shatters."

"Nelthraun," the darkly handsome man said gently, to the face flickering between his upraised hands in the air before him, "I truly don't care if the timing is inconvenient, or how many coins this will cost you. I need your warriors armed and hurrying to Ironthorn *now*. Or I'll need a new Lord of Stelgond."

He strolled across the room, the floating face hanging in the air staring at him going slowly pale, and added casually, "If that brutally unsubtle threat isn't sufficiently clear to you, I can make another. This, for instance: gaunch-eels eat humans very slowly, from within. I'm sure you'll find it entertaining to watch your daughter die—it will take days—and then your wife, all the while knowing you'll be next. Unpleasantnesses that can all be avoided, if you just obey me. As you swore to do, when I named you Lord, remember?"

"Y-yes, High Lord Malraun! Of course! I was merely informing you of the effects of mustering my armsmen at this time, not disputing your command! I'll be leading the swords of Stelgond north before nightfall!"

"That's *very* gratifying to hear," Malraun purred, and flung his arms wide, ending the spell. The face vanished into a brief-lived cloud of whirling sparks; he strode right through them on his way to the meal that was now waiting for him. Or should be, if certain servants wanted to retain their heads.

In the meantime, his armies were gathering and converging. Armies no other could match—or hope to stop.

The bracelets on Malraun's wrists crackled as the poison-seeking spell awakened. He had not outlasted Arlaghaun, and withstood Narmarkoun all these years, by being careless. The newest Doom had come at last, true, but his scryings had long since told him that Rod Everlar was a blundering weakling who hailed from a far place indeed, who knew very little about magic or Falconfar. There was no need to worry about anything Rod Everlar might do.

Wherefore a relaxed and smug Malraun the Matchless went to enjoy his repast without further care, unaware of one silent, hidden little problem known as Lorontar.

DYUNE SHOOK HER head. "Burrim has sons, and a daughter, too, but his real strengths are his fearlessness and clear wits, and his three loyal warcaptains: Darlok, Tarlkond, and Syregorn. He is the strongest, and holds most of Ironthorn—all the northern part—for good reasons."

"Lyrose is the hated one," Iskarra murmured.

"Hated by outlander merchants who tell their hatreds to wider Falconfar? Yes. Wanton cruelty, sneering at everyone who's not kin to you, and seizing any traders' wares you like the look of, without paying a lone coin for them, earns such regard. Moreover, the current Lord Lyrose, Magrandar, is driven to outstrip the deeds of a more famous—and far more capable and level-headed—father. His wife Maerelle is as hotheaded as he is, and so are their children. Some summers back, they seemed not only to be rushing to accomplish their own doom, but to have very nearly reached that cliff. Whereupon Magrandar did the only wise thing I've heard of him doing, in all his life. Perhaps he was bullied into it, and perhaps he seized upon it in desperation, after Hammerhand slew his father and came after him, intending to eradicate House Lyrose whatever the cost."

"He accepted the aid of the wizard Malraun," Iskarra murmured.

"Eagerly. Malraun's spells hurled back Hammerhand's forces, shattering most of his knights. The Doom gave Lyrose a personal shield that heals wounds dealt by metal weapons and by poison—though he feels the agony and momentary debilitation of the wounds. As far as we Aumrarr can tell, Malraun has been largely absent from Ironthorn since, but he may have given Lyrose far more—or installed his own hidden creatures in Lyraunt Castle, as some whisper. Yes, Lyrose is best… avoided."

"I care naught for how Ironthorn tears itself apart, and who tries to lord it over the place, once I'm not sitting in the heart of it," Garfist rumbled. "What of the last lord—the one who has the gems all the rest of Falconfar cares about?"

Dyune shrugged. "Lord Irrance Tesmer rules over the valley of Imrush, supported by perhaps the most ruthless and informed Ironthar of all: his wife Telclara. Whose manner is icy, and whose will is stronger than most swords. We suspect another Doom is working through her."

"Narmarkoun?"

"He's the only one left, if it wasn't Arlaghaun or the Dark Lord—and if there are no other fell wizards of power who are wise enough to act more covertly than the Dooms."

"Why," Iskarra asked curiously, "do the Aumrarr suspect a wizard is behind Telclara? Can't Falconaar be evil or ruthless all by themselves?"

Dyune smiled. "Well, does this seem, ah, *usual* to you? Given Telclara's unhesitating cruelties? She no longer admits Tesmer to her bed, but herself selects bedmates for him from beautiful slave-girls she purchases from Stormar slavers, who in turn procure them in raids on the most southerly cities of the Sea of Storms. She slaughters each of them after they bear him a child. Children she deems acceptable are named heirs of the blood Tesmer, and trained to war; they have three daughters, followed by six sons, all by these means."

Garfist sighed. "Could ye Aumrarr have chosen a *slightly* less crowded snakepit to toss us in? War-torn Galath, for instance? Or are ye determined to hurl us all over Falconfar?"

Dyune smiled again. "No, that's a fate we reserve for the newest Doom. The Lord Archwizard of

Falconfar, Rod Everlar."

"Oh? And what's he ever done to ye?"

"It's not what he's done, so much as what we fear he will do. Very soon now."

Chapter Eight

HALF A DOZEN strides after they'd passed under the raised portcullis of Hammerhold and marched straight ahead into the open center of an echoing, bustling entrance hall—that had promptly fallen into a hush, as hurrying courtiers had stopped to stare—Briszyk stepped right in front of Rod, forcing the Archwizard of Falconfar to come to a hasty, unsteady halt. Their noses almost banged together.

"This will go best," the senior guard said very firmly, keeping his voice low and quiet, "if you obey calmly and say almost nothing, this next little while. The Lord Leaf will be less than pleased at our bringing *any* stranger into the presence of Lord Hammerhand, let alone a wizard. To say nothing of someone calling himself the Archwizard. Many bows will be aimed at you, but rest easy, and none of them should be loosed at you. For now, stand right here and move not."

He and Urlaun scurried off into the depths of the castle, in opposite directions, without waiting for any reply.

Rod was only too happy to obey, even under the deepening, unpleasant feeling of being stared at by curious and fearful Hammerhold cooks and retainers who poked their heads out of various doors and panels to level hasty stares at him ere swiftly vanishing again. None of them looked happy; a sadness seemed to hang over the castle.

As he stood waiting, heavily armed and armored Hammerhand guards came trotting quickly up to him in twos and threes. They were uniformly grim-faced and silent, and avoided meeting his gaze as they hastily readied crossbows. More of their fellows promptly followed.

By the time Urlaun came hurrying back, Rod was ringed by so many ready bows that the Hammerhand defensive strategy was clear. Not even a battle-ready Archwizard could work much harm—they hoped—before he'd be fairly torn apart by war-quarrels speeding in from all directions to pincushion him.

The younger guard had someone with him. Someone older. Tall and impressive in the most ornate armor Rod had ever seen, this white-haired warrior stared down his long nose right through Rod, grounded the great iron-shod staff in his hand loudly on the flagstones, and whirled around, leaving the outlander with a grand view of his back.

Quelling a momentary urge to blow a raspberry in loud imitation of flatulence, to crown the ostentatious insult, Rod watched with interest as the elderly warrior started to stride slowly away, pausing to ground his staff gravely on the stones at each step—and the ring of crossbowmen carefully moved with him, not shifting the shape of the ring around Rod in the slightest. Briszyk came puffing out of a side-passage in bent-over haste and fell into step just behind the man with the staff, matching

Urlaun's position on the man's other flank.

Somehow they had become a solemn procession, with somber, silently-staring Hammerhand folk lining the walls of the rooms they passed through. If someone painted this parade, they might well call the result *Bringing the Captured Beast Before The Glowering Lord*, Rod thought wryly—as doors five times his height were drawn open in front of the Striding Thunderstaff, who swept slowly on into the grandest chamber yet.

About ten paces away on either side of Rod walls soared up, curving inward well above hanging candle-wheel lanterns, presumably to meet somewhere in the darkness above. The floors were of glossy-smooth black stone—not marble, but looking a lot like it—and there were tiered benches along both walls, all of them crowded with haughty-looking folk in all manner of rich robes.

Rod was entirely unsurprised to see two lines of guards ahead—each of four warriors, in identical black-and-silver armor—flanking a three-broad-steps-up dais that jutted from the far end wall of the room. A high platform that had closed doors behind it and a massive dark stone throne on it. A burly, bearded man in half-armor was standing in front of that throne, legs apart and hands on belt, glaring at the procession as if it was an unwelcome foe. There was a sadness on his face, too.

Lord Burrim Hammerhand, unmistakably. Looking just a bit older than Rod had described him, with tinges of white joining the gray along the edges of his close-trimmed, jaw-fringe beard.

What Rod hadn't expected were the pair of identical high seats two steps below the throne, on

111

either side of the dais, and the two frowning persons standing watching him from in front of them.

One was a tall, slender woman with surprisingly broad shoulders, startlingly dark eyebrows and snapping blue-black eyes to match, framed by a long fall of pale brown hair. She had been weeping, but some time ago, and her face was now a cold mask of strength. She wore half-armor to match Lord Hammerhand's, and had a frown on her face that was the exact echo of his, too. This must be Amteira Hammerhand, despite her leather breeches, swordbelt, and small arsenal of weapons.

So where were all Hammerhand's sons? Jarvel and Glaren had fallen years before, yes, in books Rod had written, but that should still leave the eldest, Dravvan—a taller, broader-shouldered version of his father—and... and... wait, hadn't Holdoncorp done something with the other three? Turned them into horrid monsters in some dungeon for game players to slaughter? Yes...

So who was this *other* guy standing before a throne? Someone Rod knew he'd never conceived of or written about before, someone entirely unfamiliar; a thin-faced man with hard eyes and flaring nostrils, who wore a green-black cloak and robes of brown so dark as to be almost black.

Who was glaring at Rod right now as if a lone, rather bewildered SF writer was his oldest, most fiercely hated foe in all Falconfar.

Marvelous. Rod let his sarcasm swirl through his mind and fade, as he tried to smile faintly at the man. Leather boots with a hint of mold on them, and on the man's belt, too. A priest, perhaps, of the Forestmother?

The Striding Thunderstaff halted abruptly, about six or seven paces away from the lowest step of the throne-dais, and slammed down the butt of his staff as if trying to shatter it or the black stone beneath it, or both.

"A stranger is come to Ironthorn. Alone, your loyal guards say. He demands audience with you, and has used magic. He calls himself Rod Everlar, Lord Archwizard of Falconfar."

The old man delivered his words in ringing tones, but kept his delivery neutral and terse, devoid of judgment.

All around the hall, a murmur of hasty exclamation and conversation arose from the excited folk. "The Last Doom" was one phrase that rose above the rest, though the thirty-some lips whispering it did so sadly out of step with each other.

In the midst of the hubbub, Lord Burrim gravely inclined his head to the elderly man, and the Striding Thunderstaff responded with a deep nod of his own and a smoothly-whirling departure, taking his staff with him. The ring of crossbowmen remained.

The Lord of Hammerhand took a step forward, to the very edge of his topmost dais, and the courtiers fell silent in an instant. In the tense silence that followed, the ruler regarded Rod wearily. His face was a curious mixture of sadness, hostility, curiosity, and uncaring, as if Rod was an unwelcome addition to a long, bad, crowded-with-weighty-matters day.

"So you are the missing wizard the tales speak of? Why come you here, to this hold in the backlands of Falconfar? In the Raurklor, where we are used to being left alone by the wider world, remembered only by a few bold traders?"

"Magic brought me here," Rod said cautiously. "Not my own, but of the gods. Magic that has marred my own spells. It snatched me here, to your woods, when I sought to follow and rescue an Aumrarr, a friend and guide who was taken from me by one of the Dooms, and remains his captive, in torment. I can only conclude that the gods sent me here for their own purposes. Aims they will soon reveal to me, just as they have told me their will before."

Careful, he reminded himself. *Say little. That glaring guy over there is ready to pounce.*

Said glaring guy chose that moment to snap, "The Forestmother tells me this man *lies!* Lord Hammerhand, have I your leave to question him?"

"*Question?*" Rod thought. *Does this involve whips and chains? The rack?*

Lord Hammerhand sighed. "You do. Bowmen, down your shafts."

The raging priest whirled around. "Lord, is that wise? I—"

The lord of Hammerhold was very much a master of cold stares. "You never tire of trying to convince me, Lord Leaf, that I should put all wizards to death, Dooms included. If I do, but other lords and kings do not, what then will protect House Hammerhand, and all we hold dear, from the spells of other wizards who've been left alive? *Your* spells, Jaklar. And if we must all trust in them, surely they are powerful enough to protect you against this one man, who stands in our midst, with our best bowmen still in attendance—yes?"

The Lord Leaf started to say something sharp in reply, then closed his mouth, nodded, and instead replied, "*Yes*, Lord," as he turned back to Rod.

To favor the writer with a glare that looked as if his eyes were two flaring flames.

This is my true foe here, Rod realized. *If I don't fight him now, and fight hard, I'll soon be put to death. Painfully.*

"Are you using any magic right now?" Jaklar snapped.

"No," Rod said truthfully.

"Why not?" the priest snarled, stalking forward at Rod as if readying himself to drive a sword through this unwelcome outlander.

Rod blinked. "One should never use magic if there's no need. It's like fire, or the sword. Too powerful—too dangerous—to use lightly."

"Oh? And who told you that?"

Rod shrugged. Time to push back. "Many wizards. The Aumrarr. The Forestmother herself."

"*Whaaat?* You *LIE*, man! Blasphemer! Foul spewer of untruth!"

Rod drew in a deep breath, concentrating on doing that to keep himself from flinching away from the raging, spitting priest. Looking past the man—who was now dancing about waving his fists in incoherent fury, inside the ring of bowmen but carefully *just* out of Rod's reach—and asked Burrim Hammerhand politely, "Lord, are your Lord Leaf's wits... his own? Does he often do this?"

The priest shrieked and sprang at Rod, who sprinted aside, only to find the bowmen drawing together to bar his escape. They were trying to look stern, but he could see some of them struggling not to grin. The Lord Leaf, it seemed, was not well liked.

"Cauldreth Jaklar!" It was a new voice, young and female, and it cracked like a whip. "Another *step* toward the outlander, and prayers will be said for you before the Forestmother's altar this night!"

The priest whirled. "What d'you mean?" he asked, aghast. Truly astonished, Rod saw, his foaming rage gone in an instant. Meaning it had been an act.

"Meaning we'll plead to the Goddess we all revere to drive your madness from you," Amteira Hammerhand said crisply. "So that we need not take your life, to protect ourselves against your mad wrath."

The priest ducked his head like a growling dog. "You *dare* to raise hand against the anointed servant of the Forestmother?"

"I dare to *pray* to the Forestmother, Jaklar. Who is *my* goddess as well as yours. I said nothing at all about raising hands. Though perhaps it's time to remind you that I am a Hammerhand, and that Hammerhands rule here. We dare just about anything in the service of Ironthorn."

The Lord Leaf grimaced and shrank back as if her words had been an icy blast searing his face, then turned pointedly away from the lady heir of Hammerhand to look to her father.

Who gave the priest a steady gaze, and said firmly, "You were *questioning* the wizard Everlar, Holy Lord Leaf. Before you started screaming that his answers were lies. Remember?"

"I—I—" The priest sighed, closed his eyes for a moment, then said quietly, "Yes, Lord Hammerhand. The Goddess sent her fury into me, and I—it overwhelmed me."

He whirled around to glare at Rod again. "Wizard," he commanded flatly, "invoke the Forestmother no more. Your lies enrage Her."

"That's odd," Rod said, trying to keep his voice calm and confident, but raising it to make sure the courtiers at his end of the hall, at least, would hear. "That's *exactly* what she told me about you. Your lies enrage Her."

More than a few snickers and sputters of hastily-suppressed mirth rose from all around Rod, and a distinct—though mirthless—smile crossed Burrim Hammerhand's face. It was gone, however, by the time the priest whirled back to face him, and implore, "Leave, great lord, to have this foul outlander punished!"

Nor was the lord alone in his amusement. Amteira Hammerhand's eyes were dancing with sour mirth, though her face was carefully expressionless.

"*No*, Lord Leaf," the lord said firmly. "I am *not* eager to make an enemy of any Doom of Falconfar, or risk facing any lurking spell that may protect the person of this one. What I need most are spellhurling allies, despite your oft-stated desire to destroy all wizards. What I value most after that are huge armies I needn't pay nor feed, and after that, information. This outlander may aid us with the latter—perhaps even with the others—and your rage, holy or otherwise, helps us little just now. So let us have an end to shouting and threats and talk of punishment. This man met with two of our guards in the forest, and Briszyk and Urlaun are neither harmed, nor turned to toads. That proves this outlander can stay his spells long enough to talk and bargain and even walk peacefully. Let us try that first."

"You are wise, as always, Lord Hammerhand," the priest said quietly. "Would you prefer to question the outlander?"

"Yes," Burrim Hammerhand replied simply, and turned his gaze to Rod. "Lord Archwizard," he asked flatly, "what do you know about Ironthorn?"

"That it is a hold in the Raurklor, most famous elsewhere in Falconfar for its gemadars and the swords they produce. That it has three lords who all claim to be Lord of Ironthorn, but that you, Burrim Hammerhand, stand foremost. That Ironthorn seems to be all river-valleys." Rod shrugged. "That's all. Truly."

The Lord Leaf pounced again, his sharp words coming out in a rush before Lord Hammerhand could ask something else. "Yet you claim the Forestmother sent you here for some holy purpose?"

Rod shrugged. "No. As I said, magic that was not my own brought me here. I know not whose magic, or why. I am trusting that the gods did this, and now await their message to me, to tell me what I should do. I will be happy to talk with you—all of you here—honestly and openly, to learn all I can of Ironthorn. I am seeking a particular Aumrarr, wherever she may be. I intend no blasphemy, nor any attack on any Hammerhand or ally of the Hammerhands."

"Doesn't sound like a wizard to me," a courtier muttered, loudly enough for everyone to hear.

"Liars never do," someone else grunted.

Lord Hammerhand cast a sharp look in the direction of that comment, and silence fell again in his throne chamber.

"Lord Archwizard," he asked Rod, "how well do you know your fellow Dooms, and what do you think of them?"

"Not much," Rod replied, "and... not much."

Someone chuckled, in the courtiers crowding the tiers of benches.

"Lord Hammerhand," Rod added, "all of the Dooms, I think, have tried to kill me. One imprisoned and tortured me. That was Arlaghaun—"

There was a collective intake of breath that almost rose into a shriek. Rod rushed on.

"—and he is dead now, I believe, though what Lorontar—"

Another gasp that was almost a shriek. There was open, quivering fear on the Lord Leaf's face, and he was drawing back from Rod as if from a snarling wild beast.

"—has done this last little while hints that dead Dooms can be as active as the living. The one called Malraun is openly my foe—"

This time, an almost-approving murmur arose from the benches.

"—and I only know Narmarkoun exists at all because he and Malraun fight each other so fiercely. All of the Dooms, so far as I can tell, are cruel and manipulative tyrants, and I like none of them. I am not like them."

"Oh? How so?"

"Power seems to be everything to them," Rod replied, casting a meaningful look at the priest. "Power, and destroying their foes. I come from... very far away, where we do things differently."

Lord Hammerhand merely lifted his eyebrows in query to that, and Rod explained, "All men and women have rights—are held to be equals, under the law—and those who wield power ruthlessly must do so with more subtlety. Where I come from, we see magic very, very rarely. If the Dooms behaved there as they do here, they would be regarded as dangerous madmen."

"Very much as they are here," the lord said gravely. "Do you think your spells can defeat them?"

Rod met Lord Hammerhand's gaze and said firmly, "No."

That caused another stir among the courtiers, and made the Lord Leaf's eyes flash.

"I... believe one or more of the Dooms has cast fell magic on me," Rod lied, choosing his words carefully as the priest strode forward again, triumph clear on his face. "Magic that prevents me from remembering all of my spells. Yet as your two guards who found me can attest, I *can* work magic. Powerful magic. Not wanting to blast down castles unintentionally, change something that should not be changed, or kill someone who may be a friend, I am trying to be very careful. Which is why those who threaten me, like the Holy Lord Leaf—"

Rod bowed gravely in Jaklar's direction.

"—endanger us all. I have no desire whatsoever to do *any* harm to Hammerhold or anyone in it, but I fear smoking ruin may be its future if someone wounds me or tries to do me harm."

Some of the bowmen had started to raise and aim their weapons, but lowered them again hastily, frowning and casting looks at their lord, to learn his will.

Lord Hammerhand was frowning. "Your spells— can you bring the dead back to life?"

Sudden, tense silence gripped the room.

"No, Lord," Rod said sadly. "Though more than once I have fervently wished I could."

Courtiers sighed, and the lord's shoulders slumped, as if he'd been clinging to a slender hope that had now been snatched away.

"You came out of the forest," he said quietly. "Tell me; aside from Briszyk and Urlaun, did you see or fight any armored men there?"

There was a sudden, tense silence in the throne chamber.

Rod shook his head, knowing his answer was very important yet not hesitating. *The truth. All I dare give is the truth.* "No, lord. I saw an Aumrarr—*not* the one I seek—killed and eaten by a lorn. I attacked and wounded it, but it flew away."

His words had caused another murmur of excited talk. The lord of Hammerhold raised his eyebrows as if he wanted to hear more, but instead asked, "So this Aumrarr you seek to rescue is the captive of the Doom called Malraun?"

Rod nodded.

"And magic brought you here to Ironthorn—that you know so little about—when you sought to reach her?"

Rod nodded again.

"Then, Lord Archwizard, be aware that we see little of the Dooms in Ironthorn, but all Ironthar know this much: that Malraun openly aids Lord Magrandar Lyrose, our hated rival. If this Aumrarr is in Ironthorn, she is in Lyrose hands, and can only be won free by your spells—or force of arms. We would welcome your doing battle with Lyrose knights, and so will aid you, if you dare go a-seeking her. Food we can give you, and guides; some few of our knights who face punishments, and can step aside from such fates if they do us this service, rendering you aid and the strength of their swords. Go with these bowmen now; they will take you to one of my most trusted warcaptains, Syregorn. Though grief hangs heavy on us just now, Hammerhold welcomes you, and will aid you in all you do against Lyrose."

"Grief, lord?" Rod asked gently. "I—"

"I do not wish to speak of it," Lord Hammerhand said curtly, and turned away. "May you prevail, Lord Archwizard, and destroy our foes in doing so." He strode across the throne dais, heading for the leftmost of the closed doors opening onto it.

"Amteira, Lord Leaf? Attend us in the Map Chamber," he ordered, laying his hand upon its handle.

Then he was gone, and courtiers were rising from their seats to stare curiously at Rod. The bowmen closed in around him, grim-faced, almost rushing him back out of the chamber again.

"What happened?" Rod asked. "Who died?"

The nearest bowman gave him a curious look, half disbelief and half disgust. "Thought you were a mighty wizard," he snapped. "Y'sound more like an idiot outland drover lost in Irontarl, to me."

Rod shrugged and looked away. *I AM an idiot of an outlander lost here and just blundering his way along. I wonder when everyone will realize that, and pounce?*

Chapter Nine

A LARGE, PAINSTAKINGLY-DETAILED map of Ironthorn sprawled across the circular table that filled the center of the room. More maps hung from the low rafters in cloth dust-gowns, each sewn to fit the map it guarded.

Among these dusty hangings, the warcaptains of Hammerhold stood silently waiting in the still air, their thoughts hidden behind guarded faces, just as they had stood in this map chamber many times before. Along one side of the table they stood: Syregorn, balding, scarred, and senior; swift, capable Darlok; and darkly handsome, stolid Tarlkond. Three patient statues.

A door opened and Lord Hammerhand shouldered in, his daughter and the priest of the Forestmother silent shadows in his wake.

Amteira Hammerhand stopped at the door, setting her shoulders against it, but her father and the Lord Leaf strode forward, trading brief, silent glances ere they stopped across the map table from the warcaptains.

Then Lord Hammerhand looked at Syregorn. "Take a few trusted knights, and get this Lord

Archwizard into Lyraunt Castle. He seeks his Aumrarr and the fell wizard Malraun, who may well be lurking there. Once inside, concern yourself before all else with slaying those of the blood Lyrose. Killing wizards is work for other wizards."

The priest drew forth some small, slender metal vials from his belt and proffered them to Syregorn. "Leaf powders. Introduce them covertly into the Dark Lord's food—and *only* his food. They will keep him drowsy and biddable."

"When," Syregorn asked carefully, "will we have time for stopping and eating?"

The Lord Leaf looked for a moment as if he was going to fly into one of his rages, then relaxed and snapped, "Before heading to Lyraunt Castle, get well away from the Vale, back into the forest—say, to the old fire clearing—and there stop and feed this Archwizard. He looked hungry enough, but make sure he eats something. Tell him eating before battle is our tradition, and we need to keep the favor of the Forestmother."

He looked to Lord Hammerhand, who nodded again.

The priest smiled the briefest of tight smiles, went to the wall, and undid a loop of chain, lowering the five-candle lantern over the table.

Each of those candles burned in its own wax-filled bowl, all of the bowls thrusting forth on their own metal arms to flank a larger central bowl that served to reflect and magnify the light of their flames. Jaklar reached into the central bowl, supposedly empty of all but dust, and drew forth a small wooden coffer. Opening it, he lifted out a fistful of matching sheathed daggers, and handed three of them to Syregorn.

"Poisoned," he announced curtly. "Wear one, and give the others to men you trust."

"With them," Lord Hammerhand added grimly, "you are to kill whichever of the two wizards survives their battle with the other. A Falconfar with two fewer Dooms in it is a much safer Falconfar for us all."

THE FOUR AUMRARR shivered from time to time; no matter what height they chose to fly at, the air was chill and damp. Ironthorn seemed somehow farther away than last time... but then, as they all separately and silently remembered, it always did.

There came a time when Juskra looked up from her constant peering at the land below to ask, "Time for Orthaunt's skull?"

"*More* than time," Ambrelle said severely. "We must get the mindtrap gem from Stormcrag first, though. Malraun is probably watching us, and I can cloak his spying only for a *very* short time; I know a few spells, but he's a Doom of Falconfar!"

"And we all tremble accordingly," Lorlarra commented.

A bare moment later, she was tucking in her wings and banking sharply aside from something blossoming in the air right in front of them.

Something large, dark, and flickering, born out of nothing and growing with astonishing speed.

A rift in the air, its ragged edges as dark as a stormcloud, its heart a brightness out of which flying shapes—lorn!—were streaming.

Magic, of course... and of a size and power that only a Doom could wield. Oh, many a wizard could open a small rift for a moment or two, to thrust through a message, a burning brand, or perhaps something as large as a newborn babe or a sword...

but this, in the midst of empty air, a tear in the sky as tall as many a keep...

All four Aumrarr were cursing, and all four had swords out and were swooping and darting their own racing ways through the air, seeking to get past their foes before the lorn—there were two dozen or more, easily, all of them waving swords or spears as they came—could reach them.

"Together!" Ambrelle shrieked, as Dauntra dodged one way and Juskra went another. "Sisters, *stay together!*"

Dauntra was already past the foremost lorn seeking to intercept her, and Juskra was growing a savage grin as she ducked aside from a spear-thrust and slashed with her sword across one of the lorn arms wielding that spear. Blood sprayed, and another lorn was blindly trying to thrust a spear through that gore when—

A *second* rift opened in the air, angled to half-face the first one, with the Aumrarr caught between.

This rift was spewing forth its own rushing horde of armed, Aumrarr-seeking lorn, too. Scores of the cruel winged beasts.

The four sisters cursed in disbelief, for all of three breaths.

Then the sky all around them was crowded with jostling, snarling lorn, and they were too busy frantically hacking just to try to stay alive, to have any breath to spare for curses.

* * *

AMTEIRA HAMMERHAND WATCHED the last of the three warcaptains stalk away down the darkened hall, firmly closed the door, and whirled around.

"Father, this is *madness!*"

Lord Burrim Hammerhand looked up from the part of the map of Ironthorn he most liked to stare at—the Lyrose lands, that he'd vowed so often would be his, every tuft of grass and fresh-plowed furrow of them—and asked with just a trace of weariness in his voice, "How so, dearest?"

Amteira had intended to be no more than sternly sorrowful, but she found herself striding forward in as loud a bluster as her father ever trumpeted, anger rising like a warm red tide to choke her, before she could stop herself.

"Poisoned weapons! Lies about the gods! Risking Syregorn on a sneak-thief raid on a castle all our warriors have failed to take, dozens of times! Are not *all* of these things foolish, dangerous, and dishonorable?"

Her father's face turned stony. "Daughter mine," he said curtly, "hear this, and know it well: to preserve Ironthorn, and free Falconfar of wizards, *nothing* is dishonorable, or too foolish, or too dangerous. Nothing."

The Lord Leaf smirked at Amteira. "Best you should find calm, Lady Hammerhand, and keep silent, and learn. The Forestmother—"

Fury flared. Amteira fought it down enough to keep from snarling or screaming, so her voice came out as something very close to her father's curt snap.

"*You* be silent. You are no Hammerhand, priest. Concern yourself with what the Forestmother charges you to watch over: warding off wolves and worse forest beasts, guiding those lost in deep woods safely home, and looking after woodcutters. Who rules in a Great Forest hold and how they rule is *not* your affair."

Cauldreth Jaklar stiffened, his eyes blazed up like fresh-kindled torches, and he strode toward her, snarling, "Do you *dare* to tell me what the Forestmother does or does not say or do? Am I actually hearing such blasphemy from your fair lips, young—and thus far spared all holy wrath—lady heir of the Hammerhands? You *dare* to speak so?"

"Priest," she replied, striding forward to meet him, until they almost crashed together chest to chest, "spare us your staged tantrums. Quite obviously, I *do* so dare. Nor is it blasphemy or presumption on my part. The Forestmother's teachings have never been about what befalls in castle, town, or market-moot, but rather out in the—"

The priest interrupted her in a tight whisper that managed to stop just short of a shout. "*You* hear only what I tell you of what She says to me, child. To spare your very sanity, I keep from you—from all faithful Ironthar—much of the dread secrets she reveals! The truth is that She has whispered to me of cleansing Ironthorn enough to hold a Holy Moot here, that all Ironthar personally know Her love and blessing, and—"

"What will *that* mean?" Amteira snapped, interrupting Jaklar in turn, emboldened by the cold look of disgust in her father's eyes, as he stood with arms folded glaring at the priest's back. "We Hammerhands sacrificed on altars, you sitting on my father's throne, and wolves and bears roaming the farms and every last alley of Irontarl, devouring Ironthar at will?"

"Pah! Such wild fancies are always flung by those who—"

The door behind Amteira opened, bringing instant silence. The Lord Leaf glared murderously over her shoulder at the intruder, but that warrior was unabashed.

Panting a little, he looked at Lord Hammerhand and blurted, "News, lord! The wizard Narmarkoun has vanished! His tower of Helnkrist stands empty, and no one knows what has become of the greatfangs he breeds there!"

"Well, they're a little large to have slipped away unnoticed, what with all Helnadar cowering down whenever they flap overhead," Lord Burrim said flatly. "No other news? My thanks, Bramlar."

He inclined his head in a clear dismissal, and the warrior bowed and withdrew, pulling the door firmly shut again. He clinked his scabbard against the wall as he walked away, again and again, to let the three in the map chamber know he wasn't tarrying to eavesdrop.

"One less wizard for us all to worry about," Jaklar said triumphantly as those clinkings died away, turning to give Lord Hammerhand a grin.

It died away along with his voice, as he caught sight of the bleak look on Burrim Hammerhand's face.

"*Think*, priest," the lord said bluntly. "Is this Doom dead? Fled? Captured by one of the other Dooms? Or staging some ruse we can only guess at? Was the 'Dark Lord' we just met with Narmarkoun in magical guise, trying to learn all he could of Ironthorn's strength? Or hiding from a greater pursuing foe?"

Silence fell, as the two Hammerhands and the Lord Leaf stared at each other, truly aghast this time.

THEIR AGILITY AND the fact that they were only four, and so few enough to pass between jabbing spears, twist around the shafts of those weapons, and fling one lorn into another—or onto the sharp edges and points of countless gleaming lorn weapons—was all that was keeping the Aumrarr alive.

Juskra loved to fight, and was hewing and stabbing in glee, lost in the red and bloody moment. Lorlarra fought with nostrils flaring and lips tight in distaste, as usual, grimly doing what she must.

The minds of Ambrelle and Dauntra lay between those extremes. They were fighting for their lives, but had time enough—in the panting instants when lorn stiffened and spewed in death against them, and they were tearing free their swords, or fighting to win free of the dying—to mark one grim realization: only a Doom of Falconfar would have power enough to craft *two* rifts in succession. There were legends of Archwizard Lorontar doing so twice or thrice, of old, sending armies into the castles of their foes, to smite those who'd thought themselves safe behind walls...

Not that this being the work of a Doom was all that much of a surprise. Or that it really mattered much who had caused these rifts, if they died here in this sky full of endless lorn.

Lorn who seemed confused and hesitant, thanks to the only useful spell Ambrelle could call to mind. A magic that made the four Aumrarr look like lorn, except to each other.

It was not a magic that made mere looks slow sharp steel. Lorlarra moaned in pain as a spear-blade laid open her side, racing along ribs that had lost all protection to earlier slashes and thrusts. She twisted around to thrust her free hand into her own gore, holding her side as if her fingers could quell pain.

Her wings faltered, she fell below a drift of swarming lorn—and Juskra, dropping beside

Lorlarra to protect her, wrested a spear from dying lorn hands and shouted in glee as she found a dozen lorn bellies and backsides within easy reach of it.

Dauntra raced past overhead, drawing the attention of many lorn as she hacked and thrust, darting and swerving in a wild, swift progress that few lorn could turn quickly enough to follow, though it drew all eyes.

Juskra thrust her spear again and again into the nether parts of lorn, jabbing swiftly and moving on rather than risking plunging her borrowed weapon in deeper and getting it stuck and torn from her hands.

Not far away, Ambrelle was diving in behind the lorn who were starting to pursue Dauntra, flying just above them and using her sword to slash wing-tendons. A helplessly-tumbling lorn who can't fly is one less lorn for outnumbered Aumrarr to fight.

Dauntra gasped as a lorn spear caught her ear and sliced it away. Some of the lorn beneath her raised a liquid, laughing roar of triumph and anticipation—but were drowned out, almost instantly, by the dismayed sigh of scores of others.

The first rift had closed, as abruptly as the passing, air-slicing blade of a hard-swung sword. Only one vast darkness now hung in the air.

The four Aumrarr were fighting for their lives, so they fought on uncaring. All that mattered was that the rift, when it had vanished, hadn't helpfully sucked all of its lorn back through it.

Leaving them behind for four increasingly weary winged women to hack and hew as best they could, with arms growing heavier with each stroke, and fingers more numbed with each crashing meeting of blade and foe.

Then Ambrelle found time and breath enough to notice that a lot of sky around her was blue again, more or less. Empty of flapping, clawing lorn, anyway.

Had they—?

Lorn were wheeling away from her now, drawing back for the first time, their bloodthirsty eagerness to jostle each other aside to take part in slaughtering these four outnumbered foes gone.

Behind and below the midair battle, dozens of wounded lorn were tumbling toward the distant ground, some of them struggling to fly and others plunging, limp and dead.

Drenched in blood and sweat, half-blinded, the winded Aumrarr fought on viciously, snatching wild-eyed lorn to use as flapping, frantic shields against lorn spears, swords, and claws. Living shields that did not cling to their lives long.

More lorn swooped away, fleeing the fray.

As something happened that did make the four weary sisters smile.

Silently and swiftly, without any sound at all, the second rift closed and was gone, leaving perhaps two dozen lorn still sharing the sky with the Aumrarr.

Lorn that now, in silent accord, turned and flew away.

THE LYROSE WAY was the sneer and the biting comment, not snarled oaths or angry shouting.

Yet the four surviving Lyroses had forgotten and flung aside their customary manner long ago, so heated in the disagreement that had followed their smallmeat tarts and wine that they had ordered servants and guards alike out of earshot, then stormed up to the long-disused topmost turret bedchamber of Lyraunt Castle so they could shout and spit at each other freely without being overheard.

What the family Lyrose was arguing so heatedly about was what to do in the ongoing war with Hammerhand.

Lord Magrandar was furious, and had taken to repeatedly saying so.

He was saying so right now, in roars that echoed thunderously around the small, round stone room.

"I am *furious* that Eldred and Horondeir were so rash and stupid as to get themselves killed!" He ran out of room to angrily stride across the small bedchamber and whirled around, half-cloak swirling. "To say nothing of hurling aside the lives of a lot of my best knights! They were like eager children!"

He whirled around again. "Why, *anyone* could have foreseen that the Hammerhands would fight to avenge their heir, not flee hand-wringing and shrieking! What were Eldred and Horondeir *thinking?*"

Pelmard knew very well how much he'd led his father's opinions astray in his twisted retellings of what had happened on the forest trail, but he dared not change his tale again now. He'd been busily blaming his two dead brothers for every last little misfortune, and if a Lyrose was going to be blamed for something, let it be a dead one, and not a far more favorite family target: the sullen youngest son, Pelmard Lyrose.

He hadn't known his icily-calm, nasty father *could* grieve, but grief must be the fire behind Lord Lyrose's wild scheme.

Unless Lord Magrandar Lyrose was given to bouts of sudden madness he'd hitherto managed to hide from his family.

Two of his sons might now lie dead as a result of testing them, but—Dooms take us all!—the Lord of Lyraunt Castle actually thought the ward-piercing crossbow quarrels the wizard Malraun had given them had worked so well that he wanted to strike at Hammerhand *right now*, so as to do the most harm he could.

Not by besieging Hammerhold, mind, but by seeking to capture Irontarl, and so luring Hammerhand's troops into street battles in the town, where they could readily be slain with the new quarrels, by Lyrose archers aiming along streets and alleys and down from rooftops.

Pelmard tried to keep his incredulity off his face, but he knew all too well where this was heading.

Sly, craven coward he might be—he knew that was every last Lyrose's opinion of him—but this *was* madness.

Madness he wanted no part of, yet was quite likely to be hurled into the heart of, if he knew his kin.

This rash attack on Irontarl would doom them all, when just sticking to their defenses and patiently waiting a season or so longer would see Hammerhand overreach himself.

He said so, trying to sound calm and wise, as if he'd observed and considered this very matter for months. "Hammerhand is a warrior—he must be in the thick of the fray, sword in hand. So we give him frays, of our choosing, and wait for the moment when he rides too far, and we can surround and overwhelm him. If we can kill Burrim Hammerhand, he has no heir left now but his spit-shrew of a daughter. And I know *just* how to handle her." He kept his leer soft and slight.

Yet found himself staring into three coldly hostile gazes.

"Your problem, my son," his mother said icily, "is that we all know you rather too well. We look upon Pelmard Lyrose, and see a coward who would betray—even slay—us all in an instant if doing so aided you in any way."

Did they know the truth about Eldred and Horondeir?

Pelmard waited, but she said no more, letting the silence lengthen until he filled it by sighing, shrugging, and saying, "I disagree with your judgment of me, yet I doubt I can unmake it in any great hurry. What would you have me be?"

"A battle leader," she said crisply.

"And a worthy heir of this house," Lord Magrandar Lyrose added heavily.

"And failing that," his sister Mrythra said silkily, "I'd like to see you killed while *trying* to become those things."

Pelmard kept his face as expressionless as he knew how, as he gazed back at her.

So this was the trap at last, yawning before him, and all three of them seeking to thrust him forward into it. He knew very well Mrythra and his mother Maerelle both believed Mrythra would make a much better Lyrose heir anyway—and one who could shrewdly marry a Stormar lordling to drag new allies into the endless Ironthar wars, so as to defeat and slaughter Hammerhand and Tesmer once and for all.

"And so?" he asked quietly, lifting one eyebrow in sardonic challenge.

He knew what was coming.

His family stared back at him. So did they.

Chapter Ten

"AND SO," LORD Magrandar Lyrose replied quietly, "we're expecting you to stride forward into firmly and properly doing the right deed. For once."

"And just what would this 'right deed' be?" Pelmard tried to sound as unconcerned yet silkily menacing as his mother or his sister ever had. He would be damned before the Forestmother and all the prancing Dooms if he'd give them the satisfaction of seeing him crawl. Or show fear. Or rage in desperation. "Getting myself killed trying to become a victorious-in-battle heir of this house?"

His parents and his sister answered him with shrugs, silently smiling nods, and sneers.

"I see," Pelmard drawled, trying to sound far more nonchalant than he felt. "In my judgment—as heir of this house and a loyal Lyrose son who has dared much for my kin, unlike my only surviving sibling, whose daring very seldom reaches beyond the walls of this castle—that seems to be a view that's very *wasteful* of family resources. Almost, one might say, the act of a foe. Hammerhand swords claimed the lives of my brothers, not Lyrose treacheries. Yet all of you cleave to this decision?"

More silent, smirking nods, broken by Lady Maerelle Lyrose saying coldly, "Put away indolent cowardice and obey your father, Pelmard. It is far past the time you should have begun doing so. Lead this foray into Irontarl or be a Lyrose no more."

Pelmard met her cold stare for a time that would have been less than comfortable for anyone not so well armored in hatred as those of the Blood Lyrose. Then he said lightly, "Very well. If you are all resolved to be this wasteful of kin, I shall do the same."

He held up his right hand and slid an ornate ring off his middle finger, to reveal a second ring that had been concealed beneath. It instantly kindled into a sullen glow.

"The wizard Malraun favors me," he told his family gloatingly, "and gave me this, for use should my life ever be threatened. I can blast all of you where you stand—or as you dare not oppose me, I can stride out of this castle, hie me straight to Hammerhand with all of my knights riding at my back, and fight *against* Lyrose henceforth. Making your deaths slower, but probably far messier."

"Think you so, foolish boy?" his mother said sweetly. "What have you ever done, that a Doom should favor you over the rest of us?"

Sneeringly she drew a locket on a fine chain up out of her bodice into view, and flipped it open to reveal an identical warning glow of magic. On either side of her, her daughter and husband unveiled their own glowing rings to Pelmard; mirrors of his own.

"As you see," his father said, "we all have our little secret weapons, tokens of the *special* esteem our patron Doom holds all of us in. Given to each of us privately by the wizard Malraun, in return for our various personal promises, yet seeming very much alike to me. Wherefore know you, Pelmard my obedient son, that these three arrayed against you overmatch *your* little gift from Malraun."

Lord Lyrose smiled and took a step forward, dropping one hand to the hilt of his sword. A gem in its pommel promptly took on the same glow as his ring. "You may try to play the traitor as you threaten," he added softly, "but I promise you death will be your reward for any such attempt."

A tension had built in the room as each of the little glows had waxed brighter; now, every dim corner of the little turret chamber crackled with power. Although it could be seen that there was nothing but dust under the high, uncurtained bed, this risen power seemed to gather there, pulsing or thrumming in a way that could not be heard, yet made all ears ache.

"Loyal son," Pelmard's mother sneered in quiet triumph, "there's one thing more. Your father's sword and this locket of mine can both fly after you, seek and find you no matter where or how you hide, and smite you down from afar. If ever you succumb to treachery, you are doomed."

"They blaze up prettily the more you wave them at me in clumsy threat," Pelmard replied, "yet forgive me if I believe not your claims. Malraun said noth—"

"*Listen*, brother," Mrythra said scornfully, "and learn. Learn to believe, or you'll soon be very dead. Your ring is the least of the Doom's tokens, because he trusted you least. We *all* bear two of Malraun's favors, thanks to your carelessness over stripping magics from the bodies of your dear brothers.

Behold, before you in folly cling to further defiance, what my 'other' can do."

A glow kindled in her bodice, eerily lighting her face from below, and Pelmard abruptly became aware of a burning pain in his manhood, a searing so intense that he choked, reeled helplessly, and found himself panting and clutching at his cods as he staggered across the room, whimpering.

"Every gladsome inch the sullen son and heir," his mother murmured sarcastically.

"Scorching from a distance," his sister announced, her voice idle and carefree. "Have you ever worked with your ring, Pelmard, and truly mastered all it can do? This ring was Eldred's, and in but moments I learned how it can burn from afar. Stop whimpering long enough to heed me, and hear this: brother, I promise you far worse agony if you displease me in any way, from this moment on."

On his knees, drenched in sweat and lost in teeth-chattering pain and terror, Pelmard barely managed to gasp out, "Mercy! I hear and heed! Oh, by the Three Thorns, *stop!*"

"Am I hearing you promise your obedient loyalty?" his father asked gloatingly, from very close by.

Through welling tears Pelmard stared at his own left hand, splayed on the flagstones in front of his nose. It was bone-white, which surprised him not in the slightest.

"Y-yes," he managed to sob. "I'll lead your mad-foolish attack on Irontarl. And die heroically, along with loyal Lyrose knights you'll thereafter urgently *need*, but then no longer have. You're hurling us all to our deaths."

No one replied to that bitter opinion, but the air crackled above Pelmard, and he felt the roiling, vaguely sickening flows of restless magic. His father's wards were all active, no doubt to prevent a desperate heir erupting in knifings—or a tripping followed by frantic flight.

Pelmard shook his head, sweat spattering the smooth stone floor nigh his nose. He could barely *stand*; violence and sprinting out of his family's clutches were... far beyond possible.

Somehow he found his feet, the floor yawing alarmingly in front of him as he clutched at nothing... then bent low to keep from crashing face-first back to the floor.

"Come," his father said, the sharp note of impatience barely overriding an overall smugness. "If it's falling you crave just now, many steps await yonder to afford you more spectacular descents. I'll take you to join the knights I've chosen. You are to prepare this foray, so you can move in at dawn and take Irontarl before the sun's truly up—to say nothing of yawn-a-bed knights of Hammerhold. Show me a true Lyrose, son, and I might just manage to forget most of the words I've heard out of your mouth here this day. *Might*, I said."

Shaking, Pelmard mumbled out a few words more foul than anything he'd ever said before.

* * *

"I'M THE STRANGER here," Rod said politely, as they came to another fork in a narrow forest trail, and took the smaller and more tangled way on, "but surely the Lyrose lands lie back behind us? Down the valley from Hammerhold, across the river?"

"They do," Syregorn said curtly. "Yet it is not Lord Hammerhand's will that all of us be slaughtered when the echoes of our boots on Hammerhold's cobbles have barely died away. We're making a wide loop through the forest, along older, nigh-forgotten back trails, to come at Lyraunt Castle from a less-than-expected direction."

Rod's stomach rumbled loudly. Again.

"Nor has it escaped my attention," the bald, scarred warcaptain snapped, "that you are more than a little hungry, Lord Archwizard. Hungry men have little patience, and do foolish things. This way will take us along the flank of a hill to a clearing— where we will eat, and wait for night to come. Now, silence. Idle talk carries far, and warns many."

Without another word the small band of leather-clad knights set off again along the trail, flitting like shadows through the treegloom. The way was barely more than a line through the thick thornbushes, and the lead knight stalked along it slowly, peering carefully and stopping from time to time. It dawned on Rod, with a little shiver, that the man was seeking snares and trip-lines and hidden pitfalls.

None were found, as the trail rose along the hillside, then forked again. Without hesitation the lead man turned left again, upslope. The slope became steeper, then rock-strewn, and then came out into a place where rising rocks burst out of the trees at last, and bright sunlight dazzled.

Syregorn tapped Rod's chest and pointed where he should go, across a drift of loose, tumbled stones that were sprouting tiny vines and creeping flowers. Rod followed one of the knights, and found himself in a little hollow amid the soaring rocks.

Shaded by a great toothlike slab that soared overhead, it was about the size of Rod's kitchen—

minus the cupboards, fridge, and stove. Two leaping strides could have taken Rod from one end clear to the other, and halfway up the waiting stone wall there. Amid the lowest rocks underfoot, a spring gurgled faintly, rising up to run away again to unseen depths.

"Can we talk now?" he muttered, as Syregorn and his six knights settled into the rocky bowl around him, all facing each other.

"Yes. You have questions," the warcaptain said flatly, accepting a helm from one knight and various small cloth-wrapped bundles from others. Upending the helm to make it a bowl, he set to work mixing together various powders and green leaves from the bundles in it. "I'll give few answers, so ask sparingly."

"I—well, forgive my asking, but if darkness is cloak enough for a foray like this, why isn't every night full of knights creeping about Ironthorn, daggers drawn, and every morning after having its harvest of corpses?"

"Once, they were," Syregorn told the bowl, "and many Ironthar died. Then came the wizards and their nightmists, and cold iron seared and poisoned at a touch, wherever light or wardings did not reach."

He looked up with a glance both cold and sharp. "How is it that the Lord Archwizard knows not such things?"

"Nightmists," Rod replied in a voice that was as grim as he could make it, as he invented magical "facts" off the top of his head, "are not my way. They poison the land. What price a feast, if you've tainted all the food to get it?"

Several of the knights nodded acceptance of that, and Syregorn's voice was the barest shade warmer when he said, "You use words as swords." It cooled again when he added, "Like the Lord Leaf."

Someone passed him a belt-flask, and the warcaptain poured its contents into the mixture in the bowl, stirred it with the blade of his dagger, then looked to the only one of the knights who looked older than him.

That Hammerhold veteran unwrapped three gigantic, many-veined leaves from around two long, thin loaves of dark bread that he'd already sliced— into thick, generous slabs—and wordlessly held them out. Syregorn started slapping the contents of the bowl pinned between his knees onto the bread, and passing the slices around, Rod's first.

Rod wasn't unobservant enough not to notice the thick sprinkling of dark powder on Syregorn's knife before it spread his slice—powder that wasn't on the knife when it spread any of the later slices.

Yet he also wasn't unobservant enough not to feel the wary gazes of all the knights fixed on him, and the drawn daggers ready in their hands or across their laps. Keeping his shrug an inward, private thing, he bit into the slice without any hesitation.

Whatever was in the mixture—lots of herbs and fragments of crushed leafy greens, plus a wet paste that might have been crayfish mixed with quail, but was almost certainly something else—tasted very good. By the way the knights ate, and their faces, they thought so, too.

In what seemed no time at all, Rod's slice of the dark, nutty bread was gone, and the curt warcaptain was wordlessly handing him another. He ate that one just as eagerly, even as the first threads of warmth and strangeness started to stir in him.

Well, whatever that powder was, here it came. He didn't think they'd go to all this trouble just to poison him, when a dagger in the back could have delivered the same fate many, many trudging strides ago.

No, this was something else. Drugging, intended to... what? Rod wasn't feeling sleepy. On the contrary, every inch of him was starting to tingle, his fingers curling and twitching by themselves, and a fire was rising in him.

He felt more awake than he'd done in years. It was like the shock of plunging into icy waters—without the shock, or the cold. Rod felt hot all over. Not burning, *hot*. He reached for his brow, to wipe away the sweat he knew would be there... but his trembling fingers came away dry.

Then it *really* hit him.

Whooooo! His heart was racing, adrenalin surged through him like a flood of mint-laced water, his mind started throwing up visions, memories racing past so wildly and swiftly that he had to fight to keep a grasp on here and now...

Rod gasped aloud, staring all around at knights. They sat still, daggers in hands, staring expressionlessly back at him. Except for the old one, who gave Syregorn a glance that asked as clearly as if he'd shouted it: "Mixed it wrongly, aye?"

The only response the warcaptain gave was to look at Rod and ask, as gently as any concerned chambermaid, "Lord Archwizard?"

"I—yes, ah, that's me, yes indeed, Rod Everlar, creator of Falconfar, every castle and Aumrarr and glowing sunset of it, well, except for the Holdoncorp stuff, and that's—and the—uh, the Dark Helms, uh—ah—"

He was babbling, and couldn't stop! Syregorn's powder—or, no, it would have come from the Lord Leaf, that icy, nasty worm, wouldn't it?

From the shocked expressions some of the knights were now wearing, and the half-grins twitching about the mouths of the rest, Rod gathered that he must have said those thoughts aloud. Shit, he *was* babbling.

"Drowsy and biddable, hey? I'd say Lord High Holy has crashed down proper," the old knight whispered to Syregorn behind his hand. It was faint, barely more voice than soft breathing, but Rod heard every word clearly. Jesus, he could hear the *heartbeat* of the knight closest to him! Whatever this powder was, it was mighty stuff!

Fire raged through him and roiled within him, burning nothing but hurling him to his feet, straining on tiptoe, thrusting him up on its own warm tide. Knights hefted daggers watchfully, but did nothing as Rod danced awkwardly in their midst.

I must look like a proper dolt.

He was bobbing on his toes like a child's balloon bouncing, too light to fall as the buoyant surges within him gathered strength...

"Lord Archwizard," Syregorn said soothingly, though he was now wearing a dark-browed frown of exasperation, "rest easy. You are in no danger, I assure y—"

"No danger? *No danger?*" Rod's uncontrollable eruption of bubbling laughter was almost a howl. "Since first walking Falconfar I've faced *nothing else!* Everyone wants to kill me, or harness me like a prize bull, and *no one* will believe me when I tell them there's a lot—*a lot!*—about Falconfar that I

146

just don't know! So hear me, men of Hammerhold! I don't want to rule you or use magic to force you to do anything! I don't want to use magic at all! I just want to rescue Taeauna from the wizard Malraun!"

"Malraun," one of the knights muttered, wary eyes fixed on Rod and dagger raised and ready. "Syre, he's raving."

Syregorn sighed. "I believe I'd noticed that already, myself," he growled, raising nervous chuckles all around the hollow.

"Somehow, that is," Rod added. "No magic, not if I can help it! I'm not like the Dooms, I don't *want* to rule Falconfar! I don't! I—"

"We hear you," Syregorn said sharply, reaching out a hand to pluck at Rod's sleeve and drag him back down to sit on the rocks. "We might even begin to believe you."

"I—but I don't, I assure you! Please, you must believe me! God, hell of a hero I'm turning out to be, babbling like an idiot and—and—"

"Lord Archwizard," the warcaptain said sternly, "speak more slowly, and say less. We are well away from Ironthorn, but talk *does* carry. Is there anything we can do for you, to set you more at ease?"

"I—" Rod started to shake his head and wave his hands dismissively, but then a sudden bright thought struck him. "*Yes!* Yes, there is! I need ink, quills, and something to write on! Straight away! I—"

He sprang forward, caught hold of Syregorn's shoulders, and shook him. "Now! Here and now! Writing—"

"Archwizard," the warcaptain snapped, letting go of his dagger and clamping his hands around Rod's wrists in what felt like a grip of iron, "sit *down*. Do

147

you think, faring forth on a raid, we would carry ink and quills with us? When none of us can read or write?"

Rod saw on some knights' faces that this was a lie, that Syregorn himself could read and write, but—but did he dare say that? When these grim knights almost certainly didn't have any writing necessities with them, anyway?

"Why do you want them?" the warcaptain snapped, staring into Rod's eyes almost nose to nose, Rod held like a doll in his strong grip.

"I—ah—"

"*Why do you want them?*"

"Uh, ah, to Shape Fal—uh, I—ah, don't want to rule or oppress anyone! I only want to free Taeauna, so she can guide me! I, ah—"

"This, too, we have heard and understood," the warcaptain said sternly. "Lord Archwizard, *be still.*"

The old knight chuckled. "Heh. *You* gave him the powder."

"Thalden," Syregorn snarled out of the side of his mouth, eyes still boring into Rod's, "be still."

The old knight nodded, smiled, and fell silent.

"I—just a scrap of parchment as big as both my hands, or vellum, and a quill that—"

"I promise you, Lord Archwizard," the warcaptain said firmly, "that we shall seize any such things we find in Lyraunt Castle, and procure them for you. If we find nothing, and win our ways back to Hammerhold, the Lord Leaf shall provide. Or else."

"I—yes, I—that's wonderf—"

"Lord Archwizard, you have my promise. Now by the Forestmother, *be still* about ink and quills and writing!"

"I—ah, uh… yes," Rod managed, sitting back down on the rocks as Syregorn rose and shoved, forcing him down. "Now about Ironthorn—why is Hammerhold grieving? What—"

The warcaptain spat out a string of oaths so swift and harsh that Rod couldn't make out the words. There was open laughter around the hollow.

"Syre," one of the younger knights said, through it, "we *can't* take him skulking up to Lyraunt Castle like this. If he's going to hurl out questions like a youngling until it… wears off, we may as well answer him—or he'll just go and get answers from Lyrose folk, in the castle, and they'll fill his head with all their lies. I'd say the Forestmother—or some great calamity—has made a simpleton of this wizard, and he'll be as dangerous as a pranksome lad until he knows what is what under the sun and moon. So…"

"Perthus," Syregorn replied, still holding Rod firmly down, "you see things swift and clear. Not that I like the truths you're telling me overmuch."

He let go of Rod, sat back, sighed, and said, "Lord Archwizard, all Hammerhand grieves the loss of Lord Burrim's only son and heir, Dravvan Hammerhand. He was slain in a fray in the forest. I was there. He was struck down with the aid of fell Lyrose magic—doubtless from the Doom Malraun, who backs House Lyrose, and uses them as his witless tools."

"Only son? So if Lord Hammerhand falls, who—?"

"His daughter, Amteira. Who swings a sword and rides into battle as well as any of us. Lyrose lost heirs in that bloodshed, too: Eldred and Horondeir. Only the youngest brother, Pelmard, survived—by fleeing like a weeping child. So I suppose those of Lyrose are grieving, too. If any of them know how. There have been days when Ironthorn has been stronger."

"Assuredly," Rod agreed hurriedly. "Please believe me when I say I have not come here to rule, nor to force my will upon any Ironthar! I don't want to work any magic or tell anyone what to do! I only want to—"

"Yes, yes, *yes*." Syregorn's snarl was louder than any of Rod's babbling had been. "Archwizard, we know this."

"—Taeauna—"

"*Yes*." The snarl became a roar.

"Yet Ironthorn," Rod babbled, "tell me of Ironthorn. Why should wider Falconfar turn its eyes to Ironthorn? What does Malraun want *here?*"

"Huh." The warcaptain let out his breath in a dismissive snort. "As to that, Lord Archwizard, you'll have to ask him yourself. I'm a mere swordswinger, who serves a foe at that; he doesn't talk to *me*."

He shrugged. "Myself, I think those of Lyrose are toys to him, idle amusements. The rest of us Ironthar are but ants for House Lyrose to grind underfoot— good for us that they're such arrogant fools as to be bad grinders—and he watches, when he bothers, just to see us die."

Chapter Eleven

"**B**UT IRONTHORN MUST have interested Malraun for some reason in the first place!"

The urge to talk, the restlessness that made him want to get up and *move* was still strong, but Rod found that he could govern his tongue now. Not that he saw any need to make that obvious, if the warcaptain still felt like talking. "Is it your farms, in the midst of all this forest?"

Syregorn snorted. "Hardly. There are farms beyond counting across Falconfar. It's the gemadars."

Rod didn't quite dare to seem ignorant of what gemadars were, but the warcaptain was already doggedly embarking on educating this simpleton of a Lord Archwizard. Doing a terse but accurate job of it, too.

Gemadars were busy Ironthar smiths, the sons and prentices of those who'd first learned how to bond sharpened gemstones to the edges of swords to make them astonishingly sharp and strong. The sort of swords that had recently become the rage among the wealthy of the Stormar, the black-bearded, dusky-skinned folk who dwelt in their hot, crowded cities along the coasts of the Sea of Storms.

Syregorn seemed personally insulted by this interest taken in his home hold by outlanders from afar. Rod decided to try to steer him back to Ironthorn itself.

"I—I confess I know not enough of how things stand in Ironthorn just now," he interrupted, waving his hand in a way that had the more spell-fearing knights rising to hurl their daggers. Thankfully, in the suddenly tense silence, none of them did.

Into it, Rod spoke earnestly, playing the innocent dolt for all he was worth, rueful that the act wasn't much of a stretch. "Lord Burrim I had heard of, and liked what I heard. Yet tell me of his rivals; who are these Lyroses, really? There are others, too; I can hardly aid you if I know not who I'm fighting."

"That's true," Syregorn admitted, as knights started to relax and sit down again. "I..." he sighed, obviously at a loss over where to begin.

"Syre," Thalden spoke up gently, "let me."

The warcaptain gave the older knight a hard stare for a few moments, then nodded.

Thalden turned his head to meet Rod's eyes directly. "Lord Archwizard, as we sit here Ironthorn is ruled uneasily by three rival lords. We serve the best of them, Lord Burrim Hammerhand. His badge is the iron gauntlet, on a field of battle-blood. Of living kin, he has only Amteira left, now; his wife, the Lady Venyarla, was raped and butchered years ago by Melvarl Lyrose—"

There were growls and the hisses of indrawn breath from all around Rod, as knightly faces went hard and cold.

"—father of the current Lord Magrandar Lyrose. Lord Hammerhand avenged her, slaying Melvarl blade to blade."

More growls, of grim satisfaction this time.

"From Hammerhold, our lord rules most of Ironthorn: its northernmost three valleys, with all their farms, and Irontarl, the vale's market town and ford over the Thorn River. Lord Hammerhand is and has long been the foremost lord of Ironthorn— because of us, his loyal warriors. Yet he dislikes and shuns magic, and so has suffered in recent seasons as his rivals Lyrose and Tesmer have used magic against him; wherefore his recent embrace of the faith of the Forestmother."

There were some muted mutterings; these knights were not overjoyed by the Lord Leaf, it seemed.

Thalden's voice rose a trifle. "It is needful," he said firmly, "that you know why House Hammerhand are the rightful rulers of Ironthorn, and other claims are empty."

He leaned forward, staring hard into Rod's eyes to make sure the Lord Archwizard was listening. "Long ago the wizard Orthaunt, who then ruled Ironthorn by cruel force of magic, proclaimed the Hammerhands rulers in his stead when he went off to war against another wizard. That other was Lorontar, who mockingly sent the talking skull of Orthaunt back to Ironthorn to tell of Lorontar's victory and Orthaunt's doom. The skull was, in time, stolen. So of course the Lyroses and Tesmers now say it was but a hoax, enacted by some hidden wizard hired by the Hammerhands to advance their claim to rule."

"Lorontar," Rod could not help but whispering, a moment of chill rising inside him amidst all the warmth. The first Lord Archwizard—the *real* Lord Archwizard—had been a busy man, to be sure.

"Across the Thorn River," Thalden went on, "is our most bitter foe, whom we go up against this night. Lord Magrandar Lyrose sneers at us from Lyraunt Castle, that stands just south of the Thorn River. His badge is the Three Thorns—a pinwheel of three steel-gray thorns, joined at their bases, on a yellow field. Looks like a caltrop. His wife, Maerelle, still lives, but he has now—thanks to our blades, Syregorn's here among them—"

Grim murmurs and mirthless chuckles of approval arose around the hollow.

"—but one son, Pelmard the dashing coward. A daughter, too, Mrythra by name, who is as cold a schemer as any wizard I've ever met. Uh, begging your indulgence, Lord Archwizard."

Rod nodded and managed a weak smile. These knights might call him "wizard," but he was hardly striking fear—or respect, for that matter—into any of them.

"Real daggers 'neath her garters, that one," Thalden growled, shaking his head in disgust. "Not that her mother's far behind her. So these Lyrose serpents reign over southwestern Ironthorn. Which is three vales that flank monster-roamed Harstorm Ridge, where none but Lyrose's bravest foresters dare go. And none of them set boot near haunted Stormcrag Castle, atop Harstorm."

"Tell me," Rod said quietly, as the old knight sat back to reach down a cupped hand to the spring by his feet, and drink. "The Lyrose sons who were slain; what did you do with their bodies?"

"Burned, and the ashes scattered," Syregorn snapped. "No wizard or priest will be bringing *them* back."

"And that's the real power behind Lyrose," Thalden said urgently, swallowing hastily so as to lean forward again, to be sure Rod heeded him. "The Doom Malraun is Lord Lyrose's spine and fire. When our lord slew Melvarl Lyrose and came after Magrandar, seeking to slaughter the whole family and take Lyraunt Castle, the wizard offered Lyrose his aid. Now, Magrandar is a snake and a wallower in cruel pleasures, but he is not a fool. He accepted. It made him a slave to come, aye, but kept him alive then. The wizard's spells hurled back our lord's forces, felling many brave knights. Yet, mark you, Malraun did not hound us, or seek to scour out Hammerhold; he is no great friend of House Lyrose or their aims. He gave them magic, though, to keep them alive. Little things, shields that heal and banish poison and the like. Then he vanished again, and has seldom been seen in Ironthorn since."

The old knight drank again, cleared his throat, and added, "Yet Ironthorn has a third lord. Lord Irrance Tesmer, who dwells in his castle of Imtowers, holding sway over the valley of Imrush. The largest, most lush farms in Ironthorn; the River Imrush winds through them, down to join the Thorn at Irontarl."

"Uh, ah, does he matter?" Rod asked, more to try to make Syregorn think he was still babbling helplessly than to goad Thalden into telling all.

"He is the reason Hammerhand and Lyrose didn't hurl themselves at each other and into death long ago. The reason we skirmish and glare instead, and Ironthorn staggers along wealthy and crowded, with three lords, rather than being a graveyard ruled by one."

Well, *that* was emphatic enough.

Thalden wasn't done, though.

"Tesmer's arms are a purple diamond on a light gray field. That diamond shape represents gems, for every rock crevice in the Imrush was once full of gems, and they are still to be had to this day, albeit scarcer, and only in deep crawl-mines."

Rod frowned. "So why isn't Tesmer the strongest Ironthar lord? Why didn't Malraun aid *him?*"

"Well," the old knight said slowly, "there you have hit on a mystery. There's some as say another Doom was lurking in the minds of the Tesmers already—a trap for Malraun, belike—and others hold that Tesmer's wife Telclara—who rules him as harshly as he lords it over the Imrush farmers—is set against Malraun, and has some power or thing of magic he fears, to keep him at bay. I know not, and I doubt any jack or knight of Ironthorn does, whatever truths they may claim to know."

"And Tesmer's heirs? How well does she rule them?"

"Well, now," the old knight growled. "That's the part that's worth listening to me ramble, to hear. Lady Telclara, they say, no longer admits Tesmer to her bed, but herself selects bedmates for him from beautiful slave-girls she buys off traders who come in a steady stream to Imrush-vale from the cities of the Sea of Storms. *They* get them in raids from more southerly cities across that sea."

He took another drink, shook his head at what he was about to say, and added, "And after they bear him a child, she slaughters them. The sickly or defiant babes she kills, too. Those she deems acceptable are named heirs of the blood Tesmer, and trained to war. Wherefore there are now three Tesmer daughters, followed by six sons, all gained by this means. From eldest to youngest, they are—"

He counted them off on his fingers as he listed them, to be sure of missing none.

"Maera, a cold and haughty one who never lets anyone forget she's foremost; Nareyera, a scheming beauty whose eyes actually flash when she's raging; the tall, quiet one, Talyss, and then the sons."

Thalden cleared his throat again, and went on. "Belard, the handsome master swordsman; Ghorsyn, who's big and loud and a bully, so of course witless lasses love him; Kalathgar, who just might be the smartest of them all, and doesn't think much of his kin; and Delmark, a lazy cheat and spy who'd slit your throat for an idle instant's amusement."

He shook his head, waggled the two fingers still upthrust, and added, "Two more. Ellark, who's ugly and clumsy. His brothers sneer at him, but he's strong as an ox and perhaps the only Tesmer who knows how to be kind. Last and youngest: Feldrar, another coward, liar, and prankster like Delmark, but busies himself being the dashing swindler instead of lie-a-bed lazy. Quite a House, hey?"

"By the Falcon, I don't want to rule Ironthorn!" Rod said feelingly, by way of reply. "I take it House Tesmer has few knights?"

"Aye, and we take care to keep it that way. Poisoned arrows from the trees, if need be. Not that we often see the need; Lyrose usually has his archers in there slaying, first."

"I cannot help but see," Syregorn said firmly then, "that your fit of talking has passed, Lord Archwizard. Sunset is not all that far off, now, and it will take us much of what's left of the day to work our way around and into the Lyrose lands unseen. They are *not* unguarded."

157

"Patrols like swarming flies," one of the knights commented, earning himself a sharp look from the warcaptain.

Ah, yes, Rod thought. *This was supposed to be when the Lord Leaf's little powder made me yield up answer after answer to you. Not a time for me to ask and ask, and so hear all that befalls in Ironthorn.*

The hard, steady stare Syregorn gave Rod then made the Lord Archwizard of all Falconfar wonder if the warcaptain could hear his thoughts.

Perhaps magic was among the secrets the Hammerhands were still guarding.

After all, it wasn't as if he was wizard enough to find out.

"THERE GOES THE sun," Garfist grunted. He turned away from the castle window like a restlessly prowling bear. "Can't help but feel this's not going to be a restful night."

Iskarra nodded. "So my bones tell me, too." She made a face. "I am beginning to hate one thing most of all."

"That is?" Gar rumbled, flexing his fingers as if a handy throat was waiting for them.

"There's not a glorking thing we can do but sit and wait," his lady said bitterly. "'Tis like being a sworn soldier again."

"*Ye* were a sworn soldier?"

Even after all these years, Garfist was used to Iskarra being able to surprise him.

"No, but after you've killed one for his cloak and armor and put them on, one idiot who can march, dig shit pits, swing a sword, and die is enough like another for a warcaptain not to care. Especially when he can thrust his little warrior into you whenever he pleases, under threat of revealing what you've done and having you put to death slowly and painfully. With all your fellow soldiers helping."

Garfist grew a slow grin. "What'd ye do to him, in the end?"

"The short tale? Put him to death slowly and painfully. With all the other soldiers helping."

Garfist waved one large and hairy hand. "Tell me the longer tale. 'Tis better than just waiting."

Isk gave him one of her more twisted smiles. "Well, farther away and longer ago than I care to remember, I was born in a muddy field during a lightning storm…"

"No talking, now," Syregorn murmured into Rod Everlar's ear. "We are well inside the Lyrose patrols. No noise, whatever befalls."

Like a ghost in the darkness—it had grown dark amid the trees with frightening suddenness—the warcaptain rose and moved along the line of Hammerhand knights. Rod could barely see the nearest of them, ahead and behind, even though he knew exactly where to look.

The forest was still thick, and alive with small rustlings. None of them made by Syregorn or his men, so far as Rod could tell.

Scarcely daring to breathe, he froze only for a moment when a hand patted his arm. It was the third time he'd felt that signal, and knew what to do: rise from the tree he was crouching against, and move on along the trail without making a sound.

He did that, and so did the Hammerhand knights behind him.

The last of them had been gone for the time it took the Lord Archwizard to draw in three of his new, careful, oh-so-quiet breaths before something rose silently up the other side of the stout old tree Rod Everlar had been crouching against, and started to skulk after them.

GAR AND ISK stiffened when someone stepped into the room, but it was only the Aumrarr, and she gave them a smile, not a brandished blade.

She'd gone off to walk about Stormcrag Castle some time ago, telling them firmly she did not want them along, for their own safety.

"Lurking beasts? Traps?" Garfist had growled at her challengingly, whereupon she had nodded and replied simply, "Yes."

A look from Isk had quelled whatever defiance Gar might have offered next, and Dyune of the Aumrarr had walked off alone.

Now she was back, her hands empty. There were cobwebs in her hair, and smudges and smears of dust all over her. "Find whatever it was ye were looking for?" Gar rumbled, raising one bushy eyebrow.

"No," she replied, and went to sit beside Iskarra, where they could both look out the window into the night.

Silence fell. Garfist lurched a few steps, threw up his arms in exaggerated exasperation, spun around, and returned to where he had been sitting, facing Iskarra. He stared, however, at the Aumrarr.

She gave him a nod and went back to staring out at the night.

Silence stretched.

"So," Gar asked thoughtfully after a time. "How

many Aumrarr are there left, after Highcrag, d'ye think?"

Dyune stared at him, shrugged, and asked in defiant reply, "How many lorn are there in Falconfar, d'ye think?"

Garfist gave her a sour look. "I'd never have a way of even guessing that, but Aumrarr have always been few, have always worked together and had much to do with each other, and so…"

Dyune gave him a tight smile. "And so would never answer questions like that."

"*Very* few, I see," Isk said softly, from beside her.

"I didn't *say* that!" Dyune snapped.

"You didn't have to," Isk replied, even more quietly.

Dyune turned her head away, and said not another word.

THERE WAS A tiny sound in the night right in front of Rod Everlar, and he froze and crouched down. It was followed by a thud, the briefest of thrashings in grass, and then something that might have been a sigh.

What seemed like a silent eternity later, that hand patted his arm again, and then took firm hold of his shoulder and pulled. Rod allowed himself to be led—off the trail through the grass, in a little half-circle that brought him back to the trail again.

He suspected he'd been led around a body. Of a Lyrose guard who'd just been killed.

The moon was rising, and he could just make out shapes, now. One of them was the grim face of the Hammerhand knight still guiding him.

The other, soaring like a dark and endless cliff right in front of him, must be Lyraunt Castle.

"BRIGHT MOON RISING," the Aumrarr whispered, as if to herself. She had not moved, nor stopped staring out the window.

Garfist rumbled deep in his throat, as if about to point out that he had eyes that worked, too, but it was Iskarra who spoke first.

"Dyune, there is something I would know. Something I hope you can tell me."

The Aumrarr turned her head. "An Aumrarr secret?"

"Perhaps."

Iskarra let that lone word fall into a silence, and waited.

Until Dyune shrugged and said simply, "Ask."

"Time and again Aumrarr warn that this new Lord Archwizard is going to do something terrible, soon. Now, I'll grant you, terrible things are what wizards—*all* wizards—do, darned near every time they really try to do anything. But just *what* are you afraid of? What can he do, that the others can't?"

Dyune grimaced. "We Aumrarr don't speak of such things, and—"

"Then ye Aumrarr are fools," Gar rumbled. "How many secrets and wise remembrances were lost when the Dark Helms slaughtered everyone in Highcrag? If ye tell us, then mayhap when ye're dead, one of us can shout to some handy hero what he has to stop the Lord Archwizard doing! Now *tell* us, glork ye! We healed ye, didn't we?"

The Aumrarr regarded them both thoughtfully, looking slowly from one to the other, then nodded. "Very well. There's an enspelled gem—we call it the mindgem—that scrambles the minds of wizards who get too close to it. Made long ago, by a forgotten enchanter. It's long been one of the treasures we

Aumrarr keep secret—and has always had a tale clinging to it: that it sears the minds of wizards too close to it, until they're dragged back away from it or it's taken away from them, because it's waiting for just one wizard. The right one. The Lord Archwizard. So it could make him like unto a god, able to hurl mountains into nothing at a whim. That's why we guard it."

"And where is it now?" Iskarra asked softly.

Dyune shook her head, her lips tightening in might what have become a mirthless smile.

If, in that moment, she hadn't heard or felt something they could not.

Stiffening, the Aumrarr suddenly moved as swiftly as any striking serpent. Snatching up her weapons from where Iskarra and Garfist had laid them near to hand, she tugged hard on something hidden in her hair, tore forth a fine but now-broken chain that had been looped around both of her ears, and flung it to Iskarra.

Who caught it out of habit, and was still staring at the sparkling gemstone she now held as Dyune sprang out of the window, eluding Garfist's oath-accompanied grab at her, and flew fast and hard up into the night, warsteel ready in her hands.

Chapter Twelve

GARFIST HURLED HIMSELF at the window, but as always, Isk was faster. Like a lightning-swift serpent she was there and pressed to one side of the window opening, to give him ample room to do what she was doing: craning his neck to look sharply up into the night.

The light of the rising moon was strong, despite the countless trees blocking much of it, and they could make out what blotted out so many of the stars overhead.

The huge bulk of a greatfangs hung across the night sky like a vast ceiling—a ceiling that swooped, beating wings so massive that their cleaving of the air could be *felt* more than heard.

Dyune was swooping all around the vast beast, darting and stabbing, as its fearsome head sought her but turned too slowly to close on her jaws that three dozen Aumrarr could not have filled.

There were other Aumrarr swooping and stabbing too, their wings curling and flapping as they fought to keep too close to it to be easily reached, but just far enough away that it couldn't slam into them in the air, and leave them falling, broken or stunned.

As they watched, one of the winged women got struck glancingly, and tumbled down through the air, that great neck sweeping around to—

"Bright nipples of Nornautha!" Garfist swore, clenching one fist and using his other hand to stab a hairy pointing finger into the night. "That's Dauntra, one o' the wingbitches as brought us here! An' that's Juskra, yon! By the Devouring Worm, all four of 'em!"

"Aptly cursed," Iskarra murmured. "It *will* devour them, if it can catch them. Hmm. They weren't all that far off all this time, those four, I'll be bound."

She watched the desperate dance in the sky for a few breaths longer, then snapped, "There's someone riding the beast! The third Doom, Narmarkoun, I'll lay you a gleaming gold broon."

"No, I'll lose no coins to ye this night," Gar growled, pounding his fists on the sill in frustration. Almost directly overhead, rolling in the air above the battlements of Stormcrag Castle, the great wyrm twisted, snapping its jaws but *just* failing to catch a desperately-diving Aumrarr.

They saw the rider on its back shaping air with his hands, in the strange fluid gestures that meant magic was being worked—and then the air in front of those hands blossomed into shadowy shapes that bit and snapped and darted in an echo of the bitings of the huge, arrow-shaped head of the greatfangs. Phantom spell-jaws reached hungrily for the flying Aumrarr, trailing the little winking lights of fresh-spun sorcery, and bit down. Hard.

An Aumrarr reeled in midair, the magic that had savaged her sapping her strength, and fell... and as Gar and Isk watched, hard-eyed, the huge head of the greatfangs swung up to finally catch a darting foe.

Teeth as long as the falling Aumrarr's body closed on the winged woman, blood sprayed in all directions, and severed limbs came tumbling down out of the sky in the wake of that many-fanged, busily chewing head.

Another Aumrarr rushed up to stab at a large and heavy-lidded eye, howling in rage and grief—and the head drew away from her and then thrust back, slamming its snout into her. She spun helplessly away across the sky, wings curling and convulsing, and the great wyrm lunged after her and bit her apart, too.

Gar and Isk saw a third Aumrarr swoop up from beneath the greatfangs to slice and stab at its rider, and—

Brightness burst across the darkness, an explosion that rocked Stormcrag Castle and tore the night sky asunder.

Gar roared in pain, clutching at his eyes, and Isk whimpered beside him. They could see nothing more.

Blindly, they groped for each other, hoping their sightlessness wouldn't last long.

"Lass," Garfist rumbled, as his arms went around a familiar bony shape, that clung to him and nipped at his shoulder lovingly, "I'm thinking *we're* now the guardians of this mindgem that's waiting for the right Lord Archwizard to come along."

"I'm thinking that, too," Isk whispered, nigh his neck. "Glork. Glork and be-frawling *bugger*."

A FLASH OF light split the sky above Harstorm Ridge, driving blinded knights on the walls of Hammerhold to curse or cry out. They had scarce clutched at their eyes and shouted for fresh watchers to come up from below when Hammerhand's castle rocked and shuddered under them in the throes of a second great crash.

This one was coming from behind them, and it was *moving*. As knights pounded up stairs onto the battlements to peer into the night, it groaned on for a long, rending time in which trees shrieked aloud as they were torn apart, snapped like so much kindling, and hurled down amid many smaller crashings. Then it all faded.

The hard-eyed watchers on the walls of Hammerhold saw that something had smashed a path of devastation across the Raurklor above them, on the forested heights that looked down on Ironthorn. An eerie glow—flames?—was flickering up there now, and silhouetted against it were tumbled and broken trees that should have towered unbroken up into the starry sky.

It was then that Lord Burrim Hammerhand came up onto the battlements in a growling rush, to glare all around at the surrounding forest as if he held it personally responsible.

"Darlok," he snapped, knowing without turning to look which of his warcaptains had hastened up the steps after him, "gather some knights—enough to hurl back three Lyrose patrols—and get up yonder to see what's befallen. If it's some dread spellhurler or other, fill him up with arrows for me. If it's something worse, get word back to me, or get yourself back to tell the tale, just as fast as you can run."

"Lord," Darlok agreed with a nod, and plunged back down the stone stair. Hammerhand followed him, slamming one shoulder against the stone as he always did when he came to the archers' bend, and cursing—only to fall silent, aghast, as a guard's shout arose from below: "Lorn! Lorn in the castle!"

Swearing, Lord Hammerhand hurled himself

down flight after flight of stairs, collecting a trotting Tarlkond and almost a score of knights by threes and fours at each floor.

They snatched out their swords when they reached the still-shouting guard, and flung just one question at him: "*Where?*"

At the sight of his lord that knight gave off crying his warning and spun around to point down the passage that led to the forehall. Hammerhand and the rest were streaming past him almost before he got his arm aimed properly.

"This is Lyrose mischief," Tarlkond snarled. "Who else can call down lorn?"

"Tesmer," another knight gasped.

"Or wizards," the Lord Leaf snapped darkly, from where he was suddenly panting along beside them, come from out of some dark side-passage or other.

He turned his head to catch Burrim Hammerhand's eye, and said urgently, between gasps for breath, "We will never see any limits to the evil and the wanton slaughter done by wizards. We must kill them, Lord! Kill them all!"

"Lorn first," the lord of Hammerhold growled back at him. "One foe at a time. All the wizards in the world will just have to wait; my swordarm isn't getting any younger."

THOUGH THE MOON was well risen and they were both within reach of the soaring highlance canopied bed they were wont to share, Lord and Lady Tesmer were still up and dressed. As the fairest flower of Imtowers had put it to her lord earlier, she was not in the habit of receiving spies—no matter how deeply trusted nor well paid—in her bed-silks. Or less.

The spy, a slender and softly-murmuring man of nondescript looks, had slipped out of the best bedchamber in the castle of Imtowers a bare few indrawn breaths earlier. Presumably he was now hastening back to his scullery in Hammerhold, before his absence might be remarked upon.

He had not borne overmuch news, and the most interesting of what he'd imparted came not from Ironthorn, but from Helnkrist in Helnadar.

It had taken Lord Tesmer, who loved maps but thought slowly when he was aware of his wife's disapproving glare and trying not to meet it, all this time to recall just where the small market-moot town of Helnadar was. On the easternmost edge of the Raurklor, of course; he'd remembered that much the moment he heard the name, but it had taken until now to bring to mind that—unsurprisingly—it straddled the Heln River, where that narrow, winding water flowed out of the forest into Sardray.

Helnkrist was the tower of the fell wizard Narmarkoun, the Doom who bred greatfangs. Until the wizard had slain them all to take possession of that keep, it had been the safehold of a consortium of Stormar merchants—a refuge in the green heart of nowhere they could retreat to in times of war, or retire from their rivals when old age crept into their bones. Well, Narmarkoun had saved them that most feeble of fates.

Now, it seemed, Helnkrist stood empty, the wizard gone.

Gone but not dead. Lord and Lady Tesmer knew that much without exchanging a word.

They were under Narmarkoun's sway, and right now he was just as he had been to them every moment of these last few seasons—a dark, heavy, everpresent, stifling weight in their minds. Watching their thoughts whenever he pleased, steering them when he desired. Yes, the breeder of greatfangs was very much still alive.

Just as they were very much still awake, and conferring together.

"This is not helpful," Lord Tesmer muttered worriedly, running one hand through his stylishly long, but thinning, hair. "Malraun's army advances without pause or check. No lorn harry it, no foe can stand against it; the best chance of destroying it would be greatfangs attacks, by night—and what chance of that now, if the Master is a fugitive, wandering and hiding somewhere in the Raurklor? Just when we need him."

Narmarkoun had told them long ago that Malraun was behind this "Horgul out of nowhere," and if Malraun saw into minds as often and as energetically as the Master did…

"Don't be a *fool*, Irrance," Lady Tesmer hissed sharply, leaning forward. Her long black hair, unbound for slumber, fell forward off her shoulders like a glossy waterfall. Her dark brown eyes seemed to blaze up into amber coals when she was angry, and they were smoldering now. "Narmarkoun is no such thing. Malraun's army is certainly something to be worried over—hence my strict orders to the men to withdraw from all frays with Lyrose and Hammerhand—and I know as well as you do that if they arrive in Ironthorn as strong as they are now, we are all doomed. We would be even if you, Burrim, and Magrandar were lovers, and all the Ironthar knights one united and superb army, against the numbers this Horgul leads."

Lord Tesmer grimaced in disgust and got to his feet, chamber-gown swirling out behind him like a cloak. He was tall and graceful, for all his broad-shouldered brawn, but the years had streaked his hair with white and etched lines of worry across his face. "Lovers, Clara? *Must* you say such things?"

"Blood of the Falcon, Irrance, will you stop thinking about *trifles*? What matters is not a few words of mine that happen to nettle you, but our lives! You've been worrying about what will happen to Ironthorn if Malraun's army comes, among all the *countless* things you worry about, all this season! Listen to me, Lord of Imtowers, and listen well: the one thing you do *not* have to worry over is the Master's fate. He is not some fugitive wandering the Raurklor, cowering or hiding. You can feel him in your head as well as I do; does he seem any the weaker? Well?"

"But Chansz—"

"*Irrance Tesmer!* We do *not* use his name! Never! Not here, just this once, where no one can hear us, because we never truly know when no one can hear us, do we? Call him 'spy' and and naught else!"

Lord Tesmer put a despairing hand over his handsome face, sighed loudly, and murmured, "Spy, then. The *spy* said Helnkrist stood empty— ransacked by the overbold when they found its doors open and nothing living within but birds and rats that had strayed inside before them. As if it had been abandoned in such haste that the Master had owned not time enough to take a thing with him! It follows that all he had time to do was take himself out of there, saving his skin in the face of some great foe! This Archwizard of Falconfar, or Malraun, or someone more terrible!"

"My lord, there *is* no one more terrible. Now stop babbling like a chamberlass and heed: the Narmarkoun in Helnkrist was not our Master."

"What?" Tesmer whirled around incredulously.

"Close your mouth, Irrance. You look like a drooljaws village lackwit." Lady Tesmer's voice was as sharp as her flawless nose and cheekbones, the beauty that still drew Tesmer's eyes and snatched at his breath every time he gazed upon it. Even now, when he stood agape in disbelief.

Her eyes blazed brighter, and he hastily closed his mouth.

Whereupon his wife nodded in satisfaction and informed him firmly, "The missing Narmarkoun was a *false* Narmarkoun, a lesser wizard serving our Master and wearing, through magic, the shape and seeming of the Master. A double set there in Helnkrist by the real one."

"What?" Tesmer's mouth dropped open again.

His lady didn't bother to hide her scorn. "Irrance, have you paid *no* attention at all to the Master's words, these last few years—and what can be gleaned from what he does *not* say?"

Lord Tesmer closed his mouth hastily, paced across the room as anger rose in him, and snapped at the wall that loomed up in his way, "Of course not. I'm too stupid to do so, of course. You miss no chance to make *that* abundantly clear."

"Now you are being churlish, like one of the stable lads when he's been caught at something. Tesmer, *enough*. I need you to be Lord of Imtowers—rightful lord of all Ironthorn—now, and set aside your boy's trifles and *learn*. Irrance, I need your promise."

Tesmer sighed at the wall. "Of course. You have

it." *You always do*, he added silently, as he turned to stride back across the room, slowly and bitterly, still not looking at his wife. *You ask for it often enough*.

"Irrance, look at me!" Lady Tesmer snapped, like a swordcaptain hurling an order at a disobedient spearboy.

And, Falcon take him, he looked.

Right into her coldest, most satisfied smile. The one that had trapped and fascinated him all these years.

"Heed," she repeated, almost gently, holding him with her eyes. Little flames were leaping in them, by the Falcon. "The *real* Narmarkoun dwells in Closecandle, in the westernmost Raurklor. He has several false selves, all underlings who serve him—so that Malraun and other foes can watch and betimes smite them, whilst our Master goes about his work unregarded and free of their attacks and meddlings."

Tesmer blinked at her in real amazement. "What is Closecandle, and why have I not heard of it? It's not on any of my maps!"

"And well do you love and trust your maps, my lord." Scorn was clear in Telclara Tesmer's voice again, but it was soft, almost affectionate. "Know you that Closecandle is neither a castle nor a wizard's tower. It is a mountain, reshaped and hollowed out by the Master's magic. How could you hide breeding greatfangs in anything smaller?"

"A mountain." Tesmer shook his head, and then mimicked her voice: "And how would you hide a mountain?"

"Amid other peaks, of course," his wife said sweetly. "The Howlhorns."

He frowned, seeing in his mind that part of his best map where the westernmost reaches of the vast Raurklor gave way to the Howlhorns range, mountains so named for the constant Howling Winds that roared through them. "So remote," he protested. "No roads, no…"

"There are no roads leading to it, and no settlements near it," Lady Tesmer confirmed crisply. "It looks like… a mountain. Very much like the other peaks all around it. And now you know perhaps more than you should know."

The Lord of Imtowers stiffened. "More than I—? Lady, I thought you were my wife."

"I *am* your wife, Irrance, and we are equals. Yet I seem to have managed to keep secrets, and you cannot even keep yourself from blurting out the name of a common spy. See that you guard *this* secret rather better. Or it won't be my rebuke you'll have to fear."

Lord Tesmer stiffened again, recalling the utterly cold eyes of the Master—and the dead, ice-cold wenches that had been caressing him and massing menacingly behind him, some of them grotesque rotting things and some of them almost all the way gone to walking skeletons. Not just the fleshless skulls among them had been grinning in endless, ruthless promise. He swallowed, and said quickly, "Tell me more of these false Narmarkouns. I—I should know such things."

"I suppose you should, at that. Do you recall Sornspire from your maps?"

"In southwestern Galath, in the mountains… of the barony of Chainamund. A wizard's tower. Built by the mage Malagusk Sorn, who's been dead for centuries. Abandoned, I thought."

Telclara nodded. "Until the Master installed a false self there."

Lord Tesmer found himself remembering that chilling gaze again, the blue and scaly skin... he managed not to shudder. "Tell me more."

"Irrance, in truth I know only three places: Sornspire, Telnkrist, and Mrelgates."

"Mrelgates," Tesmer said sharply. "In the Taur Waste." The swampy eastern arm of the Rauklor where he'd never been; a dismal, mist-shrouded place. He knew Mrelgates as a fortified merchant's manor, so remote that it must have been built where it was to squat atop a gem-mine, or a lode of gold, or to hide a veritable herd of slaves. "Why there?"

His wife shrugged. "The Master does not tell me such things. I know only that his forces took it by storm. Perhaps he was riding greatfangs, and wanted to give them some experience of striking from the sky under his command."

Tesmer nodded. "Yes, I can see that. You know only these three places, you said; he has others, with a false Narmarkoun dwelling in each?"

"So I believe."

The Lord of Imtowers started to pace again, anger gone but fresh worry rising in him, instead. "Yet if he has so many false selves, why did he not quell all these tales of his destruction by having one of them appear with thunder and hurled spells, to make all Falconfar think him stronger than Malraun?"

"He's trying to feign dead, for some reason," Lady Tesmer replied firmly. "Perhaps until Malraun overreaches himself, somehow."

"But if Malraun's armies come here..."

"We flee or die," Lady Tesmer said crisply. "Unless Narmarkoun awakens in our heads to compel us to do one or the other—or something else—our fates will be in our own hands. Which means the sooner we plan how we'll escape Ironthorn alive, the better!"

Lord Tesmer winced. "Flee? Leaving the gem-mines and…"

"Dead men can't gloat over gems," Telclara Tesmer told him sharply. "And though I doubt you've noticed, Irrance, live Falconaar women are seldom foolish enough to gloat over *anything*. Doing so always seems to goad the gods, or fate, or greedy neighbors to come and take whatever we're gloating about away from us. Along with our lives, usually."

Lord Tesmer winced again.

Chapter Thirteen

HIS SWORD STILL drawn, Darlok led the way.

The eerie glows that had lit up the hilltop were now feeble, dying things, but flames—real flames, not strange magical radiances—were flickering here and there among the fallen, splintered trees.

Ironthar knew better than to trust in moonlight when in the woods, so the knights hastening along behind their hard-striding lord—and the sweating priest struggling to clamber over fallen trees fast enough to keep up with him—had brought torches.

Darlok's report had been vivid enough. A gigantic winged beast, probably a greatfangs, had crashed to earth, thankfully dead, and there were signs of battle. Specifically, other bodies. Human.

For the taciturn warcaptain, that was eloquent. There had been only three lorn. So, spies rather than an invading force, to Hammerhand's thinking. The lord and his knights had made short work of them.

Not that the slaying had left Lord Burrim Hammerhand in all that bright a temper. He had welcomed the chance to follow Darlok up into the shattered part of the forest to see matters on the hilltop for himself, and hadn't sheathed his sword.

It was still drawn now, as he came out into a clearing that hadn't been there before. A long scar of devastation clove the forest from east to west, wide enough to park three wagons or more, tail-to-tail, as if some titan larger than a greatfangs had driven a plow through rocks, trees, and forest loam alike, turning them aside in a great furrow. The scar was a good three bowshots long, a path of heaped and broken trees that shone like so many pale broken bones in the moonlight.

"A new place we'll have to guard," Hammerhand growled aloud, "or we'll have Lyrose massing up here for mischief every day."

He took a few steps around a massive tree-limb, to where he could tramp around that fallen waerwood tree and along the scar in Darlok's wake. Stifling a curse, the fearful Lord Leaf followed, still panting from all the clambering up through the trees, and shaking a numbed hand he'd slammed into a very solid bough in the insufficiently torchlit darkness.

After a dozen more breaths of lurching along climbing on his knees over hard yet splintered wood and bruising himself against branches too strong to give way before him in the blinding tangle of leafy boughs, the priest came out into the westwards end of the open area. And stopped, aghast at what he saw.

A great scaled bulk stretched from near his boots for a long, long way to where the scar ended, in a clump of trees leaning perilously over the open area as if anxious to topple into it. It was the largest beast Cauldreth Jaklar had ever seen, and it lay in a sickeningly deformed heap. Broken-off treetrunks, dark with glistening gore, thrust up out of its rolling, twisted flesh like spears here, there, and over yonder.

It was dead, all right.

The lord of Hammerhold came tramping back along the huge corpse—Jaklar's stomach heaved as he realized what he'd thought was an upthrust, splayed tree in the distance was actually the talons of one large, dark dead claw, frozen in a last, futile clawing of the air—to growl, "Well, Jaklar? Know what you're looking at?"

"A greatfangs," the Lord Leaf managed to say, though he was certain his voice quavered. "Or what's left of one."

Hammerhand nodded. "It had a rider."

"Oh. You found the body?"

"No. Which means we may have a Doom lurking near us right now. I hope you've magic enough, Lord Leaf."

"Narmarkoun," the priest murmured, too afraid to bristle at Hammerhand's words.

The lord of Hammerhold nodded. The Doom called Narmarkoun was known to breed and ride greatfangs, and this great bulk beside them, all scales and tail and a dark, spreading lake of blood that was starting to stink, was the shattered corpse of a greatfangs.

The Lord Leaf swallowed. He knew of no priest of the Forestmother—not even Loroth the Highest— who could hurl magic enough to fight off a Doom. Fight off, not destroy.

"Lurking near us, right now," he whispered to himself.

Hammerhand looked at him sharply, then turned to a knight who was hastening up with a torch, and pointed in silent command.

The knight nodded, stepped forward, and bent to let torchlight fall where his lord was pointing.

Something small, pale, and bloody glistened in the flickering radiance. It took Jaklar a moment to recognize what he was seeing: bloody fragments of bitten-through human bodies. His stomach lurched.

Lord Hammerhand bent down and picked up the largest lump as calmly as if he'd been a butcher gutting boar in his own kitchens. It flopped in his hand, heavy but shapeless, rows of shattered ribs protruding from dripping flesh. One shapely breast thrust forward from the gory piece of ribcage.

"Female," Burrim Hammerhand said grimly, holding it up for a better look.

Jaklar vomited violently, staggering aside almost blindly as his stomach emptied itself in a hard, unstoppable, heaving rush.

When he could see again, the lord of Hammerhold had dropped that obscene lump and was holding up another, severed scraps of leather war-harness dropping from it. It was part of the shoulder of a sleekly-muscled woman's back, with the base of a bitten-off limb that shouldn't have been there protruding from it.

"Aumrarr," he added tersely.

The priest swallowed. Hammerhand thought he was trying to ask a question, and explained, "A wing."

Jaklar's stomach heaved again, trying to rid itself of meals that were no longer there. He drooled bile helplessly, swallowed, then gaspingly turned back in time to see Hammerhand hold up the most grisly thing of all: a head, minus jaw and everything below.

The Lord Leaf caught sight of a face, all smeared hair and blood across dark, forever-staring eyes, as Burrim Hammerhand held it up and calmly looked into that dead gaze.

Then the lord of Hammerhold shook his head and let it fall back into the darkness with a wet thud. "No one I know."

Cauldreth Jaklar found himself fighting to be sick again, though there was nothing still down him left to come out.

"Lord Hammerhand!" It was more of a breathless gasp than a shout, out of the forest below. Back toward Hammerhold, whence they'd come.

"Here," Burrim Hammerhand replied, turning, his sword coming up.

"Lord!" It was a Hammerhold knight, gasping hard after a hasty climb through the dark forest. "News!"

"What is it?" Hammerhand sounded as calm—and grim—as ever.

"Horgul and his army have taken Darswords!"

Hammerhand nodded as if he'd expected this, and said only, "There's more. Worse." It was not a question.

The knight nodded, gasping for breath, then blurted, "Nelthraun, Lord of Stelgond, has marched through Yuskellar, the valley of the Gold Duke—and right through all the Gold Duke's guards, too, when they disputed his passage, though he did *not* stop to plunder the Duke's mansion or harm the Gold Duke himself—with the stated aim of conquering Ironthorn just as fast as he can get here!"

"*What?*" The word burst out of Hammerhand in disbelief.

"Six message-birds, lord, all from merchants we pay for news. All bore the same tidings," the knight replied grimly.

Darlok had joined them out of the night, and now snapped, "Stelgond up in arms to come here—where no Lord of Stelgond has ever been, nor wanted to be—

183

and Horgul in Darswords, three holds away from us if he marches on in the direction he's been going. They're coming here because of the Lord Archwizard, lord!"

"Harlhoh, then through the wild Raurklor to Darkriver, then east along the Long Trail to Burnt Bones... and on, to us," Hammerhand mused aloud. "Stelgond alone is more than enough for us to handle, what with the two vipers here in the Vale biting at me day and night to see who'll be lord and who'll be dead. If we must cross swords with this Horgul, too, we'll need all the Forestmother's luck—and anything else the Aumrarr or lorn or anyone else can spare to aid us—to have any hope of holding onto Ironthorn and our lives."

"Where's Stel—" the Lord Leaf started to ask.

"In Tauren," Hammerhand snapped. "A small hold, but wealthy."

"Ah. I have heard," the priest murmured, "that a Doom rides behind this Horgul. The same wizard who aids Lyrose, Malraun the Matchless. If that's true, we are all... doomed."

"Heard where, and from whom?" Hammerhand growled, watching the knight who'd brought the news go pale and flinch back at Jaklar's words.

"In altar-visions, of far-away priests of the Forestmother talking to each other," the Lord Leaf replied.

Hammerhand shot him a hard look, but the priest seemed both sincere—and scared.

He was.

"I have prayed to the Forestmother for guidance," Jaklar whispered, "in case we must flee into the arms of the Raurklor around us. All of Hammerhold, that is. But She has sent me no sign."

Lord Hammerhand rounded on him. "Of course

She hasn't. She knows we'll fight to hold Ironthorn, and die doing it. No Ironthar will flee anywhere. If we lose what's dear to us, what is 'living on' worth? Nothing. We stay here, our swords sharp in our hands, and defend our Vale against anyone who comes to try to take it from us."

He stared out into the night, past the torchlight. "Even if every last Stormar or Galathan took up arms and came here, in hosts beyond counting, I would take a stand and try to kill them all. It's glorking near all I know how to do."

WARRIORS WERE CLIMBING the hill from all sides, torches flickering wildly in their hands. With the moon now so bright, the flames they carried served more to make them superb targets than to aid their way over the heaped and strewn bodies, but Malraun didn't even bother to shrug at that passing thought. He had more important matters to concern him.

Blasting down these last few wizards before any of them managed to spin a magic to flee this place, for instance.

Darswords had fought furiously against his army. Furiously but hopelessly; they would all die, or were dead already. The children had been hurried away into the forest, of course, by a few of the crones and youngest women. Everyone else would perish.

Malraun was not in the best of moods. Amaxas Horgul had been more boar than man, a brawling, rutting lout governed by his lusts and rages—but he had been a giant on the battlefield, and a man warriors looked to and obeyed.

And now he was dead, and if Malraun was to hold this army together, he would have to lead it himself. Falcon rut and spew! Riding across half Falconfar—the backlands, fly-infested half—was *not* how he'd planned on spending the next score or so of days. Which meant he'd have to get to know a lot of thick-headed swordswingers rather too well over the next day or so, and hope he could find a war leader among them who could lead them all half as well as Horgul had.

However, there was one task in hand to finish with, first. Scouring out Horgul's slayers.

The Stormar had been a surprise. Who'd have thought a remote Raurklor hold like Darswords could have coin enough to hire wizards from distant Sea of Storms cities, let alone known how to contact them?

Lesser mages or not, they'd been far from overconfident fools, too. They'd hidden among the defenders of the hold, avoiding hurling magical fires and lightnings in favor of peering hard to find the right man, and then hurling mind-lances. By such means they'd slain Horgul and some of his warcaptains, then tried to seize control over the minds of the rest, so as to take over command of the whole host.

If there'd been no Doom standing unseen behind Horgul, it would have worked. As it was, Malraun the Matchless was in the habit of often prying into the minds of Horgul and his captains from afar, and was warned. He'd learned all this from the mind of one startled Stormar mage, then given that unfortunate the same death that had been visited on Horgul, and then magically taken himself and Taeauna to this blood-drenched, moonlit hill nigh Darswords.

The hold itself crowned a hill beside the one he stood on, with the wingless Aumrarr by his side. This hill had been left bare of homes and barns because, fittingly, it was where they buried their dead.

There'd be a lot of burying to do, later, though he doubted anyone would be alive to do it. The slope they were cautiously climbing was heaped and strewn with the dead. The folk of Darswords must have spent every last coin that had been buried under every dirt floor, to hire so many mercenaries to stand shoulder-to-shoulder and fight. And die.

Taeauna raised her sword, peering past it at the last few Stormar huddled atop the hill. They were now hurling all the fires and lightnings they'd avoided using earlier, hence the caution of their ascent. She was shielding him with her body, something that almost brought a smile to Malraun's face. She was his creature, now, in truth; that wasn't something he'd coerced her into doing. When Aumrarr served, they *served*.

Now she was rising and striding on, a few swift, bent-over steps that took her to the next heap of dead they could shelter behind.

Malraun scrambled to keep up with her, ignoring a groaning, feebly-moving warrior underfoot. Whoever it was lacked the means to harm him, and would die soon enough of his wounds or under the claws and jaws of lurking beasts who'd come out of the forest—or down out of the skies—to feast on the dead.

The Stormar wizards were still hurling death of their own, a roiling wall of flames this time, that marched down the slope, licking empty air, until it engulfed the foremost torch-bearers. Their screams were raw and terrible, but didn't last long.

Malraun smiled. That fiery wall had faded away to nothing already, and the very use of it told him the

Stormar were running out of real battle-spells. This would probably take no time at all, once he got close enough to smite them all at once. They knew he was here—or at least, *something* that could burn out the minds of their fellows was. Hence all the shieldings they'd so hastily conjured. Yet he'd been careful not to hurl fires and lightnings of his own, to give them a target or to frighten them into flight, when he was too far off to trap and hold them.

He wanted every last one of them.

Taeauna turned to look at him, her hair swirling about her shoulders. Malraun gave her a smile, letting his growing fondness for her show through their linked minds, and her answering smile was dazzling. She gasped and shook in rapture, shuddering briefly and biting her lip ere she turned away to return to the careful climb up through the dead.

Malraun's smile went away. What did she think of him, really? If his hold over her mind was taken away?

He'd find fear, and hatred, and a desperate drive to murder him as swiftly as she could, no doubt. Falconaar all seemed to think of their Dooms the same way.

Yet she was a splendid creature, if he could ever trust her. He knew not if any Aumrarr could ever be trusted, or if there was something deep and innate within them that would goad them into striking out against all rulers and tyrant wizards when they saw a good chance to really do harm.

If he worked on her mind with his spells, not to control but to alter, a little here and a little there, could he avoid driving her mad? And truly change her, until she loved him? Or would she always remember what he'd done in her mind, and hate him for it, and wait for her chance to lash out in revenge?

And what was the love of one female worth, bought at such time and trouble, when he could mind-ride and coerce so many with such ease, and have a new and different one gasping willingly under him every night?

The torches were converging now, the small bare hilltop ringed closely by grimly-advancing warriors. Taeauna bore no torch, but her sword was raised and ready. Malraun admired her catlike grace as she stalked from one heap of bodies to another, using the last cover on this stretch of slope to full advantage. Then he reached into her mind and brought her to a shuddering halt, sending her his fondness to give her pleasure and quell her flare of resentment at being reined in as sharply as any snorting warhorse.

It had been a good plan, this army of his. Covertly aiding Amaxas Horgul in his first few victories and spreading word of it, subtly twisted so as to communicate a yearning for more under his banner that Horgul—who had no banner, nor thoughts of needing one—had no taste for. When the lawless and landless men came flocking, Malraun had set to work on the minds of many to see that the gathering warriors gained food and drink, and more victories, and captains whom he made staunchly loyal to Horgul.

Then he dived deep into the minds of Horgul's encamped warriors, plunging into a weight of minds that no Doom—and certainly no one lesser—had faced or weathered before, emerging drained but triumphant, having sown dreams wherein monsters aided and fought alongside Horgul's army, and were things too useful to be attacked on sight.

So when he then gathered in the monsters, in their slithering, flapping, or softly padding handfuls, no butchery erupted, and Amaxas Horgul found himself, without quite realizing how it had befallen, leading an army of monsters and mercenaries to attack one hold after another.

A host that had conquered hold after hold in a way never possible when three Dooms had worked in watchful, wary opposition to each other.

Now, Horgul's army had lost Horgul, but had almost conquered Darswords. There was just this last, savage little slaying to see to, first.

With a shout, some of his men gained the crest of the hill and charged the Stormar, hurling a stream of weapons they'd plucked from the dead, seeking to disrupt any spells the wizards were trying to cast until their own swords could reach Stormar throats, and it was too late.

It almost worked, but they were still two or three sprinting steps away when all the flung warsteel whirled back into their faces, in a slicing, darting storm of points and edges that visited on them the same lacerating deaths they'd sought to give the Stormar.

Malraun smiled grimly. Fools. That ploy might well have worked on hedge-wizards, but these Stormar were far beyond such feebleness.

He raised his hands, stretching his arms wide, and worked the spell. Not the one that would slay the Stormar, but the one that would unleash that deadly, already-risen spell—that even now was shuddering through him, prowling restlessly back and forth like a hungry caged cat—and let him put on a little show.

Armies, after all, need to be impressed.

A burst of power thrust Taeauna flat on her face in front of him, thrust aside a few of the battle dead, and lit him from ankles to the tips of his fingers with a bright white light, a radiance that drew all eyes and trailed an aura of curling ruby-red smoke out into the night.

"Hear me, doomed wizards, and all others who would dare to defy me!" he thundered, his magic making his voice roll thunderously out across Darswords and echo back from wooded hilltops all around.

"I am Malraun the Matchless, whose magic triumphs over all other spells, from one misty end of Falconfar to another! I avenge Horgul now, just as I assure all Falconfar that his army will fulfill its destiny, marching on to victory after victory, until every warrior who fought for Horgul gains gold enough to retire fat and happy, living in idle luxury all the rest of his days! No wizard can stand against my might, and all who seek to do so will be served *thus!*" He turned to face the wizards alone, and added, "*Die!*"

The light cloaking him rose around him, like a snake rearing up to strike, and then rushed away from him through the torchlit, moonlit night, to crash down on the Stormar on the hilltop in an inferno that blazed up fiercely. His power had pinned them there even before he'd spoken, and it held them there now, arms waving in futile attempts to weave spells that would whisk them elsewhere, as their bodies were consumed in a few breaths of roaring fury, and collapsed into ash.

A faint radiance flickered momentarily over a hilltop that had been scorched down to bare, blackened stone, then died away into darkness.

There was a long, stunned silence. Then the surviving warcaptains, up and down the hill on all sides, raised a ragged cheer.

Taeauna hurled herself at his ankles, kissing his boots and reaching up to caress him.

Malraun smiled down at her, at first out of mere fondness, but then more broadly as a thought struck him.

He would stay with the army long enough to enjoy their "taking" of Harlhoh. As it was under his rule, that would be mere feasting and reprovisioning, not fighting. Then he would leave Taeauna in charge of these ravening beasts and warriors, as they went on to conquer Darkriver.

So he could get back to his real work. Finding and destroying the real Narmarkoun, and watching this "Lord Archwizard" Everlar dolt to learn what he was *really* up to, and what hidden power he was seeking, before the right moment to destroy him came.

Not that destroying *this* Lord Archwizard would be anything more than childishly easy.

If it had been Lorontar, now... Malraun shivered inwardly, just for a moment, setting Taeauna to whimpering softly.

Then, reaching down to soothe her with a caress or two, he firmly put *that* unpleasant thought from his mind.

Chapter Fourteen

WINGS SUDDENLY BLOTTED out the moon, making Garfist swear in startlement and rear back from the window. A flapping moment later, there were two Aumrarr in the room.

Iskarra and Garfist could see that much, though in the wake of the flash that had split the sky, their eyesight was still blurry. Yet the two winged women were clear enough—as tall and slender black shapes, silhouetted against the cold brightness of the moon flooding the room.

"Who are ye?" Gar growled, settling into a menacing swordsman's crouch as he faced them, as if his hands bristled with warsteel rather than hanging empty.

"Dauntra and Juskra, of the Aumrarr," came the curt reply. "We brought you here, and we'll be taking you away again. Now."

"Why?" Iskarra snapped, from behind the table. "I'm finding I *like* Stormcrag Castle."

"The time is come," said the other Aumrarr, in a slightly kinder voice. "We need you."

"For what?" Garfist asked suspiciously. "Just how quickly is this going to get us killed, hey?"

"No time for that now," Juskra snarled, her sword starting to grate out of its scabbard—whereupon Isk held out the mindgem above the table, swinging her arm sharply to warn them she could at a whim swiftly bring it down, and shatter what she held.

"Oh," she told the two Aumrarr softly, as they stared at her with thinning lips, "I think there is."

Juskra's eyes blazed, and she strode forward almost panting in rising fury—only to stop abruptly, hissing, as Gar moved to bar her way to the table and drew back one arm, as if a solid punch could prevail against her sword and dagger.

"Dyune," he said firmly. "She left us. *Just* left us. What's befallen her?"

The two Aumrarr looked at each other, and then back at Gar and Isk.

"She has… perished," Dauntra said reluctantly. "In battle with a greatfangs. Along with our sisters Ambrelle and Lorlarra."

She shuddered as she fought back tears, then swallowed, sighed, and added, "Ambrelle died so we might live. She used the flame of life that burned within her to work a great magic."

"That blew the beast's brains apart from within," Juskra said grimly, "and slew it."

A little silence fell, until Garfist said into it, "Tell us more."

When neither of the Aumrarr spoke, he sighed and waved a hand at the mindgem Iskarra was holding over the table. "We know what we have, but where's the skull?"

"The skull?"

"*Orthaunt's* skull," he growled disgustedly. "An' just for that, ye can tell me what ye're planning to use it for—or we, an' this oh-so-precious mindgem with us, stay right here."

The Aumrarr traded glances with each other again. Juskra was visibly itching to bury her sword in Garfist, but Dauntra gave her a glare, shaking her head.

"I know where it is," she told Garfist, slowly and reluctantly, "but we've not sought to recover it, yet. *That*—" She pointed at the mindgem. "—we came seeking first. Dyune was supposed to have hidden it here at Stormcrag and then departed without the two of you—or anyone else—ever seeing her."

"Ever kings scheme, yet the Falcon rends all bright plots awry," Garfist quoted an old ballad archly. "Even, it seems, the clever plans of Aumrarr."

"Enough of this," Juskra snapped, glaring at Iskarra. "Give us the gem, or I'll start cutting large slices off your man, here!"

Garfist grabbed for her sword then, barehanded. She backed hastily away and brought its point up to menace his face and throat.

He gave her an unpleasant grin. "Threaten someone it'll work on. For us, save yer breath. Ye need us, not just yon stone and the skull. Hey?"

Dauntra sighed, shoulders sagging. "Yes."

Garfist gave Juskra a sardonic look, arching one eyebrow. She grimaced in disgust and lowered her blade.

"That's better," he growled. "Now, the two of ye, heed: Isk and I may well be quite willing to aid ye. *If* ye speak truth, and keep nothing back from us. Ye Aumrarr love to keep secrets, but there's none but us to say ye didn't, hey? If you speak truth, the Falcon might even smile on ye, for once! So speak. We know ye need us, so what we're to do is something no Aumrarr can succeed at. We know 'tis dangerous and urgent, or ye wouldn't be here in the dead of night drawing steel on us. So spill all, lasses! What d'ye need us for?"

"If we tell you," Dauntra said quietly, "the mere knowing leaves you standing in danger."

"Sister, *no!*" Juskra snapped. "We dare not—"

"You daren't *not* tell us," Iskarra snapped out, her voice louder than the scarred Aumrarr, and ringing with the iron of command, "or you lose your chance. Either we refuse, you slay us, and you go out into the night with no gem and the need to hunt down more humans who'll aid you—or you tell us all, and we can begin whatever task you need us for. I will *not* aid and serve captors who hurl us hither and yon like old cloaks and tell us nothing, but I could very well fight alongside someone who trusted me, and treated me as worthy to know *what is going on.*"

Her words rang out into a sudden stillness, as the two Aumrarr turned to lock eyes with each other.

A swift and silent war was fought in a few unfolding moments, through their sharp eyes, and then Juskra tossed her head, sighed loudly, and announced, "Very well. The truth. We, yes, need humans, because the warning-spells on Lyraunt Castle are keyed to rouse the place if any Aumrarr comes within their reach."

"Malraun's spells," Garfist rumbled. Both Aumrarr nodded, so he asked, "And ye need to get into Lyraunt Castle why?"

"To put the skull in… a particular place, therein," Dauntra replied, "and the gem in another specific spot."

Letting the weariness of worn-thin patience sound clearly in his voice, Gar asked flatly, "*Why?*"

"The Doom you named has created gates—magical ways to and from far places, traversed in a step; waerways, some call them—in the castle," Juskra replied. "Two of them."

"We know what gates are," Isk said softly. "You seek to close them."

Dauntra nodded. "The spells on the skull will disrupt the enchantments of the larger gate, yes. The second, smaller one we believe to be the Doom's secret; his 'back door' if you will. If we can place the mindgem in it, and he later tries to use that way into the Castle, quite likely to find out and fix what happened to his other gate, the powers of the gem will affect him."

Garfist glared at her ere asking patiently, "And do what?"

"Scramble his mind to drooling idiocy, if the luck of the Falcon is with us," Juskra muttered.

"And if it isn't?"

"Enrage him into setting aside his schemes for as long as it takes to come after us, and destroy us," Dauntra said quietly.

Iskarra frowned. "So the gem won't close the gate?"

"No." Juskra grounded the point of her sword on the floor, leaned on its quillons, and sighed, "Yon stone will just sit there *in* it, waiting for Malraun to get too close."

Garfist nodded. "So, now, where are these gates?"

She fixed him with a hard, direct stare. "Telling you where the larger one lies is a waste of breath if you haven't been inside Lyraunt Castle, until we're flying above it and I can point the right roof out to you. The second one is in a bedchamber at the top of Lyraunt's tallest tower. The bed all but fills that room, and the gate awaits anyone squeezing under the bed, right at the back, by its headboard."

Acquiring the ghost of a smile, the sword-scarred Aumrarr added, "You're too fat to use that waerway, unless you've brawn enough to heave the whole thing up on your back."

"You welcome would-be allies *so* charmingly," Isk told her sharply.

The reply was a shrug, but Dauntra said, "Juskra, *please*. Garfist, Iskarra; we need you to be the ones who place the skull and the gem for us. Now."

"Why now?" Garfist asked, suspicion sharpening his voice from its usual growl.

"Because," Juskra told him grimly, "the armies of monsters and mercenaries Malraun has sent flooding across all Falconfar this side of Galath will reach Ironthorn soon enough. Then it'll be too late, and you can die smug and secure, knowing you could have saved the world. But chose not to."

TAEAUNA SMILED UP at her Master, there on the hilltop. Looming above her, the gloating Doom threw back his head to laugh at the stars, and compelled his wards— the spells that would turn aside any arrow, hurled weapon, or hard-swung blade the more ambitiously treacherous of his warriors might decide to send his way—to glow more brightly, outlining him in eerie flames that burned nothing and gave off no heat.

He blazed coldly on that blood-drenched hilltop, awakening mutters of awe and wary regard among his warriors. Behold Malraun the Matchless, triumphant in victory. The overconfident fool.

Behind Taeauna's smiling face, too far down in the dark depths of her mind for Malraun's light hold over her to sense, Lorontar chuckled in glee.

Malraun's decision to let his playpretty, this wingless Aumrarr, lead the army was brilliant, of course.

And it was a notion he, Lorontar, had planted in Malraun's head, working with slow, deft patience through Malraun's mindlink with Taeauna. The Matchless One had swallowed the idea as his own without any suspicion... without even beginning to suspect Lorontar's influence.

So, now, if Malraun did depart, with Taeauna in charge, Lorontar would cloak himself even more deeply, and happily exert a little more mind-control over the Aumrarr.

Making her lead the Army of Liberation in an attack on Galath.

That would draw preening little Malraun into a frantic effort to quell the fighting. He would want to salvage some part of this army, after all, and seek to conquer Galath not on the battlefield, but by storming and coercing the mind of its new king. Thus gaining dominion over a Galath as undamaged as possible, not a kingdom ravaged by war or plunged into fresh and ongoing civil strife as this or that ambitious arduke or baron sought the throne.

Yet thanks to Lorontar's deft reminders, worked in one mind here and another there, King Melander Brorsavar of Galath was now protected by the diadem given by the meddling Aumrarr to a long-ago predecessor, to keep the mind of he who sat the Throne of Galath shielded from hostile magics.

Malraun might get an unwelcome surprise or two. If he was foolish enough to bring Taeauna along with him as he sought to master Brorsavar, one of those surprises might be a long, cold length of warsteel plunged up his backside a long and bloody way inside him.

Then he could put his Matchless mastery of magic to work trying to save his lifeblood, before it all ran out of him. While a certain not-dead-enough Archwizard of Falconfar tried to put *his* magic to the task of teaching Taeauna how to cast a spell that would turn her Master's blood to fire in his very veins, and cook him alive from within.

Now, *that* would be fun.

Above her, still brightly aglow, Malraun looked all about over the night-shrouded carnage of Darswords, eyes boyish-bright with excitement at all the bloodshed, exulting in his victory.

Abruptly his fingers tightened on Taeauna's head, digging in with cruel force to drag her upright. She rose willingly, not to escape the pain but out of ardent desire to please and obey him.

Showing all his teeth in his most hungry smile, Malraun swept the wingless Aumrarr into a tight embrace and bit her throat lightly. "Do off your armor," he murmured, releasing her. "Quickly."

She unbuckled, wriggled, and shrugged her way clear of war-harness in deft, supple haste, but it was still heaped all about her knees when he growled, freed himself, and started to make love to her, brutally, there on the moonlit hilltop in the midst of all the blood-drenched dead.

Embracing him, yielding and urging him on wordlessly with her caresses, Taeauna smiled. She was beneath him, and his ardent kisses were below her chin, so he never saw the smile on her face.

It was the deep, triumphant smile of Lorontar.

AHEAD OF ROD Everlar there was a brief, almost soundless commotion, a straining and whispering of cloth and boots, and then something that might have been a long, trailing groan under firmly-clamped, muffling hands. Then there came a sort of thud, and a louder scrape of a boot heel being dragged across stone.

One of Syregorn's knights had killed another Lyrose guard, and they were another step closer to setting foot in Lyraunt Castle.

Its walls loomed over them, almost unseen here in the deep darkness beneath these trees, but the moonlight was almost frighteningly bright back behind them, on the lawn that separated Lord Lyrose's fishpond from the scullery port. A side door too small and simple to be called a gate, the port was set deep into the wall. It was tall but narrow, was sheathed entirely in thrice-banded oiled iron, and was about two feet thick, to boot.

Rod doubted Syregorn's men had been stretching tales to impress him; now that they were settled into stone-faced readiness to slay, he doubted this lot would seek to impress their own grandmothers. In any way, and for any reason. They were like foxes padding through the night. Silent and patient, until they were close enough to pounce.

Ahead of them, there was a brief flicker of lantern-light as the scullery port swung open again—and the hand on Rod's shoulder forced him down onto his knees. He froze there, seeing the knights ahead of him doing the same, as a muttering of low voices rose briefly by the port ere it swung shut once more.

Oblivious to the stealthy doom fast approaching them, Lord Lyrose's guards seemed to be busily engaged, this night, in their usual habits of visiting some of the maids to trade coins for their embraces and for leftovers from Castle feasts. The scullery port had swung open and shut seven times now, just since the Hammerhand band had rounded the fishpond.

Though it was now too dark for Rod to see Syregorn, he knew the warcaptain was frowning like a grim mourner at a funeral. An entire Lyraunt Castle guard patrol was missing.

Usually, according to Thalden's latest whisper nigh Rod's ear, there were guards stationed outside the scullery port, to prevent this nightly commerce becoming a vulnerability to any skulking warbands from Hammerhold and Imtowers. Yet not a guard had they found, aside from those waiting their turn to shuffle briefly in through the scullery port.

"Come *on*, Larl," someone growled resignedly, startlingly close at hand. "Rut with her *faster*. I'm getting cold."

A gentle breeze arose then, covering the faint sounds the Hammerhand knight in front of Rod made as he rose to clamp a firm hand over that Lyrose guard's mouth.

Then the quickening wind shifted some branches, making them dance and let in moonlight just long enough to let Rod see the knight's dagger slice across the back of one of the struggling guard's hands.

The knight held the man tight, holding the knife high rather than trying to stab him again.

When another moment of moonlight let the hard-swallowing Lord Archwizard see the struggling pair again, long seconds later, the guard was sagging and the knight was trudging a few steps across the lawn under the man's dying weight, to let him down out of the way.

That knife was poisoned. It had to be.

Rod swallowed again, finding his throat a more rough and dry place than ever. Poison cared nothing for titles or high station.

Certainly not for a title like "Lord Archwizard of Falconfar."

"WE'LL DO IT," Isk told the Aumrarr quietly. "But then, you knew that."

"We could not be sure. We compel no one against their will," Dauntra replied with dignity.

Then she froze, as Garfist's loud snort turned into barks of derisive laughter. As that harsh laughter rose to roll about the moonlit room, Juskra joined in, the same disbelief in her bitter mirth. A moment later, Isk chuckled.

After a long, reddening time, Dauntra chuckled, too.

* * *

THE SCULLERY PORT closed again. The wind had died, and the night was very quiet.

"Now what?" Thalden whispered, his voice the faintest of ghostlike murmurs. "There are none of Lyrose left alive out here, but surely they'll send a patrol around the outside walls *some* time."

Syregorn nodded, and reached out to tap the nearest knight in a certain manner Rod couldn't see. The signal was passed along, and in a few almost silent moments, the band that had come from Hammerhold were crouching on hands and knees in a ring, faces almost touching. Someone's breath was foul with fish.

"I dislike the standing guards who aren't here, and should be," someone whose voice sounded rough and old muttered. "This feels like a trap to me."

"I am just as uneasy over that," Syregorn replied, "yet suspicious or not, it's let us get very close to Lyraunt before we had to do much killing."

"You dislike killing? You surprise me," a deeper voice muttered.

Syregorn sighed. "Slaying bothers me not, but every killing is a chance you'll be discovered, and the alarum raised. Hence the..."

"Poison," Thalden murmured. As Syregorn's furious hiss arose, he added, "The wizard knows, Gorn. While he was watching us use it, and realizing what he was seeing, I was watching his face."

"Ah yes, *the wizard*," the deep voice muttered again. "So here we are with the great Lord Archwizard, and do we blast the castle apart? No. We go creeping in like thieves, in the mud and thorns, and him with us!"

"Use magic, when there might be a Doom inside those walls? You *are* a dolt," the old voice hissed. Then it came to Rod's ears a trifle louder, as its owner turned to Syregorn. "What'd you do to the outlander to turn him into Lord Wizard Babbling-Tongue, anyway?"

"Followed orders," Syregorn snapped. "Now *silence*. Or he'll start with the questions again, and get us all killed! Quick, now! To the port—to the walls on either side of it. Tarth and Reld standing, steel ready; everyone else farther along and lying flat. When yon port opens, I want us there and ready. Let the man get out before you fell him, so those within hear and see nothing amiss. Then we slip in, as the latest lusty guards. If a maid screams, mind, we'll probably all die."

The ring melted away into moving shadows, so quietly that Rod blinked in disbelief. He stayed where he was until the familiar firm hand tightened and tugged on his shoulder in an unmistakable "come with me" signal.

Obediently he went, crouching low and making so little noise that the owner of the hand sighed in disgust only twice on their way to the wall of Lyraunt Castle.

I thought this castle had a moat, Rod thought to himself as he went to his knees and then down to rest on his chest and stomach in short-scythed grass, a moment before Thalden whispered, "Malraun's ward-spells did one good thing, anyway: let the Lyroses fill in that stinking moat." The whisper changed, sounding amused. "They regretted it soon after, when they had to start digging graves, not just rolling their dead off the walls and into the water."

Then the scullery port opened with a brief flare of light, a man was butchered in swift and efficient silence in front of Rod's eyes, and the night was full of swift-moving Hammerhand shadows.

The firm hand returned, and a moment later Rod Everlar was bruising his elbows on hard stone as he was thrust forward. The terrified eyes of maids feeling poison burn inside them stared at him helplessly over the brutally-tight hands that covered their mouths and noses.

Then he was past them, turning to try to watch but seeing only the night outside vanishing behind the closing scullery port ere he was wrenched around to face forward and shoved into a dark chamber.

Where the Lord Archwizard came to a stumbling halt, well and truly inside Lyraunt Castle.

Nearby in the darkness, someone laughed. Coldly and menacingly, of course.

Chapter Fifteen

"HAMMERHAND VIPERS," THE unseen man who'd laughed greeted them. "Welcome to your deaths. You won't last aaaaaaa…" The voice trailed away in a dying, fading moan.

"That wasn't necessary," Thalden chided someone. "He was a prisoner, chained to the wall. Probably a Tesmer man, who hates Lyrose as much as we do."

"He was being too loud," came the hissed reply. "What if he'd shouted for guards, hey?" The whisper turned less fierce. "This poison works *fast*."

"So keep your blades pointing down, not out," Syregorn said grimly, from somewhere behind Rod. "Now silence, all of you. If this Lord Archwizard is to have any chance of defeating the Doom Malraun and getting the Aumrarr he came for out of here alive, it's best he arrives in Malraun's lap as a surprise—not in a grand confrontation, after all Lyraunt's been roused."

Those words were barely out of his mouth when a Lyrose man in livery came around the corner, head down and hurrying, hands already busy at his codpiece. "Falcon bugger *all*," he was growling to himself. "Late relieving me, taking his own sweet sated time over telling me a jest I didn't want to hear any—"

His words trailed off forever then, but he'd been doomed since Reld's kissing-sharp dagger had sliced him, on his hurrying way by. He'd never even noticed, and he had time only to gape in wonder at all the unfamiliar armed men in the passage before—still gaping—he started to topple.

Syregorn put out an arm, gathered him in with casual strength, plucked him off his feet, and carried him into the cell where the prisoner now hung silent and dead in his chains.

The warcaptain came back out immediately, shrugging the dead man's Lyrose tabard over his head and slapping Tarth's arm on the way past in an obvious signal. As one—with the usual exception of Rod Everlar—the men of Hammerhold moved to follow Syregorn, striding boldly down the passage as if they had every right to be there.

Rod was marched along with them, Thalden's hand in its usual place where Rod's right shoulder turned into his arm. Most of them had sheathed their poisoned knives, but he suspected the little rolled bundle of cloth Syregorn was carrying in both hands concealed his dagger, held ready in the heart of it. Around them, Lyraunt Castle seemed deserted, and that had all of the Hammerhand knights frowning in suspicion.

Rod thought back over all he'd written about Falconfar, knowing he'd never penned one word about daily life in Lyraunt Castle, but... yes, of course. Guards and the day-servants would be few in the heart of a castle in these wee hours, but there'd be—*should* be—other servants busy everywhere. Those who cleaned, those in the kitchens who baked and roasted, kitchens that should be not far from the scullery port, and those who laid fires in every hearth. Probably lots of others he couldn't bring to mind just now, too. There was something else, though. An air, an *atmosphere* that was alert and awake... that was it: awake! The castle felt awake around them. Not "the very stones are watching" magically awake, nor yet the bustle and wakefulness of day, but a tension that hinted they were expected.

Oh, *shit*.

Ahead, their passage met a cross-passage and ended there. A glow of light was coming from the right, toward the front of the castle, but to the left all was dark. Syregorn waved a quelling hand at the floor, and his knights slowed and started moving quietly. Their warcaptain strode on ahead, with an air of bored unconcern.

Reaching the passage-moot, he turned left without hesitation, took a stride, stopped and smote his forehead as if he'd forgotten something, then turned and came back, shaking his head as if in self-reproach and moving faster.

"Guards under the light," he murmured, "so we go left. Casual-like; no stealth, but keep it *quiet*."

They did that, Rod's back a-crawl with apprehension as he turned in the wake of the rest, expecting shouts and pounding feet from behind him at any moment.

The outcry he was dreading did not come. The Hammerhand knights had followed Syregorn around another corner before he let out his breath in a great sigh—and only then realized he'd been

ED GREENWOOD

holding it. Ahead of him, some of the other knights were sighing too.

They were crossing through about the midpoint of the back half of the castle, as far as Rod could judge, and all around them was dark silence—that waiting stillness—and closed doors. Again a meeting with a cross-passage, though the hallway they were in continued across it this time, and this time the glow of light was coming from the left.

Syregorn repeated the same little tactic he'd used before, with the same result. They headed to the right, away from the guards, all striding along with apparent unconcern.

"He's trying to remember where the stair up is," Thalden muttered to Rod. "There's one somewhere around here that's not as narrow as the servants' stairs at the back, nor quite as public as the grand staircase in the great rooms at the front. As you might imagine, we don't come strolling through Lyraunt Castle often."

"And you never will again," a calm, sardonic voice remarked, out of the darkness near at hand.

Thalden and all of the nearby knights whirled, daggers flashing out, but there was no one there, despite their hard scrutiny and peerings for concealed doors or spyholes. The voice seemed to have come from empty air.

"Sorcery," one knight muttered. "*Malraun.*"

"No," Rod told them firmly. "That wasn't his voice."

Tarth and Reld both hissed curses under their breaths, and hastened to catch up to Syregorn.

The knights were trotting hard after them before the deep-voiced knight observed sourly, "Great. Lyrose has another wizard, too."

"Well," someone else observed merrily, "at least our deaths will be *interesting*."

"So they will," the sardonic voice agreed pleasantly, from far behind them. Rod stiffened, but it seemed only he and Thalden had heard it.

And Thalden's response was to dig his fingers into Rod's arm like so many iron-hard talons, and trot the Lord Archwizard along faster.

THIS WAS FUN.

More fun than he'd had in years, in fact.

Lord Magrandar Lyrose smiled to himself in the darkness, and took his hand off the speaking-sphere. It was time to join his wife and daughter, in case the more violent of the magics the Doom had given him were needed. He was wearing his best black boots and his most dashing new garb—by the Falcon, the mirror had shown him back a fine figure of a man!—and his chased and polished gorget gleamed at his throat.

His fingers strayed to the familiar, comforting lines of that curving triangle of bright chased metal. He never took it off, these days, even to bed with his lady wife and despite her caustic remarks about it. She felt it shouted to all Falconfar that he trusted her not.

He shrugged. What of that? He trusted no one, and hadn't done so for as long as he could remember. Only fools trusted in others.

And only a fool would take off a personal shield enspelled and given by Malraun the Matchless. A shield that would heal Magrandar instantly of all wounds dealt by metal weapons and the ravages of poison—though it did not spare him the agony and debilitation of such hurts, ere it banished them.

Oh, yes, he could handle a few Hammerhand raiders. Even with most of his guards gone from their posts to muster into Pelmard's Irontarl-seizing force. If the cleverness he'd thought up worked, he'd manage it without even spilling much Lyrose blood. Huh. Pelmard would no doubt see to *that*.

Patting the hilt of his sword and the bracer hidden beneath the splendid cloth on the forearm of his free hand, he hurried out of his study.

This was a most important social engagement. It wouldn't do to be late.

"THIS WAY," SYREGORN whispered, and boldly opened the door on the right. The veteran knights kept their stares on the other six closed doors that lined the small, rounded end of the passage, but none of those doors burst open to spew Lyrose knights at them. Syregorn's door led into darkness, and silence—to Rod, that same waiting, listening silence, as tense as a taut bowstring—reigned.

One after another, doing nothing to break that silence, the Hammerhands followed after their warcaptain.

Through the door, into a large open space; a great high hall. A set of doors at one end of it stood just a thumb-width ajar, letting in faint light enough for their eyes, accustomed to gloom, to see two tiers of balconies above, a wide, sweeping staircase ascending to the first of them, tapestries hanging on the walls wherever there were no doors—and there were a lot of doors, all of them in tall, grand pairs.

Except one. It stood open, breaking the only curving stretch of wall that bowed out into the room. This was evidently the base of a tower, because the door opened directly onto a spiral staircase that ascended steeply, entirely filling a cylindrical space beyond. They could tell that much, because faint glows arose from the painted edges of each step.

Right across the room was a gap in the wall, a large open archway rather than a door. It opened into another huge room, so dark that only the nearest end of three long feasting-tables could be seen, stretching away lined with chairs.

The hall itself, if one didn't count the tapestries and four braziers clustered together near the base of the grand staircase, was empty of furniture. Its flat, smooth bare floor was glossy and new-washed underfoot, a small sea of black tiles surrounding the Three Thorns of Lyrose, inlaid in tiles of some lighter hue.

Syregorn did not stride far out across that glossy floor.

"We've been herded here," he said suddenly, darting hard glances in one direction and then another, all around the hall, as he started around the room, keeping close to the walls. "This has been too easy—time and again, no servants where there should be, and too few guards. Lure in one direction, herd in another… Lyrose has meant us to come here, to this room."

"So this would be about the time their archers would come out onto the balconies, casting torches down on our heads to make us targets, and their knights burst in on us through every door," Tarth said bitterly, as the Hammerhand knights followed their warcaptain around the walls.

They all looked up as they did so, as if expecting all of those things to happen in answer to his words, but the dark silence hung unbroken.

Except in one direction. From beyond the doors that were letting in the light, from where that bright radiance was, nearer the front of Lyraunt Castle, there rose sudden loud voices. Voices that came swiftly nearer, accompanied by a bobbing light that could only be a lantern, and the noisy scrapes of boots scuffing along the floor.

"Every *one* of them? Why, there must be six-score! Why can't the Master Steward rearrange his own plates? I'm supposed to set up the braziers around the Thorns, and have all the bowls polished before—"

"I don't give the orders, Greth! Just do it—braziers first, mind!—and do it *right* for once, and mayhap he won't break any bowls over your head, this time! Not that I can even promise that, after what you—"

Greth and his lantern were almost at the doors, bare moments away from thrusting them open and discovering a room full of Hammerhand knights. Syregorn darted for the dark feasting-hall, and his knights hastened at his heels.

As they passed through the arch, there was a white flash, a purple flickering as strange, surging power awakened and gathered them in—power that reached out a long tentacle to englobe and snatch Rod and Thalden, who were still some strides away—and then the air itself swallowed them all.

Stealthy knights or not, every last one of them, the Lord Archwizard included, shouted in alarm.

But by then, of course, it was too late.

THE SHOUTS OF the Hammerhands were cut off as sharply as if severed by the edge of a descending sword. In the alcove behind the tapestry, mere steps away from the gate that had swallowed the hated foes, Lord Lyrose unhooded the glowstone and smiled an unlovely smile.

His daughter, who had been peering through a gap in the tapestries to make sure the magic of the gate had snatched away all the intruders, turned, nodded reassurance that they were all gone, and smiled a matching smile right back at him.

"So much for *that* clumsy Hammerhand attack," he murmured. "I wonder how many others will come, and how soon?"

Mrythra shrugged. "What boots it? We'll crush them all."

Lord Lyrose heard a door open in the distance. His wife, on her way to join him. He seized the moment, before she was within earshot, and could forbid what he was going to order. Ah, suggest.

He leaned forward. "Daughter mine, Pelmard will be expecting me to ride the high whip-wielding lord over him, in this Irontarl foray. I'd like to hand him another little surprise, and have *you* do so. Flog him literally, if he dares to flee."

"Lord and father," Mrythra replied softly, as she glided to the tapestries to depart before her mother's arrival, "*nothing* would give me greater pleasure."

THE MOON WAS shockingly bright; dangling like a heavy grainsack from Juskra, Garfist felt like a brightly-lit archers' target, and said so. Adding with a fierce hiss, "An' ye could fly a mite higher! That's the *third* tree ye've dragged me through!"

"The moonlight is precisely why I'm flying this low," Juskra snarled back at him. "*One* of the reasons."

"Hey? What d'ye mean by that?"

"She means you're fat and heavy, Old Ox," Iskarra said scornfully, from not far behind him, where she dangled beneath Dauntra on a single leather strap (Garfist was strapped to Juskra's waist by three).

"Not much farther now," Dauntra said soothingly, as Garfist started to snarl a less than pleasant retort. "Yon's Lyraunt Castle. So we come in low over the forest, from behind and in the shadow of those tall trees just ahead, then land yonder, in the shadows behind that thick stand, there. Things'd be easier if Lady Lyrose didn't have this love of open, expansive lawns."

"Oh, aye, the unbroken sward," Gar muttered. "And why is that?"

"How would you ever get through a day without that word 'why,' Gulkoun?" Juskra muttered, but Dauntra hissed at her sister and made courteous reply.

"Likely it was to make sure the stink of the moat was gone forever, so ponds and herb-beds were kept far from under her windows," the fairer Aumrarr said. "Watch, now; draw up your feet, Gar."

They skimmed low over—or cracklingly through, in Garfist's case—a last few trees, and descended to the earth in a running, flapping thump and thud of a landing.

Garfist growled wordlessly, but Juskra whirled around and hissed fury back at him, right in his face, as her fingers tore at the leathern thongs that bound them together. "Gods, how does a man get so *fat*?" were the last words of her furious whisper.

"Not flying about all Falconfar meddling in the business of others," he whispered back hoarsely.

"*That's* true," Isk put in soothingly. "We walked."

Dauntra snorted in mirth, then thrust slender fingers under the noses of Garfist and her sister.

"Drop it, both of you!" She and Juskra were quickly reknotting the leathern thongs, to bind their carry-straps in place around their waists.

"You wait right here," Juskra hissed at Gar and Isk. "We'll cause tumult soon, at the foregate—the front gate. Then you go down *there*, over that little bridge by the pond, into the gardens. That side door should be unlocked; it's how the guards and the maids get out into the garden for their trysts. If anyone sees you, act like a panderer come from Irontarl with a wise one who sees to maids' complaints."

"Maids have complaints?" Gar growled. "More than other servants, I mean?"

Isk slapped him, an instant before Juskra gave him a look of withering scorn and snapped, "When women bleed below, and other things men never want to hear about. Just walk in there as if you belong there, and put the gems where we told you; the castle's simple to get around in. Any *proper* questions?"

"Just one," Garfist asked thoughtfully. "How many of you Aumrarr are still alive?"

"We don't—" Juskra hissed, but Dauntra put a hand on her arm and told her firmly, "Those who made such rules are all dead, and I'm obeying them no longer, no matter what it costs us in influence."

She turned to look at Garfist. "Gulkoun, I know not. All I can be sure of are the two of us, and I *think* Taeauna is still alive, though whether her wits are her own is another matter. So, three I can be certain of. Perhaps as many as six, or even nine. No more."

Garfist swore in astonishment.

"So that's why Dyune wouldn't say," Iskarra murmured.

Both Aumrarr nodded. "We aren't—weren't—supposed to. So no one would ever suspect how few we were. That's how we managed to wield any influence at all in places like Galath; scaring brawling barons into thinking a flying army could show up, any time, to chastise them."

"So you're telling us now because we'll likely all be dead before dawn," Garfist rumbled. "Well, thankee. Always nice to be sent to death by honest folk."

And without waiting for a reply, he set off down the hill, toward the little bridge.

The two Aumrarr hissed curses and sprang into the air. Hard and fast to the front of Lyraunt Castle they flapped, to create their promised diversion.

STILL BELLOWING THEIR startled fear into the night, Rod Everlar and the knights from Hammerhold suddenly found themselves—somewhere else.

Somewhere outside, under the bright moon, in a place that by the startled looks on Hammerhand faces all round him, Rod knew wasn't Ironthorn at all. They'd stepped through a magical gate, of course. Not one he'd ever written about, but he was beginning to realize that his books seemed to be more about bringing kingdoms and mountain ranges into being, here, and not the finer details. Even if he'd been the only Shaper ever to work on Falconfar, it seemed the sweep and strivings of everyday Falconaar life set about changing little things, the moment you'd lifted your pen, or your fingers from the keyboard.

The moment your Lord Archwizardly back was turned...

They were standing in a moonlit walled garden, at the base of a soaring castle keep larger, grander, and newer than any Ironthar fortress. The garden seemed to occupy the crest of a long hill that dropped away in the bright moonlight down to a small village. It was a Raurklor hold, by the familiar trees making up the seemingly endless forest all around. That slope was a long series of tilled fields outlined by hedge-walls of heaped stumps and boulders.

Syregorn and the oldest knight were both looking disgusted and hissing out curses.

"You know where we are?" Tarth asked him.

The warcaptain nodded. "I've been here before, on Hammerhand business. This is the hold of Harlhoh, hard-riding *days* distant from Ironthorn along none-too-safe forest trails."

He turned and waved disgustedly at the soaring tower whose garden door seemed to be the only way out of their enclosure, bar clambering up the stone walls. "Which makes *this* the tower of Malragard, abode of the wizard Malraun."

It was Rod's turn to curse bitterly, and he did so.

When he ran out of colorful things to say, Syregorn was standing close to him, and wearing a grim smile.

"So, Archwizard," the warcaptain asked softly, "when will you blast down this fortress, and Malraun the Matchless with it?"

Rod swore again, clumsily repeating himself. As he saw faces go hard and unfriendly all around him, he broke off and snapped, "Get me some parchment! And ink, and some quills, and a lamp and something flat and smooth to write on! *Then* you'll see some blasting down of things, I promise you!"

The knights exchanged puzzled glances. "Don't sound like the ballads much, do it?" Tarth asked Reld.

"Never does, when you're in it," came the laconic reply, as Reld stared through Rod Everlar as if the Lord Archwizard of Falconfar was some sort of earthworm he'd just fished out of his soup. "Never does."

Chapter Sixteen

"READY?"

"Skull... mindgem behind yer buckle... darklantern," Garfist whispered hoarsely, waving the cloth-wrapped helm that held the skull, nodding at Iskarra's midriff, then thrusting forward the closed-shuttered lantern.

"That's not what I meant," she replied softly, and kissed him. At first the fat former panderer sought to squirm away, growling gruffly incoherent protests, but then shrugged and surrendered to her insistent lips. The kiss went on for a long time.

When at last she released him because they both needed to breathe, he looked at her with a dark fire dancing in his eyes, as they stood nose to nose, and asked, "An' what was *that* for?"

"In case it's the last kiss we ever enjoy together," Isk whispered, eyes very large and dark.

"Oh, for the Falcon's sake," he said disgustedly. "Been reading too many o' them firelust chapbooks, ye have! I *thought* ye were wasting coin when we were last in the Stormar cities!"

"Wasting coin?" Isk snorted. "I was *writing* them,

Gar, not buying them!"

"*Writing* 'em? An' drawing on what, for yer, ah, inspiration?"

"My memories of our earliest trysts, my lord love," she breathed, in wide-eyed mimicry of a love-struck young lass.

Garfist growled amused dismissal and chucked her under the chin. She belted him back, rather more forcefully, leaving him blinking.

"As for *your* inspiration, Garfist Gulkoun," she added severely, "I am well aware of what you got up to, every glorking moment my back was turned, with the dusky and all-too-willing wenches of—"

"*Lass*, lass, lass, that was *work*. A panderer can't sell wares he can't fairly describe, hey? I—"

Isk used only two fingers to whack Garfist's windpipe, but they were two very firm fingers. Instantly he fell silent, to tend to the task of busily clutching his numbed throat.

Which was just as well, considering how many heavily-armed Lyrose guards came rushing past the slightly-open door of the cell just then, and out through the scullery port into the night.

Lord Lyrose was well aware that other eyes besides those loyal to Hammerhand watched Lyraunt Castle by night for signs of lax vigilance. Wherefore it was high time to restore the regular patrols in the castle grounds.

Or so Iskarra read matters. Garfist wasn't troubling his head over it, of course. He'd be thinking just of the task at hand. Which was trying to breathe, just now.

Well enough. Isk devoted herself to the task at hand, too. Thinking for him, as usual.

The Aumrarr had given them directions that were

clear and simple enough, but they still had to get to the right places, in an unfamiliar and unfriendly castle.

Nor did she feel overmuch like standing here in the darkness much longer. There were at least two dead men sharing this chamber with them, and a less than pleasant smell was beginning to rise.

Drawing in a deep breath despite the foul air, she stepped forward and swung open the door.

The passage outside was quiet again, and she tugged gently on the nearest part of Garfist—his left forearm, as it turned out—to tell him to be ready to move. Then she stepped boldly out the door.

The passage was empty. She faced the heart of the castle and started walking unconcernedly, trudging with the weary, slightly bored air of a servant who was supposed to be there, but Gar came out of the room in a rush and pounded past her, trotting along swiftly and gathering speed as he went.

Isk gaped at him in astonishment, then shook her head in exasperation and sprinted after him.

When she caught up to her man and clawed at the arm that held the lantern, he whirled with a growl, swinging the helm that held the skull at her like a weapon. She'd been expecting him to do just that, and ducked easily aside.

"Fool!" she hissed. "If we go racing through the castle, we *look* like intruders! Walk slowly, and if we see someone, embrace me and cozy up to the wall as if we're lovers who just couldn't wait to get somewhere more private!"

Garfist grinned. "Why do I get all the hard jobs, hey?"

"Gar, *heed*. This is serious! Our very lives depend on it!"

"Isk, lass, our very lives depend on *everything* we do. Yet grab at yer temper and douse the flames in those eyes; I'll go slowly, look ye. I'm—I'm running out of breath."

"I should think so," Isk muttered back. "Now come, we haven't got all—"

There were faint shouts from distant, unseen chambers off to their right, nigh the front of Lyraunt Castle. The Aumrarr were at the foregate.

Dauntra and Juskra had given warning that although they'd seek to draw the foregate guards out of Lyraunt and butcher them, they dared not press their attack if the defenders stayed inside the fortress. They could fight in the foregate, where they'd offend only against the outer ward that cried warning—but if they tried to pass through the crackling, waiting inner wards, Malraun's magic would both harm them and send warning not just to Lyrose eyes and ears, but alert the Doom himself, wherever he might be, that Aumrarr were trying to enter Lyraunt Castle.

That might make him merely shrug—or it might mean that Garfist and Iskarra would face the light entertainment of trying to defy an annoyed Malraun the Matchless, possibly the most powerful wizard in all Falconfar, with not much more weaponry than their smiles. And a skull whose grin could match theirs.

Yet if the winged women drew all the guards to the front of the castle, Gar and Isk just might be able to pull off this unlikely double task, and even get out again alive. Might.

"Well, we have to find this high hall to get to the turret stairs, right? So leave the skull in the arch there and *then* do all the climbing. My knees aren't what they used to be."

"Yes, and 'tisn't just your knees," Isk murmured darkly.

"Hoy!" Gar protested. "Ye've not complained before!"

He caught her darkly scornful look, and amended his words hastily. "Er, much."

Up ahead, guards sprinted across their passage, hurrying down a larger hall to the front of the castle. Close on their heels came more guards; one glanced in their direction, but his attention seemed rapt on a spear that seemed to be sliding out of his grasp.

Isk swiftly drew Gar against her, embraced him, and used her thin, bony hips to thrust him, stumbling, against the wall. "Kiss me," she hissed. "Look love-struck."

She'd positioned them so she could look past his arm. The next guards to rush past did give them a good look, but didn't slow.

"That's chance enough," she snapped. "We take the next side-passage. Walking along this one is like prancing out on a well-lit stage in any Stormar ladydance club you might care to name! *There!*"

Garfist obeyed, swerving into the dark passage she indicated. Before them loomed closed doors on all sides, an ornate little table under an oval mirror, and their new passage running only a little way before it ended in stairs, going up. Isk took them without hesitation.

"But—" Gar growled.

"They said the hall had balconies," Isk hissed back over her shoulder. "Well, once we're on one of them, we can toss the skull down into place, yes?"

"Ho-*ho*," Garfist replied thoughtfully, indicating agreement. The Aumrarr had warned them not to step into or through the arch, for fear of being plucked away to a "terrible doom in a terrible place" by the gate. Isk's idea bid fair to dodge that little pitfall just fine...

By then Isk had turned right along a passage at the top of the stair, and was about to step out onto... a balcony.

It overlooked a grand, high room with another tier of balconies above theirs, a largely empty room lit by four braziers, identical curved wrought iron standards, each as tall as a man.

The great chamber was deserted of people, thank the Falcon, but its far side held a grand staircase sweeping up to their level, a door on a curved wall that must from the Aumrarr description be the way to the turret stair, and, yes, the Three Thorns of Lyrose outlined in the center of the glossy black floor.

This could only be the right place to find the archway, unless Lyraunt Castle had *two* identical high halls.

Well, Lord Lyrose was thought to be crazed—or had that been his father? It had been seasons upon seasons since they'd last been in Irontarl—but neither Gar nor Isk thought he was *that* sort of mad. Which meant, if this was the high hall, the archway they sought was right underneath them.

Isk leaned out, looked down, then drew back and nodded.

"Give it me," she murmured. "You tend to hurl skulls about like weapons."

"When I hurl skulls about, they *are* weapons," Gar growled, unwrapping for all he was worth.

Isk put her fingers through the eyesockets of Orthaunt's skull the moment they were uncovered, lifted it up to face her, and murmured his name

226

as tenderly as if saying farewell to a beloved relative. Then she leaned out, swung her slender arm, and threw the skull, gently and carefully. If it shattered...

The wizard's brain-bones plunged toward the floor, arcing in smoothly beneath the balcony to pass through the center of the arch.

Where it suddenly stopped in mid-flight, a halo of white sparks briefly appearing around it and then as swiftly vanishing again, and hung motionless, grinning endlessly out into the deserted hall.

Which was when Garfist, leaning out to watch, lost hold of the helm they'd brought it in, made a grab for it too late, and stared in dismay as it plummeted to the glossy black stone below.

It landed with a terrific echo-raising crash, bounding up high off the floor with the force of its strike, only to crash down again. And again. Bouncing with loud enthusiasm to a raucous rolling stop.

Tapestries twitched below, as if someone was plucking them aside to see the source of the noise, and Gar and Isk hastily backed off the balcony. A door slammed open in the hall behind and below them. They froze, back in the gloom of the open curtains that flanked the balcony door, as a Lyrose guard burst into the room, spear clutched in both hands.

He saw the still-rocking helm—and then the skull.

Which promptly told him, in a deep but quaveringly ghostly voice: "Beware!"

Its tone was mocking, and the paling Lyrose guard grimaced and hurled his spear.

The skull ducked aside in its hovering, to let the spear whistle through the arch and crash down on distant crockery and what sounded like ringing, bouncing metal flagons somewhere in the unseen distance below.

A fell greenish-gold light kindled inside the skull, drawing a fascinated Garfist back to the balcony rail to watch what befell. He was in time to see it shoot out of one of the skull's eyesockets, in a bright ray that struck the guard high in the chest.

The Lyrose warrior fell over backward, or tried to. The moment his boots were off the floor, he was caught in the skull's magic—and hung quivering in midair, leaning back but unable to fall, as his chest swiftly blackened… and started to melt away.

There were gasps of fear and amazement from beneath the balcony—from behind where those tapestries had been plucked aside, no doubt—but they were lost in the sudden, raw shrieks of the guard, as terror gave way to agony.

Those screams were as frantic and high-pitched as a bewildered child's, but they faded away almost immediately. And no wonder; the flesh of his throat and lungs had melted away, leaving blackening bones. As Garfist stared, wincing, they suddenly slumped to the floor with a clatter.

Isk was already plucking at his arm, wearing a look of relief.

Ah, that they'd not have to stay and try to protect the skull, aye…

Willingly Gar followed her around the balcony, hastening along in the same awkward crouch she was using, to keep low and hopefully out of sight of anyone watching from below.

There was a door at the end of the balcony that opened into the tower they sought, and Isk was clawing it open.

To reveal another Lyrose guard, rushing up its curving steps to reach the landing where the balcony met the stair. As the door swung open, he glared at Garfist along the balcony, and charged.

The warrior never even saw Iskarra behind the door. One of her long, slim legs took him across the ankles as he sprinted—and he crashed down helplessly in front of Gar with such jaw-shattering force that Gar's leap to bring both boots down hard on the back of the man's neck seemed almost unnecessary.

The guard spasmed and writhed silently under Gar for a few moments, then went limp; the fat former panderer snatched up a Lyrose dagger and sword and rushed to join Isk, who was crouching on the tower stair landing, using one knee to hold the door open for him.

Then they heard the thunder of many boots descending down that stair. It was almost loud enough to cloak the rising noise of more hurrying boots approaching from somewhere behind Garfist. He met Iskarra's dismayed gaze with a grim look of his own as he rushed toward her, and pointed down the tower stair.

She uncoiled out of her crouch like a striking serpent and was down those curving steps a bare stride in front of him. Together they rushed around its bend and found... that it ended in a stone floor, at a door that opened into the grand chamber they'd just been looking down into. The way on down into the cellars beneath the tower was a barred and locked trapdoor—and its lock was a massive thing, almost as large as the helm Garfist had dropped.

Iskarra was already snatching open that door. A guard came rushing at her from somewhere, grinning—but had to duck away as Garfist's blade slashed at his face. The fist of Gar's other hand, wrapped around a solid Aumrarr hilt, took the man in the throat, sending him staggering down to his own hard meeting with the floor.

The great chamber looked even grander from where they were now, racing across its glossy-smooth black tiles, seeking a way out. Yonder was the great arch where Orthaunt's skull hung in the air grinning at them, over there was a pair of double doors that obviously opened into a wide passage heading to the front of the castle, and behind—

The tapestries that they'd seen being plucked aside, earlier, parted again as half a dozen Lyrose warriors—knights? Well, they wore the best darkly-gleaming plate armor Garfist had seen this side of Galath, from head to toe—strode forward into the room. Some of them were unshuttering hand-lanterns as they came, and the others were drawing long, gleaming swords.

Behind them were two menacingly-smiling, grandly garbed people who could only be Lord and Lady Lyrose.

"So two alley-dregs intruders have dared to burst into our home," the lord purred, "undoubtedly to steal." As his wife's sneer became a cruel smile of anticipation, he added softly, "No need to keep these alive to question. Use your poisoned blades, loyal warriors of Lyrose."

It was cold in Yintaerghast. The place was a massive stone fortress, yes, with gaping window-holes aplenty in its walls to let the winds whistle through, but the ruined castle of Lorontar wasn't just dank and chilly. Its dark, looming walls and floors held a deeper, bone-numbing, somehow *alive* cold, that seeped into one's body and sapped alertness and feeling, and… and life.

Narmarkoun grimaced. His lips had long ago tightened into a grim line; even after he'd slain the last lurking beast in the deepest dungeons, and shattered the last clever trap-magic he could find… and long after the magics he'd devised had clearly triumphed over Lorontar's great shield-spell.

He could still feel the silent thunder of that fell and mighty magic all around him. It twisted the minds of all living creatures who entered Yintaerghast, slowly stripping away any magical knowledge—wherefore wizards less brilliant than Narmarkoun dared not enter.

It also, far less slowly, sapped any magics at work on intruders, which freed servitors sent in by wizards from the magics that controlled or saw through them.

Almost as an afterthought, it did one more thing, that made finding a way out of the castle again difficult. It caused all of the castle's empty windows to look out into a swirling void that allowed no creature to leap, fall, fly, or climb out; those who tried were thrust back in again by the suddenly-thickening, surging mists.

Narmarkoun had never witnessed this last effect before now, but then he'd never dared set foot in Yintaerghast before.

So he was immune to Lorontar's greatest magic—and so were his dead playpretties, so pale and silent as they stood yearningly outside the chamber door, watching him—but anyone else who might come to the cold castle in the dead wood would still face its harms.

Which made it the ideal hide-hold, for now, if he could pierce its mists. With Malraun's armies on the march and his own false selves being hunted energetically all over Falconfar, Lorontar's fortress made a great place to hide. And from that hiding, to magically spy from afar on Rod Everlar.

Or he would do, the moment he got the details of this last magic sorted out, and could see through that misty void—that "otherwhere" that wasn't really gathered around the outside of Yintaerghast, at all—whenever he pleased.

If Malraun hadn't conquered everything else and decided to come exploring Yintaerghast for himself by then.

Ah, well, nothing in life remains the same.

Narmarkoun smiled wryly at no one, and bent his will again to adjusting incantations and the subsumptions of certain herbs and powders, to give himself the means to spy on Rod Everlar as freely as he'd been doing for months, now, before coming to Yintaerghast.

He had already filled several tomes with careful notes about the so-called Lord Archwizard. Who was no wizard at all, but a Shaper, and a naive buffoon at that. Some "Dark Lord" to quake in terror at!

Yet Everlar *was* mysterious, and in those mysteries might well lie his own bright future.

Rod Everlar had come from somewhere, a world or place that was not Falconfar. A place where Narmarkoun could take refuge, and build power, and perhaps even conquer, while Falconfar was ravaged in Malraun's ever-widening war.

The army of monsters and mercenaries raised by Horgul, with Malraun standing behind him—and

Lorontar quite likely standing behind the unwitting Malraun—had attacked one hold after another, conquering territory in a manner never possible when three strong Dooms stood in opposition to each other.

That uneasy balance had held for too long, as Falconfar had simmered beneath it. Now, with the lid off the cauldron and Malraun charging through the Raurklor, swords were coming out everywhere. City against city on the far southern shores of the Sea of Storms, Galath about to rise into civil strife again, and the new faiths—the Forestmother, and the rest—goading men everywhere to visit fire and sword on each other.

Distressing for a Doom who desired the cold, quiet caresses of the obedient dead, and simply a quiet place to study.

He might have to conquer a world to get those things, yes, but if it was a world as full of dolts as Rod Everlar, how hard could *that* be?

Chapter Seventeen

ISKARRA AND GARFIST stared at the six Lyrose knights advancing in slow, menacing unison, with Lord and Lady Lyrose sneering from behind them. They were tarrying rather than charging, and Isk and Gar could hear why.

The thunder of boots was growing louder down the tower stair, and Lyrose guards were rushing along the balcony Isk and Gar had just traversed, too. Dark-armored and eager, they seemed to have spears in plenty, but no bows. Thank the Falcon for small glorking favors.

Gar bent, plucked up the still-hot sword from the blackened bones of the guard slain by the wizard's skull, and ran to the tower door juggling it and swearing as it scorched his fingers, the charred remnants of its scabbard falling away in his wake.

A spear hissed down at him, and then another—but Orthaunt's grinning skull saw those as attacks, and lashed out with more green-gold fire. Two guards shrieked up on the balcony, and one of them toppled forward over the rail, to hang motionless, head-downwards, as he cooked. No more spears were thrown.

Aside from ducking low and running as far around the curve of the tower wall as he could get from the balcony, Gar paid no heed to any of this. He was too busy hurrying—and then thrusting the burned guard's weapon through the door-rings to try to bar the tower door shut. He doubted one blade could hold back all the guards in the tower and on the balcony, but it might take them some time to break it and force entrance. Oh, they could jump down over the balcony rail, aye, but that wouldn't be a flood he couldn't stand up to, and carve as they landed.

Isk snatched open one of the doors in the wall behind where he'd been standing with her, to try to get out. Discovering a trio of grinning guards waiting in the passage beyond, she flung herself at their ankles and tripped them helplessly forward into the room.

Gar whirled from the tower door in time to see them fall. Snarling, he unshuttered his darklantern.

As Lord Lyrose's bodyguard knights raised shouts, deciding to charge him after all, he flung it—high, hard, and flaming—into the tapestries just above and behind the sneering lord and lady.

Fire flared amid the folds of the old and dusty cloth in an instant. Lady Lyrose shrieked in dismay, Lord Lyrose roared out his anger, and a knight spun around and hurled his sword vainly at the flames.

Orthaunt's skull took that as another attack, and lashed out with another deadly green-gold beam.

As that doomed guard burned, Gar sprinted back to aid Iskarra.

She had already efficiently daggered her three guards as they crashed to the floor, sprawling atop each other. He joined her just as the blades of the

foremost rushing bodyguard knights reached her—
and the bone-dry tapestries *really* caught alight.

Flames rushed up the walls with a hungry roar,
racing along the tapestries in a growing, deepening
thunder to ignite lesser draperies tied back around
pillars all along the balconies.

The knights hacked and thrust enthusiastically at
Garfist, blades ringing off his frantic parryings, but
Lord Lyrose shouted, "*Knights of Lyrose!* Back from
him, you *fools!* Go get the maids and the steward
and *everyone* from the stables, with all their buckets!
The rooms back yon are all timbers and paneling!
Hurry!"

The knights hesitated, looking to their lord to
be sure they'd heard rightly—and Garfist managed
to slice the throat out of one of them with a wild,
overbalancing slash.

He staggered helplessly, desperate to regain his
balance, but the knights were no longer heeding him;
more of Lyrose's roared commands were sending
them obediently dashing off in all directions. One
flung a dagger at Iskarra as he went. She eyed its
whirling, oncoming blade, seeing there a blue, sticky
sheen no steel should have.

"Darfly poison," she murmured, deftly plucking
the dagger out of the air in front of her nose. "Nasty."

The tower door thundered again as guards behind
it tried to wrench it open, and the sword Garfist had
thrust through its rings resisted them.

Again they tugged, the swordblade bending slightly
and shrieking in protest as the door buckled a trifle. A
guard ducked between flames to vault down over the
balcony rail and run to pluck out the sword from the
hall side of the door, and Gar grinned and went for him.

Only to see Lord Lyrose himself charging to intercept his unwelcome guest.

"Burn my home, will you?" he snarled as he came. "Die, thief! Slayer! *Bastard!*"

"Well, it's nice to meet a pompous backwoods lordling who's so *eloquent*," Gar taunted merrily, slashing aside the running guard's sword and driving his free fist hard into the man's throat.

Choking, the guard reeled, and Gar flung himself across the man's front to get around him and put him in his rushing lord's way, tugging at the guard's sword at the same time. He came away with it as the man spun sideways under his jerking, then hopped, stumbled—and toppled helplessly to the tiles.

The tower door thundered again, nearby.

Lord Lyrose never slowed, trampling his own guard without hesitation to get at Garfist. The splendidly glittering Lyrose sword and dagger slashed out with a deft speed that made the fat, gruff swindler grunt in surprise, and hastily back away.

"Kill him, my lord!" Lady Lyrose shrieked, eyes blazing in fury. "*Kill him!*"

"With pleasure!" her husband roared back, adding a bellow of laughter that sank into a grinning sneer as he stalked forward, seeking to corner Garfist.

Across the great hall, the wizard's skull spat magical fire at another running guard, and Gar could see Iskarra dodging, darting, and stabbing with her poisoned dagger at six or seven more who'd rushed in the door she'd opened. Smoke was thickening in the air now as flames reached the roof-beams, and shouting could be heard from all over Lyraunt Castle.

Garfist gave way thoughtfully as his noble foe pressed forward. Well-trained with a blade this

Lord Lyrose might be, but the lord was far more gloatingly confident than anyone but an utter fool should be—given that he'd rushed eagerly in to take on Garfist alone, when he could wait for his seeming scores of guards to take care of that slaying for him.

So Lyrose was trusting in something more than sword-skill. Probably magic.

No glowing rings, though the man wore quite a few, heavy gaudy things of gems on gold, and… hoy, now, that gorget looked out of place on a man otherwise unarmored… and it stood in the way of Gar's handy fist downing his lordship as easily as he'd sent yon guard choking and strangling to the floor, too, so…

Garfist sidestepped the next Lyrose thrust, skipping lightly sideways like a Stormar table-dancer to shift his bulk faster than sneering lords would expect. Lyrose gaped at his foe, then rushed to close the gap that had opened between them.

"*Die*, dolt! I am Lord Magrandar Lyrose—and I am the best swordsman in all Falconfar!" he hissed.

"Oh?" Gar asked mockingly, beating the lord's gleaming blade to the tiles with his own sword. "*That* declaration'll look nice on yer casket! Lord Maggot Lyrose, one more idiot who thought himself the best bladesman in the world—but was, of course, wrong about that."

Their blades rang off each other twice and thrice. Then Lyrose was snarling at him and thrusting viciously, but Garfist caught that splendid sword again with his own rougher blade, forced it down, and leaned deftly in toward the lord. Lyrose brought up his dagger with a triumphant "Hah!"

But the growling adventurer had timed his lean just right. Lyrose's dagger flashed between his arm and side.

Leaving him easily able to reach the target he sought. He wanted to slash—with more force than elegant deftness—away the lord's gorget.

His blade spun in, under its edge, slicing flesh and straps alike, and sent it ringing and flashing away through the air.

Bleeding copiously from his throat, Lord Magrandar Lyrose staggered back, staring at Garfist in open-mouthed shock.

Whereupon Isk smiled thinly, tossed her newly-acquired, poisoned dagger with her customary skill—and the lord of Lyraunt Castle suddenly sprouted steel in one eye.

He went down to the tiles in silence, two stumbling strides later, leaving Lady Lyrose to shriek out her own rage and rush forward.

For two wild strides before she realized her peril—and abruptly ducked aside, darted across the hall, and out a door.

Leaving Garfist and Iskarra momentarily alone—though ominous cracks were spreading across the still-thundering tower door—as the tapestries blazed on, and flames billowed up everywhere in the ceiling overhead. Unconcernedly the floating wizard's skull grinned at them as shouts arose behind the tower door, and guards boiled back up onto the balcony.

Gar had lumbered forward to loot Lord Lyrose's body of all those golden gem-bedecked rings, but Isk plucked at his arm.

"Come," she commanded. "Bring his sword and *come*. We have a task, up yon stairs, and burning castles have a habit of falling down. I'd rather not be up there when this one decides to collapse!"

"Bah! Always right, y'are!" Gar growled at her,

hastily clawing up Lyrose's sword and dagger. Shoving himself to his feet, he took her hand.

Ducking aside from the spears now hurtling at them from the balcony in a quickening rain, they ran for the nearest door.

MALRAUN FOUND HIMSELF rising out of a fading but unpleasant dream of flaming tapestries and rushing guards, to blink up at an unfamiliar ceiling, in silent darkness.

He was lying on his back, linens thrown off him, in a large but sweat-soaked bed—soaked with *his* sweat—with the bare, beautiful form of Taeauna warm on his shoulder. He was in... oh, yes, the best bedchamber in conquered Darswords.

And he was now thoroughly awake.

Though his head ached cursedly and he felt as tired as if he'd not slept a wink. Lyrose had... had what?

Something had flared in his mind. Falcon rend all.

With a grunt of disgust that awakened Taeauna, he rolled over and away from her. "Idiots," he growled into the darkness. "If that castle burns, I'll lose all I've hidden there, and the Lyroses besides. And I've plans for them."

Ignoring Taeauna's reaching, soothing hand, he angrily clambered out of the bed, strode naked across the room until he was far enough from where his clothing and carried magics were all heaped together, and worked a swift spell.

Light flared briefly around his limbs, leaving him a glimpse of Taeauna kneeling on the bed staring at him in sleepy concern.

Then that radiance took him to distant Lyraunt Castle in a glowing, tingling instant, and faded away.

He was standing on the Three Thorns in the center of the great hall, with flames blazing away above him, smoke and corpses everywhere, and—

Malraun waved both hands in a mighty magic that swallowed the tapestries and hall ceiling alike, hurling them high and far up into the starry night sky, and leaving the fires nothing to feed on.

Above, the last few flickering flames fell toward him, slumping into sparks as they came, and… were gone.

Something struck the tiles right beside his leg. Malraun sprang aside and turned, even before a second spear cracked off slightly more distant tiles and skidded away across the hall.

The balcony rail was crowded with hard-eyed guards, glaring at him and hefting spears. With a silent snarl, the naked Doom waved his hands again. Magic surged out of him—and the balcony was suddenly empty of men, its ceiling and back wall dripping and glistening with fresh red gore.

He turned on his heel to peer around the hall. It no longer had a ceiling, but then fire was no longer raging in Lyraunt Castle. Yet someone had set that fire, and—

Malraun spotted an all-too-familiar face among the nearest bodies on the floor, and cursed bitterly.

Gorget gone. Taking two swift steps, he drew the dagger up out of Lord Lyrose's eye. Darfly poison, and a Lyrose blade at that. A family slaying, then.

He thrust the dagger right back into dead Magrandar's eye—and yawned, rage ebbing before a sudden rush of weariness. *Idiots.*

Well, at least this wasn't Hammerhand work. So it could wait until morning, when he wasn't so workmule-tired from killing wizards. And when he wasn't standing naked in a castle far from home, with only pitiful remnants of magic left. Another balcony full of guards with spears wouldn't be all that welcome, just now...

Stifling another yawn, he cast another spell—and vanished. Sleepily padding across a dark bedchamber where Taeauna's arms awaited, back to his bed in Darswords, having never noticed a certain silently-smiling floating skull—or a bone-thin woman and a fat, gruff man who were decidedly *not* of House Lyrose.

A handful of moments later, a dozen maids and stablehands rushed into the room, water slopping from their buckets as they slowed.

They stared around in the gloom, smelling smoke and scorched stone, but seeing nary a flame that wasn't in a brazier.

Then they saw the bodies on the floor, the balcony a-drip with blood, the floating skull, and the lack of tapestries.

It took another few gasps and oaths before a shriek went up from one maid—as she pointed tremblingly at their lord, lying dead on the tiles with a dagger sticking up out of his eye.

There were other screams, but more than a few of the maids stole reluctantly forward for a better look. And when they'd looked, and were sure, they gave the corpse of Lord Magrandar Lyrose some good, hard, heartfelt kicks.

"THAT WAS MALRAUN!" Iskarra hissed, panting from their long climb. "A glorking Doom of Falconfar!"

"Don't look like much bare-assed, do he?" Garfist growled back, pausing for breath three steps above her. "He'll be back come morning, mind—after he's finished rutting with whoever he so hastily left to come here and blow the roof off the hall! So let's thank him, *very* quietly, and be done with setting our trap and get *gone* from here! At least he took care of all Lyrose's guards!"

"I'm not so sure his kills were anywhere near 'all' of them, Old Ox," his partner panted, "but yes, let's do it and begone! Do we try to find the Aumrarr and use their wings to get well away? Or try to hide in the forest, and make our own way back to…"

"Heh," Garfist agreed, "*that* needs more thinking on, don't it? The Raurklor's dangerous for a band of less than, say, twenty armed knights at the best of times. Given what the wingbitches said about his warning-wards, d'ye think Malraun the Matchless has an Aumrarr-sniffing spell?"

They looked at each other in the faint magical gloom that filled the upper reaches of this tower, until Iskarra spread her hands and shrugged to signify she could not even mount a worthy guess.

Then she looked up the spiraling tower stair past him and hissed, "Not much farther. Who was this bedchamber built for, anyway? A babe who was a family monster? Child princes or princesses kidnapped from elsewhere? An Aumrarr, perhaps, so she'd learn to fly?"

Garfist shrugged. "Who knows why lords with castles do *anything?* I think they're all more'n a little mad; all that gold and power rots a man's brain."

Isk smirked. "So when did *you* have lots of gold and power, that I missed noticing?"

Garfist was above her on the stairs, so he didn't bother with a clever reply. He just broke wind into her face. Noisily.

The stairs ended in a plain stone door that wasn't locked. Gar and Isk traded glances over that before Garfist warily turned the door-ring and pushed the door gently open.

Inside they found no lurking monster, nor any guard. Just a high, uncurtained bed that nearly filled the room, and dust in the corners.

"Under it, right up nigh the headboard," Garfist rumbled, before Isk could remind him. "Give me the gem."

"No, my fat beloved," Isk panted gently. "Let's catch our wind first, and then I'll do the crawling beneath. Someone may want to find this bed intact— and a Doom arriving and finding it broken will be wary, for sure."

"No Doom's going to climb all those stairs," Garfist growled. "Not when he has spells to spare." He held out one hairy hand. "The gem."

Ignoring him, Iskarra strolled along the far side of the bed, both hands on her belt buckle, fingers undoubtedly touching the mindgem she'd slid into the little pouch she'd sewn behind it some seasons ago.

Halting at the head of the bed, she turned and gave him a strange little smile. "I've decided something."

"Aye?" Garfist asked warily. That sweet tone of hers was not one he liked overmuch; it always betokened something bold. And dangerous.

"I'm going to step *through* the gate, and drop this little mindtrap-stone behind me. After you precede me through, of course."

Garfist stared at her. "*Now* who's gone crazed? *Without* any gold an' power, too!"

Isk shook her head, still wearing that odd smile. "*I'm* not a wizard. Nor are you. So we'll be fine, yes?"

"If 'fine' means happily stepping into the unknown, when that unknown is a wizard's lair!" Garfist growled.

"Well, Malraun won't have made a gate that would hurt him, if he came home from here through it," Iskarra replied, the mindgem now gleaming in her hand, "for isn't this a bolthole he might use when hurt, or desperate, or in haste, or when trying to sneak into his own home because, say, another Doom has broken into it? And if we stay here in Ironthorn, half Falconfar—the armed, warlike half—are either in our laps already or will soon be here. Arriving ready to kill everyone, even before all the wizards start blasting. If we stroll quick and quiet *out* of a wizard's tower, we might well make it. It's folk trying to get *in* that have all the trouble."

"Wizard's tower," Garfist rumbled slowly. "Gems, wine, gold... Isk, ye're going to get us killed some day, ye are!"

He let his wagging, reproving finger fall—and grinned widely. "So let's be about it!"

He held out his hand, Isk took it, and he pulled, hauling both hard and upward. She came flying into his arms like the scrawny sack of bones she so nearly was, and they embraced amid chuckles.

Then they went down on their knees together. Isk promptly gave way until he was lying atop her on the floor, their arms around each other. Garfist glanced at the bedframe beside him, then at the dim dustiness beneath it, and grunted, "Don't think so."

"Doesn't look heavy enough that you can't heave it up," Iskarra murmured, from just beneath his chin. "I can always worm out of your arms and let you flatten out."

"Right, wench—lead us on to our deaths," her man growled, and they rolled together.

Almost immediately, Garfist's shoulders got stuck.

So he grunted, heaved to shove the bed up from beneath, and won them space enough to roll over again.

Into a tingling that snatched away their eyesight into swirling mists, and made the mindgem glow like a pale eye.

"Hurry," Iskarra hissed, and they rolled onward.

She let go of the mindgem, heard it drop onto a floor that sounded very far away, and they left it behind and fell together through endless, welcoming mists.

Chapter Eighteen

ROD EVERLAR LOOKED up at the moon, serene in a nigh-cloudless sky that was alive with more stars than he'd ever seen before—and then down at the moon-drenched roofs of silent Harlhoh. No dogs barked, no wolves howled, and no nameless night things called. It was very still.

Except for what was bubbling up inside him again, warm threads stirring like reaching fingers. The drug they'd given him earlier…

He reeled, and Thalden flung out an arm to steady him and snapped, "Gorn! The wizard's under attack! Some magic of Malraun's, belike!"

The knights scattered into a ring, swords and daggers out. Their points were thrust toward Rod, not out at the shadows in the garden.

"No," Rod protested weakly. "Whatever you gave me earlier, that made me babble so… it's back."

He sank to his knees before Thalden could shift his grip, and then to a crawling along one of the soft garden paths.

Moss, he thought to himself, suddenly acutely aware of the look and feel of what was under his palms. *It's all moss. Thicker and grander than any I've ever seen before...*

The garden was all snakelike curved beds, each one different, each a ridge of heaped earth drenched in shrubs and natural-seeming stones and little shade trees, wandering its own way through the ribbons of moss... Rod crawled along the path like a dazed, unsteady babe, as whatever Syregorn had given him returned with a vengeance, rolling like silent surf through his mind.

Its thunders submerged him, and he was only dimly aware that he was talking again, fast and wildly and about anything and everything, the words tumbling over each other as he ranted on—and the knights slowly closed in around him in a looming ring, grim disgust on their faces.

"Strike him senseless," Reld muttered.

"We daren't have him making so much noise, right here next to where a Doom may be sleeping!" Perthus hissed, looking to Syregorn.

"Aye, silence him," Tarth agreed.

The warcaptain held up one hand at them in a clear signal to desist, and ordered, "Pick him up. Gently. Carry him back there, to yon farthest corner, and set him carefully down, where he has space to lie on his back. No talking."

Rod babbled on as they took him carefully under the armpits and around the legs, and lifted. "So then the Aumrarr showed me a greatfangs, dead and stinking, and God it reeked, like all the open cesspits and rock concert vomit put together, so foul that—"

"What about *him?*" Reld whispered at Syregorn.

The warcaptain's reply was flat and cold. "Magic has prevented me obeying one order from Lord

Hammerhand—for this night, at least. I will therefore do my utmost to fulfill his other commandment, and learn *all* I can from this one who calls himself Lord Archwizard."

"You mean—?"

"I mean I'm going to sit and listen. The rest of you can explore the gardens if you'd like—in pairs, and with at least two of you standing guard over our babbler with me. Oh, and I want someone watching yon door at all times."

"There're only six of us—seven with you, Syre."

"And eight, with this Rod Everlar. I learned to count too, Perthus." The warcaptain's voice was quiet but very dry, and his youngest knight flushed dark red in the moonlight, and said not another word.

Rod did, though. He couldn't help himself, though what he was revealing was embarrassing him into squirming, blushing depths of humiliation. "No magic at all, but Taeauna insists I'm the Lord Archwizard, greatest of the Dooms, and I don't feel heroic, don't feel lordly or that I have any right to tell anyone to do anything. I can't swing a sword, can't hunt, can't even light a bloody fire…"

The moss was just as soft in the deep gloom where two of the garden walls met, and bushes flourished in that corner and on the bed two steps away, across the last, looping-nigh-the-walls path. They lowered Rod Everlar onto his back as gently as if he'd been an honored corpse being laid on an altar. Syregorn sat down beside Rod's head, plucked a long shoot from a nearby bush he evidently recognized, and started chewing on it.

It protruded from his mouth, dancing gently, as he leaned over Rod's face and asked into the helpless, endless flood of words, "So, were you born in Falconfar, Everlar?"

"No no no," Rod found himself saying eagerly. "I was born on Earth, in the *real* world. In a hospital that's been torn down now, in the usual way, or so I'm told. I don't remember when I was really young, except standing in a garden one summer in the sun, staring at sunflowers as big as my face; they always told me that summer must have been when I was three, and—"

"How did you get from this Earth to Falconfar?"

"Tay-Taeauna came for me, and cried for my help, and the Dark Helms came to finish her off, and she told me to weave a dream-gate, and—and I guess I did. Just as they swung their swords—"

"A dream-gate?"

"Think of Falconfar, she told me. Look at me, but think of Falconfar—and it worked! We went from my bedroom to the road leading up to the keep!"

"Oh? What keep?"

"Hollowtree Keep, of course, up in the hills east of Galath. One of my favorite creations."

"'Creations'? Ah, and what else have you created?"

"Well, ah, *Falconfar*, and almost everything in it. This place. Ironthorn and the Raurklor and Galath and all."

Someone who wasn't Syregorn snorted in disgust, and Rod became vaguely aware that some of the knights were standing nearby, listening.

"A madman," one of them muttered, to another. "I knew it."

Rod also became aware that the bald warcaptain was fiercely but silently waving his knights away, now, even as he bent closer to Rod to say in a gently soothing voice, "Let's go back to Hollowtree Keep. Why is it one of your favorites?"

"Ah, Syre, shouldn't we be—?"

That low, uncertain voice broke in on them from just above and behind Rod, the opposite direction from the now-retreating knights. It was Reld, and he was jerking his head in the direction of the distant door that led out of the gardens into Malragard.

Syregorn gave that knight a level look. "You're in a particular hurry to die? Alone in the undoubtedly-spell-guarded fortress of a Doom of Falconfar?"

"Alone? But I won't be..." Reld trailed off under the warcaptain's grim glare.

"Ah, but you will be. If you step through that door right now, none of us'll be going with you. Yet if you feel you must, go right ahead—disloyal knight of Hammerhold. We'll tell Lord Hammerhand you died valiantly. And foolishly."

Reld moved his mouth as if he was going to make some sort of reply, but then flushed, closed it again, bowed his head in acceptance, and stepped back into the night.

I know JUST how he feels, Rod thought, as his own verbal flood flowed on. *Humiliated, an idiot, a failure. Some fantasy book hero I'm turning out to be. Wandering along like a dimwit while others do what they like with me, smirk at me, and deem me an utter dolt. And they're right, every last one of them.*

He paused for breath, and Syregorn's gentle voice returned. "So that's all you know about the Aumrarr? Well, then, tell me more of what you know of the world you came from, this *Earth*."

Syregorn was smiling, but the smile never touched his eyes. He went right on with his careful, quiet questions—and helplessly, while fear grew inside him like a cold, awakening worm, Rod obediently babbled on and on about the real world.

The warcaptain wanted to know about everything. What people wore, how they locked their doors at night, how they spent each day.

Of course. Syregorn was learning all about a foe, so he could invade them and swiftly do all the right things to conquer. And I'm telling him, God help me.

Shit. Earth was about to become doomed.

THE MISTS FADED away, leaving Garfist and Iskarra lying on a cold stone floor in each other's arms.

They were lying at about the center of an empty, plain stone room, in a castle or fortress somewhere, and there was a singing stillness in the air that smelt of magic and emptiness. They were alone... or at least it felt like there was nothing alive nearby.

"Malragard?" Garfist whispered hoarsely. Isk shrugged her wordless reply, then patted at his ribs to signal that she'd like to be free of his tight embrace.

Gar obligingly opened his arms, and she rolled out of them and up to her feet in one supple, eel-like wriggle, to crouch and peer alertly in all directions.

There wasn't much to see. Two doors out of the room, on opposite sides and both closed, and the stillness—and that very faint, high singing sound—hung unchanged.

Isk crept noiselessly to one door, listened, then went and put her ear to the other. Evidently hearing nothing, she beckoned Garfist to join her, and he rolled slowly to his knees and then rose, stifling his usual grunts—and noticed the singing sound dying away as he moved away from where they'd been lying. When he took a step back closer, it grew stronger again.

So the singing sound was Malraun's gate, awake and ready to whisk them back to Lyraunt Castle—and witlessness, trapped by the mindgem.

Bugger all, they'd slammed their door out behind them locked-tight.

Garfist fervently hoped that wouldn't be one of the largest glorking mistakes of their lives.

Iskarra nodded to tell him she'd noticed the shift in sound, too, and promptly beckoned him to follow her back to the first door she'd listened at.

He shrugged acceptance, and obeyed.

Iskarra flattened herself against the wall beside that door, took hold of his nearest ear the moment he was close enough, and tugged him gently forward until she could whisper right into it, her breath warm and ticklish, her lips brushing his earlobe.

"Stay *quiet*, Gar, and stick with me. We go slow and try to stay back from anything that could make a noise—and we don't open things until we really have to."

"So as to not to alert any guards," Garfist whispered.

"Or worse," Isk agreed, her whisper ghost-quiet. "You know how wizards love guardian *things*. Pillars and lamps and who knows what other sorts of furniture, that all turn into beasts with jaws and claws. Usually right behind you, after you've passed."

"Unnh," Garfist grunted in unwilling agreement, unpleasant memories rising.

"Touch or take *nothing* that looks valuable until we've agreed on it. Constantly seek ways out and down. We're here to get out unseen, remember, not loot the citadel of Malraun. I'll bet he could trace us, to the deepest caves in the farthest lands of Falconfar, if we took just one coin from here."

"Aye, aye," Gar growled. "I hear ye. Ye're going to stand here and *talk* me to death—and when Malraun strides in through this door, d'ye think that'll work on *him?*"

"Idiot," Iskarra hissed, eyes flashing. "How long ago would you've been dead, if not for me?"

Garfist grew a slow grin. "Aye, but I'd've died from that smith dropping his anvil on my head, as I slept after slap-an'-tickle with his three daughters. I'd've greeted the Falcon a happy man."

Iskarra dug just the tips of her fingers into a certain bulge in his breeches, and murmured, "Do all men think only with *this?*"

"Nay, Snakehips. I make 'em use their own," Gar told her with a grin. Isk rolled her eyes at him, put a silencing finger across his lips, and bent to listen at the closed door again.

Then she straightened, nodded, mimed the motions of him drawing his sword—so he did so, careful to step away from the wall and do it carefully and silently—leaned in again, put her hand on the pull-ring... and drew open the door.

No menace they could see, and no sounds or movements. Nothing. The darkness of the revealed stone passage told them their room must be lit by magic, though the radiance was so faint, and coming from everywhere and nowhere, that they'd not noticed.

Iskarra leaned back into Gar to breathe her words into his ear. "Come, but don't let the door slam behind you, or even shut," she commanded. "We have to move as if a Doom of Falconfar is sitting reading, or dozing, in a room somewhere nearby—a room with an open door."

"We do?"

"Just shut up and humor me, Old Ox. Save your questions—and attempts to think—for later."

"Why?"

Isk answered that hoarse question with a long, cold look, holding it until Gar grew uncomfortable and started to shuffle from one booted foot to another.

"I'll be good, Isk," he whispered, finally.

"See that you are—at least until we're well out of here," she breathed into his ear, and slipped out into the passage.

Almost immediately, one of her hands returned, to beckon Garfist. Moving gingerly, with exaggerated care to keep quiet, he followed out of the door, leaving it open.

The soft light in the room cast a gentle fan of radiance out into the darkness, and he thrust a forefinger twice into Isk's shoulder, and when she turned, pointed at it.

She shrugged, captured that finger, and tugged it gently, signifying he should move onward with her. Lifting his feet carefully to avoid the customary scrape on stone of his boots, he did so.

The passage ran straight, past several closed and featureless stone doors, then became a descending flight of stairs without archway or fanfare, its smooth and featureless ceiling curving to run downward with it.

They went down the steps in slow, careful silence, Isk in the lead. She froze the moment she could see what the stair emptied out into: a large room that held an oval pool of a glowing, deep emerald green oil or water or *something* that surged and rippled in slow, constant, and silent motion, as if it were alive and lazily thrusting up serpent-like, wriggling spines or backs, large curved claws, and short-lived tentacles that always became tubes that vented out gases with tiny gasps, and then sank back into the oily green life. There was a faint, sharp smell in the air, something like soured wine, and this vinegar-like taint was almost certainly coming from the pool, but ...

Isk kept well back from the pool, and moved purposefully to the right, to where she could see a way opening out of the room, into another dark, narrow passage.

Garfist followed, sword in hand but stepping no farther from the wall than he had to. He knew what was making her hasten, because he was starting to feel it, too.

An intense feeling of being watched. A feeling that was coming from the radiant green contents of the pool...

They were almost trotting by the time they reached the passage, and Gar couldn't resist a look back over his shoulder, to make sure no tentacle was arcing up out of the glow to reach after them.

He saw none, but when he turned back again, Isk's face was turned his way and wearing a pale expression that told him, as clearly as if she'd shouted it, that she'd pictured a reaching tentacle too.

The new passage was short and dark and lined with more closed doors, running about a dozen strides ere it turned sharply to the left and became another stair down. The feeling of being watched faded as they followed it down into another room.

This one was empty of everything but a simple, smoothly-finished stone table, and was lit by moonlight streaming in a large window that appeared to be just an arched hole cut through a thick castle wall. There were no bird droppings or any stirring of moving air, though, and a faint tingling sensation built within them as they drew near to it; magic was alive here, and seemingly preventing anything passing through the opening.

Iskarra stopped three careful steps away and peered out into the moonlit night. She could see that they were fairly high up, perhaps half the height of Deldragon's battlements back in Galath. Far too high to jump out of and land alive, even if the window's magic allowed their passage.

A vast forest—the Raurklor, by the looks of it—began not all that far off, and stretched away to join the stars at the straining limits of her eyesight; nearer to the wall, the land fell away to the left in a series of walled, farmed plots, down to the roofs of what looked like one edge of a town. The Raurklor hold of Harlhoh, no doubt.

Isk looked back over her shoulder; Gar was looking out into the night with an irritated expression on his face. When their eyes met, he jerked his chin in the other direction, to where the room emptied into yet another passage, in a clear message: *Let's get on with it.*

Iskarra nodded, and led the way.

Malragard remained as still and silent as a tomb around them, as if its owner and any servants he might have had abandoned it.

Isk knew, without their trading any words at all over the matter, that Gar felt the same way she did about this silence.

It was bad, and betokened danger to come. Probably soon.

Down the years, Iskarra had learned to trust such feelings, though she often wished she was wrong to have them.

She never had been yet, though, and didn't feel like wagering on her being so, this time.

After all, the Great Falcon did have a sense of humor—and it was not a kind one.

The passage forked almost immediately, one end a short stub lined with closed doors, and the other becoming another short flight of descending steps, to a lone closed door.

Isk went down, listened to the utter silence from beyond the door, then opened it into... another large, moonlit room. Stepping aside so Garfist could see it, too, she gestured silently to indicate he should leave it standing open, too, in case they needed to retreat back this way.

He nodded, and they went on into the brightening moonlight together.

Behind them, by itself, the open door silently drifted closed. Then, with the same utter lack of sound, it started to melt, its shape shifting into... a dark oval, a... great pair of fanged jaws that gaped open, awaiting anyone trying to go back through.

STANDING ALONE IN dark Yintaerghast, Narmarkoun beheld not the dark shadows before him, but a bright eye floating in the air, a scene from afar conjured by his own magic.

One side of that scene flared bright like fire, in a continuous struggle against Malragard's wards and shieldings, a battle that blinded his far-seeing if he looked toward the fortress.

Yet he had no interest in looking at Malraun's abode. Not while there was a man lying on his back in the farthest corner of its walled gardens, babbling out all he could say, just as fast as he could.

Since hearing that the fabled Dark Lord had come to Falconfar at last, he'd hungered to know more about this mysterious Rod Everlar's origins.

Now, hearing these babblings, he chuckled in triumph.

At last he had heard enough.

Enough to craft a dream-gate that would reach into this "real world" Everlar came from, this "Earth."

Narmarkoun banished his spying-scene with a wave of his hand, strode into the room he'd made ready, and set about casting it.

Why wait? Dooms of Falconfar age just like lesser men.

Besides, he'd always wanted to conquer a world.

He flung up both hands, said a careful word, and felt Yintaerghast tremble all around him.

Then, slowly, here and there, the darkness started to glow. Lorontar's long-sleeping magic was awakening. It would feed and aid his own.

Narmarkoun took up a wand he'd left ready on the table, and said a word to it that its maker had never intended it to obey. It started to burn in his hand, like an impatient candle, its flame spreading out into the air around him. Yintaerghast's tremble became a deepening hum.

The third Doom of Falconfar allowed himself a broad, triumphant smile, and started in on the long and difficult incantations. Though lengthy, the magic was relatively simple, being a lone casting that created a single, stationary effect; the trick would be to imagine this other world vividly enough from what Everlar had said of it, so his gate would reach out to it, and not somewhere in Falconfar.

Intent on his words and the wand burning away to nothingness in his hand, Narmarkoun never noticed what briefly formed on the wall right behind him.

The face of Lorontar, first Lord Archwizard of Falconfar and builder of Yintaerghast. It looked down on Narmarkoun, smiled a triumphant smile of its own, then faded away again. Unseen by any overconfident Doom of Falconfar.

Chapter Nineteen

THE LARGE, BRIGHTLY moonlit room ended in a matched trio of windows and another stair down. To get to them, Garfist and Iskarra had to walk the length of a long stone table that had large pages of untrimmed parchment laid out neatly along it. They gave these only brief, cautious glances, mindful of all the old tales of curse-spells erupting to afflict those who gazed upon the wrong runes.

Old tales those might be, and wildly grown in the telling as such stories always were, but all old tales were born of *something*, and…

Isk's eyes were keener, and she was in the lead, so it was she who spun away from the table to catch hold of Garfist, half-turn him away from the parchments, and murmur in Garfist's ear, "Yon's a boastful little history—unfinished, of course—of the great deeds of Malraun the Matchless. I saw mention of his glorious victories—seemingly several, by the Falcon!—over the hated Arlaghaun, to say nothing of Malraun's triumphs over Stormar lords who foolishly defied him, Galathan knights too stupid to surrender to a mage, and upstart wizards and petty rulers in many a Stormar port."

Garfist grinned mirthlessly. "This is Malragard, all right. An' proclaim me unsurprised at what its master has written, Snakehips mine. Self-delusion and spinning grand fantasies would seem to be vital skills to mastering wizardry, aye?"

"Indeed," Iskarra whispered, waving at him to speak more quietly. "Yet reading that drivel doesn't make me sneer at him or count myself lucky I'm not crazed enough to become a mage. It makes me want even more to get *out* of here—speedily, and *right now*."

"The stairs," Garfist whispered hoarsely, bowing to her and gesturing as floridly at them as any powdered and face-painted Stormar palace servant might do, to visiting nobility, "await ye."

Iskarra made a face at him, and stalked soundlessly toward them. At their head she spun, pointed accusingly at him, then at the parchments, then shook her head grimly.

Gar rolled his eyes. "'Tis *coin* as might tempt me, lass, not some unfinished fancy of a book! Nor do I think he'd pause in hunting us down for *anything*, were we to take or damage so much as a scrap of this!"

Isk put a shushing finger to her lips, nodded to signify she'd heard him and agreed, and started down the stairs.

It was another short, straight flight, that at its end turned back under the table that held Malraun's writings, but a level lower, in a straight passage lined with doors, that ran to yet another descending stair.

There was just one thing in this passage, but the sight of it brought Iskarra to an instant halt. Gar, too, stopped the moment he saw it.

They had both seen more than a few hanged men before, dangling from executioners' nooses from high Stormar balconies for the sea-craws and gulls to peck at. This hung the same way, but it was a partial suit of armor, quite possibly with no body inside it, and it was hanging in the empty air from nothing at all; from the silent, invisible force of Malraun's magic rather than a noose.

Its helmed head drooped as if it was dead, unconscious, or asleep, but its gauntlets gripped two drawn swords. It floated motionless, the leggings of the armor having no feet to them and apparently no legs inside them; those empty tubes of buckled-together metal well off the ground, their lowest edges about at the level of Garfist's knees.

It looked suspiciously like a guardian of some sort, that would suddenly awaken to hack at any intruder who came too close. Gar and Isk if they dared step off the stair, for instance.

Yet step forward they must, eventually, or retreat back up through the tower. Would the armor fly after them, and try to strike at them with those swords? Would awakening it raise a magical alarm, to alert Malraun—or other magical guardians—of their presence?

"I *hate* magic," Garfist muttered, more to himself than to his lady.

Isk's reply was a shrug—and a bold descent, down the last steps and into the passage.

She kept her hands near her daggers, but held and waved no weapon. Garfist watched, his body tensed to spring at the silently-waiting armor and his sword ready in his hand, but the floating metal never moved, reacting not in the slightest when she slipped warily past it.

It hung there unmoving. Isk reached the far end of the passage and the stair leading down, and beckoned to Garfist to join her.

Warily, arm itching to draw back his sword and give the floating armor a glorking good, hard *hack* while it was an obligingly unmoving target, he trudged past it, looking back twice to make sure it wasn't stealthily drifting after him and raising its blades.

It never moved.

With a shrug of wary disbelief he joined Iskarra— who promptly brushed his cheek with a kiss, and set off down this new stair, another short flight down into a passage almost a mirror image of the one they'd just traversed. The midpoint of this one held an identical footless, apparently empty floating suit of armor with swords in hand, and led to another stair.

Garfist swore under his breath, coming down the stairs slowly and glancing back at the first suit of armor for as long as he could—only to find himself staring at a second one. He retreated up the stairs a step or two, to peer and make certain the first guardian—for so he firmly thought of them, believing they could be nothing else—was still there. It was.

Two steps down, and there was the second suit of armor. Back up again. The first one floated just where it had been when they'd first laid eyes on it.

He descended all the way, this time, sword up but not slowing, to walk past the second guardian to where Iskarra was waiting in silent, nodding patience at the head of yet another stair. It was longer, descending about twice as far as the previous flights.

"Not like in the tales, this," Gar whispered to her. "No tentacles coming out of the walls, yet, nor empty suits of armor hacking at us... not that I'm disappointed."

"Hold your tongue," she breathed back, her manner furious. "We have *no idea* what might awaken such menaces, but it bids fair to be more likely that silence is safe, than that your *suggesting* things will keep them from happening."

"Yer wisdom, Snakehips, overwhelms me," Garfist growled sulkily. "As always."

Iskarra rolled her eyes, tapped him severely on one cheek in a pantomime of a slap, and went on down this new stair. Only to stop again, a few steps from the bottom, and stare all around warily.

Garfist joined her, sword up and stopping three steps up so he could swing it, if he had to, without slicing her.

Together they beheld a room, the largest they'd yet found in Malraun's fortress, that stretched away from them to the by-now-familiar descending stair at its far end. Its ceiling was twice the height of any of the rooms they'd traversed thus far, and at about its center, a podium or railed balcony thrust out from one wall at the height of the skipped floor-level; it was reached by its own stair that clung to the wall and then curved out to join the jutting vantage-point. Aside from its wooden rail, the balcony and its stairs seemed to be made of the same smooth, fused stone as the walls. At one spot, the floor of the balcony rose up into a sloping-topped table or lectern. There were books, one of them spread open, atop that sloping surface.

The room seemed to be the site of an unfinished magic... but had the casting just been interrupted, or was it some slow, long-proceeding project?

Silence reigned. Freshly-carved wooden staves leaned in an untidy bundle against one wall; two of them had already fallen to the floor.

A large white circle had been drawn in the center of the floor, and from its chalk—if that's what it was—a strong, moving glow rose, like an ankle-deep band of dancing sparks. Out from the circle projected curlicues and flourishes drawn in the same glowing substance, the largest of them forming arms that in four—no, five—cases made rings that enclosed runes drawn on the floor in glowing red and gold.

Above that central circle, items hung in the air, glowing with the same white, dancing-sparks radiance as the circle.

A helm, a cloak—spread wide as if pegged out on an invisible rack to dry—and two gauntlets, seemingly placed to await someone standing in the circle donning them. Or perhaps anyone stepping into the circle would awaken spells that would magically thrust the items onto them, like an invisible maid or manservant dressing them.

Something else was hovering in the air above those four motionless items, swirling in the air beside the little balcony. It seemed to be a slowly-turning whorl or point-down cone of tiny lights; dim radiances that looked more like water droplets than sparks. As Isk and Gar peered at them, they seemed to turn a trifle faster, and some of them winked out of existence—or visibility—while others winked in, and faint, gentle chimings arose from them. The point of their cone hung directly above the floating helm.

Iskarra spun around to glare at Gar and whisper fiercely, "Touch *nothing!*"

Before he could grumble out a reply she was down off the stair and trotting quietly across the room, keeping well back from all the glowing lines on the floor. Up the balcony stairs she went in a rush, not touching the stair-rail, only to come to a smooth halt on the top step and from there look carefully at the books on the lectern.

She nodded slowly as she read from the open book, then turned and scampered back down the steps without ever setting boot on the balcony. Going to the staves leaning against the wall, she carefully plucked up one of the toppled ones, hefted it in her hand—and then leaned out to gingerly poke at the floating helm, trying to move it.

Three careful prods left her panting with the effort of stretching out her bony frame to its utmost without letting the staff waver down into any sparks, but she'd touched no glowing white lines, and the helm now floated in a new spot, shifted sideways a little more than its own width.

Garfist sighed, and turned on the stair to face back the way they'd come, so he'd be ready if two flying suits of armor silently erupted down on their heads.

"Isk," he rumbled warningly, "ye're up to something. And telling me nothing, just as ye usually do. Give. *Now*."

"Old Ox," his longtime partner replied merrily, replacing the staff back on the floor in just the position she'd taken it from, "Malraun has left these floating things waiting for some time of great need, such as when he's in a big fight and needs to snatch up some timely aid. The cloak to shield him and help him fly without spending a spell to do so. The gauntlets to subsume certain blasting magics normally shot out at the world with wands; he'll be able to point fingers instead, and so unleash those dooms. The helm to let him see and hear far away, and pry into minds. Yon cone contains spells to sear and ravage the minds of others he touches with his own—if they're wizards, to try to enthrall them, and if they're simpler folk like you and me, to fry us into mind-slaves or walking mindless things."

"So ye moved the helm, why?"

Isk smiled sweetly. "Now, instead of the cone pouring its powers temporarily into the helm, it will unleash them right into the head of whoever stands in the circle. So if Malraun is in a great and excited hurry, and doesn't notice my little adjustment, he'll end up with his mind rocked and cooked for a bit, not smugly able to blast the brains of others. *I* think wizards in Falconfar are more than powerful enough."

"While *I* think we should get the defecating greatfangs out of here!" Garfist growled, waving his hands in mimicry of a Stormar hedge-wizard casting a spell with many a florid flourish.

Giggling, she ran to take his hand. They hurried across the room together to the far stair down, staying well away from all glowing lines.

"THE GOOD WINE, you glorking bastard," Pelmard Lyrose snarled, backhanding the flagon into a clanging moot with the nearest tree. "Golden firefalcon, to my lips, in my next ten breaths."

He did not bother to add: *Or you die.* That was understood.

It was almost dawn, and he had a gloomy feeling that the firefalcon, when he got it, would be the last wine he'd ever swallow.

Now he'd not have time to properly savor it, Falcon take the dolt. Sourly, knowing some of the knights were smirking at his haggard, reluctant face, he strode over to them, one after another, making certain there was no confusion over which archers would be placed where.

The firefalcon came—still in its flask, and sealed; Pelmard nodded approvingly at the knight's prudence, broke the seal, and drained it in a long, swallowing gasp and swig, ignoring the proffered flagon. Nodding curtly to the man and handing back the empty flask, he wiped his mouth with the back of his hand and drew on his war-gauntlet. His bodyguard thrust forward an unshuttered dark-lantern so its light fell upon Pelmard's gage, and he promptly waved it in the signal. Around him, with a muffled thunder of boots on turf, his little army set forth.

"Off to our deaths, all of us," Pelmard mumbled under his breath, as he followed them, his bodyguard moving with him like a well-trained mount. "*Thank* you, Father. Mother. Bitch of a sister."

Boots and all they forded the river—amid splashings that Pelmard thought would rouse the town, but didn't seem to—and trudged up into the misty gloom.

Irontarl wasn't yet fully awake; all they met were a few sleepy cooks and stablemasters wandering about getting various cauldron-fires going, spitting thoughtfully into the darkness, hissing curses at their own sore backs or stiff limbs, and emptying their bladders over the piles of refuse alongside walls or behind buildings. The Lyrose knights moved among them like shadows in a hurry, using their daggers here and there, and ignoring those who ignored them.

Soon enough, he heard a *clink-clink* of sword tapped on sword from a nearby rooftop. It was answered by the same sound, several buildings over—and then by a sporadic chorus of many clinkings, each signaling that Lyrose archers had reached the rooftop they'd sought.

Well, *that* had been easy enough. Dawn was just about to break—or creep in across the Raurklor, shedding shadows, as it always did in Irontarl—and it seemed all his men were in place.

Some of the ground-mists were stealing away down to the river already, and if he peered hard at where he knew they were, he could almost make out the frowning walls of Hammerhold.

Pelmard allowed himself a shrug and a smile. "Well, at least we'll be dying in style," he murmured, too low-voiced for his bodyguard—Baernel, a veteran knight who would gladly die for Lord Magrandar Lyrose, who'd been assigned to guard Pelmard for that very reason—to hear.

He heard the creaking of the cart before he saw it. The first rumblewheels of the day had been sent forth from Hammerhand's castle in the fresh dawn, down to Irontarl to buy whatever they were shortest of, in the Hammerhold kitchens.

In the swiftly brightening light on the steep hillside, Pelmard could see the open cart was crowded with sleepy-eyed scullions and an even sleepier-looking pair of guards. Those two armsmen didn't even get up when the wagon halted—and were pinned to the wagon, right where they sat, when Lyrose bows started to twang.

Pelmard grinned at that—and at the more than dozen scullions who fell, wearing arrows, just after they'd jumped down from the wagon to head down to various shops.

A few survivors turned and ran back up the hill. Pelmard's archers felled two of those fleeing folk of Hammerhold, but the range was extreme; most of the shafts fell short.

As a bright morning unfurled and shutters began to roll up and night-gates squeal back from in front of doors all over Irontarl, the Hammerhold hostler whipped his horses frantically and got the cart rumbling in a hasty, bouncing half-circle, to try to make his escape. It almost turned over, but ended up thundering back up the hill, the driver desperately lying flat and the rumps of his kicking, rearing horses taking the arrows that had been meant for him.

Pelmard barked out his mirth as he watched, knowing he'd have nothing much to laugh at, all too soon.

About now, for instance, as a warhorn bellowed out from the walls of Hammerhold.

The castle looked even darker and taller than usual in the brightening morning. As he watched, mood darkening swiftly, its gates were flung wide and a small flood of men emerged.

Forty bowmen, perhaps a few more, on foot. Men in helms and leathers or even less, hastily mustered and sent forth. They came trudging down the hill, splitting up into groups of three and four.

"Closer, you fools," Pelmard growled at them, willing them on into the reach of his waiting archers. "Just a few strides *closer*."

As if taunting him, the men of Hammerhold halted just out of bowshot, and waited.

By now folk in Irontarl had seen them, and the arrow-bristling bodies in the street, and some of the shop shutters were hastily slamming down again. There were shouts, and some scurrying back to homes.

That Hammerhold warhorn rang out again, and another forty-some bowmen came striding out. Helmed and armored, all of these, and fanning out on the hillside into trios and foursomes. Down they came, not hurrying, as Pelmard's heart sank.

He could see arms lift to point at this rooftop of Irontarl, and that one. Marking his own bowmen.

They slowed and readied their bows. More than two to his one, now—and glork if that warhorn wasn't blatting again, and now Hammerhand's spearmen were starting out of his gates.

Pelmard watched them in deepening despair, then turned on his heel to cast a look back behind him at Lyraunt Castle. Just one figure was visible, on the highest balcony. His sister Mrythra, watching him. Glork it, he could *feel* her malicious smile.

Turning away from that torment, he looked back at the Hammerhand forces, now streaming down the hillside. A hundred spearmen? Or more?

"Oh, *shit*," he said aloud, knowing just how swift and messy his doom was likely to be.

"This is my father's mistake," he announced calmly, for Baernel's ears. "Though my mother and my sister can be *very* persuasive, when they speak together. I wonder how Burrim Hammerhand got to them, to persuade my father to this folly? We dare not lose this many archers—or all Lyrose may well be swept away."

He turned and looked at Baernel then, but saw only contempt in the man's eyes.

"Save your breath," the knight snapped. "I wear a gift of the wizard Malraun—crafted especially, to foil the blasting magic of your ring."

Meeting that cold gaze, Pelmard felt his sudden urge to command the man to lead him back across the river onto Lyrose lands, to observe or outflank or undertake some such vital mission, dying away.

Something tapped his shoulder gently, and he looked away from Baernel's face to seek the source of that touch.

The knight's drawn sword was waiting, steady and deadly, its point aimed squarely at the gap under Pelmard's arm, where only leather protected him.

Pelmard Lyrose looked at it, then back up at its wielder.

"Ah, well," he told the knight, managing a twisted smile. "Time to die valiantly. Or otherwise."

Chapter Twenty

MALRAUN THE MATCHLESS raised his hand with a smile—and blasted down a pleading Narmarkoun, a blubbering-with-fear Rod Everlar, and six shadowy Stormar wizards, one of them a tall and mysterious figure with the antlers of a stag and a face that was two blazing white eyes floating in a shroud of darkness, all in one blazing instant of magic.

Watching warriors of three armies moaned in fearful awe and went down on their knees to him, there on the hilltop. Malraun ignored them. Instead, he reached down to the woman on her knees before him, who'd torn open her gown in abject surrender, plucked her up as if she weighed no more than a feather, and slung her over his shoulder. With the Empress of all the distant Emaeraun Empire riding warm against him, her rear in the air as she gasped out her loyalty and obedience to the ground behind his boots, Malraun turned his back on those armies, and set off for the nearest bed.

It obligingly appeared, wide and familiar—the bed from conquered Darswords—on the hilltop right in front of him, and Malraun threw the Empress down on it and plunged into her warm, yielding depths...

There was something warm and heavy on his left shoulder, and he... he was coming awake.

To look at a ceiling he knew. He was in the best bedchamber in Darswords, on his back in the rumpled bed with Taeauna snuggled against him.

Hmmph. No blasting of Narmarkoun and the rest yet, then. And the cruel Emaeraun Empress would sit idly tapping the arms of her throne for a day or six longer. He had a few lesser and more local tasks to see to, first.

Such as enjoying the last, wingless Aumrarr in all Falconfar. Loyal she might now be, thanks to his magic, but she slept still. Powerless to resist him forcing herself upon her, that most delicious of bed-pleasures.

He crossed her wrists, one over the other, and bound them that way with the simplest of spells, then spread her ankles far apart with the same spell, reversed.

That awakened her, so she was blinking at him in surprise when he snarled, "Receive your Doom!" and flung himself on her.

"Willingly," she managed to gasp, fighting for breath as the bed creaked and groaned under his bruising assault. She tried to cradle her long legs around him, tried to reach down to caress his back and shoulders... but fell back exhausted, defeated by the iron grip of his magic.

Malraun chuckled and spat out a word, and suddenly she *could* move, and tugged hungrily at him, seeking to claw him farther, tighter, closer...

He bit her breasts cruelly, laughed, and reared back out of her yielding, arching himself in triumph as he neared his moment of greatest pleasure—

Then, in an instant, his face changed. He stiffened in astonished dismay, and became a statue above her.

Taeauna watched rapture melt into anger on Malraun's darkly handsome face, with sweat just beginning to glisten at his temples. Grimacing, he flung up a hand to clutch at his head, his fingers like talons.

"What idiocy *now?* I swear, these Lyrose *dolts...*"

Still snarling, Malraun the Matchless flung himself back from her and off the bed, landing on the floor beyond with an awkward crash. Wincing and limping, he rose and scrambled across the room to his discarded garments, snatched up his belt of wands from where they lay atop the rest, and—was gone.

Taeauna fell back on the bed, her wrists and ankles tingling, and smiled a lopsided smile at the ceiling-beams.

Her lord and Doom was making a habit of teleporting away to seek trouble without even bothering to get dressed. Now, when a *lass* indulged in such behavior, she acquired a certain reputation...

* * *

"SLAY ME NOT!" Pelmard shouted desperately, slipping in blood again. That traitor Baernel had turned and fled—sprinting back to Lyraunt, to report, of course—the moment the nine Hammerhand knights had come trotting around the corner of yonder pottery with swords drawn, and come for him.

They'd known *exactly* where he was standing, and must have run a long way wide, out and around most of Irontarl and risking arrows all the way, to avoid getting caught up in battle with the desperately-fighting, retreating men of Lyrose. Now, panting behind their helms—full plate armor, all of them, and better than his own!—these Hammerhand hounds were here for him.

"Stand back! A ransom! I am Lord Pelmard Lyrose, heir of House Lyrose!" he snapped, tucking his sword under his arm so he could use that hand to pluck off his other gauntlet and bare his ring.

A hurled dagger caught fire across his fingertips the moment they were uncovered, and clanged away. *Falcon hurl, they knew about the ring!*

"Back from me, damn you!"

Pelmard backed away himself, let fall his gauntlet, and faced them with blood-dripping hand and raised sword. "The Forestmother will curse you with ill luck for this, all your days!"

One of the knights snorted, by way of reply.

"Die," another replied coldly, as they spread wide to come at him from all sides, and cut off his retreat. Calmly, not hurrying, they closed in.

Pelmard backed away again, well aware that the river-mud was a mere pace or two behind him. He bent his will and Malraun's gift flashed, lancing out and through the eyeslits of a helm worn by one of the outflanking knights. Who staggered, and then fell.

Goading his fellows into a snarling charge.

"Malraun!" Pelmard shouted desperately. "Aid, I beg of you! Lyrose has need of you, mighty Doom! *Malraun!*"

They were rushing him now, trotting in with a forest of cold steel swung back to hack and thrust and—

Pelmard got his visor down just in time, swung desperately, clenched his bared hand and felt the ring-magic blaze forth again, and—

Steel rang on steel, jarring his arm, and cold hard steel hacked and thrust at him from all sides, squealing off his armor, flinging him back, their batterings crashing heavily against his ribs and face.

Half-dazed, Pelmard fought to see a foe well enough to use the ring again, trying to tuck his hand back into its armpit as cold blades came slicing at it, cutting away that thumb... The pain was sickening, and his helm was half-turned on his head, blood gushing out of his nose inside it and burning pain blossoming from his torn ear; he could see only out his left eye-hole...

He swung his sword feebly and blindly, as someone struck shrewdly at his ankles and sent him staggering...

Into the hard, punching embrace of someone else, who tore off Pelmard's helm with one cruelly-clawing gauntlet, hair and most of the other Lyrose ear coming with it, to snarl hatred into Pelmard's despairing face and—drive his sword home, up and under Pelmard's cods, sharp and high and so utterly, utterly *cold*...

"Mrythra!" he gasped, or tried to. "I love youuuuu—"

He never saw the sword that swept in along his shoulder-plates then, to bite deep into his neck and half-sever his head.

It wobbled obscenely, still partly attached, as blood spurted, choking him. Pelmard Lyrose reeled and went down, still struggling to tell his sister his deepest longing. The Hammerhand knights thrust and hacked viciously, seeking to get that head off its shoulders and that ring on its finger cut well free of the rest of the man ere it could unleash more deadliness.

The last thing Pelmard Lyrose saw, swimming into his darkening mind on wings of magic, was Mrythra

Lyrose standing clutching the rail of the highest balcony of Lyraunt Castle, face twisted in revulsion. She pursed her lips, eyes meeting his, and spat in his direction.

And then burst into tears. "Pel!" she sobbed, as he fell from her, down, down into echoing darkness. "Darling Pel!"

"So how are these men of Earth with swords?" Syregorn asked, as casually as if he'd been inquiring about cattle breeds.

"Using them in battle, you mean?" Rod asked, inwardly cursing the eagerness the warcaptain's drug had given his tongue. "No one does, in the countries I lived in and did book tours through, anyway. Oh, street gangs use knives, but most people, if they mean to do violence, use guns."

"And what are 'guns'?"

"Uh, like blasting wands, only they fire tiny arrowheads into you. Without needing a wizard, nor the strong arm of an archer. Anyone can use one, even children."

"Women, you mean?" Syregorn looked startled. Then the curl of contempt returned to his mouth, and he asked scornfully, "Tiny arrowheads? They'd do no harm."

"Ah, but they do," Rod burst out, helpless to hold back his words. "A gun can drive that arrowhead right into your heart. Or through it and out the other side of your body, so all the blood pours out."

"And they need no skilled archers to do this?" Syregorn looked shaken.

Then he looked thoughtful.

The knot of fear inside Rod Everlar's stomach grew a little heavier, and a lot colder.

A LINE OF broad cobbles marked where the trampled turf of Irontarl became the always-mud of the river ford. Pelmard Lyrose's head thudded onto it and rolled free of his hacked and quivering body.

As it tumbled past, seemingly seeking river water, the gift of Malraun, adorning a finger now lying severed in the mud some paces away, flared into sudden blue fire.

That tiny conflagration was echoed by a much larger flame of the same deep, thrilling blue hue, roaring up out of nothingness in the street in front of the pottery. A flame that broadened, split in the center, and widened like a hole burning in the air—if the air had been tinder-dry parchment or stretched hide—to reveal an angry naked man standing in its heart, with a belt of sticks in his hands.

Abruptly the flame winked out, leaving the man behind. Darkly handsome face bright with rage, he jerked one of the sticks out of a belt-loop, leveled it at the nearest of Pelmard's killers, and snarled, "That man was *mine!* Mine to use and slay, not yours! *Mine!*"

The Hammerhand knights took one look at the naked madman and fled in all directions, running as hard as they'd ever run in all their lives.

"Die, you stupid backland brutes!" the Doom shouted, voice cracking in his mounting rage. "*Die!*"

The wand spat fire, plucking a running knight off his feet and turning him into crisped bones and blackened, creaking armor in long, frozen moments where he hung in midair, quivering in the roiling heart of flames.

A bolder Hammerhand knight ran desperately at the naked man from behind, sword reaching.

Malraun spun around, letting the belt fall as he clutched another wand from it, brought it up, and unleashed its power right into the charging knight's face.

Which promptly ceased to exist, bursting apart in a spray of red gore, fragments of bone, and shards of shattered helm.

Malraun calmly sidestepped the toppling corpse, sweeping his belt of wands to safety with one bare foot as he did so, and told the next knight, as he fed that unfortunate the results of both wands, "I am furious. Much time and coin I've spent, shaping human tools, and you destroy them in a thoughtless moment. Well, the *next* time you might find yourselves about to make a shambles of my plans, *think*."

The by-then-headless corpse toppled, its legs burned away.

"Oh, dear," Malraun snarled at it. "I've left you nothing to think with. *Such* a pity."

He bent, took up his belt, calmly buckled it around his naked waist, replaced the wands he was using and selected two others, and set off along the streets of Irontarl, blasting every armored man or rooftop archer he saw—and turning often to make sure he saw them all before an arrow or spear could find him.

When one of the wands faltered and spat sparks rather than slaying beams of magic, Malraun thrust it back into its loop and snatched forth another.

This one didn't spit; it roared, blasting buildings as well as men. Walls and roofs in Irontarl crumpled and collapsed, spilling screaming men down to thud heavily onto the ground and taste Malraun's other wand while they were still writhing feebly.

Man after man he slew, Hammerhand and Lyrose alike. Until the men cringing behind buildings and cowering flat on roofs decided this terrible wizard was blasting everyone his eyes fell upon—and rose, took up their last arrows, and started frantically trying to fell *him*, their warring causes temporarily forgotten.

As a growing storm of shafts sought the naked man standing alone, Malraun smiled a tight smile and fed them death.

After all, when they were all dead, he could always turn and conquer Tesmer.

DAWN WAS COMING to the garden of Malragard, and the singing, urgent excitement surging in Rod Everlar was fading with the night-gloom. His tongue was slowing to its usual speed, and he found himself able to choose his words, not always instantly offering what he knew Syregorn most wanted to learn.

The drugs inside him must be nearly exhausted. He faltered, seeing Syregorn's cold eyes boring into his, and fell silent.

Whereupon the warcaptain reached out a long arm, announced briskly, "Night is fled; time to be up and doing again!" and dragged Rod to his feet.

The Lord Archwizard of Falconfar stumbled, feeling strange, but Syregorn's grip—now on his left arm, just above the elbow—was firm.

The warcaptain rushed the reeling man of Earth along the grassy garden paths, his knights grinning as they fell into step behind Syregorn.

Who dragged Rod Everlar straight to the door into Malragard—where everyone came to a sudden, startled halt.

No one had seen it open, but that thick, heavy stone door was now yawning wide, revealing a stone-lined passage stretching off into darkness broken by no lantern. A silent, waiting maw.

The knights shuffled their boots uneasily, hanging back.

"Never seen such an obvious trap," Reld muttered. On either side of him, Perthus and Tarth both nodded.

Syregorn grinned at all six Hammerhand knights coldly. "That's all right, my blades," he told them. "We've got us a bold Lord Archwizard, remember?"

His iron-hard grip on Rod Everlar's shoulder rushed the writer into a helpless, stumbling run forward—through the dark and waiting doorway.

* * *

"This has gone far enough!"

Lord Burrim Hammerhand was not a man who lived beset by fear, or shrank from thoughts of pain and battle. He had no stomach for sitting at home on a throne ordering men out of Hammerhold to stride forth and die for him.

If folk were to fight in his name, he wanted to lead them. Wherefore he was now crouching, anger warm in his throat, among prickly thistles behind the back wall of Irontarl's only smithy, with the Lord Leaf right behind him.

That anger boiled over. Standing up, Hammerhand waved his sword at Darlok, who was behind the stables across a wide and muddy street, with a score or so of Hammerhold spearmen.

"If we just wait in hiding," Hammerhand barked, "this mad wizard will blast us all dead, every last one of us! So we'd best charge him, at once and from all sides! Get every man who has a shield to the fore!"

Darlok nodded, waved his sword in salute, and turned to snap orders. Lord Hammerhand looked up. "Nelgarth?"

"Here, lord," came the low-voiced mutter from above. Archers were on the roof of the smithy, but keeping low, their bows stilled, as wands spat and roared along the street on its far side.

"I want all your lads ready," Burrim Hammerhand growled. "We're going to charge yon mage, and while he's blasting us down, I want every man to try to put an arrow through his head or his hands. Bury him in shafts!"

"Will do, lord."

Lord Hammerhand checked his own dagger, hefted his sword, and stamped down some thistles with his boots. He bore no shield. The smithy wall shook, and his eyes narrowed. He knew just where the wizard had to be, to unleash his wand through the smithy door. Which meant he just might live through this charge.

He waved his sword at Darlok in a silent but clear query, saw his warcaptain's nod, and beckoned.

The men of Hammerhold charged in a thunder of boots, no one yelling anything. Good; Darlok had given them the right orders.

Lord Burrim Hammerhand snapped, "Stay here, priest, unless you've got a blasting spell that can take care of yon mage." Without waiting for a reply, he trotted forward—and then burst around the corner at a run.

The wand-blast was fierce in its brightness. It slammed him off his feet and back around the corner in a hurtling instant, to crash to the street and roll to a stop, gasping in agony.

Then the other wand spat—right through the smithy wall at about head-height. Shedding a spray of its shattered stone, Malraun's magic raced across the street to hurl Hammerhold spearmen in all directions.

Cowering against the smithy wall, the priest of the Forestmother reached out a hand toward the man lying crumpled in the dirt a bare few strides away.

Smoke was rising from the lord of Hammerhold, and most of his right shoulder was missing, armor and all; what was left was blackened and torn, the arm below it dangling and useless.

Growling out his pain in a stream of half-formed oaths, Lord Burrim crawled back to the smithy wall, where the uninjured Lord Leaf was waiting, arms spread wide to receive him, face sharp with concern.

"Healing?" the lord grunted, as he reached the thistles again.

"What Hammerhand needs," Cauldreth Jaklar said soothingly, reaching out—to bring a knife up out of his sleeve and into Burrim Hammerhand's throat, hilt deep, before dragging it sideways.

Blood spattered the priest, and the lord of Hammerhold heaved himself up with a great, gurgling roar—only to slump down dead.

Jaklar kicked out desperately to keep his legs from being pinned under the brawny corpse's armored weight, then staggered to his feet.

"What Hammerhand needs, indeed," the Lord Leaf panted triumphantly at the lord who could no longer hear him, "so I can begin to bring the rightful rule of the Forestmother to Ironthorn."

He looked up, to see if anyone had seen the manner of Hammerhand's death—and beheld the warcaptain Darlok, helmless and scorched, staring at him from the far end of the smithy wall.

"I gave Lord Hammerhand peace," the priest snapped quickly, "as he commanded me to. The magic of the wand was turning him into something foul and evil." Spreading his hands, he added in his grandest, most pious voice, "By his blood, shed for all Ironthorn, may the Forestmother take him into Her arms and give him all pleasure, as a great stag in the forest."

Hammerhand's blood had drenched Jaklar's lap, and was now coursing down his legs, but he could see Darlok's face going from astonished hatred to awe and grief. Good. In a moment, if he cast the simple little spell that would make his hands glow, and proclaimed it as a sign from the goddess, he could—

Then, as the wands flashed and boomed again farther away, Cauldreth Jaklar saw someone else, far beyond Darlok's shoulder but approaching fast.

Helmless, her hair streaming out behind her and her eyes two dark and snapping flames of anger, Amteira Hammerhand was racing toward them.

Her sword was in her hand, and the look on her face proclaimed clearly to all Falconfar that she'd seen her father's slaying—and was now seething for the Lord Leaf's blood.

Cauldreth Jaklar swallowed, knowing he hadn't the right spells ready to blast her down like yon cursed wizard was felling everyone.

Hurriedly he spat out the words of his own feeble little spell, knowing the warcaptain wouldn't know what they were. He tried to make them sound sorrowful, so they'd be taken for some sort of prayer to guard Hammerhand's soul.

"Darlok," he snapped, the moment he was done, "I need you! *Ironthorn* needs you!"

"Command me, lord," the warcaptain said slowly, watching the conjured radiance rise up Jaklar's hands and arms, heading for the priest's face.

"The Holy Forestmother is with me," the Lord Leaf cried, letting excitement rise into his voice. "I can see now what I must do! Darlok, I need you to obey *me*, and rid us of the Hammerhands! If Ironthorn is ever to know peace, it can only be through the Holy Forestmother, and not this endless struggle of lord with rival lord, that can only and ever mean more butchery! With the Hammerhands gone, we'll have only two families to deal with—and House Lyrose weakened, at that! Darlok, I need you!"

The priest spread his glowing hands, his face now alight with radiance. "Will you obey me, and win holy glory? Or stand against me, and very swiftly be damned by the Forestmother to a horrible fate?"

Darlok stood uncertainly, bafflement clear on his face. Ridding Ironthorn of the Hammerhands? But that could only mean—

He heard the crashing footfalls of Amteira's boots, then, and turned his head.

The lady heir of the Hammerhands was enraged, her sword was out, and, panting in her haste, coming *fast*.

"Murderous *priest!*" she snarled, as she sped along the smithy wall.

Darlok swung to face her, sword rising, purely out of the habit of long years as a warrior in a valley at war.

Her face changed, and she swung at him, spitting, "You *too*, Dar?"

Darlok parried, but she struck twice and thrice, in an utter frenzy, and the third time burst through his guard.

The warcaptain lacked even time to protest before her steel slid into his shoulder, slicing in through the gap where his breastplate met his shoulder-plates.

Crying out, Darlok clutched desperately at his arm, trying not to lose his sword—and Amteira's blade burst into his mouth.

"*Traitor!*" she hissed, wrenching it free and running on, so the warcaptain was wrenched around, to stagger with blood spurting from his ruined face, dying on his feet.

The Lord Leaf had tarried to watch none of this. He was sprinting away, ascending a back street of Irontarl just as fast as he could, heading for the trees.

The Raurklor was a large cloak to hide in, and just now he needed to escape *anywhere*.

Amteira Hammerhand raced after him. "Murderer," she gasped, just once, then saved her breath for running.

Once in the forest, the priest could call on the Forestmother for aid. Yet even if he eluded her this day, she would follow Cauldreth Jaklar to the very roost of the Falcon, if that's what it took to slay him.

Her father deserved that, and far more. Once she'd torn this priest's life from him with her bare hands, and returned to conquer Ironthorn, it would be time to start in on the altars of the Forestmother.

By the blood of Burrim Hammerhand, shed by an unholy traitor, she would see this done.

Chapter Twenty-One

I T BLAZED BRIGHTLY, an arch of cold white fire flickering silently in this otherwise dark chamber of Yintaerghast. Darknesses coiled like smoke in the room's farthest corners, but he already knew they were echoes of the gate's magic, not lurking menaces.

Unless, of course, he chose to make them so.

Narmarkoun folded his scaly blue arms across his chest and smiled. This was going to be sheer glee. Plundering one world—perhaps even conquering it—to master another.

He'd anchored the dream-gate in Rod Everlar's words and descriptions. The man couldn't have been lying—no one could lie with that much urlivvin in them—but he could be insane.

Narmarkoun shrugged. Yet if the man of "Earth" was, what was lost? Six Dark Helms and a lorn, and he had nigh-countless to spare of both.

He'd given those six their orders and sent them on their way jovially, letting nothing into his voice, face, or manner that could give them any hint he might be sending them to their doom.

Not that he thought he was. This Earth should be just as the weak-minded man who hailed from it said it was; the man hadn't the wits to knowingly deceive anyone, even without the urlivvin.

Yet now it was time for someone bright enough to become a Doom of Falconfar to add his little touch. A lorn, sent after the unwitting Dark Helms to spy on them and see what really befell, rather than what they'd choose to report back to him.

Smiling, Narmarkoun strode to greet his lorn. It clicked its eerily birdlike way to join him, talons clacking on the stone floor of Yintaerghast, batlike wings folded tightly about itself, barbed tail arched up its back. Respectful—in as much as a horned, mouthless skull-face could show respect. Its eyes were downcast and submissive, its slate-gray head bent, apprehensive as to why the Doom it obeyed was now approaching a second time to go over orders given earlier.

Good. Let it ponder and worry. Narmarkoun let his smile broaden.

This time, his orders would be delivered in the friendliest of manners. As affable as he could be, to leave the lorn wanting to obey him—and also to leave it no doubt at all that disobeying him would mean swift and painful death.

Yes, send a wolf to watch the foxes—after sending the foxes to spy and plunder.

"D'YE THINK THIS is really it? The way out?" Garfist's growled whisper was dark with disbelief, and Iskarra didn't blame him. They'd descended more than a dozen—she'd lost count, several stairs back—floors, without seeing or hearing anyone moving about. Anyone. And even wizards need servants.

Especially wizards need servants, if they are as busy as Dooms of Falconfar, and want to fill their bellies with more than gruel and hardloaves. Moreover, Iskarra was willing to wager quite a few coins that enspelled monsters made poor cooks. And probably worse dusters and moppers.

"I hope so," she murmured in his ear. "Now be *quiet*. Can't you see what's waiting down there?"

They both could, which was why they were hesitating on an empty landing, restlessly pacing back and forth, so heart-singingly nervous.

From where they stood, a broad flight of wide, splendid steps curved down into what looked like a grand entrance hall. A lofty-ceilinged, crimson-walled room dominated by two rows of massive, polished mottled-stone pillars that marched down its heart.

Beyond the last pair of pillars, the chamber ended in a pair of narrow but very tall matched doors, opening in the direction of Harlhoh—and, Iskarra was willing to wager her very last coin, onto some sort of terrace and a commanding view out over the hold. Malragard, she was certain, would rise like the gauntleted fist of a conqueror above the roofs of Harlhoh, in a constant, daunting reminder of who watched over everyone and ruled their very lives with every whim.

There were six pillars in each row, each one perhaps three good strides from the next, forming a promenade or passage between the two rows about five paces wide. The spaces between the pillars at each end of the rows and the next pillars inwards along the rows were empty, but the three innermost pillar-gaps in each row framed silent, motionless statues.

Or perhaps more than statues. Neither Gar nor Isk doubted that a wizard's magic could hold a living beast as motionless as any statue, and yet keep it alive—and the six immobile shapes between the pillars looked very much alive.

They faced inwards, toward each other, and weren't breathing or moving in the slightest.

Which was a good thing, because they looked to be the most fearsome monsters either Gar or Isk had ever seen, bar a greatfangs.

The nearest was a dark purple-black hulk that seemed to rear up on the ends of its many reaching tentacles, its back an ominous hump pierced by several large, sunken, weeping black pits of eyes.

Next to the many-tentacled thing was a creature that floated in midair well off the hall floor. Its body was a wrinkled carrot-like mass that could probably balloon out to hold whatever it ate, for the blunt front end of it was split by a huge, fang-studded maw. That fearsome biting mouth was fringed about with many small and staring yellow eyes, and flanked by gigantic pincer-arms shaped like those of a hot sands scorpion.

Beside the floating maw was a creature the likes of which Garfist had fought before, long ago, only this one was easily seven times the size of the one that had nearly killed him. It was a slithering, flat-bodied snake that reared up to support a bulbous head large enough for three such serpentine bodies. That head sported a forest of needle-like, overlapping biting fangs and many, many eyes. Gar happened to know that the two large "main eyes" were falsenesses: gaps in the thing's tough black hide where its bony skull showed through, in socket-shaped plates stronger than his favorite sword had been.

Across the central promenade, facing that trio of monsters, was a second: a sleek but flaring-shouldered giant cat frozen in mid-prowl, that had a hairless, bone-armored snouted head, its jaws surrounded by large, thrust-forward mandibles like those of a gigantic beetle; a three-necked and three-headed wolf; and a spindly-legged spider that sprouted four long, thin, snake-like necks from its central body, all of them ending in nasty-looking, stabbing poison-stingers.

"That last one probably drinks blood through those four stingers," Iskarra murmured, "and I just *know* they're all real, and alive—and that something we'll have to do, to get out, will rouse them all."

"Dooms of Falconfar are right bastards, ye know?" Garfist agreed, peering down at the six monsters with narrowed eyes. "Is there a door hereabouts we can get behind, and hold closed, if those things awaken and come after us?"

Iskarra gave him a forlorn look. "Do I *look* blind or forgetful?"

She waved one bony arm at the walls around them. "I've sought with these eyes, yet not found. I suspect there are quite a few doors in that far wall, across the entry hall, but I can't see them. Can you? Moreover, Old Ox, I find myself strangely unwilling to go strolling down past yon beasts to get a better look."

"Right," Garfist growled. "*I* will, then." He set off down the stairs at a lumbering trot, ignoring Iskarra's desperate hiss from behind him—even when it rose into a scream.

RAGE STILL AFIRE in him, Malraun aimed his wands at the shop that offended him—its roof was heavy-laden with Hammerhand's archers, albeit cowering flat on their faces, hiding from him—and unleashed their fires.

The shop exploded in flames, its roof torn to tatters and hurled back up the hill to Hammerhold, shedding broken or shrieking bodies all the way. The thuddings and spatterings of their landings made a brief, dull rain as he turned to glare at the next refuge where warriors were hiding from him: a large but ramshackle old barn that… ceased to exist as his wands howled once more.

There wasn't much left of the heart of Irontarl, now, and his rage was dying down. Almost as fast as the flames his wandfire had spawned, that now danced here and there, licking through blackened beams and ruined ashes beneath.

Malraun turned away from his carnage with a snarl, suddenly weary of it all. He'd blasted almost everyone he'd seen, and what had it achieved?

Well, Hammerhand would no longer lord it over Lyrose—if there was anything of Lyrose left, to stand anywhere in Ironthorn.

As he glared at Lyraunt Castle, he saw a woman turn on its highest balcony and flee inside. Mrythra Lyrose.

Malraun the Matchless sighed. Would he be reduced to enthroning a spiteful lass? Or marrying her off to Tesmer and getting caught up in endless skirmishes with Narmarkoun the Cowardly Lurker, and all his walking corpses?

Pah; fancies to entertain later. Right now, he must see for himself what little was left of his Lyrose tools.

He took off his wand-belt and held it high as he waded the river, then rebuckled it around his naked, dripping body and stalked unconcernedly up to the gates of Lyraunt Castle.

As guards fled at his approach, leaving those tall doors untended, Malraun noticed they were fire-scorched and blood-spattered.

He found himself utterly uncaring as to why, and managed a shrug. Increasingly he was uncaring and uncurious. Perhaps that was what had afflicted Arlaghaun. Perhaps it was the price of rising to rule all Falconfar.

Right now, he didn't care to even bother thinking about it. A wand found its way into his hand, roared at his command, and the great gates ceased to bar his way.

He strode through the smoke of their destruction. Let their fate be shared by all who hampered his path, or defied his will.

"ONE THING'S CERTAIN," Garfist growled, ignoring Iskarra's raging commands, "and another's likely. 'Tis certain that if we stand waiting here long enough, we *will* be discovered. Probably by a Doom of Falconfar returning home, who can blast us to ashes in half a breath, if he's feeling merciful. The likely thing is that someone will come upon us right now, if ye don't *shut up*."

He whirled around to deliver these last words right into Iskarra's furious face, with slow and heavy menace. She blinked at him—and shut her mouth.

In the resulting silence, Garfist smiled, gave her a nod of pure pleasure—and stepped off the bottom step of the stairs, turning sharply to the right to stalk along the wall.

A glow of light promptly kindled in the empty air just inside the tall front doors of Malragard.

Iskarra stared at it—and then turned her head sharply to glare at the pillars and their statues.

Had one of those motionless monsters moved?

Garfist trudged along the wall as if heading unconcernedly home down a deserted lane at the end of a tiring but satisfying day of field-work, paying no apparent attention at all to what was happening elsewhere in the entry hall.

He was watching, though. When something rose silently up out of the apparently solid stone floor in the heart of that brightening radiance before the doors, and it turned out to be a stone table strewn with gems and gold—coins, a huge crown and scepter, and an orb thickly encrusted with jewels—he veered toward it.

"*No,*" Isk snapped from behind him, in the cold tones of command. "It's a clear trap, Gar. If those are real at all, touching them—mayhap even stepping too close to the table—will mean your death. Let's just get out of here. Alive."

Gar hesitated, one boot raised. Then he put it down, turned with a snarl, and trudged back toward the wall again.

Where Isk was waiting. Together they walked along the rest of that wall, then turned along the front one to reach the door.

Where Garfist paused, looked back at the table strewn with treasure, and hesitated again.

Whereupon all of the statues—or monsters—turned their heads to look at him.

NAKED EXCEPT FOR his belt of wands, Malraun the Matchless strode into Lyraunt Castle. It should have been bustling at this time of morning—and indeed, the stink of the sizzling sliced roast boar of the morning meal wafting down its passages was strong, and setting his all-too-empty stomach to growling—but the place seemed deserted. Hall after hall he strode down, and room after room, with his wands up and ready, fully expecting to face arrows or hurled spears at every corner.

Nothing. He might have been padding through a tomb, if the singing, watchful tension of fear hadn't hung so strong all around, silently stalking the halls with him.

It was almost a relief to meet a guard at last, a dark-armored warrior standing before a closed door. Trembling, that worthy warned him away with raised sword, the despair of one who knew himself to be doomed clear in his voice.

Malraun didn't disappoint him.

Stepping over the smoldering corpse, he kicked open the door the man had been guarding, stood aside to let the volley of arrows from inside the room beyond whistle harmlessly past, and exchanged one of his blasting wands for one that would conjure a spying eye to swoop in through the open door and survey what awaited within.

A room of goodly size, with four guards standing as a living wall to bar approach to a door in the back wall, and six archers scattered around the room, two of them against the wall either side of the door he'd kicked open. Malraun sighed, put the spying wand away again, and blasted the chamber with enough destroying fire to scorch it to the bare walls, not just fell the men within.

Their raw, dying screams were still echoing around the room as he strode into it, on a force-road spun by yet another wand, an invisible bridge across floor tiles that were still cracking underfoot from the heat. A bridge that led straight to the door that had been guarded.

If he recalled rightly, it led up a stair into a gaudily luxurious private suite of Lyrose bedchambers. That held probably not much more than a guard or two more he'd have to butcher, before he finally came face to face with those he sought.

The mother and daughter. The last two and strongest Lyroses, likely to be useful to him still if they were clever enough not to succumb to any notions of treachery.

He used one wand with deft precision, causing the door to vanish with no damage at all to its frame or the walls around. Malraun smiled pleasantly at the guard who'd been lurking just behind it, poison-tipped war-trident in hand, and said, "Drop that and flee, and I'll let you live. Do anything else, and you'll join the ranks of the foolish dead before—"

The guard didn't wait to hear more. With a despairing shout he charged, hurling the trident. Malraun's force-wand spat, and the weapon spun around in midair to thrust deeply into guard's throat.

Staring and gurgling, the man went down. The foremost Doom of Falconfar sighed, stepped around the feebly-flailing corpse, and mounted the stairs.

He kept his blasting wand, but exchanged the force-wand for one that compelled instant slumber. He didn't like to take lives wastefully, and they'd be throwing cowering maids at him next...

They did. In growing disgust Malraun sent various frightened servants who were brandishing mops, bedpans, and tapestry-hooks toppling into helpless collapse, stalking on through rooms of rich draperies, soft fur rugs, and heaped multitudes of silken cushions. There was a trail of closed doors with furniture hastily heaped up behind them, and he used his force-wand to thrust these open, splintering some of them but sending no roaring flames nor shattering blasts through the rooms.

Until at last there were no doors left, and through the gaping arch that had held the last one, Malraun beheld the Lady Maerelle Lyrose and her daughter Mrythra huddled in each other's arms, cowering where the walls met in the farthest corner of that back bedchamber.

He cast swift glances at floor, ceiling, and about the room, seeking traps and lurking guards. None that he could see—not that he expected any. Silently the Doom of Harlhoh padded closer to the trembling women, his face carefully kept expressionless, his wands raised.

"Don't—" Maerelle blurted, as Mrythra mewed in wordless fear and buried her face in her mother's bosom.

ROD EVERLAR FOUND himself standing in a cold, dark, and silent room. There was no dust, and no hint of the lingering mildew that afflicted damp, long-unused stone chambers. In all other ways, the room might have been abandoned for centuries, so lifeless was the stillness.

He could barely see anything in the gloom, and so almost crashed into the chairs drawn up around a table. His knee slammed glancingly into one, his hand sought its arched back out of habit—and slowly and silently, the chair acquired a cold, green-rime glow out of nowhere, shining steadily more and more brightly, until it lit up the room.

Letting Rod—and the rest, Reld and Syregorn and the others, their swords raised and ready at Rod's back—see a closed door at the end of the room, and shelves on both sides of it that held dull metal coffers. These bore labels, and Rod peered at them.

"What say they, Lord Archwizard?" the warcaptain murmured.

"Thaedre," Rod read aloud, from one. "Muskflower." That was the next, and he turned his attention down a shelf. "Asprarr, Belphorna, Paeldoanch, Davvathlandar."

"Seeds," Syregorn explained curtly. "Is everything on the shelves these same metal coffers, or is there anything else?"

Rod looked, then shook his head. "Spade or something of the sort hanging from the end of this shelf," he replied, "but aside from that, no. Just the seed coffers."

"Then go on down the room and open that door," the warcaptain ordered gently. "Now."

MALRAUN LET ALL the contempt he felt show in his face as he said quietly, "Look at me."

They obeyed, stiffening into enthralled immobility as they met his burning eyes. His spell-probe was swift and brutal, rather than the insistent drifting deeper into their minds they were used to; this violation tore and bored on and ravaged all it found, leaving the shrieking chaos of nightmares to come.

What he found was clear enough, and surprised him not at all.

They were utterly terrified of him, so lost in their fear that they weren't far from gibbering on the dancing edge of insanity, but beneath that they were grieving the death of Lord Magrandar Lyrose— who had betimes been the lover of them both, Malraun learned, though Maerelle hadn't known that until this moment. Disgust at their craven brother was also strong in their minds, and deeper still he found ingrained fear, awe, and respect for Malraun the Matchless. They intended no treachery against their benefactor, and scorned Magrandar's small deceptions and treacheries against the Doom of Harlhoh as dangerous and futile foolishness. They believed they would have a better chance of shattering the moon than successfully defying the one called Malraun.

Learning that last belief should have left him satisfied, but Malraun found himself still angry. Soothing their minds not at all, he brusquely enspelled them both into stasis, then used the force-wand to wall them away in their corner behind an unseen barrier only someone mightier than a hedge wizard could breach, that would fade only after a day or so.

It was time to search Lyraunt Castle properly. *Someone* had been at work here, and if it was Narmarkoun, he knew his fellow Doom wouldn't be able to resist leaving a mocking little message or salute to tell Malraun who had been toying with his tools.

If he found no such flourish, another foe was at work—and discovering who would suddenly become the most important matter in his life just now.

Unless, that is, it was already too late.

Chapter Twenty-Two

MALRAUN THE MATCHLESS padded back out of the great hall, teeth clenched. Dark anger was rising within him again, so strong and sudden that it threatened to choke him—and so seethingly *futile*. He'd searched every last damp corner and gaudy chamber in Lyraunt Castle—long, wearying work it had been, too—and knew that from top to bottom of the fortress, no enemy was lurking. Just cowering maids, cooks, and guards, and the two Lyrose women who now ruled them all. Or would, if they hadn't all fled by the time Maerelle and Mrythra got awake and free of his magic—or been replaced by plundering Hammerhands.

Yet trace or no trace of a foe, someone who loved Malraun the Matchless not at all had been at work here. Witness the talking skull of Orthaunt hovering in the room behind him—and who could have managed to hide such a thing for so long, but a Doom of Falconfar or someone aided by an Archwizard of like power?—and the mindgem. Both waiting in his gates to harm or trap him, two sneering salutes from... whom?

Narmarkoun, most likely. And yet… somehow, this didn't *feel* like Narmarkoun's work. And if there was one thing Dooms of Falconfar named Malraun had proven to be good at down the years, it was hunches and feelings. Narmarkoun was busily scheming, yes, but what had befallen here in Ironthorn, to the Lyroses and to Lyraunt Castle had been the hand of someone else, some other baleful lurking mind.

Oh, he'd been wise enough not to blunder through either gate, nor try to use any magic at all on all that was left of Orthaunt, despite the skull's cold taunts, and so had suffered not a scratch. More than that, he'd *enjoyed* smiting and hurling down cattle-like Ironthar here and in Irontarl.

Yet Magrandar Lyrose was gone, and all of Malraun's magic couldn't bring him back. Which meant Ironthorn was as good as lost to this Doom of Falconfar, if he didn't spend far too much time— time he now lacked—steering and supporting these Lyrose women, shaping them into becoming what he needed them to be.

Indulging himself here in Ironthorn this morn had been costly. He'd spent magic out of these wands as if he'd been hurling dry tinder into an already-roaring bonfire, and gained nothing but guesses about who was behind it all, nothing but wind and fancies—and—and—

With a snarl of frustration and rage, Malraun spent more precious power from the wand he liked to use least of all, and took himself back to Darswords in an eyeblink.

He was not quite swift enough to get himself gone before a long, hollow laugh rolled out of the great hall. Cold and mocking mirth, meant for his ears.

By the Falcon, but there'd come a day when he'd enjoy destroying Orthaunt's skull!

ROD SIGHED, PUT his hand on the door's pull-ring, and drew it open.

Nothing happened. Silence and darkness reigned, both in the room he was standing in, and in what he could see of what looked like a small, featureless passage stretching past, beyond the door.

"Stay right where you are," Syregorn ordered, pointing his drawn sword at Rod like the wagging finger of a long-ago, hated schoolteacher.

Rod stared back at the warcaptain. "I'm the Lord Archwizard of Falconfar," he said calmly. "Remember?"

"You are a helpless coward, and a fool," Syregorn replied coldly. "Obey me, and we just might escape this place alive. Defy me now, and you doom yourself more surely than you do the rest of us. *I'll* see to that."

Rod gave the warcaptain his best expressionless look, trying to seem far calmer than he felt. Then he turned and stepped through the doorway into the passage beyond—and vanished along it.

"After him!" the warcaptain snarled, and the knights of Hammerhold boiled through the garden door into Malragard, waving their swords in thunder-booted haste.

Only to lurch to a cursing, baffled halt in the passage. They'd seen the bumbling outlander stride to the right, beyond the inner doorway they'd just come through. He'd gone right down this very passage, that seemed to stretch away from them forever into the night-gloom. Floor, walls, and ceiling, its every surface was studded with closed, identical stone doors.

"Gone" was right. There was no sign at all of Rod Everlar.

TAEAUNA WAS GONE from the bedchamber, but the bed had been neatly made. On it, three outfits—garments and matching belts and boots—were laid neatly out for him.

By the Falcon, the Aumrarr was a peerless cloak-and-boot maid, too!

Malraun grinned despite his rage, and snatched up the darkest finery. Clawing his way into it with more haste than elegance, he buckled the belt of wands around his middle, stamped the boots onto his feet, and hurried out of the room.

Morning was nigh gone, but Darswords was quiet rather than bustling. On all sides of him men were slowly gathering wood into corpse-pyres, ignoring more energetic workers: the rats that were scuttling and gnawing, the vaugren tugging at flesh and flapping their wings at each other in scores of half-hearted disputes, and the flies busily buzzing.

These vermin were at work on the dead, of course, who lay everywhere, heaped and sprawled where they'd fallen, or blasted into charred cantles and spatters. Yestereve, there had been more slaughter here than anywhere else the Army of Liberation had fought thus far. Now, most of his weary army was dozing, lounging boots-up idly playing at dice or cards, or slumped asleep in little groups among the dead, wherever they'd been sent on makework errands.

Malraun's lip curled. Out came a wand he used very seldom, as he peered this way and that, seeking the least-spoiled bowers of the grandest houses, and amid their shade… *there!*

With a cold and ugly smile, he met the startled eyes of Horgul's most trusted surviving battle-lord, and triggered the wand.

The man's face didn't even have time to slide from startlement into fear before he was lofted straight up into the air, yelling, as the foremost Doom of Falconfar pointed the wand skyward.

Malraun held him there, paying him no attention at all, as he peered about for Taeauna. And spotted her, soon enough, pointing work-crews with barrows this way and that. She was clearing the dead away from the wells, of course, trying to keep what the folk of Darswords drank untainted.

Tae, he thought firmly in her direction, feeling for, and sinking into, the familiar warmth of her mind.

She whirled around, her mind greeting his with its usual dark joy—or at least, paramount joy, for as always that emotion overlaid deeper things Malraun couldn't properly discern—and Malraun gazed into her eyes and summoned the Aumrarr to him without a word.

Taeauna hastened, coming at an eager trot around the heaped dead, threading her way quickly and adroitly through the almost-strolling warriors, and Malraun barely had to nod to get her to reach out a long arm to clutch the shoulder of another battle-lord as she passed.

That swaggering officer spun around to favor her with a sharp-eyed glare, saw Malraun as he turned, lost the glare in cringing fear in a paling instant, and hastened after Taeauna. Good.

Malraun lowered his wand to let the now silent, gray with terror battle-lord back to the ground, folded his arms across his chest, and awaited their arrival.

He was pleased to see even Horgul's brutes weren't utterly stoneheaded; by the time those three leaders of his army had gathered before him, the other battle-lords had noticed, and were hastily converging.

He waited, regarding them all coldly, until all but a handful had found a place to stop and stand in a silent ring around him, fearful eyes fixed on him.

Malraun smiled, just for a moment, and then snapped, "You will begin—right now—to plunder Darswords, burning nothing, and slaughtering only those who repeatedly resist you. Imprison all the rest in yonder barn until we depart. Then eat well; at full dawn tomorrow you will *all* march to Harlhoh. There I'll see you reprovisioned, for immediate march on Burnt Bones. You will conquer there as you did here, then march on to Ironthorn and serve it the same way. Go, and give orders in all haste; I want to see my soldiers sleeping—*sleeping!*—no longer!"

His face tightened, rage rising again. Thanks to the skull and the mindgem, he could no longer trust using the gates to "jump" his army from Harlhoh to Ironthorn. A wizard who knew what Malraun the Matchless was intending had obviously discovered the gates and made plans of his own—reducing his Army of Liberation to no swifter a mob of trudging metalhead brutes than any other predictable marauding host.

"You," he told Taeauna, "will come with me. On your knees."

Then he turned away from them all, knowing without looking that she would obey—would already be crawling after him.

All the way back to that bedchamber, where he would take her by the throat, beat her with fists and belt while thrusting pain into her mind, and command her crawling humiliation and obedience repeatedly.

As he took her to bed and used her savagely, commanding her to thank him and gasp for more, again and again, even as blood welled out of her—and he slaked his rage in enjoying every moment of it.

For he was the foremost Doom of Falconfar. And by the Falcon, he was going to behave accordingly.

"GORN," THALDEN POINTED out unnecessarily, "*that* door is starting to glow."

"Why, *thank* you, Thalden," Syregorn replied sarcastically. "Fortunate I am to have such an eagle-eyed knight along with me. Tarth, Reld: get to it and haul it open, stepping on not one of the doors on the floor on your way to it. *Move!*"

All six knights of Hammerhold flinched at his sudden roar, and the two he commanded to the door sprang to obey so precipitously that they stumbled and both almost planted boots on the doors underfoot.

They skidded to unsteady halts in front of the glowing door, waving their arms wildly as they clawed at the air to try to reclaim their balance—and in that instant, no less than three other doors along the passage were suddenly glowing, too.

"Syre," Tarth called uncertainly, "look you! Three more, I mark, are—"

"So they are," Syregorn snarled. "Yet I gave you and Reld an order, that you already seem to have *forgotten!*"

"Ah, aye, *yes*—" Tarth gabbled, whirling to join Reld, who was hauling on the door-ring in a sudden frenzy.

Whereupon the door exploded in a great gout of blinding light, whirling shards, and wet splatterings that covered the four wincing, cowering knights around Syregorn.

Splatterings that could only have been Tarth and Reld.

Syregorn glared bleakly down the passage at the remaining trio of glowing doors for a moment, and then snapped, "Thalden, go and look at what's behind where that door was. Perthus, the nearest door that's aglow. Jelgar, the next one. Onthras, the last. Touch no doors, mind, until we know what Thalden's found."

The surviving knights hesitated, then looked into the cold promise of his glare and slunk reluctantly past him and forward, walking slowly and unwillingly.

Thalden was the oldest of the four, but he reached his goal—the scorched and gaping hole where the door that had slain Tarth and Reld had been, which was nearest to Syregorn—first.

With slow, exaggerated caution, he ducked low, stretched himself forward, and peered around the edge of the doorframe.

Then he slumped down in relief, sighed heavily, and announced, "Nothing. An empty room. Dust and bare stone."

The warcaptain nodded. "Perthus? Jelgar? Onthras?" His voice was as calm and drawlingly low as if he'd been calling on them just to keep himself awake.

Perthus reached his door and stood there trembling, face grey-white.

Syregorn idly drew a dagger. They all looked back at him, watching it, and he could see in their faces they knew it was poisoned—and what he intended it for.

Perthus hissed out a curse, and suddenly, spasmodically, wrenched at the ring of his door.

Obligingly, it exploded, with the same blinding, Malragard-rocking blast, and the same wetly fatal result.

A little farther down the passage, Jelgar started to cry.

WITHOUT MUCH SENSE of surprise, Rod Everlar discovered he was trembling with fear. Syregorn meant to kill him, and had probably been under orders to do so all along. He'd seen the cold, clear promise of death in the warcaptain's eyes.

Yes, give the unwelcome outlander the drug to make him babble, learn all you can, then drag him into Lyraunt Castle in hopes he'll blast all the Lyroses to the starry sky and bring the wizard Malraun raging across Falconfar. Perhaps he'll manage to blast Hammerhand's foe down, or weaken the Doom enough that he can be dealt with. Then kill him, if Malraun hasn't already managed it in their spell-duel, or turned him into a frog—or serve Malraun the same way. If this Lord Archwizard out of nowhere is an utter failure, shrug, you face the same Malraun you always did.

All Rod had done was seize a bare moment of freedom to step through the doorway, run along the passage, yank open the first door he came to—less than four strides along a hall menacingly full of doors, like an Escher or Dali nightmare, doors on walls, floor, and ceiling!—and get it closed again, just as quickly as he quietly could.

He'd found himself in silent darkness. A dark room, L-shaped, with walls that started to glow faintly, ale-brown and only where they met the floor, all around him. A room full of tables with what looked like effigies on them: stone images of dead men and women and—and *things*, strange beast-headed, scaled creatures, all lying on their backs wrapped in shrouds. Or were they petrified corpses? They were incredibly detailed, and peering hard at them without getting too close, Rod couldn't see any tool-marks.

He had seen a door, however, around a corner at the far end of the room, and hurried to it. At any moment Syregorn's knights might yank open the same door he had, and come for him.

His trembling hands fumbled with the ring, but the door opened. The room beyond was already faintly aglow—and it held shelves of books, a desk with a high-backed chair, and—a rack of quill pens, bottles of ink, and stacked sheets of blank parchment!

Rod looked wildly around, half-expecting Dark Helms or something worse to come gliding out of the shadows to menace him. The room had two doors, one of them obviously opening out onto the passage of many doors, and the other, in the wall across from him, surrounded by bookshelves, connecting this room to some other chamber. Tiny mauve-white lightnings played across the spines of the tomes, in a clear warning that some sort of magic guarded them, killing Rod's rising curiosity in an instant.

Hesitantly he went to the desk, staring hard at it in search of lurking dangers, but finding nothing. Not that he'd probably recognize his doom, in a wizard's tower, until it claimed him...

Avoiding the chair, he leaned just close enough to the desk to pluck away the topmost sheet of parchment, watching to make sure nothing deadly was revealed beneath it. It was blank on both sides, and newly-made, with edges that weren't yet brittle— just a sheet of parchment under his fingertips, no more and no less; not writhing to change shape back into some horrific fanged monster.

Rod hesitated a moment more, than slammed the sheet down on the desk, plucked up the nearest bottle of ink, twisted out its cork with impatient speed, and plucked up the nearest quill. It had been cut sharp, but never used.

Standing over one front corner of the desk, he dipped the quill and started to write, trying to put his will behind the words, thrusting his fear and rising excitement into them.

If he could Shape himself to Taeauna, and away from Syregorn and his men...

A sharp smell arose, and a brief wisp of—was that smoke? Rod scratched and scribbled hard, his pen slicing along like the point of a sharp knife, bright sparks— *sparks?* No, tiny tongues of flame!—trailing his pen.

The parchment was starting to burn under his racing pen... and the thrilling power that surged through him when he Shaped wasn't... wasn't in him at all!

"BEG FOR IT! Beg for more!" Malraun spat, the riding whip slicing viciously across Taeauna's chest. Panting and sweating, he was riding her hard, lashing her harder and faster as she writhed under him, spreadeagled on the bed and trying to smile between gasps of love and pain. "Beg, I said!"

"Oh, Master! Oh, Malraun!" she hissed, eyes pleading for more, not for mercy. "Hurt me! *Hurt me!*"

He snarled in wordless glee, brought his whip back far enough to wipe sweat from his brow with the back of his forearm—and stiffened, incredulous rage flaring in him.

Again?

Something was tugging at his ward-spells, somewhere, something hostile that sought to destroy...

In Malragard! Something small and feeble; a hedge-wizard too feeble to emerge alive from where he'd intruded, perhaps, or one of his own guardian creatures, freed somehow from the magics that confined it...

Malraun thrust the warning flarings down deep in his mind, and brought himself back to Darswords, to Taeauna beneath him and this release he so sorely needed.

"*No,*" he snarled aloud, "not again! Not *this* time."

"Lord?" Taeauna dared to ask. He whipped her hard across the mouth by way of reply, giving her a look meant to be a quelling glare.

The leaping fire in her eyes told him she'd seen something else in his look, though; the tenderness he felt toward her. No one else cared about him, except as a foe to be destroyed; no one else welcomed his mistreatment of them. He took her by the throat, leaned down until their noses were almost touching—until the sweat now dripping from him wet her face—and growled, "It doesn't matter. Only *you* matter. Your surrender, most of all."

Her eyes danced with—joy? Something else; glee? Amusement? No, it must be love. She was smitten with him, lost in love for him.

He could still feel the warnings, faint and deeply buried, but cared about them no longer. They were the work of a failure; whatever or whoever was seeking to work magic in the very heart of Malragard was being foiled by his warding-spells even now, and persistence would end—could end—only in being burned to ashes.

ROD SPRANG BACK from the desk and watched the scorched paper smolder. Without his quill, its fire swiftly went out, leaving only a burned-through gap across it, a line of nothingness where he'd tried to write words.

Capping the ink bottle with his thumb, he snatched it up, thrust the quill into the same hand, and used his freed hand to open the door into the next room. Which was full of racks of clothing, and even a spine- and hook-studded, weirdly-curving suit of armor on its own stand.

Perhaps it had been the paper, or some spell cast on the study, or nearness to all those magical books...

It might just as easily be something else, but he hadn't a lot of choices. This wardrobe-room had its own door out onto the passage, and—yes!—another connecting door, to another room beyond it.

Rod opened that door as boldly as if Malragard was his own home, and found himself in a room that looked like a honeymoon suite bathroom in some luxury hotel, with marble steps up to a huge, kidney-shaped lounging tub—"spa" they called them, these days—full of warm, rippling, fruit-scented water. A handful of small spheres hung in the air above it, drifting aimlessly about... and flaring into bright-glowing, amber life at his approach.

Rod peered at the water just long enough to make sure no tentacled something was lurking in it or gathering itself to thrust up out of it at him with a watery roar, and then started staring at what really interested him in the room: its two doors. One out onto the passage, and one to a room beyond.

His business right now was with that second one; he swung it open as swiftly as he could, to reveal a luxurious, tapestry-hung bedchamber dominated by a huge fourposter and large, oval-framed pictures on the richly-paneled walls that held bright, moving scenes, like so many television sets tuned to different "exploring exotic global locales" programs.

Aside from a quick peer inside for Dark Helms or other lurking beasts or guards, Rod ignored the bedroom for now. What mattered was that the door connecting it to the bathchamber was open and could be held that way with the toe of his boot, and that he could write on it with his quill pen, to try Shaping again.

Calmly he dipped the quill, reached down, and started to write. He wanted to start low, in case the ink ran down the door and marred whatever he might try to write below it.

It did, but that hardly mattered. Even faster than on the parchment, his moving quill birthed fire in its wake, flames that flared up vigorously this time, blazing away merrily—and being echoed precisely, Rod saw with utter astonishment, on the bathroom's *other* door, long strides away!

He drew his quill back to stare, then tried to write again, watching that other door. Yes. Wherever his pen touched and burned the connecting door he was holding open, the door across the room that linked the bathroom with the passage that held Syregorn and the Hammerhand knights was burning, too, like he was writing on both doors at once, or as if they were carbon copies or linked by some sort of invisible tracing pantograph!

Rod cursed softly, and stopped trying to write. He was likely doomed to fail at Shaping from one end of Malragard to the other, no matter what he wrote on, or with.

Stepping back from the door, he took a long stride into the bedroom, let the still-smoking door swing shut behind him, and looked down at himself.

He wore pouches in plenty of Arlaghaun's mysterious magics, riding all of his crisscrossing belts and baldrics. Beneath and jutting out from between those many smooth bands of tooled leather were the now-hardened blobs and splashes of what had been metal armor. Rod shook his head.

No. He simply knew too little about what he was messing with to have hopes of intending to do something and then managing it. He'd literally be playing with fire, blundering about with magical effects—and unintended consequences—he knew nothing about, and wouldn't solve until too late, when it all blew up in his face.

About all Rod had that still seemed whole and reliable were his boots, the heavy war-gauntlets dangling from where he'd clipped them to one baldric, and one of his swords. It occurred to him that taking any clothing from the wardrobe-room hadn't even entered his mind. Now, he knew why. Without really thinking about it, he'd concluded Malraun would be able to trace him at will if he wore anything of Malraun's, no matter where he might go or how he might try to hide.

Rod sighed, becoming very much a scared and bewildered fantasy writer who didn't even know how to play at being Lord Archwizard of Falconfar, let alone wield the magical might of a Doom.

That was when he noticed that something had silently happened, in the few flashing moments he'd stood gazing and thinking.

A few steps away from him, the bed was no longer empty.

Chapter Twenty-Three

"STOP THAT," SYREGORN commanded coldly. "Jelgar, be *still!*"

The youngest of his three surviving knights sobbed uncontrollably, and all the warcaptain's roar accomplished was to make him flinch—and bolt down the passage, running wildly with arms flung wide and a wordless shout of terror rolling before him.

Door after door thundered under Jelgar's boots, and Onthras whirled around and looked to Syregorn for direction—should he fling out a hand to try to halt the runaway?

The warcaptain shook his head grimly, and pointed. Much nearer at hand, one of the glowing doors in the right-hand wall of the passage had grown brighter, and started to give off wisps of smoke.

As the three men of Hammerhold stared at it, the door started to bulge.

"Get back!" Syregorn bellowed at them. "Thalden, with me! Onthras, go after Jelgar! *Get away from that door!*"

The door was visibly melting now, its substance—which had appeared to be solid stone—sagging and sliding from where it was bulging, running down its smoothness in long lines of wetness, blobs that left glistening, smoking threads in their wake.

Spitting out a stream of curses, Onthras ran for his life, sprinting down the passage after Jelgar.

Who seemed to have silently and utterly disappeared.

The third door Onthras stepped on gave way, swallowing him before he had time to do more than start to scream.

Then it banged shut again, swinging back up to cut off his cry in mid-bellow. Magic, or unseen hands, had thrust it back upwards and closed again, restoring the floor of the passage.

As Thalden and Syregorn stared at where Onthras had so suddenly disappeared, the bulging door creaked almost mockingly and… stopped melting. They watched the bulge seem to sink in upon itself, the door straightening a little, as a strange reek reached them. The stink of its burning, no doubt.

"Jelgar?" the oldest knight asked quietly.

"As good as dead," Syregorn muttered. "Time to look to our own skins, Thal. I'd say our errant Lord Archwizard is as doomed as Jelgar. Let's just try to find a way out of here."

"Back outside, and over the garden wall?"

The warcaptain shook his head. "I saw someone try that in the other direction, once. Malraun's magic slices and impales anyone passing over the top of a wall, as if the blades of a dozen-some swordsmen are at work. No, we must go on and out the front doors, if we can."

"So, down this hall? What if more doors start to glow?"

"We get as far from them as we can, without stepping on a door," Syregorn said almost calmly. "I don't think they're really seeking to slay us. I think they're awakening because Rod Everlar is blundering near."

"So the Doom cleared away or hid his most useful magic, departed, and left this place as a gigantic trap for the Dark Lord," Thalden whispered.

The warcaptain nodded. "Looks that way. Now let's see how well we two can avoid becoming incidental sprawled corpses."

A smile almost touched Thalden's lips. "Is there a wager in the offing?"

Syregorn shrugged. "Not coins," he replied grimly. "Lives."

He started off down the passage, striding carefully along the left wall to avoid the doors in the floor. "Ours. Falcon be with us."

As it BOBBED and moved with every turn of Narmarkoun's head, the small, spinning brightness he'd conjured showed him a tiny Rod Everlar opening doors, trying to write on them, and birthing fire instead of words.

Narmarkoun watched with growing amusement, but less and less attention. The man was as clumsy and slow-witted as the most bumbling of wizards' apprentices; spying on him was good only for the passing entertainment.

Wherefore this particular Doom of Falconfar paid the silent little scene increasingly less heed, and bent most of his wits to exploring every gloom-shrouded crevice and alcove of what had been the castle of the *real* Archwizard of Falconfar.

Lorontar's magic slumbered—and in some cases stirred—all around him. Yintaerghast held power beyond anything even Arlaghaun had ever hurled, certainly far more than preening, swaggering little Malraun wielded now, at the so-called height of his powers.

And if watchful, patient, nigh-forgotten Narmarkoun could gain even a small part of it…

Everlar's progress through Malragard was blundering, but much faster than his own. If a wall was thicker than its counterpart, or started a hand-thickness out from matching that other wall, Narmarkoun wanted to notice.

Soon enough, his diligence was rewarded. One of the curved stones forming the foot-collar of a pillar stood the slightest bit higher than its neighbors. Pushing it cautiously down caused part of the smooth, curved flank of the pillar to descend with it, revealing a horizontal niche about the size of a long-bladed dagger.

The hiding-place was full of rolled parchment. A scroll. Narmarkoun smiled a tight blue smile and used his belt dagger to carefully lever the long-hidden treasure forth.

A stone he'd taken out of a cracked stone lintel scores of rooms away held one end of the scroll to the floor as his dagger-point teased the tight roll open. He kept his face shielded from any eruptions in the crook of his arm, working by feel; to etch searing sigils on a scroll to await the unwary was a trick that had been old even in Lorontar's time.

When he got it entirely open—without any blast, roar of flame, or rising wisp of sinister spores—the toe of his boot served to hold down the innermost edge of the scroll so he could peer at it cautiously. Then study it more closely, with rising excitement.

This was Lorontar's writing, sure enough. He owned a few scraps of it, seized and stolen from across Falconfar over years of sly spying and covert spell-slayings, and had studied them long and often.

The elegantly-woven, nameless spell it set forth—crafted by Lorontar for his use alone, beyond a doubt—was a magic that could target from afar the sleeping mind of a specific, chosen being of... *Earth!*

Sending to that target creature whatever dreams the caster desired.

Narmarkoun nodded, his smile now wide and smug. This confirmed all his suspicions. Lorontar had long ago found a way to this other world, this "Earth," and perhaps to gain riches and magic from it; and someone, not too long ago—Arlaghaun, perhaps—had found another copy of this spell, and used it to bring the bumbler Everlar to Falconfar.

And now, Narmarkoun of Falconfar could fetch folk of Earth, too, and had the basic wits to choose someone more useful than Rod Everlar!

Firmly quelling his glee for as long as it might take, he drew in a deep breath, flexed his fingers, composed himself, and cast the spell as carefully as any calmly competent apprentice, visualizing the only man of Earth he knew.

He was promptly plunged into a welter of emotions—apprehension, above all—and racing thoughts. Just as he'd expected, knowing Everlar was awake. He saw bearded men in scruffy cloth overjacks, scribes they must be, sitting at desks beside piles of identical tomes which they were writing in, and handing to lines of supplicants... and a vast city, stretching to the horizon and dominated by many fortresses whose tall turrets thrust up into the sky higher than any temple or castle Narmarkoun had ever seen... and wagon-roads smoother than any courtyard, crowded with people along their edges and with wagons that looked to be made all of armor and were pulled by invisible steeds...

He resisted the temptation to bear down and seek to share what Everlar was thinking, as that couldn't help but make even the feeble-minded Earth dolt feel his presence. Instead, he performed the age-old mental dismissal that ended a working of magic.

A loop of sparks, visualized in a night-black void, and instantly—as always—the spell was done.

There'd be ample time to work it again when the Lord Archwizard—Narmarkoun felt his lips curling with contempt at merely thinking of that title, linked to the timorous dolt—was asleep, and drift in his dreams long enough to draw memories of others of Earth from him. New victims, to be Narmarkoun's own, and a road to conquering a new realm or two. Or even all of Earth.

Then something happened that dashed all Narmarkoun's glee away in an instant, plunging him from satisfaction to terror.

The scroll was still shimmering slightly, in the aftermath of the magic he'd roused from it. In the surges of that waning power, markings were appearing across the bottom of the scroll. Writings, in Lorontar's hand but scribbled in haste, on a slight angle from the darker, neater script that set forth the spell itself.

Notes, written by Lorontar, the *real* Lord Archwizard of Falconfar, about Shapers, one such in particular: Rod Everlar.

So unless the dolt now wandering dim-wittedly through Malragard had somehow lived for centuries without showing any signs of age or experience, Lorontar was very far from being as long dead as all Falconfar had thought.

And here he was, the wizard Narmarkoun—least in power of the Dooms of Falconfar, once one discounted foresight and spells of undeath—kneeling on the floor working magic in the heart of Yintaerghast, the spell-shrouded castle of Lorontar himself.

"FALCON!" GARFIST SNARLED, trying to claw his way past Iskarra, who stood in the way, flapping her arms in a sudden flurry as if trying to fly. "*Get those glorking doors open!*"

"Yes!" Isk hissed at him, her eyes hard and wild as she watched the monsters, now looking their way and starting to move from between the pillars. "Stand back and give me *room!*"

"Stop me vitals, woman, what're ye—"

Gar found himself staring at a pair of small but deliciously familiar breasts. They danced under his nose for the briefest of instants as Iskarra finally got her worn-through vest and ragged tunic off, into a untidy bundle where her hands met above her head.

He hadn't time to do more than gape before she swung the balled-up garments down like a swordsman using two hands on his blade to hew a foe, and grasped one of the large pull-rings of the great double entrance doors.

It awakened into a menacingly-crackling cascade of blue sparks and leaping blue-white bolts of lightning, as Iskarra cried out in pain, her hair springing out rigid to stand like a halo of tiny spears, and kicked at the ground to turn the ring.

The door ground open, swinging inward with the deep tone of a bell almost too low to hear—and Iskarra lost her hold, staggered back, and sat down hard, moaning.

Watching the monsters coming for them—even faster than he'd feared they could move, of course— Garfist charged over to scoop her up, cradling her to his chest in a tangle of helplessly shuddering limbs, ran in a tight circle so as not to risk falling by trying to halt and head in a different direction with his moaning burden, and darted out through the doors, into the glimmering beginnings of dawn.

Gloom-shadowed Harlhoh rose dark and still against that brightening horizon below, and Gar lumbered down a broad wagon-path toward it, gathering speed and hoping by all the gods there were and might be that he'd not fall, nor find all those hungry horrors snapping at his heels.

Surely they were guardians, enspelled to stay in the wizard's abode and menace intruders, not go chasing off across half a Raurklor hold… aye? Please?

Behind him, bright light stabbed out, falling on his back, and something roared hungrily. The grand entry hall of Malragard had erupted into bright and busy life.

Garfist Gulkoun cursed, briefly but fiercely, then shut up. He needed all his breath for running—or rather, panting so he could keep on running.

That roar came again, and this time it was echoed by a call that was high-pitched, bubblingly wet, and more angry than hungry.

Even over Gar's loud and quickening panting, both beast-calls sounded nearer.

THAT BED HAD been empty, its dark blue overshroud unblemished by pillows or—or anything.

Now there was a naked man lying spreadeagled on that dark blue cloth, wrists and ankles manacled to the four bedposts. Naked, hairy, and unconscious, head lolling and staring empty-eyed at nothing.

Those eyes saw nothing, but the face wore a look of terror, tinged with bewildered astonishment.

An expression that was probably pretty close to Rod's own. He knew that terrified, senseless face. It was Onthras, one of the Hammerhold knights who'd been chasing him mere panting moments ago.

So how? The magic of Malragard, of course. Onthras had been caught in a trap, or had been made part of a trap for Rod Everlar. But why? What sort of Doom of Falconfar crafts spells to do such a thing?

Rod stared at Onthras—or the thing that looked like Onthras—and slowly backed away, seeking another way out of the room.

Which is when he saw that, stare and peer about as much as he might, the bedchamber had only two doors: one out into the passage where the rest of the Hammerhand warriors presumably still were, and the one he'd come through, from the bathroom.

Now what?

After a moment, Rod used his sword to thrust aside the skirts of the bed, to see if he dared hide under it, and think.

A face like a skull turned and grinned at him, out of the darkness.

It *was* a skull, Rod realized a moment later, as he fought down a scream and hastily backed away—and the skeleton in disintegrating skirts that had been lying under the bed clambered out from under it, beckoning to him grotesquely with one long, bony finger.

A BRIGHT WARNING blazed up in Malraun's mind again, rousing him out of a pleasant doze. He was… he was lying atop Taeauna in the bed in Darswords, both of them still moist with sweat. Oh, yes… he'd exhausted himself having his way with her.

Now something back in Malragard had been disturbed again, goading his ward-spells into whirling up in his mind to alert him, and—Falcon hurl, what was it *now?*

It was the undead husk of the sorceress Telrorna, whom he'd defeated years ago, and drained of life and spells but bound into his service forever, to be his slave beyond death.

She'd been aroused from the dusty spell-slumber he'd left her in, under the guest bed, by an intruder who could wield magic. Yet hadn't blasted her.

Rod Everlar, for all the thick-headed knights in Galath.

He really should do something about the pitifully blundering Lord Archwizard, but… well, it wasn't as if it was Narmarkoun, or an arduke of Galath who'd gathered a dozen hedge-wizards, or someone *competent.*

Malraun chuckled, finding himself on the edge of sinking into slumber again. He roused himself enough to clamber off the bed to where he'd left his other whips and scourges, find thongs enough to bind Taeauna's wrists and ankles securely to the bedposts, and tie her thus, arched out at full stretch and bound cruelly hard.

As he finished knotting and tugging, and sank down onto her again, she smiled up at him, mute but bright-eyed.

Part way through trying to smile softly back at her, Malraun the Matchless fell asleep again.

"So that's why we couldn't see where Jelgar went," Thalden murmured, stepping through the magic and then back out of it again.

"Don't toy with it," was all Syregorn replied, "or, like as not, it'll start toying with you."

The passage full of doors seemed to stretch on forever. "Seemed to" were the right words, because at one step Thalden had found a place where Malraun's magic crafted an illusion: the image of the passage stretching on and on, dwindling into the distance, when it actually became a short flight of stairs, descending to a door.

Closed, of course, and as featureless as all the rest of them. Malragard did not yield up its secrets to intruders, except the hard way.

They'd found no sign of Onthras, but a lone, staring eyeball impaled on a needle-thin metal spike that had suddenly thrust up out of a door as they'd passed it had been a dull olive green.

The color of no one's eyes that Syregorn and Thalden had ever known except Sir Jelgar Thusk of Hammerhold.

A little farther on down the passage they'd heard a loud, grisly gnawing sound coming from under the floor, but—not feeling foolish enough to want to open one of the doors waiting so temptingly on the floor they were walking along—had no way of knowing if they were hearing the devouring of Jelgar, Onthras, or someone else.

Some*thing* else, perhaps.

A few hasty paces beyond where the sound of gnawing faded behind them, they'd traded glances that told each other, as loudly and as firmly as if they'd shouted it until the walls rang: "I hate this place."

Syregorn had worn a bitter half-smile for quite a few careful steps after that. He strongly suspected that where Malragard was concerned, the feeling was mutual.

They reached the bottom of the steps, and stopped facing the door. Thalden looked at Syregorn, who nodded; his usual silent order to proceed.

Slowly the oldest knight of Hammerhold reached out, laid a reluctant hand on the door-ring, and pulled.

The door opened, as easily and silently as if its stone pivots had been polished mirror-smooth and oiled—and two metal war-quarrels, as long and as heavy as horse-lances, raced out of the darkness beyond the door amid the crash of a giant double-bow going off.

One of them chipped the stone stair as Syregorn hurled himself against the wall, but the other tore right through Thalden's armor and ribs, pinning the old knight against the steps.

"Greet the Falcon, old friend," the warcaptain said sadly. Spewing out a great gush of blood, Thalden sagged over sideways and did not reply.

HE HAD TO get out of here, right now!

The gate and the creatures he'd sent through it must be abandoned! To the Falcon with all the rest of his schemes, too, until he was far from here!

Anything else he did in Yintaerghast—the slightest little thing—might awaken Lorontar, or the Great Doom might be already awake and watching him right now, lurking and silently laughing—

Narmarkoun whirled around. Had that been a chuckle? A distant footfall? Coming to Yintaerghast had seemed clever enough, so long as he didn't tarry so long that Malraun got tired of conquering forest holds and grew bold enough to come looking for Lorontar's magic, but now...

Clutching the scroll, he ran back to the room where he'd left his staff of power and the few wands he'd brought along, his cloak, food, and water, his spell-tome and book of notes he was compiling, all guarded by a silent ring of his undead lasses. He had to—

Everything was gone. Even his playpretties. The stone slab that had served him as a table was bare.

At first he thought he'd mistaken the room, stepped through the wrong archway in his haste and, yes, rising panic, but—no, when he stepped back out into the passage and looked at the arch again, it was the right one. Could only be the right one...

He strode into the room again, almost running, to peer all around and make sure his things hadn't somehow fallen to where he couldn't see them, or been dragged away and left some trail.

Nothing.

He turned, wildly. Well, let them be lost, then. Crafting a new staff of like powers would cost him a year or more of work, but the rest could be replaced easily enough—if he kept his life, of course!

He found himself running, shedding scales as his deep blue arms went pale—something that happened only when he was wracked by sickness, or truly terrified.

Well, he was, fear like a cold flame rising in his chest as he pounded along the empty stone passages as fast as he could run, his rising gasps of breath loud in his ears, a feeling of being gloatingly watched strengthening around him now—

There! The door out, an archway opening into blank nothingness thanks to Lorontar's mighty shielding, but something he'd easily penetrated and mastered before, that was nothing but a moment of cold mist to him.

Narmarkoun ran faster, clutching the precious scroll like a baton. He had to get out of here, had to get away from Lorontar's long shadow, to where he could calm himself and—

He plunged through the archway and ran on, shivering at a sudden chill that had lanced deep into his bones, that clawed at his heart and his groin and his brain, now, freezing, making him stagger...

He skidded and stumbled to a halt, panting, not believing his eyes. He was in Yintaerghast, and had been running hard down the passage he'd come in by, the same hall he'd just run along to—

He whirled around. There, behind him, was the archway he'd just run through. Silently mocking him, as he stood winded and shuddering, shivering in the bone-biting cold.

Somehow, he'd run through the archway and its magic had spun him around and sent him running on, right back into the castle he'd been fleeing.

Drawing in a deep, shuddering breath, Narmarkoun fought to calm himself.

"I am a Doom of Falconfar," he said aloud, pleased at how calm his voice sounded. The word "Doom" seemed to roll away through the castle to vast and echoing distances, a very long way, ere it sank into whisperings. Whisperings that sounded like cruel mirth.

Narmarkoun walked to the archway this time, slowly and carefully, gathering his will about himself like the cloak that had been stolen from him as he stepped into its icy mists.

He would win through the shielding, just as he'd done before. He'd mastered it, and could break it again. He was Narmarkoun, a Doom of Falconfar, the *most mighty* Doom of Falconfar—

He was blinking at the dark walls and ceilings of Yintaerghast again, standing alone in its emptiness.

Turned around again. Imprisoned.

He took two steps away from the archway, turned to face it, and worked the strongest magic he knew, raising his arms when the great wall of spark-studded power was at its height, and hurled it at the shielding spell. He might well shatter this wall of the castle, but so be it.

If that was what it took to win free of Yintaerghast and its not-so-dead master, that was what he would—

Like a great ocean wave, his own spark-studded spell came back at him, crashing down over him and burying him under hammerblows that struck as hard inside his head as out, dashing and numbing and breaking him, hurling him over and over and... out.

Chapter Twenty-Four

ROD EVERLAR SWALLOWED, and retreated another step. In grinning silence the skeleton advanced, still beckoning to him in a friendly, even coquettish manner.

The grinning skull stared at him as if its dark, empty eyesockets could somehow see him clearly, and trailed—or rather, shed, at every eerie step—tresses of what once must have been a spectacular head of long, trailing hair. From the skeleton's bony shoulders hung the crumbling gray wisps and tatters of what Rod now saw had once been an elaborate and probably very beautiful gown, with flared shoulders and an upthrust collar, gathered down into a tight-laced, corset-like middle portion that descended to a be-gemmed triangular pelvic panel from which in turn blossomed out a broad, full sweep of skirts. That were crumbling, ever so slowly and sighingly gently, into dust.

Rod swallowed again, his mouth suddenly very dry. *If that thing touched him...*

... what? What would happen?

Yes, this was a walking skeleton, probably animated by, or controlled by, the wizard Malraun. And even if he hadn't seen far too many horror movies, there was something horrible, something grotesquely *not right*, about a silent skeleton beckoning to him in an alluring manner, as it—she—

The skeleton stopped, put both hands on its—her—hips, and struck a pose. Then it raised one hand languidly and drew its forefinger slowly across its lower line of teeth, parting its jaws slightly as if it licking its finger with a tongue that was no longer there, empty eyesockets fixed on his eyes.

Suddenly Rod felt his fear fall away from him like a wet and heavy cloak dropping from his shoulders. He blinked, astonished at how calm he now felt.

"Wait," he almost said aloud. "I'm a fantasy writer. I can handle this. She *looks* horrid, yes, but what if she's just a lonely walking skeleton…"

She put her head to one side, like many a movie star he'd seen in films, flirting. Rod shrugged, smiled, and offered her his hand to shake.

As smoothly as any real movie star, she shifted her hips and stepped past it without taking it, moving to embrace him.

He stood his ground, skin no longer crawling, as those bony limbs closed around him—chilling him to the bone.

The cold of her embrace was so intense that he gasped, and had to fight for breath—and by then, the empty eyesockets were staring up at Rod Everlar from just below his nose, and both of her bony hands had risen to close around his throat.

She was trying to throttle him!

"Well, that was stupid of me," Rod panted, trying to break free. Magic flared into glowing visibility up and down her arm-bones as she resisted him, its force making her grasp tremendously powerful.

Not strong enough, however, to keep Rod from hurling himself to the ground and rolling—in a sudden dust-cloud of disintegrating skirts and flailing skeletal legs that made him sneeze violently and repeatedly, sending fingerbones rattling and bouncing in all directions.

She kept firm hold of him, though, that staring skull and those searingly cold, claw-like fingers sinking deeper into his throat, choking him... and bruisingly deeper and tighter...

Lying on his side, now, one knee thrust forward to keep himself that way despite her kicking bones, Rod clenched his teeth, fought for breath, and patiently opened pouch after pouch along his hip-belt of six pouches, and started thrusting the contents of each against the gleaming bones of her wrists.

The glowing and sparkling dust from the little drawstring sacks in the first pouch made her stiffen and sigh, but loosened her grip not at all.

The magical halo around her bones flared into angry brightness at the touch of the first of the seven rings from the second pouch, but that was all it did. Feeling his way along the fine chain he'd looped through all of the seven rings, Rod touched the second ring to the skeleton that was trying to murder him. Nothing happened.

The touch of the third ring, however, made her to stiffen, and a different hue of cold fire appeared out of nowhere to race up and down her limbs.

Suddenly those strangling fingers were gone from his throat. The skeleton arched and surged against him, thrusting and shifting herself up his front just as a small and squirming neighbor's child had once tried to clamber up Rod from his lap, until their noses—his a nondescript point of living flesh, hers a grotesque hole above a line of even, ever-bared teeth—were touching.

"Thank you," she whispered, her words blowing icy vapor into Rod Everlar and chilling him into shuddering helplessness. "Telrorna thanks you for her freedom. Free to die at last... I curse Malraun for every cruelty of his binding, for every moment of my enslavement... but you... I thank you, sir, for my death..."

And as Rod fought to master his shivering and make some sort of reply, the skull broke off those bony shoulders and rolled away.

Then the skeleton slumped, crumbled, and fell apart, leaving him lying alone on the floor amid eerie wisps of what had once been a gown, with a magical ring flickering and crumbling to nothing in his fingertips.

Its sighing destruction tickled his fingers, and then was gone.

IN A BEDCHAMBER in Darswords, the wizard who liked to style himself Malraun the Matchless jolted awake atop a bound and helpless Aumrarr, shouting in pain.

Then, even before his cry could form words, he slumped down again, senseless, his wits overwhelmed by the roaring tumult within them, as a mind linked to his own burst apart at the height of silently shrieking its savage fury at him.

The dying of that mind rocked his own; Malraun was just—and only just—able to recognize the feel of the thoughts so harming his before his own mind collapsed into chaos. He was suffering the destruction of Telrorna, a sorceress he'd slain long ago, then animated in undeath, and magically bound to himself to serve as his thrall.

One among many.

Now one *less* among many.

Through the Doom's binding that linked them, Malraun's pain stabbed into the brain of Taeauna of the Aumrarr, lying bound beneath him. She whimpered, more dazed than awakened, and arched in pain not even her own, straining momentarily against her bonds... ere she fell back into limp, sagging silence.

On the far side of the chamber door, the guards who'd flung open a door at the sound of Malraun's shout and rushed across an outer room to wrench open the bedchamber door, skidded to sudden, reeling halts at the sound of the wingless Aumrarr's whimper.

The younger guard shot the older one a doubtful look, only to see that elder warrior was relaxing and starting to leer.

Barring the younger guard's path onward with the sword he'd already drawn and tapping a finger to his lips in a clear signal for silence, the veteran guard closed the bedchamber door in careful silence, then wordlessly started shooing his younger fellow back across the outer room.

He was grinning broadly and shaking his head as he did so. It took the younger guard only a moment or two to start to blush.

THE GREAT FRONT doors of Malragard boomed and shuddered as five charging beasts—with a sixth drifting past low overhead, its many yellow eyes glaring—crashed together in the doorway, each determined to be the first out to maraud, freed to slay and maim and—

Lightnings suddenly erupted from the doorframe, a score of angrily-crackling blue bolts that raced from limb to quivering muscled bulk to roaring-in-pain maw, stabbing upward to transfix the flying monster from a dozen directions at once, holding it shuddering in midair.

As beneath, lightning flashed again and again, and monsters writhed, spasmed, and sank down. Malraun's doorwarding magics, prepared long ago for just such a task, ably and brutally sought to hold his six guardians to their guardianship.

In the heart of that surging tangle of flashing pain, the wolfheads snarled and snapped at the helmcat and the slitherjaws, who snapped and bit back with fierce enthusiasm. The gliding horror's tentacles flailed everywhere, and the stabspider reared back in quivering frustration, its legs too delicate to risk amid the thunderous collisions in the doorway.

Overhead, the flying maw shuddered, vomiting showers of sparks and defecating floods of more sparks as it burned internally. Pincers clattering in pain, it reeled back into the hall, followed precipitously by five rolling, biting beasts, as the most sorely hurt among them sought to win free of their torment by driving their fellow guardians back from the doorway, so they could flee into the lightning-free hall they'd just come from.

In this, they succeeded; the lightnings fell silent as the guardians fell back into the entry hall.

There came a moment of shared, panting relief—and then a moment of dreadful silence, as all six guardians suddenly spasmed in helpless unison.

Out of the empty air around them burst the wordless shout of a wizard hurled into wakefulness by pain, then stricken senseless by that same agony.

That cry ended as abruptly in Malragard as it had in Darswords—and so was still ringing from end to end of the entry hall as the guardians burst into frantic action again—this time, striking viciously at their fellow beasts, now seeking not to get to freedom or pursue the two humans who'd fled, but just to murder each other.

IN YINTAERGHAST, A blue and scaly Doom of Falconfar rolled over, groaned once, and sat up.

How had he come to be lying on the floor, with a spell-scroll in his hand?

By the Falcon, he must have been tired...

Well, enough slumber for now! He had a new world to conquer—hopefully before Malraun's armies managed to lay waste to much more of this one.

Smiling wryly at that thought, Narmarkoun stood, unrolled the scroll, and nodded at its familiar symbols. Striking a pose and clearing his throat, he carefully cast Lorontar's long-lost spell again, his voice seeming to gather great strength during the incantation, until it was rolling thunderously through the dark vastnesses of Yintaerghast and echoing back to him like the deep roar of a buried titan.

As he finished, notes that had been scribbled at an angle across the lower end of the scroll shone forth brightly. Narmarkoun peered at them with interest. He'd noticed them before, somewhere and somewhen...

Ah, yes. They must be the work not of Lorontar, who had so boldly and ornately written the spell above them, but of some later, lesser apprentice.

He nodded, resolve hardening. When Malraun was destroyed and his own hold on Falconfar had been secured, identifying and hunting down this scribbler—if the man still lived; Lorontar probably had held little love for those who dared to comment on his magecraft—would be both prudent and entertaining.

Yet enough thoughts of the idle future; if he was to become the only Doom in Falconfar, his entire attention now must be given to the spell he'd just cast so successfully.

Narmarkoun allowed himself a faint smile. This time, he'd focused his casting not on Rod Everlar, but on a vivid scene he'd noticed in Everlar's mind long ago, at his first spying upon the man of Earth. It was a view across a vast gathering of fortresses, tall towers of stone thrusting into the sky like dead mens' fingers or the standing, limbless tree trunks of burned forests. "Skyscrapers," Everlar's mind had termed them, which must be an Earth name for these squared, many-windowed towers.

One in particular Everlar had been interested in; a tower darker, smaller, and older-looking than most of the others, where no less than seven "publishing houses" had offices.

Narmarkoun didn't know all that such a house was, but he knew what noble "houses" were, in Falconfar. Proud families born to rule, and all too often possessed of too much pride and too little consequence. He also knew that Everlar thought of them as keeping far too much coin for having too little a hand in producing things Everlar wrote: books like spellbooks, but unlike the laboriously copied tomes of apprentices, these were swiftly-created copies—*thousands* of copies—of the same book.

Was Earth then teeming with wizards? But no, surely not; if such a lack-spell bumbler as Rod Everlar could write books—aye, "books," far more than one, over a long stretch of seasons, for so the man's thoughts ran, and surely he couldn't lie to *himself* convincingly enough for this Doom of Falconfar not to notice—and not be shunned or his tomes burned as worthless, those books must be other than magecraft, and their writers less than wizards.

The spell had been a good one, ablaze with power and bright in focus. Narmarkoun could feel it racing out from Yintaerghast, all Falconfar dimming around and behind him as he kept his thoughts with it. A mighty magic, its weavings more deft and elegant than anything he himself had yet managed, something he could admire and study and trust in. Yet...

Yet this casting was as chancy as the drag of a fishing boat on the Sea of Storms, weighting a line with sacks of stones to make their hook go deep. He'd shunned the mind of Rod Everlar to seek someone else still in this other world, this Earth, whose mind held the same view of a particular city, a view centered on thoughts of the older skyscraper called the Hardy Building, where publishing houses held sway, that Everlar held in his mind.

So his spell was racing on and reaching out, a bright spark slowly falling and dimming in vast darkness, seeking... seeking...

Finding!

He was in an unfamiliar mind; one he'd never felt before.

A mind that felt warm, yet faint, a mind somehow ale-brown and worldly at first seeming, then the pale

347

green of eager youth as he sank into it. It was not resisting or even noticing him as he drifted down, yet was neither bestial nor addled. A sleeping mind, then.

Asleep and dreaming... of the Hardy Building and the publishing houses there... and thinking of them with excitement.

And dreaming of Falconfar, too!

At first Narmarkoun felt a stab of alarm, a rush of dark foreboding. Before he could mask it, it tainted the mind around him with shadowy apprehension, flowing out through the dream like ripples across a pool that has just received the plunging arrival of a stone.

Narmarkoun's momentary fear softened as he drifted deeper, learning why this sleeper was dreaming of riding hard and fast across Galath with bare and alluring Aumrarr winging low overhead. A sensual dream now darkening into fears of lurking watchers pursuing this Mike as he rode, awaiting the best chance to burst forth and do harm...

This dreamer read and re-read books written by Rod Everlar, whom he thought of as the "creator" of the "imaginary" world of Falconfar, a world this dreamer, this Mike, longed to be real.

Yes! Of course the spell would find such a mind, and seize upon it. Now, did this Mike know anything useful? Such as the names of other Shapers, others who wrote books for the houses in the Hardy Building castle?

Again, yes! A tall, lean bearded man with a waxed mustache, named Geoffrey Halsted, who betimes worked together with Mario Drake, a shorter, bespectacled bearded man who breathed out smoke constantly.

There were two other Shapers this Mike had met once, both of whom awed him more than Halsted and Drake. Lean, darkly handsome, dangerous-looking men that Mike thought might really know how to swing swords and calmly kill people, smiling all the while. Loners, not friends who worked together or with anyone. One was named Sugarman Tombs, and wore "formal suits," whatever those were, of black over white. The other wore boots and garments that were always black and silver, and was called Corlin Corey. They wrote...

As Mike started to think of various books, in a welter of imagined faces and places, his dreams thinned, and Falconfar fell away, nigh forgotten as he rose toward wakefulness.

No! Narmarkoun hastily lent his own memories of the Galathan countryside to the sleeper, his own remembrances of galloping knights, proud-spired castles, and smiling gowned women—and Mike was with him again, eager to see more, mind flaming with excitement. So much excitement, in fact, that he was soaring toward wakefulness again, and—

The spell faded, very suddenly, leaving Narmarkoun cold and alone in darkness.

He was standing in a dark and empty chamber of Yintaerghast, blinking at a scroll, the warm and excited mind he'd been drifting through utterly gone. Leaving him clinging to four faces, and the names Mike had attached to them. Geoffrey Halsted, Mario Drake, Sugarman Tombs, and Corlin Corey.

His thralls, in time soon to come.

If they were stronger of will and imagination than this Everlar, yet biddable by his own will or his spells, they could be his greatest treasures.

He, Narmarkoun, could dominate their minds, so their writings would change Falconfar in ways large and small, to be what he wanted it to be. To give him rule over it that none could challenge, or would dare to... or in the end, would want to.

Yet to do that he'd have to cast the spell again and again—and the magic of the scroll was now exhausted.

Oh, it still set forth the incantation and displayed the sigils, and so could be used to work a casting. Yet the power Lorontar the Lord Archwizard of Falconfar had bound into those sigils so long ago was gone, consumed in taking him to the distant mind of Mike.

If he wanted to work the spell again, right now, he lacked any means to power it except his own vitality.

The force of life that kept his heart beating, his lungs drawing breath, his thoughts racing, and the strength in his thews.

Narmarkoun hesitated, reluctant to take even a single stride down that road—for wizards who drain their own lives risk much, even when they have no foes, and are safely hidden from the curious and hungry prowling beasts—and then shrugged, struck his pose again, raised the scroll, smiled, and lifted his voice in the incantation.

It took a lot from him, even more than he'd expected, stealing it away with silken skill as his voice rose and his free hand traced the gestures that gathered and shaped power...

It had seemed to take much longer than last time, but the spell was cast. As it raced forth through the void again, Narmarkoun clung to it, vaguely aware that he felt weak and sick, that he was trembling and staggering forward blindly across the empty room in Yintaerghast to keep from falling, his arms heavy and ponderous, yet seeming somehow no longer fully part of him...

Find not Mike this time, but one of the four: Halsted, Drake, Tombs, or Corey. Narmarkoun mentally shuffled through the four faces, wondering which of them might be asleep right now, or drowsy, and so provide him easiest entry into their mind.

Not that he even knew if day or night now prevailed across the part of Earth where that city of towers rose. Mike had been asleep, yes, but it did not follow that the sun was down. Even in holds where hard toil was the rule and harder-eyed overseers with whips saw to it remaining so, exhausted night servants slept by day, and slaves dropped and dozed whenever no watchful eye was keeping them at work.

He clung to the racing magic, cursing silently to himself.

Were this spell to fail now, it might be a long time ere he dared cast it again. He felt weak and sick; it had cost him much—leaving him far weaker than he dared let himself get, when any weakness Malraun got hint of could bring his rival a-hunting Narmarkoun in an instant, slaying spells at the ready.

Images blossomed around him in the void, amid bright racing torrents of wakeful thoughts; the memories and workings of scores of minds, his magic gliding slowly down through them, dimming slightly, descending...

Into a bright sequence of images; the Hardy Building, then an echoing glossy marble chamber with a row of metal cages inset in one wall, behind gliding doors polished smoother than any cell Narmarkoun had ever seen; a metal box, within, that ascended as fast as an arrow sent speeding by a strong bowman; a room with a desk, and smiling women behind it; fat men in garments akin to the dark finery worn by Sugarman Tombs, books with brightly painted covers, of fanciful dragons and impossibly beautiful women and swords that burned with blue fire...

Drake! He was in the mind of Mario Drake, who was dreaming of triumphantly accepting an apology from one of those fat publishing house men in the Hardy Building office, someone called Saul Heldrake, waving fat-fingered hands and exclaiming that he'd never thought *The President's Boyfriend Was A Wizard* would sell so well—an image that faded quickly, as the mind quickened toward—*wakefulness!*

Narmarkoun tried to make himself still and dark, to pry at none of the thoughts around him and to think of nothing at all but deep, serene oblivion. The mind all around him soared, but then slowed, dimmed, and drifted down into deeper slumber again.

Trying not to let any of the relief he felt flood out into Drake's mind, Narmarkoun peered cautiously at the nearest memories, seeking to move with them rather than turn to one and then another.

Almost immediately he found a flood of very similar half-remembrances, darkly coiled and tangled like many fists of knotted snakes around the edge between dreaming and wakefulness. Memories of countless brief nightly awakenings, all of them. It seemed Drake was a writer who often came half-awake to jot down what he'd been dreaming about, and kept notebooks handy when sleeping.

That he read when awake, and called on for what he thought of as his "bread-and-butter-makers," his "Howard colliding with Burroughs by way of Lovecraft fantasies."

Well, whatever those were—and Drake seemed mightily pleased by them, and by how many of them he'd penned, down the years—they could only be improved by a little Falconfar.

Narmarkoun drifted a little deeper into the sleeping mind, until he passed through the ongoing drifting restlessness of the man's current dream, and hovered vast and dark beneath it.

Then, surging up into the dreams swiftly and relentlessly, he shared his own vivid memories, and feelings about Falconfar, pouring into Drake's mind vivid scenes of his dead playpretties smilingly yielding to him, the soaring mountains of Galath against a sunrise, flying low and fast over the vast green Raurklor on the mighty back of a hastening greatfangs—and then that same beast, on an earlier day, rising up to tower against a stormy sky, its three heads all opening their great jaws in anger, its eyes aflame...

Drake's mind shrieked, plunged into nightmare and spasming in sheer terror. Narmarkoun hastily fed out images of the great beasts he tamed and bred that he'd always found splendid and inspiring: a pair of greatfangs he'd nursed and trained, flying off together on their first hunt as he watched them from afar. Huge and terrible in their sleek, majestic dark might, great wings and necks and long, long tails silhouetted against a stormy sky—

Sudden brightness drenched and blinded the Doom of Falconfar, exploding all around his dark knot of self-awareness in the mind he'd invaded, in a wild and surging chaos of shouting fear that swept away all dream-images and threatened to overwhelm Narmarkoun himself. It was going to crash down on him, to sweep him away—

It struck, and he was lost.

Chapter Twenty-Five

BRIGHTNESS ROILED AND surged all around him, in raging tides Narmarkoun could not fight. Swept away and lost, tumbling and wincing in pain-wracked silence, he could only cling to awareness and endure… if he could…

It must have been only moments, but seemed forever, before the wild, buffeting torrents slowed into a rushing river all thundering in one direction, fear died down with the loss of that crashing chaos, and—through the eyes of another—Narmarkoun saw his first real sight of Earth.

A small, cluttered bedroom, awash in discarded clothes and overflowing ashtrays.

At the heart of it, Mario Drake was now awake, and panting in fear. He'd hurled himself bolt upright in his bed to stare at his own walls until he recognized them. The moment he did, he flung off the covers to turn and claw for a pen and his bedside notepad.

His fingers were fast—too fast—and fumbling. The pen clacked off the wall and the rear of the bedside table and was gone, somewhere underneath things and lost in the darkness.

Sweating and shivering, Drake hissed out wordless frustration and dashed across the room to a desk, to snap on a light and snatch up a pen from a mug of them, and scribble down what he'd seen in his dreams, before his waking thoughts drove him to forget it.

He did this often, though he seldom dropped the pen and had to rouse himself enough to get out of bed. Why, some of his best ideas—the entire plot of *Worm Wizards of the Red Star*, even—had come out of dreams, had burst into his mind so colorful and stirring that he could remember them still, years later...

Narmarkoun rode that fiercely happy thought like a well-tamed and eager greatfangs, bearing down hard on Mario Drake's sleepy mind, fighting to do... *this*.

The racing pen slowed, its wielder frowning slightly. What was... He'd never felt this way before. At war with himself, almost. He watched his hand move to stroke through what he'd just written and been so pleased with.

"Exhausted by endless victories, snoring softly atop his bound captive in a bedchamber in conquered Darswords, the wizard Malraun was two battles—perhaps three—away from conquering Galath, and changing Falconfar forever."

Vivid, yes, but *wrong*. How could he have been so wrong?

It should instead read: "Exhausted by endless victories, snoring softly atop his bound captive in a bedchamber in conquered Darswords, the wizard Malraun never knew that his magic was beginning to fail him. Would henceforth be too feeble, too brief, and too mis-aimed from that moment forth, to ever let him conquer even Galath. The Falcon, or unseen gods, had decided he was not to be the Doom who would change Falconfar forever."

He amended it, writing in swift, firm satisfaction and nodding with every stroke of the pen. Yes. This was *right*.

Yet his hand was still moving, adding more. "All across Darswords, warriors of his Army of Liberation silently slumped to the ground, dead in an instant, bearing no wounds. Stricken down by the Falcon, men would say, seeing no reason for the deaths they could name. Yet rumors would arise among the paltry handful of survivors that whispered the truth: Malraun's army perished that day from the mighty magic of the foremost Doom of Falconfar, Narmarkoun."

Mario Drake frowned down at his notepad. Who the hell was Narmarkoun?

RAULDRO THE COOK turned sleepily from the cauldron he'd almost nodded off to sleep into, face-forward, his great wooden spoon a-drip with the thick brown muck old soldiers liked to call "old boots and dead cat stew."

A loud and sudden metallic crash had just burst upon his ears, from not far behind him.

It had sounded for all the world like someone in full armor slamming down on his visored nose on the cobbled main street of Darswords, then bouncing limply to rest.

And—Falcon spit!—that's just what it was.

As he stared at the sprawled warrior, another pair of soldiers—who'd frowningly turned to see the cause of the noise, just as he had—pitched forward onto their faces, too, the morning quiet broken by more crashes. Then another, and another.

Rauldro gaped. As far as he could see, up and down the street, men were toppling over, for no reason that he could see at all.

Invisible arrows? Nay, for they turned visible when they drew blood, and he could see neither blood nor arrows.

Magic? Well, how could that be, with Malraun the Matchless, greatest wizard in all Falconfar, lording it over Darswords, with this army his own swords of war, besides?

The cook shook his head, utterly dumbfounded. The men lay so still. They looked *dead*.

And he hadn't even given them any stew yet.

NARMARKOUN GRINNED SAVAGELY, in the depths of Mario Drake's mind. It was time to have his newfound Shaper write something simple yet dramatic that had nothing to do with any Doom of Falconfar, something he could check easily.

Aha.

He bore down on Drake's mind again. Let the dolt write of a certain castle in Galath soaring up into the sky—and crashing back down again in rubble, killing everyone in it. Velduke Deldragon's fair fortress of Bowrock, perhaps. Or, no, it was too splendid; he might want to dwell in it himself, some day. Why not—

Drake's mind darkened around him, and Narmarkoun dashed such thoughts away and reached out into it, to see what was happening and to strengthen his hold over the Shaper's mind.

Yet the darkness came on in a flood, blotting out everything, and he could hear Drake grimly wondering aloud, "What's got into me? It's like there's someone in my mind, making me do things! *Write* things!"

Falcon! The Earth dolt was aware of him! Then there was nothing but darkness; Drake was gone.

The spell was fading!

There was something cold and hard under him. Flat stone. Narmarkoun blinked up at dim vaulted vastness, smelling a familiar slightly sharp, slightly dusty chill. Yintaerghast. He was lying flat on his back in Yintaerghast.

Feeling weak… drained. He rolled slowly over onto his hip, and sat up. The familiar lonely, empty rooms. Good; at least he wasn't facing a sneering Malraun with an army behind the man.

He felt just as empty, and his hand trembled when he lifted it.

Narmarkoun smiled thinly. No, he was in no condition to be hurling spells. Yet he *had* to know if he'd been right about Drake, had to—

He moved his raised hand in the few simple gestures, murmured the familiar words, and watched the small, spinning brightness form in the empty air in front of him.

"Darswords." he whispered, too tired to will it silently. "Show me Darswords."

In the heart of his little conjured eye the smallhold sprang into view, from the vantage point where he'd stood long ago and murmured one of the words in the incantation. His eye was looking out over the well where three lanes fanned out from the cobbled main street. As Narmarkoun turned it to peer down one street and then another, he saw dead men sprawled everywhere, and more toppling in mid-stride, here and there, as they fled in fear from the unknown slayer who was striking them down.

"*Well*, now," he gloated. Hundreds he'd seen, in

just these few glimpses. "Well, now!"

The eye was wobbling and dimming already, sinking toward the floor like a gliding soap bubble; he *was* overtired.

Yet happy. As he let himself sag back down to the floor, into the creeping embrace of slumber, Narmarkoun murmured, "*I* am the foremost Doom in Falconfar, and now all the world knows it! Flee, Malraun, flee and cower—while you still can!"

He waved his hand feebly, as if banishing his rival, as his conjured eye sank into the floor and was gone.

Behind him, across the darkest wall of that vast and dim chamber, a wry and patronizing smile briefly materialized. It was as long as the largest Stormar ship Narmarkoun had ever sailed on, but the foremost Doom of Falconfar was now snoring, and saw it not.

AT HOLDONCORP, NOBODY walked to work. From the front gates with their security booth, in the shadow of the mirror-bright silver company name that loomed in man-high letters atop a little artificial waterfall, it was a good mile along a broad and winding drive through the rolling grassy hills of the company golf course to the parking lot security booth.

"Hey, Rusty! Check this out—Monitor Three!"

Sollars's voice was more disbelievingly amused than alarmed, so Rusty finished taking the bite into his meatballs-with-mayo sub that he'd been opening his mouth to take when the usually silent security "eyes" had piped up. Chewing methodically, he strolled over to the control desk.

Sollars was pointing up at one of the long arc of external security monitors, and Rusty prepared himself for viewing an overly fat, pale and unlovely amorous couple rolling around on a blanket on one of the gently-sculpted hillsides, or perhaps two dogs doing the same thing without a blanket.

He was not expecting to see six dark-armored men, visors down and swords drawn, stalking steadily past the eighth hole bunker toward the Holdoncorp building.

At first he was alarmed—they looked so *purposeful*—but then relaxed. There was no way thieves, vandals, or terrorists would walk a mile in this heat; these had to be fans. Crazies, of course, but fans. A free beta preview sampler disk each from the forthcoming Falconfar expansion set should send them happily on their way. Still…

He flipped a switch and leaned forward over the microphone to announce briskly, "Ground Floor Security, Ground Floor Security! Six intruders, south lawn, coming in from the eighth hole. They're dressed as Dark Helms—armor *and* swords, all of them—so take the tear-gas rifle, and make sure enough of you go to outnumber them. Loading Dock Security, vehicles and your tear-gas, ready for backup."

"Roger that," one voice rapped out of the speakers, in reply.

A moment later, an older voice drawled, "Copy. You're not kidding, are you, Rusty? This isn't just you checkin' to see if we're awake?"

"Negative," Rusty said flatly. "I mean it. Six crazies with swords that sure look real from here."

"Uh-huh. Who's *their* backup?"

Rusty snorted. "Cut it, Sam, this isn't a joke. They haven't got any backup, of course…"

Yet he hadn't checked, and a *good* security chief…

He clapped Sollars sharply on the shoulder in a wordless order that set the eye-man to punching buttons and turning magnification and camera-aim toggles like a frenzied spider.

Only to spit out some words of profane astonishment as the feed from Camera South Forty-Six came up on the big monitor, and his finger mashed down a button that brought the flashing sequence of images of empty golf course to an abrupt halt.

"Holy *shit!*" Rusty gasped, staring at the large screen.

"What?" Sam's voice demanded, over the beeping of a forklift truck backing up along the loading dock.

He was echoed almost immediately by Mase, head of Ground Floor Security. "Rusty, what's all the excitement?"

Rusty shook his head, then bent over the microphone again and snapped, "Sam, Mase, listen up! I am *not* crazy and this is not a joke. Got that?"

"Copy. Tell us!"

"Well, there's something following the six guys with the swords. Well back, but it's flying. Most of the time, anyway. Keeping to cover, like it's trying to keep hidden, but keep watch on what the six are up to."

"So this isn't just fans, then. This is serious."

"More than serious, Sam." Rusty drew in a deep, unhappy breath, and asked, "You—Mase, you too—have played Falconfar, right?"

The speakers made affirmative noises. Rusty nodded, his eyes never leaving the big monitor, and asked, "So you know what a lorn looks like? The flying faceless things?"

"Yup. Oh now, hold on there, Rusty, you're not expecting us to believe—"

"I don't believe it myself, but I'm seeing it. And I am *not* shitting you. Repeat: I am not kidding or joking or lying. And it's not some guy in a monster suit, or a clumsy homemade bolts-and-car-parts robot. Unless someone has found a way to send *very* realistic animated images over these monitors that I haven't heard about—with proper perspective, lighting, the works—there's a *lorn* out there, flying right at us!"

"Roger. So I bring along the riot rifles, not just the gas gun?"

"No! No, we—yes, damn it, *yes*. I've seen too many movies to..."

"Rusty." Sam's voice was kindly. "Your mom never tell you movies ain't real?"

"Just *do it*, Sam!" Rusty shouted. "*Now!* The Dark Helms'll be at our doors in a minute, and that thing's about two little hillocks behind them!"

"Roger, Rusty. Go eat your sandwich and simmer down. Or have you gulped it already, and washed it down with a little something extra?"

"I have *not*," Rusty roared, "been drinking! Now *get going!*"

"Roger!" Sam and Mase snapped back in hasty unison. The speakers promptly burped the two loud clicks of their switching off, presumably to snatch up their high-band handphones and run.

Staring at the front lobby monitors, Rusty started swearing. Those swords, and all that glass. The six crazies didn't have to use the front doors. Thanks to his imagination—and yes, all those movies—he could already hear glass shattering everywhere, and all those long-legged, icily elegant secretaries and marketing managers in all their down-front glass box offices screaming and fleeing in all directions.

As Dark Helms with sharp swords in their hands and rape and murder on their minds ran among them.

"Shit," Rusty told the microphone, without intending to, "I need a drink."

Rod Everlar drew in a deep, unhappy breath, then squared his shoulders, lifted his chin, and flung open the door.

The passage was almost mockingly empty and silent. So where had Syregorn and his knights gone?

Ahead of him, probably, if all this time had passed and they hadn't burst into any of the rooms Rod had so fumblingly and cautiously wandered through. Perhaps they'd thought he knew the way out, and would just run as fast as he could toward it. Moving through Malragard, down the hill the fortress descended, to reach a floor or two below where he was now. Maybe.

Yet there was no reason not to believe the unhappy mutterings among the knights that death-spells would dice anyone trying to climb out over the garden walls—and there was no way to blast a hole in any wall, and so step right out of Malraun's trap, except magic that he didn't have and wouldn't know how to use if someone handed it to him. Not to mention that blowing a hole in the side of the wizard's home was more than a little likely to alert Malraun instantly about what had happened—and just where to find the guy who'd just done it.

So, walk along obediently in the death trap it was, and would have to be. Rod turned the way he knew to be away from the garden and—eventually—downwards toward Harlhoh, and the front doors, and started walking. Slowly, reluctantly, and as quietly as he could, avoiding all doors.

So when did he get to rescue the princess, slay a dragon, and accept a triumphal fanfare?

Or at least play the hero with some small degree of competence?

"LOCK THE DOORS!" Rusty roared, wondering where the *hell* Mase and his boys were; they should have been out on the lawn stopping these clowns well away from the building, not nowhere to be seen, as the Dark Helms—looking very much like dangerous thugs, now, and not awed, giggling fans—stalked up to the outer doors. "*Lock the fucking DOORS!*"

Sollars stared up at him, not knowing whether to be scared white or to grin at hearing Holdoncorp's grayhaired and straight-arrow security chief spitting out curses.

"You're in charge here," Rusty snapped at him as he unbuttoned his holster—and then sprinted away, heading for the service stairs. "Hank," he called to the largest and strongest of the custodians, "get out the fire axe and defend everyone on this floor, if any of those guys come out of the elevator!"

As he burst through the stairwell door and started plunging down flights of steps with wild bounds, the speakers at every landing crackled and came to life. Sollars had flipped a switch.

"Ah, gentlemen, welcome to Holdoncorp." Marie's usually butter-smooth and calmly professional voice sounded a little shaky, and no wonder. "Can I help you?"

365

"Yes," a deep, helm-bound voice snarled back at her. "Take us to those who know Falconfar."

There followed a loud crash of breaking glass. Amid the tinklings of falling shards that followed, and more than a few swiftly-stifled shrieks, the Dark Helm added in a loud and gloatingly menacing voice, "And mind ye do so quickly."

Rusty hurled himself down another flight of stairs. Quickly.

ROD BLUNDERED INTO the illusion of straight hallway stretching on the hard way; by bringing his foot down on the edge of the unseen descending steps and pitching forward, slamming chest-first down on the steps, and finding himself staring at the slumped corpse of Thalden bent over the giant crossbow quarrel that had torn through his innards and killed him. It was as big as a lance, and Rod realized with a start that a matching war-quarrel had struck the steps just beside Thalden, right about where his own head was now, chipping the stone ere it bounded away up the steps. He'd fallen right past it without even seeing it.

Hastily he got himself up and away from those particular steps. Picking up that quarrel, he used it to probe at the illusory passage, running on its unseen distances. There were side-walls to the steps, and an end wall with a door in it, facing the steps, and that wall ran straight up as high as he could reach; there was no gap or space through which he could move on.

So he either had to go back to the doors behind him, dare any traps Malraun had put on them, and find a way around this dead-end... or it wasn't a dead-end, but the way onward, and he had to open that door.

The door through which two oversized crossbow bolts had fired, if that was the right word, one of them fast enough to kill Thalden. The other had missed Syregorn and however many other Hammerhand knights had still been alive when they'd reached this door.

Everlar hefted it in his hand, then gingerly poked its far end through the pull-ring of the door, stood as far away as he could on the stairs, over against the wall on the far side from Thalden's body, and tugged.

The door opened with surprising ease—in well-oiled soft and smooth silence—and an unseen double-bow let go with a crash. Rod saw only blurs as another lance chipped the empty side of the steps and bounded up and on along the passage, while Thalden's body spasmed, arms and head bouncing wildly, as a second quarrel tore into it right beside the first.

Rod swallowed, but made sure to keep the door held open as he edged along the lance toward its dark opening. He could hear no sounds of reloading, a whirring windlass, or men moving about, beyond the door; the only breathing he could hear was his own. The bow had fired from about there and *there*, which meant he should be able to keep to the very edge of the doorway and step through without straying into the path of another war-quarrel.

Assuming there were no *other* little surprises waiting in, say, the doorframe.

Rod shrugged, swallowed, and carefully stepped through the door. He had to trust in his hunches, because they were all he had—and this looked to him like a mechanical trap, not manned and aimed. Unless Syregorn and the others had decided to make it so.

The moment he was in the darkness—a magical band or zone of utter pitch-black blindness, he decided—Rod stopped, lance in hand, and stood still to listen.

No breathing, no stealthy movements nearby that he could hear. Just deepening silence.

So he raised the crossbow quarrel in front of him, holding it in two hands like a quarterstaff, and stepped cautiously forward.

Here cometh the Lord Archwizard of Falconfar, with borrowed war-quarrel in hand. Tremble, all, and flee before him.

Two steps took him out of the darkness—it *was* a magical area, that ended in a wall as smooth as the black-tinted glass he'd seen in the foyers of various luxurious corporate headquarters—and on along a stone passage very similar to the one back beyond the stairs, except that it wasn't crowded with doors in its walls, floor, and ceiling.

A hall that stretched for only a short, straight run before turning into another flight of descending steps. The ceiling bent to descend on an angle with the steps, unmarked and unremarkable stone, and there were two small, closed doors on either side of the passage, just where the steps began.

Trap, Rod thought, eyeing them. But just how did it work, and what was the best way to pass those two doors?

Right beside one of them, he decided, choosing the right-hand one on a whim and walking to it as quietly and alertly as any cat-burglar, the war-quarrel held up and ready.

Use this borrowed spear of mine to bat aside anything that strikes at me out of the doors. Rush past, low and fast, with the quarrel held up like a shield.

He did that, and nothing happened. Save that he almost fell down the stairs beyond, skidding to a teetering halt on the lip of floor they descended from. Gingerly he tapped the topmost step with the quarrel, then shoved on it, hard.

Nothing happened. The stone was hard, solid, and not moving in the slightest.

Cautiously he rapped the wall beside the step, to make sure it didn't erupt with flames or a stabbing blade or anything else.

Nothing. Rod stepped down onto that step, and prodded the next one. Any corner he cut could cost him his life. As usual.

* * *

RUSTY CARROLL REACHED the door he wanted, flung it wide, and darted out onto the giant glass display case that was the ground floor front. It ended at a wall clad in black marble, right beside him, and he ran along it, down the back row of cubicles, gun in hand.

Where were th—oh.

Screams filled the air, a cubicle wall went over with a crash, and sparks sprayed from a dangling cable as a savagely-swung sword severed a johnny pole at one stroke. From somewhere he heard the unmistakable "pop" and high-pitched singing of one of the older, larger glass computer monitors bursting.

Women in silk blouses, short skirts, expensive metal spike heels, and elegantly-decorated pantyhose were rushing everywhere, hair wild and eyes wilder.

And there, behind them, came one of the Dark Helms, swinging his sword back and forth as he came, two-handed, like a teenager smashing store displays and not expecting anything to stand in his way. He was chuckling.

Rusty fired at the man's throat. The man staggered, but the bullet whined away, the screams rose even louder from all around, and the Dark Helm neither slowed nor stopped. Instead, he headed straight for Rusty.

Who felt the sudden need for a fire axe.

ROD WALKED CAUTIOUSLY along a new passage. He'd descended two levels from where he'd met the skeleton, and was wondering how much farther he could go before Malragard ran out of hillside and he found himself in an attic or bedchamber of some house in Harlhoh.

This passage looked like it ended just ahead, in another descending flight of stairs, but he was learning not to trust his eyes. The quarrel, or spear, had saved him from—

"Lord Archwizard," Syregorn's voice greeted him pleasantly, from somewhere ahead. "Left alone, you must trudge through life slowly indeed. I was beginning to wonder if your magic had failed you."

Chapter Twenty-Six

ROD EVERLAR STOPPED, the war-quarrel feeling suddenly heavy and awkward in his hands. He was damned if he was going to flee like a scared child—and really, in this house of hidden traps, where did he dare flee to?—but the Hammerhand warcaptain was a veteran swordsman. It would be suicide to try to fight him directly.

So… what to do?

"Syregorn," he asked calmly, "have you been under orders to kill me, all along?"

"Yes," the warcaptain replied gravely, stepping into view through what looked like the solid descending ceiling of the passage, sloping down with the stairs as they went down to the door. Obviously the passage—or some part of it—ran straight on, along the level Rod was standing on. "You or the wizard whose tower we now stand in. Whichever of you survived your spell-battle, after we got the two of you together."

"So why have you disobeyed those orders?"

"I've done no such thing, Lord Archwizard." Syregorn made a sneering mockery of that title.

"Oh? So where," Rod asked, "is Malraun? If there was a spell-battle between us, I seem to have missed it."

"The wizard is obviously elsewhere. Probably with his army. *The* wizard, I said; it's clear to me now that you're no mage. You can't spell-battle anyone. So there's no longer any need to wait to see who survives a battle that will never happen, before I strike you down."

"Does Lord Hammerhand know you're disobeying his orders?"

Syregorn smiled, hefted his sword, and started to walk toward Rod. Slowly, almost strolling, his eyes alert and ruthless.

"I've not told you all the orders he gave me, and won't. You are, after all, an outlander, not a sworn man of Hammerhold. Yet take whatever comfort you can from knowing that killing you fulfills my orders, not breaks them. You cringing, good-for-naught coward."

It was Rod's turn to smile. "Was that meant to be an insult? It seems to me, I'm afraid, to be a fairly accurate description more than anything else."

"So you admit it? Or is this just a ploy to delay me? Desperate words from a man who has no way of defending himself but to hope he can somehow *talk* someone to death?"

"Er, pretty much," Rod admitted. "You don't think disposing of me will throw away a weapon Lord Hammerhand could use to finally rule all Ironthorn?"

Syregorn's smile was very thin. "No, I do not."

He was closing in on Rod, slowly and carefully, long sharp sword raised to slay. "Whatever paltry magics you may be able to work are tricks. Little ploys such as I or any man could work, if we ended up with a few treasures enchanted by others in our hands. It will take a lot more than little ploys to defeat Lyrose or Tesmer—just as it will take more than a little ploy to fool me. Outlander, you are a dead man."

"Now who's trying to talk someone to death?" Rod replied, backing slowly away, keeping the quarrel up in front of him like a spear, and making his right elbow slide along the wall to keep himself close to it. He had to stay *right* against the wall, retracing the way he'd safely come already, in case walking down the middle of the passage landed him in any traps. After all, Malraun had to *live* in this place, and be able to stroll around it without facing death every few seconds; there must be some fairly simple "safe paths" through rooms and along passages. He hoped.

Syregorn stalked patiently after Rod, smiling a ruthless smile. Rod kept backing away, trying to recall how long this run of passage was.

"So you kill me," he asked the warcaptain, sounding calmer than he felt, "and then what? How are you going to get out of here alive?"

Syregorn shrugged. "Carry you, and use you as a shield. Let the traps savage *your* body. You won't be that heavy a burden, with some of the unnecessary limbs lopped off."

Rod tried not to shudder. "And if you find yourself facing Malraun?"

"Bargain for my life with all I can tell him—all *you* told *me*—of this world you come from, Lord Archwizard; this 'Earth.' A place he can rule. A place he'll need strong arms who know how to swing swords to guard and patrol for him."

"Strong arms like yours?" Rod let his amused disbelief rule his voice, to try to make his question a taunt.

"If men of Earth are like you," the warcaptain observed calmly, "my arm alone might be all that's necessary. It takes little skill to butcher—or cow—bumbling, unthinking children."

The heel of Rod's rearmost foot struck the smooth hardness of a wall, and Syregorn's contemptuous smile widened. Rod had reached the end of the passage; the stair that had led down into it had been narrower. He sidestepped to the left, kicked gently back, and felt the bottom step instead of wall. Waving his foot from side to side until he felt the side-wall of the stair, he backed into the stair.

Syregorn shook his head. "Enough of this," he remarked pleasantly—and charged.

ALL THE SCREAMING was God-damned *deafening*.

Rusty Carroll winced more than once as he dodged frantically-fleeing secretaries, who slammed into him and clawed their way past him almost blindly, not even seeing the gun in his hand as they sought to get away.

He caught glimpses, as he struggled through the flood of terrified Holdoncorp staffers, of what they were fleeing. The men in black armor were striding everywhere through the maze of cubicles, smoked glass dividers, potted palms, and brightly-glowing flat-panel monitors—and they were hacking at things indiscriminately as they went.

Glass tinkled and shattered, earth spilled across the floor as hewn plants toppled, and sparks spat here and there as cables were severed. Somewhere a fire alarm went off. Not the incessant ringing it was supposed to emit, but a hiccuping brring-off-brring-off-brring annoyance that made Rusty heartily wish he'd insisted on headphone-style earplugs as part of full-crisis company security uniforms, not just infrared goggles and gas masks.

Neither of which he'd bothered to scoop up before running down here, he remembered, which meant using tear gas on these Dark Helm clowns was out— until he could get back to the security closet where the gas canisters and a dozen masks were stored.

That closet that was clear across the far end of this floor, of course. Put in entirely the wrong place so an architect could give the Senior Brand Overmanager of Strategic Marketing Initiatives who'd engaged his services for the Corporate Headquarters Ground Floor Front makeover a nicer view of the nearest green hillside, a neatly manicured slope across the encircling drive that only a very wildly-hit golf ball might ever roll down...

Snarling under his breath, Rusty ran toward that distant closet. He'd have preferred to keep right along the marble wall, but at least a dozen executives had wangled permission to extend their offices across the back fire route corridor to meet that wall. Of course.

So in three places he had to dodge out from the wall, following the winding passage that left the black marble temporarily behind to run out and along the curved glass fronts of their offices, separating them from mere peons in the company hierarchy. Right now, though, they and said peons were all crammed together in this same passage, shrieking in terror and punching, kicking, and clawing at each other to try to get past. Co-workers as inconvenient obstacles...

Rusty wasn't sure where they all thought they were hurrying to, being as the only ways out that didn't involve going up or down in the building (using the stairs he'd just come down, or the far more palatial adjacent bank of elevators) were straight at the Dark Helms and out the front glass doors, or through one of the locked doors in the marble wall into the luxurious offices of upper management, the Inner Sanctum with its floating-glass-steps rear stair. Unless you were bold enough to make your own exit *through* a glass wall somewhere— an escape route quite likely to sever heads, arms, or otherwise prove fatal to an unprotected and terrified secretary trying it. Just thinking about that made him wince.

A particularly hard knee nigh his crotch brought him back to the here-and-now with a jolt, and left him facing a rather more immediate truth. Head of Security or not, he was damned cold certain of one thing: these long-haired, well-dressed, uppercrust cubicle mice were all in *his* way, and determined to scratch, claw, and even bite him to get past him.

And if he hit back at just one of them, just one, he knew the lawsuit that would eventually follow— from whoever he hit, no matter what she'd done to him, or from her next of kin—would ruin his life more thoroughly than—

One of the great electronic locks hummed and clicked, in the black wall right beside Rusty's elbow. Just now, he was hurrying down one of the doglegs in the fire route corridor that swung back to run along the marble for long enough to go around the curved back wall of an office shared by four Executive Graphics Facilitators. Clawing at that glass to halt his rush, he only *just* had time to hurl himself back, and against the black marble.

So the large, rarely-used 'side door' into the Inner Sanctum, constructed for rolling large pieces of new machinery—such as the monster photocopiers and color plotters—in and out of the executive offices with relative ease, didn't break his nose or toes when it swung open.

It did knock three running, shrieking secretaries flat. Only one of them was still moaning and feebly moving on the floor as three grandly-suited vice presidents, resplendent in gleaming designer shoes and Ivy League ties Rusty happened to know came from institutions they'd never attended, strode out into the tumult, regarded all the running or sprawled and senseless underlings with clear distaste, and demanded of the world at large, in only slightly-varying queries: "What the *fuck* is going on?"

The only answer they got was more screams.

"You!" the florid Vice President Finance boomed, pointing at a particular gasping, sprinting young woman. "If you want to remain employed here an instant longer, *come here!*"

The terrified secretary obviously decided she did not desire to continue employment with Holdoncorp if it meant getting sliced open with a broadsword in the next moment or so, and kept right on running as fast as she frantically could.

So did the panting, one-shoed woman behind her—and right behind *her* came striding two Dark Helms in armor, visors down, and swords up and hacking at everything handy.

"What's going on? Is this someone's idea of a *joke?*" the Vice President Legal demanded, jowls quivering. He peered wildly around, then poked his glasses back up the bridge of his nose, as he did every few moments of his waking life.

Again, no one deigned to reply. Rusty was quietly keeping hold of the door, both to hide behind it and to prevent it from swinging closed. The escape route it offered might very soon be urgently needed.

Then the screaming was elsewhere, and fading into distances fast. The secretaries, clerks, and clerical supervisors who normally populated this part of Holdoncorp's Ground Floor Front had all fled, leaving two Dark Helms—with more coming up behind them—striding to meet the three gaping Holdoncorp vice presidents.

Executive Vice President Jackman Quillroque had not reached his exalted position by being indecisive— or slow to confront potential trouble. He had always been tall, loud, and fearless. No waiting for inconvenient results of marketing surveys for him.

"Swords? Dark Helm costumes? Who *are* you, and just what by all the smoking pits of Hell do you think you're doing? What's going *on* here?"

* * *

Rod Everlar hastily backed up two steps, caught his heel and stumbled on the third, and sat down on the fourth hard and helplessly, his improvised spear clattering from his grasp.

He grabbed for it desperately, managed to snare its end in his fingertips, and looked up—into the grinning face of Syregorn, who'd drawn back his sword for a roundhouse beheading slash, and was now taking a long stride forward, to right at the foot of the steps, to put his entire weight behind his blade.

His boot came down, the floor sank about an inch under it, the beginnings of a look of alarm arose on the warcaptain's face—and the floor sprang up behind him with a sound like thunder.

An iron arm Rod couldn't properly see thrust the flagstones of the floor up and aside like a huge trapdoor. A revealed row of barbed iron spears much larger than the war-quarrel in his hand shot upright with such force that all three of them burst through Syregorn's body—neck, chest, and belly, right through his war-leathers—before the knight could even finish bringing his sword around to hack Rod open.

"Glaaaagh!" Syregorn cried, or tried to, around the blood bursting explosively from his mouth. He stared at Rod in enraged and incredulous agony, then struggled to say, "Gglord Archblughizard—"

Then his stare became fixed, and he said nothing else at all.

As Rod watched, the warcaptain's body sagged, and the sword clanged down out of his hand.

Syregorn went right on staring at nothing, blood trickling down his chin and dripping from him. His slumped body was now hanging from the spears.

Rod Everlar looked away from Syregorn's face, slowly whispered out all the curses he could think of, and tried to stop the spear—quarrel—in his hands from shaking so uncontrollably.

He was alone now in Malraun's tower; every last one of the Hammerhand knights he'd come into Malragard with was now dead. He was on his own.

"So," he mumbled aloud, fear rising in his throat like a sudden hot flame, "what sort of horrible trap will get *me?*"

A PLATE-GLASS WALL makes a deafening noise when it shatters. A noise loud enough to drown out and sicken even hardened executives. Holdoncorp was a company both wealthy and young; in its brief history it had always had rising stock, and money to spare to out-lawyer trade rivals, so its vice presidents—however bright and veteran they might consider themselves—were far from truly hardened.

Moreover, the shattering of the front wall brought other shocking sounds flooding to the ears of the vice presidents. Screams and shouted curses from the second truck crammed with Loading Dock Security men, as the lorn darted low at their heads, and nearly caused them to crash into the front wall of the corporate headquarters the way the first truck had. The truck now disgorging dazed and bleeding men in all directions—some of whom barely had time to shout before Dark Helm swords found their throats.

Movies to the contrary, it takes a lot of strength to sever a human head—and a *very* sharp sword.

It seemed at least one of the Dark Helms had both, and a savage sense of humor besides. He caught up Sam Hooldan's head, now permanently wearing a gaping look of utter astonishment, and threw it hard and high over the cubicle walls.

Where it landed, bounced wetly, landed again, and started to roll. Almost right to the gleaming shoes of Jackman Quillroque, where it gaped up at him in unseeing, utter astonishment too.

The Executive Vice President stared down at it, then lifted his head to look firmly away, jaw set and mouth tight and grim. He was fighting hard to keep from throwing up.

He had been lucky to get this far.

More and more, Malragard seemed like one great trap around him. Rod sat on the stairs in its empty silence, trying not to look at the forever-staring Syregorn, and fancied—or was it more than mere fancy?—that Malraun's tower-fortress was *listening* to him, waiting for him to do or say something before it pounced.

Leaving him as satisfyingly dead as all the rest of the intruders. Rod swallowed, finding his throat dry with fear, and wondered just what by all Falconfar he was going to do.

Well, *not* blunder on until he got caught in some trap or other, for starters. Which meant he'd die of thirst or starvation or whatever cruelness Malraun could think up, when the wizard came home—whichever applied first.

Hmmph. He had no magic to speak of, and only in wild fantasy books did magic "just conveniently happen" when you needed it. There was, for example, fat hooting chance he could get himself whisked back to Ironthorn—to a guard-filled Lyraunt Castle, and likely death!—just by finding the right spot in the walled garden and waiting for the magic to work again. No; if the teleport magic worked that way, half the Lyrose warriors would have tramped through that garden to die bloodily all over Malragard already, or Malraun would have set up some sort of nasty welcome in his garden, or *something* like that.

He couldn't go on, unless he wanted to die. So he'd better retrace his steps, right now while he still had some chance of remembering just where he'd put his feet. Back until he got to that bed where the skeleton had been, and the room beyond that, with all the clothes. Make a bed by heaping clothes on the floor and using more to cover himself, go to sleep on it, and try to dream.

If he could shatter Malragard in his dreams, he might be able to destroy it for real, and so break himself a way out.

Or get himself killed when it collapsed.

Rod shrugged. What other hope did he have?

And he *had* managed to go from his bedroom to Falconfar, the night Taeauna had literally fallen into his life, just by being upset and thinking of Falconfar hard enough. While Dark Helms were trying to kill them both, too.

So… well, if this didn't work, he'd be in the same boat he was in right now, and he could sit and despair, seeing no way out, all over again.

Or he could get lucky, and find something in those rooms he could write on, and with, and do his Shaping thing.

To get Taeauna back, and Falconfar free of wizards forever.

Except one: Rod Everlar, Lord Archwizard of Falconfar.

Well, fatuous that title might be, but it beat being Rod Everlar, unhappy writer. Sitting home alone wondering what was happening in the world he now knew was all too real.

Sitting home alone, without Taeauna.

"CAN'T…" GARFIST GULKOUN huffed, wobbling almost to a halt, "carry ye… much longer… Snakehips."

He promptly turned his ankle on a cobble, and fell headlong—thankfully into a night-shadowed Harlhoh garden. Iskarra flung herself from his arms, covering her face and throat as she rolled. Some folk left sharp stakes and worse in their gardens.

"Gah! Grrr! Hah!" Gar snarled, lashing out around him with his fists at imagined foes.

Thankfully, no one shouted back, and there were no barks or howls. Folk in Harlhoh, it seemed, kept no dogs, and spent their nights behind secure shutters and heavy barred and bolted doors.

Malraun was probably the reason for that.

Iskarra smiled wryly at that thought. She'd never expected to be thankful for the Matchless Doom of Falconfar, even briefly and in passing. She found her feet, got back to Gar, and hissed at him to shut his row, except to tell her if he was all right.

"I am *not* all right," he growled, lurching to his feet and stamping hard on someone's flowers to see if his ankle would bear him. It held up, though a wet rustling told Isk that the half-seen tharda bush behind the flowers hadn't. "I inhabit a world ruled by crazed wizards and their minion-monsters. I'm supposed to be happily retired by now, settling into my dotage with young things bringing me sweet meals and snuggling into my arms—"

"A-*hem*," Iskarra interrupted him meaningfully.

"Oh, lass, lass, worry not!" Gar rumbled, waving one large and hairy hand. "I'll share 'em with ye!"

"Pray accept my deepest thanks," Iskarra told him icily.

Garfist blinked at her. "Isk, what's got into ye? I rescued ye from yon deadly monsters, didn't I?"

Behind them, the garden rose up into a dark and towering mountain, spilling them both off their feet as the ground quivered and then erupted under their boots.

"It seems not," Iskarra panted into her man's face, as she dashed past him, tugging at his arm as she went. "*Run!*"

"That's all we ever do, it seems," he grumbled mournfully, as he turned, lowered his head, and burst into a surprisingly powerful sprint.

THE TRIO OF Dark Helms advanced menacingly, swords ready in their hands—and the three Holdoncorp vice presidents abandoned all notions that these were crazed fans in homemade costumes. Every movement made by the men in black armor told anyone watching that they were killers, cold-eyed fighting men who knew very well how to use their blades, and daily swung them with brutal efficiency.

Vice President Legal Morton Morton Herkimer the Third completed his assessment of the situation, came to his judgment, and acted with his usual brisk efficiency.

He whirled around, jowls quivering, clapped one hand to his face to hold his glasses firmly in place, and was sent flying by a bone-shaking smack from the moving edge of the door he'd planned to flee back through.

On the other side of that door, Rusty Carroll smiled thinly. He'd shoved the massive thing with perfect timing, and was now dragging it to a halt so he could haul it back open again.

Vice President Finance Sheldon Daumark Hollinshed stared at Rusty, his already florid face going fire-engine red. Before he could wave his arms in his favorite windmilling wind-myself-up-into-a-towering-rage-for-maximum-show tactic and boom forth demands and commands, however, a storm of gunfire and shouting erupted behind the Dark Helms.

Mase's Ground Floor Security men had arrived, and were firing at everything that moved, and bellowing at the walls, floor, ceiling, and nearest wastebasket to "Get down! Get down! Get down NOW!"

Three of those everythings were the other three Dark Helms, and a fourth was the lorn.

The lorn, swooping and darting above the cubicles where everyone could see it, was riddled with semi-automatic fire in less time than it took Mase to draw breath to shout again. It flapped, sagged, flapped more weakly, and crashed down heavily inside a cubicle.

The Dark Helms, who figured out how to throw chairs and computers in that same catching-breath moment, and who saw that these new arrivals were a real danger, responded with swift ruthlessness. All manner of objects were hurled, cubicle walls were toppled, and swords and daggers were thrown and thrust with desperate speed.

As bullets laced ceilings and smacked into windows and pillars in all directions, men started screaming in agony, or fleeing—and they weren't men in medieval-style armor.

As he saw one man crash face-down on the floor and slide to sprawled stillness, blood beginning to flow from under him like a lake, the Executive Vice President of Holdoncorp went white. He turned to dash back through the open door into the Inner Sanctum—but one of the three Dark Helms, now facing him from only a few strides away, plucked out a dagger and threw it so deftly that it passed under both of Jackman Quillroque's expensive shoes, and upended him as if he'd been a kids' television cartoon character encountering a banana peel.

He rolled over to sit up in uncustomarily undignified haste, panting in fear—and stopped, staring at two very sharp-looking sword points that were almost touching his nose.

"W-what do you want?" Jackman Quillroque stammered up at the two men behind those swords, his eyes wild behind his half-glasses and his expensive silk tie caught over one hairy ear.

"Who here has worked on Falconfar, or *could* work on Falconfar?" the tallest Dark Helm boomed, his voice coming eerily out of his full-face helm.

"Uh, well, ah aha, everyone here at Holdoncorp *could* work on Falconfar. It's one of our foremost properties, a brand known and valued—*eeep!*"

Jack Quillroque was infamous in industry circles for his "We can break you!" bluster, but a sword swung viciously at your neck is a very telling argument. Moreover, it's an argument that seems unimpressed by, and even impervious to, bluster at all.

Chapter Twenty-Seven

AMTEIRA HAMMERHAND CAME to a grim, panting halt atop a mossy boulder somewhere deep in the Raurklor, and admitted to herself at last that her father's murderer had gotten away.

Cauldreth Jaklar, Lord Leaf of Ironthorn until this morning, and priest of the Forestmother, could be anywhere in this forest, this deep green wilderness of soaring trees and endless gloom and damp, moldering leaves underfoot. Anywhere at all, and it stretched away from her in all directions larger than any kingdom.

He'd escaped, Falcon curse him, and she knew of no way to find him. After all, he was a priest of the Forestmother, and he was deep in the greatest for—

Wait. That was it. That, or nothing...

Jaklar himself had told her to always pray to the goddess in the forest and in her own bare skin—except for the little bit of it she covered with a mix of a little of her blood, some drops of dew or water from a forest pool, the same amount of tree-sap, and a pinch of forest earth.

Well, so she would. Find the sap and the water, bring it right here to this rock, strip, and kneel here to pray.

She would pray to the Forestmother to deliver Cauldreth Jaklar into her hands, so she could slay him for killing her father and betraying the House of Hammerhand—for that serpent must long have been slyly scheming to weaken Hammerhold and deliver its rule into his hands...

Amteira laid down her sword and reached for the first and easiest buckles of her armor.

"Do this," she told the air around her fiercely, "and I'll believe in you and serve you more fervently than he has ever done!"

Her words seemed to echo away across vast distances, in a sudden, deep silence.

All around her, the forest seemed to be listening.

THE EXECUTIVE VICE President of Holdoncorp flung himself desperately down and sideways, reacting faster to a situation than he'd done for some time.

However, he kept his life at that moment not because of that shrewd strategy, but only because Rusty Carroll—who'd just ducked under the hard-swung blade of the third Dark Helm, and sprinted through the closing Inner Sanctum door—delivered a hearty kick to the backside of the Dark Helm seeking to decapitate Quillroque, as he passed.

In Rusty's wake, all of the Dark Helms leaped after him, the fallen vice president forgotten. They were now intent only on getting through that door before it could be closed in their faces.

The security chief had already ducked past the other two vice presidents, but the Dark Helms dodged no foe. Viciously they hacked aside the large and florid form of Vice President Hollinshed—who was already toppling, arms windmilling wildly, over the fallen form of the Vice President Legal. Yet that obstacle, and their own collisions with each other as they converged on the diminishing opening at the open end of the door, delayed them long enough that only one managed to thrust his sword past the door-edge to keep it open.

And that was the man Rusty Carroll promptly emptied the roaring contents of a handy fire extinguisher up under the helm of.

The Dark Helm convulsed and roared, trying to claw off his helm as his sword fell clattering to the floor—and Rusty launched a roundhouse kick to the man's throat that slammed him into the other two Dark Helms beside him.

Then, stepping on the fallen sword and kicking it back behind him into the Inner Sanctum, Rusty dragged the door closed, threw its heavy bolt—and lunged at the nearest fire alarm. The firefighters would probably end up butchered as ruthlessly as Mase's and Sam's men, but cops would come with them, and—

"Carroll," the President of Holdoncorp snapped, from where he stood frowning in the door to his office, golf putter in hand, "kindly enlighten all of us as to what's going on."

Rusty scooped up the sword, hefted it in his hand, and glanced from it up at the supreme boss. The look on his face made many of the white-faced secretaries standing at the doors of the various offices of the exalted flinch back from him. He brandished the sword.

"See this, sir? It's real, right? Well, there are six *very real* Dark Helms on the other side of that door, right now. They've killed a lot of our people."

"You're joking, surely—*where are you going?*"

Rusty burst past the President, heading for the back stairs as fast as he could run. "Back to my post, in Security. You might want to come with me, all of you who want to stay alive."

The President sputtered his utter disbelief. "This—this sounds like a bad movie!"

"Or one of our games," Rusty couldn't keep himself from replying. However, he muttered those words at the full run, and the metal-shod stiletto heels of dozens of secretaries sprinting frantically after him made quite a din. It was possible, just this once, that the all-knowing, all-hearing President of Holdoncorp hadn't heard.

Rusty couldn't do anything about the "all-suspecting" part of the President's character. Not without letting the ready arm and sharp sword of a Dark Helm reach the man.

It was a tempting thought, but...

Good security men, he reminded himself more than once before he reached the stairs, rise above temptation.

As FLEET AS any frightened rabbit, Iskarra dwindled into the night, bounding along the dark and deserted lanes of Harlhoh. "*Run!*" she called back over her shoulder.

"That's all we ever do, it seems," Garfist grumbled mournfully in reply, as he turned, lowered his head, and burst into a sprint that started to close the gap between them rapidly.

He doubted that whatever the emerging-from-the-earth beast of Malraun back there was, it would have expected him to able to run this fast.

But then, he doubted that it cared. It might be nigh-mindless, or might be as cunning as a wolf, but the wizard's orders would have its wits in an iron-hard, unbreakable grip. It would probably come after them, never tiring, for as long as it could. Which might well be forever.

"So we're doomed," he told himself aloud, overtaking Isk steadily. "Again."

That last growled word seemed more a wry jest than a comforting reminder of all the times he and Isk had managed to escape grim fates in the past.

Just ahead, Iskarra spat a brief, startled shriek into the night—and was plucked up off her feet into the sky. Garfist stared at her, and found himself gazing into the grinning face of one of the Aumrarr they'd last seen in Ironthorn, heading for the foregate of Lyraunt Castle.

The beautiful one, Dauntra. Then she'd stopped looking at him over her shoulder to turn and hurl herself into flapping hard, now, lifting Isk up into the sky.

"Come back, Falcon take ye!" he roared, shaking and stumbling as his lungs told him that they'd needed that wind to keep running, not to shout at sleeping Harlhoh. "Come—"

"Would you mind being *quiet?*" a rapidly-approaching voice snapped in his ear, an instant before two strong hands took him under the armpits and snatched his staggering feet off the ground. "Some folk hereabouts will have bows and some skill at using them, look you! And you're rather a *large* target!"

Garfist quelled his shouting in mid-word, and clawed at his wits to try to remember the name of the

Aumrarr now beating her wings hard to get him up and over the low and swaybacked roof of a shed.

"Uh... Juskra?"

"The same," that voice said from above him, sounding pleased. "At your service. At least until we can get you out of this hold. Forgive me, but you're too heavy for me to carry all the way back to Ironthorn."

"I'm not sure I want to go back to Ironthorn," Garfist growled.

"Good, because we have other plans for you," the winged woman replied sweetly, as they soared up over the rooftops of Harlhoh.

Gar watched the other Aumrarr gather Iskarra in her arms so they were flying face to face. They were obviously chattering busily, but he couldn't hear more than the occasional murmur of their voices.

"Plans for us, hey? I'm not sure I like the sounds of that!"

"Well," Juskra said calmly, "we could abandon them—and just drop you, instead."

Garfist spat out several very filthy expressions before he grunted, "Ye win. Again, by the Falcon. How do ye Aumrarr do it?"

"Unlike many overclever thieves and vagabonds who end up having to flee the Stormar ports in a frantic rush just to cling to their lives, we Aumrarr tend to think about what we should do before we rush about doing foolish deeds. Most of the time," came the tart reply.

Garfist Gulkoun could think of several very cutting replies to that, but the air was cool and the ground looked very far away, now. Silence seemed wiser.

COLD, SMOOTH, AND very hard. Yes, undoubtedly. His cheek had never lied to him before.

About then the wizard Narmarkoun realized that he'd been feeling the floor against his face, and vaguely noticing the chill rigidity of its surface, for quite some time.

He'd been drifting slowly back to wakefulness, he supposed. Narmarkoun worked his mouth open and shut—his tongue felt dry and dusty—blinked a few times, then found where his hands were, spread them out on that same floor, and cautiously heaved himself up. A little.

Yes. As before, he was alone, lying on the floor of a vast chamber in Yintaerghast, fortress of the dead archmage Lorontar.

Reassured—and yet not—he let himself sag down to the floor again, and examined how he felt.

Beyond "terrible," that was. He was still weak, and sleepy… well, no, not really sleepy so much as *mind-weary*.

Yes. That was it. He was too weak and mind-weary to cast the mind-controlling spell again anytime soon.

He was also hungry—his stomach promptly growled in loud confirmation, like a competent courtier smoothly anticipating his lord's signal—and appallingly thirsty.

The foremost Doom of Falconfar made a sour face, heaved himself to his feet, and stumbled a little dazedly out of the room, to wander once more through cold and empty Yintaerghast.

He couldn't stay here forever. He'd starve, if thirst didn't kill him first. Nor was the location of Lorontar's great castle a particular secret. Only lack

of daring—all right, tell truth and call it "fear"—
kept wizards and many a home-poor warrior away
from its halls; he might not be alone here forever. If
Malraun learned of his whereabouts, that sly little
Doom would be inside Yintaerghast just as swiftly
as he dared, to see what Narmarkoun was up to—
and stop it.

Narmarkoun passed through an archway he'd
stepped through twoscore times before, and came to
a sudden stop. What was happening to him?

He stared down at his blue flesh, at the scales that
began at his wrists and grew heavier as his gaze
moved up his arms. When he sat in Closecandle or
any of his other citadels and hideholds, surrounded
by his playpretties and their cold caresses, he felt so
strong, so confident.

Here, though, among the still and bare bones of
the might of the greatest mage Falconfar had ever
known, he felt... weak. Soft, vulnerable, foolish;
unaware of approaching doom, watched closely yet
unable to feel that scrutiny, somehow... as unwitting
as a coddled child.

He had reached out to Earth, had done more than
Arlaghaun or Malraun had ever managed, and was
a step ahead of the latter with the former fallen and
gone—and *still* he felt this way!

It was this place, it must be. The cold weight of
dead Lorontar's enchantments, riding him...

He *had* to get out.

Yet he'd failed to break through the shielding-
spells before. Not so very long ago. When he'd been
much less tired, and had still had some magic left.

Which meant he had to search this place once more.
Old tales told of Lorontar's fabulous wealth, hidden

everywhere behind the stones of Yintaerghast. The walls of the black castle, the legends insisted, hid chambers of luxury, magical doorways to far places, and tunnels that led far out into the forest around the castle.

So far, he'd seen none of these things. The tales were old, and most of them were rooted in things said by wizards who'd worked with Lorontar. They almost certainly held embellishments, yes, but they couldn't *all* be lies.

There was one tale he'd deliberately been ignoring all along, pushing to the back of his mind since he'd arrived here. The old, old story that insisted once you were inside Yintaerghast, you never got out. Unless you happened to find some of Lorontar's magic, and used it to win free of Yintaerghast.

So it was time to go looking. Seeking however the cleverest wizard in all Falconfar would hide things from his apprentices, enemy wizards, and intruding thickskulls who came marauding with swords in their hands and theft and butchery in their hearts.

Wall-sconces that turned, as levers—if there'd been any wall-sconces. Steps in stairs that could be lifted up or pushed down or slid side-wise. Stones in the side-walls of archways, that moved to let someone into a passage hidden in the thickness of the wall...

Narmarkoun looked around him, swallowed a groan, and started tapping, tugging, and prodding.

Falcon defecate, but Yintaerghast held a lot of archways.

As Rusty sprinted up the stairs, more than a few frightened Holdoncorp managerial secretaries at his heels, the security loudspeakers spaced up along the wall above crackled into life.

"Just... just what do you want?" Executive Vice President Quillroque's voice was so distorted by gurgling terror that it was almost unrecognizable.

"We serve a master who seeks sole control over the Great Transforming Magics some of you here have been wielding over Falconfar," came the flat reply, echoing coldly out of a colder metal helm.

"You *what?*"

"Those in this fortress who bind things in Falconfar, making matters befall by their commands, must be eliminated."

"*Killed?*"

"Ah, that word at least you grasp! Deliver them to us!"

"Them?"

"Those who control Falconfar. You are a lordling here, are you not? They serve you?"

"Uh, ah, they serve Holdoncorp, and I—I can give them orders, yes, but—"

"Then order them to assemble here before us. Or die."

"But—but—you'll kill them!"

"You comprehend at last. My words have been clear enough, so your wits must be weak indeed, lordling. Go give your orders, or we'll demonstrate our impatience. The smallest fingers on both your hands, first. Then your nose. Then ears and more fingers."

"You're *mad!* And if I refuse?"

"We kill everyone."

IT ONLY TOOK twelve archways before Narmarkoun found it. His hunch had been right: try down low. No passage in the thickness of the wall, only a loose stone that could be slid out to reveal a massive metal lever, mottled black with age despite the enchantments he could feel around it. It was upright.

He pulled it down without hesitation. A grinding sound ensued, as the floor in the *next* archway, across the room, dropped down out of sight. He looked cautiously in all directions before walking to the hole to look down, expecting hurled missiles, unleashed guardians, or *something*.

Nothing but heavy silence. With a shrug he stopped a good two paces away and peered at the hole. Stone walls, and a faint, flickering glow from below.

He took a step closer, and peered again. A small stone chamber, under the floor of the one he'd been walking in, the glow coming from something small and round floating in midair at the center of it. No other doors, no way in but a crawl-hole in one side of the shaft, revealed when the floor had dropped. Wedge something between the dropped stone and top edge of that hole to keep it all open, so he couldn't get entombed in that little room if it rose again?

Wise idea, but wedge what?

He could think of nothing suitable he could lay hand on. What was really needed was a stout timber long enough to stand as tall as his chest.

Back in Closecandle, he could snap his fingers and summon such a thing, and with two waves of his hands slice it to the right length if it was too long. Here in empty Yintaerghast...

Narmarkoun stared down into the opening, shrugged again, and dropped down into the shaft. The stones under his feet felt as firm and unmoving as solid rock. He hesitated for a moment, in case the weight of his landing triggered some magic or other to raise them again, but they moved not at all.

After a few breaths of waiting, he turned and ducked down into the small room, where he found no doors, no lurking menaces... nothing but magic, radiating so strongly around the floating object that it beat at him like storm-driven ocean waves. He winced, ducked his head, and shuffled closer, fighting the soundlessly throbbing might that seemed strong enough to drive him to his knees. If all this power was something he could take and use...

He could see what it was at last, close enough now to stare past its wildly flaring glows. It was like trying to see one twig in the heart of a roaring fire, but... he was looking at no ring or dagger or crown, but—a brain!

The brain of a man—or, no, the semblance of one.

Narmarkoun frowned at it, fighting the surging, pounding magical flows to stand motionless so he could peer intently.

He'd seen brains often enough when opening up corpses with his spells, back when he'd been working on mastering undeath. This was no glistening, dripping real brain, floating at about the height of his chest in the heart of this little room. It was an image born of magic, a seeming spun by spells surging into and through a real brain that was somewhere else.

He could see through it, watch the ruby and crimson hues of powerful spells at work as they flooded through it, ebbed, and seethed into it again. The image had the shape of a man's brain on all sides, and the forces shuddering and slamming through it were almost sickening to feel. Not only did he not want to thrust his hand into those powerful magics, he doubted there was anything solid there for him to touch.

Yet he had to know what this brain—or these spells, working on the real brain—did. This might be how Lorontar had controlled Yintaerghast, and if that was so, this might well be his only way to affect its shieldings long enough to get out.

That these were Lorontar's magics, he didn't doubt for a moment. This was nothing he could begin to craft, let alone cast, so it was no work of Malraun's. And these enchantments, for all their briskly flowing energy, were *old*. They smelled old, they felt old. Old, despite blazing with more power than he'd ever hurled in a single magic...

So reaching out into *that* with his hands would be folly. Almost certainly fatal folly.

If Lorontar lived yet, reaching out with his mind would likely be just as foolish.

This looked very much like the means by which Lorontar had long and forcibly controlled someone's mind—a mind that still existed, even if the Lord Archwizard was long dead. There were, of course, many who whispered that he lived on still, somehow...

Narmarkoun sighed. This might be his only way out, so he had to know whose mind was linked to these enchantments, who was still controlling them—if anyone—and how to take control of these surging magics.

Or he would probably die in Yintaerghast, alone and despairing, helpless to depart.

Narmarkoun drew in a deep breath, uttered a curse with slow, precise diction, then slowly and reluctantly reached out with his mind, in an inward drifting so slow and cautious that he should be able to snatch his probe back in a trice if—

The first trice told him that there was no "should" in these racing, surging magics.

The second trice told him that the mind that was elsewhere was very much alive, ablaze with long-felt rage and fighting savagely against these magics controlling it.

The third trice was when their minds met, his and the elsewhere one, and that rage blasted into his mind like a bolt of fire.

It was the rage of "Taeauna," he learned, in the fourth trice, just before he, and all Falconfar around him, was hurled away into shrieking oblivion.

ON A GRAND bed in a dark room, a man snored faintly.

Someone was lying under him, spreadeagled and bound that way. She was as bare as the sleeping man, but bruised and bleeding where he was not.

And her eyes had just snapped open, literally flaming in fury.

Taeauna knew just where she was and what Malraun had done to her. She also knew the blundering of his rival Doom had just freed her from Malraun's control.

Worst of all, she knew again who *really* held her in thrall.

Lorontar. A greater wizard than both of the Dooms working together, who had just reached out from where he'd been hiding in the depths of her mind for so long, to take over that shattered control so smoothly that Malraun the Matchless had not even paused in his snorings. Let alone noticed, even as a shadow in his ongoing happy dreams of forcing himself upon her, that anything was amiss.

She was appalled at how long ago she'd first fallen

under his—by the Falcon, how subtle!—sway. Using her as his tool to influence her fellow Aumrarr, to reach out to a Shaper on Earth named Rod Everlar...

Her appalled anger awakened quiet amusement in the mind now gripping hers.

Lorontar smiled at her, in the depths of her mind. As he held her mind in a grasp so strong she could do nothing but his will. Right now he was keeping her still and silent, and hooding the fires of her anger, gently returning her eyes to their usual appearance.

Seething inwardly, Taeauna of the Aumrarr lay silent and helpless under the exhausted and obliviously snoring Malraun.

Rod HAD SPENT sleepless nights before, tossing and turning, but he'd never realized just how uncomfortable a bed could be. The cloaks, tunics, and breeches he'd heaped on the floor slid and shifted under him, repeatedly dumping his head low while his feet stayed high. Buttons, pulls, and sewn-on carry-rings galore jabbed at him bruisingly, and the gowns he'd pulled over himself demonstrated a distressing tendency to wait until he was just drifting off to sleep—and then slide, all in a heavy heap, down to bury his face and leave him fighting for air.

It was almost as if Malraun or some impish apprentice left behind by the Matchless Doom was laughing at him and casting one taunting, toying little magic after another to keep him awake, even now that a vast weariness had risen to conquer him.

He could *not* get to sleep, could not...

What was that?

There had been a stirring sound, or sounds, in the other room. About where the bed was.

Oh, bloody hell—*another* Telrorna? Did the bed magically spit undead skeletons out, or was there some sort of hidden trapdoor underneath it, that they could come up through?

He grunted his weary way to his feet, and strode unsteadily to the door, to see what was making those faint noises. Before it came for him.

Then he stopped, stared, and chuckled.

Some magic of Malraun's had failed, or faded away—and what did *that* mean?—and all the cloth and leather on and about the four-poster bed were melting away to nothingness, leaving only a bare bed and a bare and hairy man on it, waking bleary and bewildered.

Onthras blinked at Rod, extended a sleepy hand to point and growl, "L-lord Archwizard? Weren't you s'posed to be—"

Just then a wave of half-seen magic rolled through the air and snatched him away, leaving the bed empty.

And taking away Rod's mirth, too.

Was Onthras dead? Or snatched away somewhere else? Or had he been some sort of illusion all along?

Rod doubted it. Yet there was no way, by the Falcon, that he was going anywhere near that bed now.

It was back to his uncomfortable heaps of clothes, and trying hard to sleep, to dream of destroying this tower behind Malraun's back.

Or so he hoped. Rod collapsed back onto the heaped garments with a sour sigh.

Could *anything* be managed behind Malraun's back?

Chapter Twenty-Eight

"I RRANCE," LADY TESMER'S voice came coldly out of the darkness, "come back to bed. All of this lordly striding about in the darkness disturbs my slumber. And just *what* do you think you'll need that sword for?"

"I—I was thinking of war, and... and ruling Ironthorn," her husband mumbled. He waved the slender naked longsword with both hands as he spoke, but he was brandishing it a little less flamboyantly than he'd been flourishing it a moment or two ago. For an instant, as it sliced empty air, it caught moonlight through the tinted window-panes, and its edge blazed up a cold bright blue. "It... it found its way into my hand, somehow. Felt good there."

"Time was when *other* things would find their ways into your hands at this time of night, and more than one of us would feel good, thereby," Telclara Tesmer said bitingly. "But the years have wrought changes, haven't they?"

"Clara," her lord replied quietly, his voice a little sullen. "I wish you wouldn't do this. I really do."

"I wish I didn't have to do it, but if I don't, you start to swagger like a game-cock and strut around spewing nonsense. *Dangerous* nonsense."

When he made no reply, she added sadly, "One of the maids heard you talking to our warriors this evening. Calling yourself 'Lord of Ironthorn' again."

"Well, and so I shall be!" Lord Irrance Tesmer said sharply. "Soon, too, from what the Master gave me to understand! At long last, to rule this—"

"Irrance, the Master gave you *nothing of the kind*. I heard his every word, remember? Now put down that sword before you hurt yourself or break something, and get over here!"

"I—" Lord Tesmer was not a foolish man, no matter how often his wife proclaimed him so. Nor did his temper tend to ride down and trample his caution. With foes and threats he knew well, his wisdom steered his gallop time and again into prudent ways. Telclara's voice was more familiar to him than anything else, and he knew that particular tone very well.

"Yes, dear," he replied meekly, carefully laying the sword down on the crudest and least expensive of the three seats in the room—the one she wanted replaced, the moment she found just the right chair to serve in its place—and wending his way through the concentric arcs of hanging tapestries to their great new fortress of a bed.

The bed, grandest in all Falconfar, for all he knew. It was what Telclara wanted—*everything* was what Telclara wanted—and towered up in the center of the room like a great Stormar temple idol. Lord Tesmer felt like a thief slinking into a castle every night. Telclara's castle.

A glow was kindling in it. When he ducked past the last tapestry, brushing aside its translucent fall of white silk, he saw his wife had awakened the light of her enchanted mirror and held it under her chin so he could see her smiling at him in welcome.

It was a kind smile, devoid of sneer or anger, but the warm affection she meant to convey was marred by the coldly steady radiance of the mirror lighting her face from below. It gave her an eerie appearance, as if some fell spirit had stolen inside his wife's body and taken it over, to use it to lure him into its clutches.

Irrance Tesmer forced a smile onto his own face and held out his hand, but was unable to keep the gesture from seeming tentative.

"Lady?" he asked gently, feeling once more the uncertain courting lad he'd been, so long ago.

Her smile widened and went tender. She beckoned him, deftly undoing the catch at the throat of her bodice so it fell open, baring her to her waist.

Lord Tesmer swallowed. By the Falcon, but she was still beautiful!

"Tel," he whispered, daring to use the pet name he'd called her by when they were both young, as he put his arms rather gingerly around her, "you look... look so..."

She was deftly drawing apart his night-wrap, thrusting the long robes back over his shoulders to bare him, too.

"Tell me," she murmured. "Not how you think I look, but what you want to do to me."

"Take you," he said hoarsely.

She drew her knees together against his chest, to hold him at bay. "There will be a price, Lord Tesmer,"

ED GREENWOOD

she said gravely, sounding gentle but firm—neither teasing nor scornfully dismissive.

Irrance frowned, not knowing how to take this. "My Lady?" he asked gently.

"Treat with me as an equal, Rance," she replied, addressing him as she had when he was a young and splendid lion among men. "You hate the bite of my words, and how I rule you; you think I know this not? So in return you give me sullen silence, and play the war-commander behind my back, and tell me little of how you order our soldiers and what they do. Little enough, and less truth."

Lord Tesmer was still and silent against her knees for a long time before he brought the edge of one hand down between them to ease them gently apart, and murmured, "It will seem odd to discuss tactics, as I would with my warcaptains in the stables, as we..."

"Couple," she murmured helpfully, and added in a whisper, "Let's try it."

He smiled, shaking his head in rueful wonder, then commanded sternly, "Begin."

"You have been readying our soldiers for war," she replied without hesitation, parting her legs and reaching for him between them, the mirror in her lap now.

He surged forward, lowering himself onto its glow, and replied, "I have. Mindful of what you said earlier, of mayhap fleeing Ironthorn rather than conquering it."

"Meaning, I hope, you're taking every care *not* to get caught up in fighting?"

He hesitated, then lowered his mouth to her breasts rather than replying. She smiled thinly as he licked, nipped, and sucked, then closed her fingers around his most tender of areas, tightened them into a claw that made him stiffen and gasp, and said pleasantly, "My Lord Tesmer, I do believe I have somehow failed to hear your answer."

"Falcon, Clara, don't—" That gasped protest ended in a little cry as her fingernails almost met through his flesh.

"You no longer want to try it?" she asked him sadly, putting all the reproach she could into her gaze.

Their noses were perhaps the length of her hand apart; she saw him wince as much as she felt it.

"I... I do neglect to tell you things," he admitted. "Out of habit, it now seems."

"It does indeed," she agreed softly, letting go of what she'd clawed and stroking it in gentle apology. "*Please*, Rance."

He drew in a deep breath, nodded in very much the same manner as her favorite gelding customarily tossed its head, and said in a rush, "Well, we can't dwell in Ironthorn and not daily draw blade or bend bow when those of Lyrose and Hammerhand menace us, surely?"

"Of course not. Yet you seem strangely reluctant to tell me just what frays our warriors have tasted these last few days. I'm neither blind nor an idiot; I would know if we were besieged, or many of our soldiers were rushing off elsewhere in the vale—and we are not and they are not. Which means whatever fighting they've been doing can't be more than a skirmish or two, at most... wherefore I find myself puzzled indeed at your reluctance to discuss it. Irrance, *what's going on?*"

He made as if to pull back from her and sit up, but she moved with him to keep them joined, clasping her arms and legs about him with sudden strength. They stayed pressed together on the bed, the radiance of the mirror leaking out from between them.

Lady Tesmer's movements made her lord growl with pleasure and grin at her. She smiled back, then took his lips in her own and kissed him every bit as aggressively as minstrels always insisted conquering lords forced kisses from captive wenches.

When their lips parted again, both of them had to gasp for breath, but Irrance Tesmer couldn't keep a widening grin off his face. His lady moved under him again, making him groan with delight and setting him to moving, too. Rocking, slamming into her.

As that surging rhythm built, he gasped, "Let me... let me say this *my* way, Tel. The Hammerhands are dead; the father, or vanished; the daughter, and their warcaptains are *enraged* at that. Too furious with Lyrose to have anything to do with us but loose arrows our way if we dispute with them or bar them passage; they're bent only on besieging Lyraunt and taking it. They carve up dead Lyrose warriors and send the flesh into Lyraunt tied to flaming arrows, and they slaughter Lyrose horses and roast them under the Lyraunt walls. Word is that House Lyrose is now reduced to just mother and daughter. Magrandar and his last and most worthless son, Pelmard, are both dead."

Telclara Tesmer frowned. "So how then are the men of Tesmer caught up in this? It would seem to me that until Hammerhand exterminates Lyrose or dies in the trying, they have no time for us."

"True," her husband admitted, looking away from her fierce gaze for a moment, "but I... I am weak. I could not resist."

"Resist what?" Lady Tesmer could not quite quell a sharp edge from creeping into her words.

"Sending our best bowmen to watch the siege from afar, and slay the best of their warcaptains and boldswords—just a handful I've marked, mind—with well-placed arrows."

"Their best officers."

"Yes," he murmured, bowing his head as if expecting a storm of her fury to explode in his face.

Two strong hands caught hold of his ears and dragged his face down to meet hers. She kissed him hard—and bucked under him, harder, until he exploded with a roar of release.

"Gods above and below, Rance, but I'm proud of you!" she panted, eyes shining. "*Just* the right thing to do! Keeping our blazon out of sight and no arrayed Tesmer force for Hammerhand to glare at, yes?"

"Yes!" he panted happily. "Exactly thus, yes!"

She twisted and arched under him then, moaning and biting her lip, and her hands tightened like claws on his shoulders. Irrance Tesmer found himself gripped firmly in many places at once, and froze just as he was, sweating happily as he grew the beginnings of a fierce grin.

Under him, his lady growled low in her throat, like an angry hunting cat, her fingernails raking him. It was a sound of pure pleasure, loud and long.

He flinched not under her clawings, but kept still and silent, holding her until they both calmed back to gentleness—which was when she interrupted her own slowing pants to say smilingly, "So now tell me what you're keeping back from me. What darker thing haven't you said yet?"

Her lord stared at her, then shook his head and laughed ruefully. "You're beyond the Falcon, Tel, you are! *How* did you…"

"I've been reading your face and voice quite well for more than a score of years now, Irrance Tesmer," his lady replied meaningfully. "Now *give*, Rance."

"I just did," he jested, then met her mock-angry gaze with a raised finger and the graver words, "Earlier this night, and I tell you true now, some of our bowmen watched the Hammerhands howling at the walls of Lyraunt Castle—and as we put arrows into a few Hammerhand backs, lorn flew out of Lyraunt and commenced to savage the Hammerhold knights."

"Malraun," Lady Tesmer said quietly. "Sending them at the last to try to salvage something while his spell-might and attention remain elsewhere."

Her lord nodded. "I saw it in that wise, too. It stands as proof of the danger you warned against, yes. Yet, Tel, I still hunger to be Lord of Ironthorn; I think I always will, until I am."

"Ah, but Lord of Ironthorn now, just in time for Malraun to arrive and blast and burn you, me, and all this vale? Or Lord of Ironthorn in some year to come when there is no more Malraun lording it across too much of Falconfar? I still say we must very soon be ready to flee into the Raurklor—all Tesmer folk, our warriors with us—if need be. *Try* not to get caught up in any wider fighting yet, so we can stand ready for anything."

Irrance Tesmer nodded. "You have always been the shrewder of we two, and any man can see the wisdom of being ready for anything. Yet tell me, if you would, the thinking that led you to this counsel."

Staring gravely up into her husband's eyes, Lady Telclara Tesmer murmured, "I see the Master's hand in this, but I've not yet seen what he desires. When he tells us, then we'll know if ruling Ironthorn is a stride ahead from us—or if our lives are going to be turned toward something else altogether."

Lord Tesmer nodded slowly.

"We've trusted him these many seasons," his wife added, "and are still alive and reigning over gem-mines that many a Stormar lord or Galathan velduke drools to have. We must trust him now."

"Do you trust any of our children?"

Lady Telclara Tesmer snorted. "Of course not." A look of disgust passed over her face, and she said, "We forge what tools we must, at the Master's command. Now love me again; I'd much rather not think of them."

Her lord grunted heartfelt agreement and lowered his head to her breasts again.

She chuckled and twisted under him, trying to buck him off. Mock-struggling, yes, but with surprising speed and strength. Lord Tesmer had to move in great haste to catch her wrists, then use all his strength to hold her down.

When their eyes met again, his were once more ablaze with delight.

"HAND ME THE flask. Making love to you is hot work, sister."

"Warmer than you anticipated?" Talyss Tesmer purred, stretching to let the moonlight trace her every sleek curve.

She was sitting up on their cloaks, settled into the curve of a tree-bough as sleekly at ease as if she'd been lounging on a grand chair in one of the great rooms of Imtowers. Looking down her shapely length, from lambent eyes to long, long legs, Belard Tesmer licked his lips all over again.

They were here, in this shady and spell-guarded hollow far out in the Raurklor, to scheme. Nigh the tiny, tinkling headsprings of the Imrush, in a dell half-cloaked with overhanging tree boughs, surrounded by the invisible fires of the strongest ward-magics they both carried. Wards to keep prowling beasts at bay as they honed their plots over wine—and, it had turned out, a little lovemaking. Coupling with each other for sheer pleasure despite being brother and sister.

"Relieving my burning itch," Talyss had termed it.

The wine and their excitement had spurred it, but it was more than sheer release. Both of them had been hungry for it, and more than hungry, feeling the lack of skin on skin. Neither dared trust any non-kin—or anyone else of the blood Tesmer, for that matter—enough to play the bareskinned bedmate, no matter where or when.

Now sated, it was time to relax, sip wine, and discuss what to do.

In a single smooth, graceful movement, Talyss Tesmer took up the flask and conveyed it to her younger brother's waiting hand. Her movement was swift, but seemed languid, not hurried. Her movements always seemed languid.

The youngest and most vicious of the three Tesmer daughters, she was less than a year older than dark-haired, handsome, sardonic Belard, scourge of young lasses everywhere he rode—and their mothers, too.

She smiled now at that thought, still aglow; he'd been every bit as good as his reputation, and much,

much better than she'd expected. It seemed there was one Tesmer, at least, who knew how to use his tongue for more than mere foe-lashing.

He was using it now to answer her, voice softly breaking the companionable silence. "Much warmer, and gladly so. We are sadly out of the habit of thanking each other properly, we Tesmers—probably because fitting occasions for gratitude among us are so few—but let me thank you now, Lyss. You were... magnificent."

She gave him a real smile in return, making sure the moonlight was full on her face so he could see she'd laid aside her usual arch, ready-to-pounce manner, and told him, "Thank you, Bel. So were you. Consider yourself welcome in these arms any time."

Belard Tesmer ducked his head, doing something he'd not done in four seasons of wenching, facing down angry husbands, and sparring with rivals: he flushed, the blood rising to his face dark and swift. Then he nodded to cover his sudden lack of words.

Utterly relaxed, Talyss kept her instinctive little smile of satisfaction off her face. Hooked. As every man was, yes, but she must treat Bel differently, or ruin his usefulness to her.

"Let us speak of plots once more," she said gently, letting reluctance taint her voice. "Do you agree—in the main—with these admittedly over-simple assessments of our parents? Father is a weak fool, utterly ruled by Mother, and she—for all the fearsome reputation Falconfar accords her—is a blinded-by-ambition schemer who will sacrifice everyone and everything to get more power for herself, no matter what the cost to the family, to Ironthorn, or for that matter to all Falconfar?"

Belard smiled mirthlessly, and nodded his head. "I cannot help but agree. I would have agreed with you seven summers ago, or more. How matters stand between Lord and Lady Tesmer is not something all that hard for anyone to see."

"And where will knowing this obvious state of things profit us, if we seek to govern all affairs Tesmer?"

"That control over Mother is essential, control she does *not* see as taking power from her or frustrating her will and rule. Rather, successful control must come through arranging events and what she learns of them to appear to offer her greater and greater power, so she does and decrees what we want her to as likely steps in her own reaching for more power."

Talyss nodded. "Well said." She reached out wordlessly for the flask.

"Yet so much *is* obvious," Belard murmured, returning it to her. "Our brothers and sisters know it, the lowest of our servants knows it—even the dead Lords Hammerhand and Lyrose knew it. How can we use this, that all know, to move Mother and therefore all Tesmer the way we desire—yet not get caught at it?"

"There's where you struck the shield-wall, brother, and saw no way past it, yes?"

"Yes," Belard admitted. "Wherefore I risked..."

"Much, and more when you got here and I gave you my smile," Talyss said quietly, taking a swift swallow that sent fresh comforting fire down her throat. "I value that more than you can probably believe, Bel. You're not the only one who knows loneliness as a knife that's never far away, and ever sharp and cruel."

Belard chuckled. "Even our brothers and sisters would be surprised to hear these words from us, so well do we play our parts; me the rake, and you the claws-always-out cat, both of us too eager to hurt, in our separate ways, to feel hurts."

Talyss let her catlike smile reach her lips this time. "Yes, and we must use their judgments of us to give us chances to do the unexpected. Our first chance must be good, and we must *use* it, mind. Mother's no fool; the slightest hint that we're working together— or that either of us is able to step out of being what the world sees us to be—will have her watching us sharper than the Falcon itself. We—"

She broke off, looking up sharply, as dry branches snapped underfoot not far off in the forest.

Their wards started to sing, that rising note of resistance to an intruder, and on its heels sounded the crackle of dead leaves, crushed under foot or paw by something moving forcefully. Something the size of a hunting cat, or a man.

Belard was on his feet with sword in hand, bent forward to get out of the moonlight and try to peer into the night-drenched forest.

They heard a stifled curse—a man, trying to keep his oath to a whisper—and more snappings of trodden dead wood. By then Talyss had snatched up her own slender sword and the best-balanced of her poisoned knives, and had the smaller fang poised for throwing.

The wards were almost shrieking now, the shrill sound they made when fighting someone who had his own magic to counter them.

For the intruder, striding closer to the hollow would be like wading upstream against a strong current, or forcing his way onward through a biting wind—not the stabbing pain the wards would force on the unprotected, where to advance far enough would be to die.

Belard felt for his boots. Seeing him made Talyss look for her own, and—

Light was blazing up in the darkness now, the wards starting to burn with the fires that both warned ward-owners and seared imprudent intruders. Most men would have turned back long since, and many of the rest would be screaming by now, plunged into agony by the flames streaming over them.

They could see him, or rather his outline, trudging rather unsteadily toward them through the thick trees. One man alone, hands apparently empty...

"Forestmother, defend me!" he declaimed, in the manner of a priest.

Boots on but otherwise still stark naked, Belard Tesmer strode to the edge of the hollow, sword raised and ready. "Halt," he snapped, "or die."

The burning man, who must not be feeling the flames, to have a voice so free of pain, never slowed.

"We all die, lord," he replied calmly, "and I would rather speak to you—both of you—than flee emptyhanded. Put up your sword; I mean you no harm."

Belard shot a look at Talyss, who nodded, and gestured with her sword that he should let the stranger come.

Or not-stranger; she knew that voice. She couldn't place it, just yet, but she'd heard it a time or three before, she knew she had... in Ironthorn, of course, yet who—

Belard backed away, and a man came staggering down into the hollow, the ward-flames falling away from him into nothingness as he reached the protected area within the wards.

As he came out through the lowest, still-dancing boughs—the limbs overhead were thick, as large in some spots as some full-grown trees along the banks of the Imrush—the moonlight fell full upon him, and both Tesmers gaped in astonishment.

They were staring at Cauldreth Jaklar, the Lord Leaf of Hammerhold. He looked bedraggled and grim, and his hands were empty. He raised them in a palms-out "I'm unarmed" gesture, and came to a halt amid their discarded garments.

"Lord and Lady Tesmer," he said, shooting swift looks at both of them, keeping his eyes carefully on their faces, his own face betraying no opinion at all about their lack of dress and likely reason for that, "I am pleased to have found you this night, for I have an offer to make to you that should please you both and lead to a bright future for Ironthorn."

Belard took a step forward and brought his sword up. "Priest," he snapped, "how did you know we were here?"

"I... you are in the forest, and I serve the Forestmother, who told me where you could be found."

"And why did you *want* to find us?" Talyss asked silkily, stepping back so moonlight no longer reached her raised arm, and the knife held ready to hurl in it.

"I need your aid, and your talents. *Ironthorn* needs your aid and talents."

"Oh?" Belard snapped, taking another menacing step forward. "Ironthorn's been slow to say so, thus far!"

"Lord Tesmer," Jaklar said quickly, stepping back and to one side, "please hear me! I can hurl spells to strike you both down, yet have not! Please! Hear me out!"

"Speak," Talyss commanded. The priest's sidestep had brought him closer to her, yet she was mindful of his winning his way so swiftly through their combined wards. He was protected by his own magic, and it might serve to turn aside blades. Or even send hurled ones back at the one who'd thrown them.

"Yes," the Lord Leaf agreed. "Hear me: the Hammerhands are dead, yet House Lyrose survives—with the wizard Malraun standing behind them. So I need new rulers in Hammerhold."

He took a step forward, and tried a smile. "Such as the two of you. With any mates you care to take, of course."

Chapter Twenty-Nine

TWO TESMER JAWS dropped open again, incredulity ruling them this time.

"*What?*" Belard asked disbelievingly, shaking his head.

Talyss had a swifter, surer tongue. "Rule as lord and lady? Over those who hate and mistrust us? While our parents sit a short ride away in their own castle, with their own claim to rightful rule over *all* Ironthorn?"

Jaklar met her eyes and nodded hard, as if accepting her view. "Yet hear me still!" he snapped. "The Lyrose women will soon be dead, punished by Malraun for their laxity, and your parents—who are, admit what you well know, the pawns of the other Doom, Narmarkoun of the greatfangs and the walking dead—will flee Ironthorn even sooner, running before Malraun can catch them."

"Leaving us to be blasted down by the *both* of them!" Belard protested. "To say nothing of what we'll have on our hands from all Ironthar—brother and sister ruling as husband and wife!—and our own kin! If none of them accept our rule, we'll soon be corpses, lord and lady of no more than a coffin each.

If we're lucky enough to be slain cleanly, so there's something left of us to put in a coffin, that is!"

The priest looked to Talyss and then back at Belard, almost beseechingly. "What if your brothers and sisters rallied to you, and upheld you as Lord and Lady of all Ironthorn?"

Talyss shook her head, lip curling. "Man, you know nothing of House Tesmer, do you? Our darling kin wouldn't do that even if both Dooms, the Falcon and Forestmother, and our parents *all* ordered them to!"

"What if I used magic on them? Do any of them have influence over the others? I could—"

"Priest, you are a fool."

Those words were uttered by a new voice, that struck everyone in the hollow to startled silence.

It was loud, cold, scornful—and came from above their heads.

Cauldreth Jaklar's hand gave off a sudden glow as he looked up, but an answering wink of light blossomed from one of the great tree limbs overhead, and the voice spoke again.

"No, Jaklar, not this time. You're not the only ambitious snake in Falconfar able to lay hands on a little magic, you know. I've half a mind to blast you now, just to make sure you'll never again dare to think of using spells to control any of we Tesmers— or have mind enough left to do so."

"Nareyera!" Talyss spat.

The younger of her two elder sisters smiled sweetly down at her through the leaves. Nareyera Tesmer had long, glossy black hair; right now it was framing eyes that were dark with malicious glee.

"Talyss, dear, where did you learn to pleasure a man? Watching mares being serviced in the stables?"

Fire rising in her eyes, Talyss hefted her knife threateningly.

Nareyera sneered. "Even if I wasn't spell-shielded against warsteel, your poison is nothing to me, dear. You use dellarra—so lazy of you—and I've tasted it for years. All it does these days is give me a headache. Enough to annoy me, nothing more. Bury it in yon lying priest if you must feed it someone."

She shifted silently along the bough until she could glance clearly across the hollow—whereupon her smile broadened. "Now *there's* a dagger," she said, licking her lips. "I wouldn't mind a ride or two myself, Belard, if you've finished with Little Cat Spiteful, here."

Her brother glared up at her. "How long have you been here, Nareyera?"

"From the beginning. *Two* family wards walking together, out here in the dark, dark Raurklor, arouse my curiosity—and when I'm curious, I like to get up high to watch and listen. When those two wards obligingly stop right under me and start to interweave, I get *very* interested. As it turns out, I got more than interested—I got entertained. Mmhmm, did I. Enough to make a swiftly-aging woman warm and wet, even if it is my own brother and sister."

"Lady Tesmer," Cauldreth Jaklar snapped, "you would be wise—"

"I *am* wise, priest. You're the one who should learn to become wise. You can begin by shutting your mouth, right now, and putting aside all thoughts of using any magic at all on any of us. Then, perhaps—just perhaps—I'll let you live."

"I—"

Belard took another step toward Jaklar. "Lord Leaf," he growled, "I very seldom agree with my sister Nareyera, but in this one matter I find that I do. Very much so."

"One moment," Talyss said then, raising her voice a trifle. "Jaklar, I believe it would be best if you left this part of the forest, very soon and walking briskly. However, I would have an answer from you first, and an honest one, if you're capable of telling truth. I believe I would like to hear you swear by the Forestmother on this."

Cauldreth Jaklar gave her a glare, but raised his brows and tilted his head to one side as if inviting her query.

"You put a proposition to us," Talyss Tesmer said to him, as calmly as if she was clad in finery, with armed Tesmer knights surrounding her, drawn swords backing her every word, rather than standing nude in a forest hollow, clad only in her long hair. "Tell us now: Why? Why did you want to see a Tesmer brother and sister ruling Ironthorn? What were you looking to gain from this? *What hold did you plan to have over us?*"

A slender, black-clad arm pointed down at him from the tree-limb above, rings on its fingers suddenly kindling to glowing life, and Belard sidestepped smoothly, to menace Cauldreth Jaklar from one side, almost from behind him. An instant later, Talyss moved too, her bare feet utterly silent, to put the priest squarely between her sword and Belard's.

The Lord Leaf's face slowly went pale.

"By the Holy Forestmother," he said slowly, "I—"

"No tricks, priest!" Nareyera snapped, from overhead. "No calling down your goddess on us! Just answer my sister's questions!"

Cauldreth Jaklar closed his eyes, let out a long, shuddering breath, and seemed to dwindle a little, before their eyes.

"The Forestmother," he said quietly, "wants me to tend to the forest, and not meddle as much in the lives of castle-folk and farmers as I have been. Yet she has charged me to make very sure that Ironthorn remains a place of modest farming and woodcutting, and is never home to folk who would even think of burning trees to cut into the Raurklor and expand beyond the vale. So I cannot rule Ironthar, but I need those who do to know the will of the Goddess, and agree with and uphold it."

He spread his hands. "I know well that Ironthar most like and trust other Ironthar, so I wanted those rulers to be of Ironthorn, not outlanders. I hoped you Tesmers would be my rulers. Yet it seems I was wrong."

He lifted his head, eyes all cruelty now, and spat a word none of them understood.

A moment later, every living tree branch and twig that was in, around, and over the hollow trembled violently. Then, with a hissing like the sound of a thousand angry serpents, they all started to grow, thrusting forward with frightening speed.

The priest smiled at the heart of it all, untouched, as the feverishly-growing branches reared up and stabbed at the three Tesmers like striking snakes.

ROD EVERLAR STOOD alone above the by-now-familiar heap of clothes that seemed determined to grant him no rest, and sighed.

Some Shaper of Falconfar. A prize fool, more like, rushing around trying to rescue Taeauna without knowing what I'm doing.

"Yes," he said aloud, sighing again. "Looking back, it's hard to see it as anything better than one blundering foolishness after another. I suppose that's one way to describe the career of a reckless hero as well as an utter failure, but… I'm no hero, that's for sure."

He started to pace. "Not that I ever claimed to be a hero or wanted to be a hero. I just wanted to help Taeauna… and right now, to help free her."

He clenched his fists, remembering that moment of thinking of Falconfar so vividly he'd managed to bring himself and Taeauna here… or had he? Could it have been Taeauna, working with him, that managed it?

Well, he had to try. Clenching his teeth as well as his fists, Rod shut his eyes and strained to picture Taeauna in his mind. Her every movement, her smell, her eyes when they looked at him with scorn—and admiration—and amusement—and exasperation, and a dozen other occasions… and the feel of her skin against his when they'd been in that bed together in Bowrock, and…

Rising pain distracted him. Looking down, he saw blood dripping from between his fingers. He'd tightened his fists so hard that he'd driven his fingernails into his palms.

And for nothing. It hadn't worked. He was still here in Malraun's tower. Alone.

Or so he hoped.

Letting out his biggest sigh yet, he flung himself down on the heap of clothes, and tried again to get to sleep.

So he could dream of destroying Malragard and striding across Falconfar like a mighty colossus, smashing castles and Dooms of Falconfar with snarling blows of his fists, and reaching down to pluck up Taeauna, the wingless yet beautiful Aumrarr of Falconfar.

Hoping, as he did, that she'd not spit at him with rage and disgust, and spurn him on the spot.

SILENCE, AND A pale white glow.

All around him, yet far away as he floated, screaming but silent, agonized but numb, staring but blind...

Narmarkoun. He was Narmarkoun, wizard... Doom of Falconfar. And he was in Yintaerghast, chill and empty... yet somehow *watchful*, all around him...

Yes, he was... he was floating in tangled and torn spells, drifting in midair, their pearly glows the radiance he'd been seeing. Shieldings, by the looks of their ruination, all bound up around him against one wall of the small, hidden chamber where...

Yes, where spells that must have been cast by Lorontar himself, long, long ago, were still at work on a distant living mind.

He remembered shrieking rage, and being blasted and hurled away by a furious mind that wanted him dead yet barely perceived him, and knew him not.

Yet now he felt... splendid. Not cold or bruised or hungry, not tired, and not hurt in any way. The shieldings—and where had they come from? Magics of Lorontar, left waiting for just such a moment of calamity?—seemed to have spent themselves not only keeping him from the slightest harm, but in healing and renewing him!

He felt marvellous. Narmarkoun swung his feet down, flexing one scaly blue arm and marveling at its fresh, gleaming, *new* appearance. The moment his boots touched the floor, he was upright and standing calmly amid the shieldings—which were fading away now, and growing dim as they settled toward the floor and vanished before they reached it…

He made no move toward the bright floating image of the brain. It was as alive as ever, magic surging around it and pounding through it in a soundless tumult of power. He shook his head in admiration, and more than a little fear. This could only be the work of Lorontar, and as such it must be older than the oldest Galathan noble lineage, yet it was as powerful, as vibrant, as if it had been cast mere moments ago.

The mind it was keeping conquered was alive and aware and seething at being enslaved, and in the instant he'd tasted its regard it had seemed somehow female… and human but strangely, subtly different than human—or most humans.

A mind that was in Falconfar, and active—not sleeping in some tomb or in the spell-frozen guise of a statue. Active somewhere distant from here, and— he somehow knew, as he gazed on those rushing, humming flows of magic—long under the control of this spell.

It was a mind of power, too. Not necessarily a wizard, but someone who had known and wielded magic enough not to be awed by the very thought of it.

Perhaps, if he—no. He'd been blasted once before, smashed down helplessly in a moment of passing thought. He might well not survive a second contact, if he probed with any determination and gave that captive brain more of a mind-moot to lash out at him through, and longer to do it in.

Best to just withdraw, healed and hale. It was enough to know that Lorontar had left magics behind to control and compel, spells that worked yet, and that held entrapped the mind of some female creature—it could well be a beast rather than human, perhaps a dragon Lorontar had desired as a steed—somewhere in Falconfar. Flight... yes, it was a mind that had known flight. And a mind that had influenced others of its kind, so that by working through it, Lorontar had held a measure of influence over them, too.

Yet he'd best stop thinking about that captive mind, *right now*, lest he draw its attention again, and taste another, harder, lashing-forth.

Turning his gaze from the glowing image of the brain at the heart of its eternally rushing whirl, Narmarkoun made his way quietly along the wall and out of the little hidden chamber not nearly as cautiously as he'd come in.

Up into a Yintaerghast as quiet and deserted as before, yet seemingly now familiar and welcoming. It seemed now to be *his* castle, not Lorontar's.

It wasn't that he suddenly knew its every chamber and passage, but rather as if they were forgotten parts of his home, not unfamiliar menacing corners of the most forbidding fortress known to Falconfar.

Hmm. The shieldings must have done this to him. Not just the healing; they'd left something behind in his mind that he was noticing only now that he was away from those rushing flows of magic.

A new spell was emblazoned in his mind.

Shining new and unfamiliar among his deepest, oldest memories. A magic he *knew* had not been there before, one he'd never mastered or cast.

A spell for overcoming and compelling a mind.

427

Like the mind whose control spell was humming and swirling down in the hidden chamber. Or perhaps not. As Narmarkoun peered at it more closely, letting his thoughts follow its workings to see what it was designed to enact rather than just marveling at its unexpected presence and its shining entirety, he perceived that it was a spell for controlling the minds of creatures of Earth, from here in Falconfar.

Though this arm of incantation, *here*, coupled to the larger spell with yon binding, made it also, when cast *thus*, into a means of conquering the minds of creatures of Falconfar while they were in the world called Earth.

So it was not a means of walking down a Stormar port street and compelling merchants to thrust all their coins into his hands, or forcing a Galathan noble to surrendering his daughter to a smiling Narmarkoun upon sight. It would work on lorn or Dark Helms he sent to Earth—or the man called Rod Everlar, here in Falconfar.

Yet even with these limitations, it was a wonder.

And best of all, it was *his* now, burned into his mind so deeply and securely he'd never need a scroll or to read the glyphs set down in a spellbook to cast it. Just thinking it through, letting his mind follow its intricate paths, would be enough. So long as he was conscious, and unharmed enough to remain strong of will from end to end of its casting.

Right now he felt stronger than he'd ever felt before. Brimming with vigor, on the verge of prancing through these empty rooms out of sheer joy at feeling so... alive.

No longer despairing, or longing to get out of this place and back to Closecandle before Malraun caught him here.

Now, somehow, half a dozen Malrauns alarmed him not in the slightest.

Not that this grim and empty castle around him was in any wise better than his Closecandle.

Nay, Closecandle was *his*, its every cavern and tunnel, chute and stair hollowed out of the heart of a great mountain by his magic. His work alone, every casting. His was the hand that had measured every handspan of rock melted away, and so tamed the greatest peak of the Howlhorns.

Just as his spells tamed and gentled every greatfangs he'd captured, and in time guided them as patiently as any greatfangs elder into breeding, one with another.

Beasts as large as villages and as deadly as armies, and they were his. His to ride, to goad them into hunting and making war at his command.

Six of them, though only the aging parents and the oldest of their hatchlings were full-grown brutes who could smash into a turret and live, toppling the castle's stone fang in their wake. The next-hatched was big enough to ride but still fighting his training, and the two younglings were little better than greedy fledglings, more interested in devouring and play-brawling with each other than obeying anyone.

Them, he missed. Not the younglings, but the elder three. Just as he ached for the caresses of his playpretties, no matter how swiftly Narmarkoun their Doom tired of them when he was nigh-buried in them.

Oh, the longings were there. Yet somehow, as he exulted in feeling stronger than ever before, they paled before the sheer joy of being here. Here, in Lorontar's ancient lair of secrets. Here, in the hidden heart of elder magic. Here where he could quite well abide for now, and spy on anyone he desired to from afar.

Rod Everlar, for one.

Oh, he now knew half a dozen Shapers he could call on, to alter Falconfar with their dreams and writings; Everlar was no longer *the* prize.

Yet still, Everlar was the Shaper most familiar with Falconfar—and the lone Shaper *in* Falconfar. So he'd bear watching, if only to make sure Malraun didn't sidle up and cast a net of spells to control the Earth man utterly.

Perhaps it was time to alter some of his playpretties into false Everlars, so Malraun would have a merry dance to lay hands on the real one...

Narmarkoun found his face aching from the wide and unaccustomed grin splitting it. He laughed aloud, clapped his hands together, and strode to the very center of a great empty chamber.

It was time to work magic. Lots of magic.

Swiftly conjure up another spying globe of magic to watch what's happening to Everlar, then cast spells to link again with the minds of his lorn and Dark Helms on Earth, to spy on their doings through their eyes.

Nor would that be all his spying and prying. It was high time to look in on the Tesmers back in Ironthorn—and time to awaken Deldragon, too. Even a Doom of Falconfar, after all, would need at least one army to invade and conquer Earth.

Let Malraun think he'd won Falconfar for now.

Fewer places ruled by Narmarkoun meant fewer places to defend. Even Closecandle could be sacrificed as a Malraun-trap now that the greatfangs were all grown enough to fly, and the elder three wise and mighty enough to defend themselves against even the spells of the Matchless.

Aye, let Malraun gloat, and turn to conquering Galath. A Galath without Deldragon and his knights.

Then, when the time was just right, appear unlooked-for in his very lap and smash him utterly. Letting him know, as he died, who was destroying him.

FAR AWAY ACROSS Falconfar in the dim and silent chambers and passages of Closecandle, dead faces started to smile, not knowing why.

NAREYERA TESMER SPAT out a curse, and then a flood of stranger words. The rings on her slender fingers obediently blazed and winked in wild fury.

An instant later, the night exploded in fire.

Great rolling balls of flame, erupting out of nowhere to light up the night as they thundered away from Nareyera in all directions. The tree that held her caught alight with a great roar, hurling her down into the hollow as it blazed up angrily, warming her back.

Everywhere she looked, as she crashed down and left her breath behind, fire was racing along black, writhing branches. Through many leaping, hungry amber tongues, as she rolled over and up to her knees, gasping, Nareyera saw her brother spring at Cauldreth Jaklar. Mindful of blazing branches stabbing at him, Belard bounded aside at the last moment to thrust with his sword at the priest's side rather than sinking into a face-to-face lunge.

The priest ducked away and ran, fleeing across the hollow as the tree boughs moved by his magic dipped at his back to form a flaming wall—and flail at Belard. He staggered back from their rushing flames, but behind him Talyss was momentarily free of reaching limbs and branches. She glared at Jaklar through the flames and hurled her knife, hard.

It bit home deeply, striking to the hilt in the priest's shoulder. Nareyera saw him falter, arch over backwards in pain for a frozen moment—and then stagger forward with a great sob and run on, up out of the hollow into the night-dark forest. He was bleeding freely; there'd be a trail of blood to mark where he fled.

Yet the Lord Leaf was still very much alive, for the tree-limbs governed by his spell were reaching even more wildly for Belard and Talyss, thrusting in from all directions despite quickening flames dancing along them, seeking to throttle and entwine.

In the space of a breath her brother and sister were back to back in the heart of closing claws of living wood, hacking desperately at the burning branches that jabbed at them, fighting to stay free and alive.

They were doomed.

Nareyera triggered the ring that quelled magic. If she called on all of its power at once…

It exploded, taking her finger with it and leaving her shrieking in pain, startled and in agony—amid a sudden great hissing, that heralded the return of the night-gloom.

All around the hollow, the fires she'd caused were sinking down into smoke, leaving behind only the hissing of their dying. The smoke-wreathed tree limbs were falling limp, no longer growing or moving purposefully anywhere. They started to creak and groan as they cooled. Amidst the cacophony, the ward-spells of all three Tesmers flickered—and failed.

The *pain!* Falcon Above, it hurt! Nareyera could not seem to stop weeping. On her knees, she wrung her hand wildly, trying to quell the pain, trying not to look at the twisted and blackened ruin of where her finger had been. The rings on her slender, unmarked neighboring fingers winked and gleamed almost mockingly.

Out of the sagging boughs strode Belard and Talyss, swords glittering and faces grim.

Two swordpoints menaced Nareyera, who stared up at them in teary disbelief. "What're you—fools! I just saved your lives!"

"So you could use us as your little spell-driven dupes," Belard sneered. "Well, behold my gratitude, sister!"

His sword swung back—and then down.

Still weeping, Nareyera spat out a word that took her far away.

Her brother and sister saw a ring wink, and their sister vanish, the winking ring becoming a fading spark in midair. Belard's blade swept through empty air.

He turned to look at Talyss. She was turning slowly on one boot heel to peer at the forest all around. Seeking any sign of Nareyera—or Jaklar—standing nearby in the night, looking murderously back at her.

Belard lowered his sword and waited in silence as she looked, slowly and thoroughly, going around twice.

"Alone," she breathed at last, turning to look at him.

Belard set his teeth in a snarl and sliced away the nearest smoldering branch.

"Good," he spat. Jabbing his blade into the soil, he opened his arms.

Talyss smiled, planted her own sword, and sprang into his embrace.

Their cloaks, still draped over the boughs that now thrust aggressively out into the hollow, were giving off plumes of smoke. He bore her down onto them regardless, almost clawing at her.

She *did* claw at him, thrusting her loins up to meet him.

"We should get away from here," she panted. "Nareyera knows where we are; she could hurl spells! Our wards are down; that priest could turn the trees against us again, or the beasts of the Raurklor come a-sniffing, to see what meals the fire served them up…"

"Let them," Belard growled. "The danger makes me all the hungrier!" He bent his head and bit at her breasts.

Talyss moaned. Cupping them in her hands, she offered them to him, to bite all the harder.

"Yes! It does!" she hissed. "Take me—and may the Falcon take Nareyera!"

"Oh, it will," Belard snarled, sweat running down his face as he rammed into her. "The way she's going, it undoubtedly will!"

Chapter Thirty

AMTEIRA CAME AWAKE shivering. Small wonder; she was lying curled up on her side on the great mossy boulder, still wearing nothing at all. Falcon, how long had she been here?

She didn't remember falling asleep, didn't remember anything at all after starting into her prayer…

Knuckling her eyes awake, she sat up—only to have her arm fail her, so she almost fell back to greet the rock with her face.

Wincing, she rolled over on her back, rubbing one arm with the other, flexing both of them, and wiggling her fingers. They were stiff—all of her was stiff—and she found herself shivering. Stars were glimmering overhead through the dark cloak of leaves, and the night air was damp as well as cold. As she rolled over again, Amteira could see her breath for the most fleeting of moments, as a fading, drifting mist caught in the moonlight.

The moon was low, and around her the Raurklor was alive with rustlings and faint, distant hootings and calls. It was full night.

She sat up. Well, so much for her blood and prayer and all. Either there was no Forestmother and Jaklar was a hedge-wizard lying about his holy beliefs and deeds, or the goddess of the Raurklor wasn't disposed to listen to the entreaties of Amteira Hammerhand.

Most likely Jaklar was lying. "Lord Leaf," indeed. He wasn't a priest at all, but a clever fox who knew who to taint with his berries and ground roots, and when and how to sway or slay folk that way, with a few spells to back up his claims of serving a mighty goddess. Leaving Amteira Hammerhand as just one more fool who'd believed him.

There was her war-harness, just where she'd dropped it. She'd best get dressed before something with fangs came along and decided—*hold!*

What was that?

Where she'd shifted herself off the great mossy boulder, there was a faint glow.

It was coming from a spot smaller than the palm of her hand, amid the old fissures in the stone. It was the moss she'd wet with her blood, fallen from her skin to the rock, shining in moon-silver silence. A small radiance, but a steady one.

She reached out to touch it but drew back before her fingers reached it, and couldn't stop herself from turning about to shoot swift glances out into the dark forest all around her. Glances that saw no skulking men or beasts, nothing but trees and their leaves.

She looked back at the glow, half expecting it to rear up and lash out at her.

So was this some trick of Jaklar's, or is there a Forestmother after all?

The moss hadn't moved or changed. Staring down at it, Amteira decided she should pray again to the

Forestmother. Just a few words this time, no more moss and blood. Just to ward off the disfavor of the goddess, if there was a Forestmother.

Considering what she'd just been thinking, it was only prudent. And would take her but a moment, before she'd get her armor back on and think about what she should do next.

"Holy Forestmother," she murmured, thrusting out her hand to put her fingers firmly on the moss.

She caught her breath and almost pulled them back again; the moss was *warm* where it should have been cold, dry where it should have been damp with dew. The doing of the goddess, or—ah. The heat of her own body. She'd been lying on it, of course, warming it with herself.

Smiling at her apprehension, the last of the Hammerhands sat up straight, looked to the stars and then down at the deepest, darkest trees around her, and firmly began a simple, respectful prayer.

"Forgive me what I have done in harm to the Raurklor and all forests," she whispered. "Guide me in what I should do henceforth. Show me some sign, to make me believe and heed."

The world exploded.

Amteira's ears rang and seemed to split under a great cracking sound, even as the darkness was lost in a blinding white flood of light.

In the whirling silence, she found herself on her back on the rock, staring up at what was crackling down out of the clear and starry night sky.

A lightning bolt as thick as an ancient tree, that was stabbing down into the boulder. The great rock that was shaking under her, a great numbing shuddering that—

Ended in a great shriek of riven stone.

I *can* hear.

As Amteira thought that, she was hurtling through the air, tumbling over and over amid dark shards of rock.

All of us, being hurled into—what had Jaklar so often said? Oh, yes: oblivion.

In the blinding light rose darkness. Dimly Amteira Hammerhand clung to one fading thought.

So there *is* a Forestmother.

VELDUKE DARENDARR DELDRAGON strode along his high battlements, restless and not knowing why. Spread out below him, Bowrock stood tranquil in the moonlight, a light glimmering here and there among its roofs and towers. Modest when considered by an eye that could at the same time gaze upon his castle, yet far more prosperous than most places in Galath—or even the Stormar cities, with their reeking backstreets and grasping, desperate rib-daggers. Gaunt and starved and glaring out at the world with no hope.

"There's none of that here," he told the night aloud, in almost fierce satisfaction, his words startling one of his sentinels into stepping out of his embrasure to peer along the wall to see who'd spoken.

Deldragon gave the man a nod and smile, pausing in his striding where the moonlight would fall full on his face and front, so he'd be recognized. And so he was; the man gave him a hasty salute and stepped back again.

Deldragon felt his smile widening; he strode forward again, heading for the corner, still far ahead, where this great keep ended and the wall-walk turned down its end wall for a few paces, ere sloping down to a lower, newer hall that ran on to the two turrets all Bowrock liked to gaze upon of nights like this one, when they stood awash in moonlight. He—

Faltered and almost stumbled. Why had his mind been suddenly full of blue skin with scales, skin covering an arm that might have been his own?

What could possibly bring such a scene into his mind, and so vividly? A spell, sent from afar? A whim of the Falcon, or some malicious Stormar god he'd never heard of? A wizard nearby, dreaming?

He knew of no wizards in Bowrock right now, mind, but that stood as nothing beside such a vivid mind-seeing, aye? Most hedge-wizards strode through life grandly proclaiming their magic to all, to make themselves seem mighty where the truth was far feebler, but *real* wizards—not just the fabled Dooms, but all their apprentices, and the sorcerer-lords across the Sea of Storms, too—could hide what they were, if they cared to.

All contentment gone, Velduke Deldragon stood in the moonlight frowning, wondering what to do. What *could* he do?

Was this a deliberate warning, or the Falcon's way of alerting him to a hidden menace? Blue scaled skin should tell him something, remind him of someone, but he couldn't—couldn't—had never known, his mind told him coldly.

He stared at nothing, seeing a blank stone wall and emptiness beyond in his mind. The empty field or chamber was its old, old way of telling him he knew nothing at all about something—but the stone wall was how he'd always known he was forgetting something. A broken down, ruined stone wall, under an open sky, but this was inside, a tall and strong barrier in front of his nose.

Something was being hidden from him. By whom, and how, he had no idea, but the very thought frightened him, leaving him shivering.

"Lord?" the sentinel asked hesitantly, from just behind him. "Are you—is aught wrong?"

Deldragon lifted his head, set his jaw, and snapped, "No. Not yet."

He spun around, barely seeing the man, only vaguely aware that his sudden movement had made the man dip his spear menacingly and then hastily raise it again with an apologetic mumble.

Instead, he was seeing himself in bright armor again, riding among the tents of a great encampment. Inspecting an army; *his* army. His knights were coming forth from the tents to salute him, his men looking up at him with smiles on their faces, all the might of Bowrock arrayed across a great meadow and filling it...

"Yet I know what I must do," he heard himself telling the guard, not really knowing why, and seeing no foe or battlefield. "We must ready ourselves for war. All Bowrock must stand prepared to fight."

The sentinel said not a word, but the moonlight was on his face, and Deldragon could read it well enough.

"Yes," he said wryly, knowing his lips were twisting. "Again."

ROD FOUND HIMSELF falling gently down through a red mist, a mist of flowers—flowers?—to stand before a stone gate he'd never seen before, in a misty forest. It was a gate with a fortress behind it, and warm firelight was flooding out around the chinks in the old and ill-fitting wooden doors of that keep. Doors that were suddenly guarded by nude women holding drawn swords. Women bare from the throats down, who had the dark, menacing helmed heads of Dark Helms.

"Who are you?" they challenged him, stepping forward to point their glittering blades at him.

"Rod Everlar," he replied, bubbles flooding out of his mouth. Had they heard him?

"I *thought* so," the foremost said fiercely, and tore off her helm. It was Taeauna, but she thrust her thumbs under her chin and peeled the flesh up and off, too, in a drifting mist of blood, to reveal—

The mouthless face of a lorn.

The other guards all laughed, and it was the shrill, cruel mirth of women who hated him.

"What is this place? Who's lord here?" he asked quickly, as they all started toward him.

"Zundarl rules here. We kill you in his name," was the smugly chanted reply.

Zundarl? Who the hell was Zundarl?

Not a name he knew, nothing of his writing, but "hell" was familiar enough. Hell meant a great dark gulf, and despairing shrieking from shattered skulls that still had eyes, staring redly at him as he fell into it, joining the general plunge down to—

Land lightly on his feet, on a high platform of stone, a great slab that shuddered under Rod's boots with the deep, approaching roar of the great winged beast that had just landed. The clap of its great wings set his red cloak—red cloak? Where'd he acquired a red cloak?—to swirling, buffeting him with gusts of wind that made him stagger. Cloak flapping, he hastily drew his sword, and had to thrust it far out into the air, just to hold his balance.

That blade was in his left hand, suddenly, and there was a quill pen in his right, a great white plumed feather larger than any he'd ever seen before, trimmed to a point that dripped dark red blood.

No, *streamed* dark red blood, in a constant welling that came from nowhere he could see. No feather could hold that much gore...

There was nothing to write on, though, and the monster was turning to regard him, slow and massive, baleful menace in its great gloating eyes even before their gaze found him.

Turning, so huge that its tread and throat-rumbling were shaking the high landing where he stood, sending small shards crumbling off the steps below and tumbling down to...

It was a greatfangs, the largest he'd ever seen, bigger than any dragon, and there were more of its kind—smaller, but each one still easily larger than a castle as they glided past—filling the sky behind it.

The greatfangs was reaching out its huge neck, crashing through a space in the castle in front of Rod that wasn't large enough for it. Its great bony beak of a snout came at Rod like a thrusting dagger, the flaring ridges of the widening head behind all those fangs hurling down stones with an ongoing clatter.

Folk were screaming and running out of the groaning, leaning keep now, as shattered stone-work plunged down around them.

Rod found himself staring in fascination at the forest of upthrust horns atop the head of the greatfangs, the many spines that defend the head of every greatfangs from the closing jaws of larger greatfangs and of dragons.

Staring as it all came nearer... he could do nothing

with his bloody pen or his puny sword... the eyes of the greatfangs kindled into the bright glee of the devourer, its forest of fangs parted, and the snout came for him...

Rod came awake shouting.

Or had he cried out? The echoes of something were ringing in his ears, he thought, but Malragard seemed silent and empty around him.

He was sitting upright atop his heap of clothes, sweating, his heart pounding in fear as he stared into the darkness.

Fear... and anger, too, like red coals under it getting ready to flare. He'd not dreamed so vividly and so, so... *energetically* for years, and never had a dream held so much of the astonishing and utterly unfamiliar.

Malraun. It must be Malraun tampering with his dreams.

Oh, not deliberately, riding his mind and meddling—why bother, when a Doom of Falconfar could so much more easily blast any mind he could enter, or conquer will and thought and memory, to enslave the owner of the mind?

No, this was more, uh, *automatic*. As if it was happening to him just because he was inside Malraun's fortress, and so within reach of spells the wizard had cast to affect everyone like this.

Rod swiped the back of his arm across his drenched face.

So, were greatfangs flying through the skies above a keep somewhere in Falconfar, or smashing open the front of that fortress to turn and menace a man in a red cloak, who was standing alone on a high stone terrace one moment and gone into empty air the next?

Just because he, a Shaper, the Lord Archwizard of Falconfar, dreamed matters stood thus?

Or was he just a sleepy, deluded writer of thrillers and fantasy trilogies who had no real power at all? A bumbler who could do nothing in Falconfar unless some lurking wizard or other worked magic to make things happen, hiding behind Rod Everlar as a cover for their deeds...

TAEAUNA FOUGHT TO scream out her rage, but managed only the faintest of gasps. Lorontar's will was a great fist of power against her feeble infant's fumblings, flooding through her and leaving her dazed and helpless.

Flooding through her not to slay or savage, but to soothe.

Caress and cozen not the mind of Taeauna of the Aumrarr, but that of the man sprawled atop her, the wizard who styled himself Malraun the Matchless.

To keep him deeply asleep, no matter what guards came shouting or seeking to shake him out of slumber, as morning came to Darswords.

Bound and helpless under him, Taeauna lay silent. Seething, but held in a grip that wouldn't allow her to so much as curse softly.

She'd never thought she'd miss cursing so much.

ISKARRA SHOOK HER head again, trying not to spew what little was in her stomach. She'd just plunged out of spiraling red mists, a long and sickening fall that had ended—none too gently—in a landing on hard stone battlements in the gray and misty chill before dawn.

The battlements belonged to an unfamiliar keep that stood in a narrow green river valley, that was part of a labyrinth of side-vales, somewhere in the vast Raurklor.

She'd seen that much while hurtling down to… here.

Iskarra shook her head, wincing. Everything she looked at swam a little around its edges, and looked a trifle greener than it should. "What did you do to us?"

"Took you through a gate," Dauntra said tartly. "Wizards and high priests aren't the only ones who have a little magic."

"Yours came from something you carry, not a spell," Isk said calmly, trying not to show her horrible queasiness. "I was watching."

Dauntra shrugged, her smile fading not a whit.

"So where are we?" Garfist's grunt, from above and behind Iskarra, was as sour as it was resigned.

"Ironthorn," snapped Juskra, as she flapped her wings hard to slow her plunge—and dropped him the last foot or so onto the battlements. "The other end of it. Tesmer lands."

"This is Imtowers," Dauntra added softly.

Gar's grunt told all listening Falconfar that he was far from impressed.

He lurched to the rampart, looked down, then turned away. No escape there. Not and keep hold of life. He started the long trudge to where the battlements turned a corner, heading for where the hillside loomed and the drop would be less.

A dark shadow glided over him before he was halfway there, landed in his path, and folded her wings rather grimly.

The scarred Aumrarr wasn't in the best of humors. Garfist Gulkoun wasn't the lightest of men, and had the irritating habit, when dangling in the air as a burden, of twisting and kicking just as a side-gust struck. Wherefore her shoulders ached abominably.

"In there," Juskra told him, pointing.

Gar spared the stair-hutch she'd indicated not so much as a glance. He kept right on lumbering along the battlements toward her.

"Garfist Gulkoun," she added, voice sharpening, "that's the way down. Or rather, the only one that doesn't involve your neck—and probably most of the rest of you, too—getting thoroughly broken."

Face set, eyes flickering everywhere but at her as he strode, he gave no sign of having heard her words.

"Those stairs descend past three bedchambers that're very likely unoccupied this night, unless various of the younger Ismers have very swiftly returned from mischief they looked quite happy to be part of, in various elsewheres. The third step below the landing giving onto the main floor lifts up. The catch under it opens a door in the stairwell you'll never find otherwise, into the room where Lord Irrance Tesmer keeps the greater part of his spending-gems. In handy carry-coffers."

The striding man lifted a hand and firmly favored her with a gesture that was both dismissive and decidedly rude, and kept right on coming.

"Garfist," she added warningly.

He did not slow.

The Aumrarr sighed, bounded into the air in a violent clapping of wings that sent him staggering, and landed right behind him. He whirled with an oath, fists coming up, but it took her only a passing moment to slap the side of his neck as he turned.

His eyes went out like two snuffed candles, and he kept right on turning, plunging silently to the floor.

Iskarra darted forward, eyes wild. "What did you—?"

"Hush," Juskra replied soothingly, raising a hand on which a ring was glowing softly. That faint radiance certainly hadn't been there before. "He'll be able to move again very soon. And breathe."

Isk gave her a cold look. "If you've harmed him…"

"*Very* soon," Dauntra murmured, from just behind her.

The gaunt woman was unmollified. "We faced and fought Lyroses for you; why are you doing this to us?"

The scarred Aumrarr shrugged. "Your work in this isn't done. That which you were intended to affect hasn't yet arisen."

"Can I have that in plain tongue?" Gar growled weakly, glaring up from the flagstones by her feet. "Ye sound like a sly merchant trying to sell a new cure-all-ills ointment! *Plain* talk, wingbitches! Plain talk!"

"You need not fight, for this one," Dauntra told him, waving at the stair-hutch. "If the Falcon smiles, no Tesmer will even see you."

"Nor any of their guards," Juskra added.

Iskarra put her hands on her hips, disbelief large on her face. "You want their riches," she said almost primly, "and daren't risk your own precious necks going down in there to steal it. So the traps are? And the guards?"

"There are none," Juskra said flatly. "Nor do we *need* their riches; we wingbitches have always had more than enough coin to buy the best spies. Which is why we know there are spells waiting all down that stair that will cry out when Aumrarr—or lorn, for that matter—come too close. Hence your present usefulness."

"Tesmers shorn of their ready wealth," Dauntra added calmly, "are Tesmers looking over their shoulders for thieves, or assassins following where the thieves came in knowing so much. They are also Tesmers now lacking coin enough to work certain mischiefs better not promoted. Whereas Garfist and Iskarra enriched are... Garfist and Iskarra enriched."

Garfist shook his head. "Were either of ye priests, in younger days?" he asked sourly, finding his feet unsteadily and not shaking off the swift assistance of his lady. "Such verbiage!"

"I can be blunter," Juskra said with the faintest of smiles, her voice dry. "Both of you are thirsting hard to be free of us and everyone else who's been chasing you and forcing you to do this and that. You want food, rest, and riches."

Garfist and Iskarra both nodded.

Juskra held up her hand to show them her ring again; the glow had quite fled from it. She drew it off and put it carefully into Garfist's hand. "You awaken it by thinking of a vivid sunrise. It should work twoscore times more. It belonged to an Aumrarr who's now too dead to feel the lack of it. I give it to you freely."

He glared down at it, then lifted his glare to her. "So just what're ye playing at, hey?"

"If you do this thieving for us," she replied, "and come back up these stairs, we'll fly you safe out of here. To a ruin—an Aumrarr wingbitch ruin no others dare approach, though none of us are left to guard it now—where we can all rest. Then come the next day, aloft again and on to an inn in Galath we know, where you can have all the food and drink you want, and no one will ask who you are or who you may be running from. Safe we'll take you, just as I've promised; no treachery and no lies."

Dauntra nodded, and the battlescarred Aumrarr spoke again.

"We'll swear this by any bindings you desire; we want to know you as friends, henceforth."

"Because ye'll be needing us again, in time to come," Gar growled.

Juskra did smile, this time. Sweetly. "Of course."

THE MOUNTAIN SHUDDERED again, a deep, teeth-jarring rumbling that was loud and long. As its din deepened, rocks as large as human heads came crashing down in a hard rain from above, amid the usual dust and grit.

None of Narmarkoun's undead shrieked or cried out. Without the Master to empower them to do otherwise, they remained mute.

Yet their agitation was clear to each other by the ways they stiffened and hastened to vantage points in the great open interior of Closecandle, to peer in all directions to try to see what was happening.

Solid stone rocked beneath them, under heavy blows. In the great central well-shaft where Narmarkoun was wont to ride his greatfangs up into the chill mountain sky or come plunging down out of it to thunderous landings, a jutting balcony cracked off the wall and fell. One of the Master's favorite playpretties clung silently to its sheared-off fragment of railing, staring all around in wild despair, as she plunged to shattering oblivion below.

Another balcony cracked and crumbled away, spewing smaller stones down the shaft. Then, quite suddenly, there was no room for more stone to fall down that great opening, as huge scaled bodies burst into view from below, thrusting upwards wedged together and struggling, each one furious to get to the light first. Huge claws raked the ancient stone walls as if they were made of butter, and wings strained to find space enough to unfurl.

The eldest and strongest of the greatfangs suddenly prevailed, clawing its way up the surging body of the rival it was wedged against. Kicking off from its rival's head, it took wing in a great bound up the shaft.

Wings clapped wind in their wake, a blast of air that made a great roaring bellow of exultation ring deafeningly around the shuddering shaft as the greatfangs tasted freedom, climbing fast into the sky.

The second greatfangs raced up the shaft after it, and then the third, as Narmarkoun's undead watched.

Not knowing what to do, with the Master absent and sending no commands, they stood mute and helpless, doing nothing more than staring, as every last greatfang soared up out of Closecandle and flew away.

All in the same direction, long necks stretched out in raging haste.

Chapter Thirty-One

AMTEIRA DRIFTED FOR a long time in dreams laced with the everpresent gentle rustle and earthy smells of the Raurklor. They were cold dreams, full of shivering, and frantic dreams, too, often bursting into desperate running. Barefoot, through the woods, sometimes as a doe, betimes human, and from time to time as stranger things... but always female, always bare-skinned, and always fearful.

Abruptly she came awake, huddled on her side on a bed of blackened stone shards. Lifting her head, she found it to be part of the great boulder she'd prayed on. The rest of it, riven into chunks great and small, lay all around her. She *was* cold.

Yet even as she stood, shivering, she cared nothing for that discomfort. The Raurklor was all around her, vast and wonderful, and she stared at it in awe, seeing it keenly for the first time.

Many, many smells cradled her and nigh overwhelmed her. The normal smells of a forest, it seemed, but she'd never before *really* noticed them all. Always, before, one scent—the smoke of a fire, or the sharp tang of bruised pine needles, the rotting-leaf mud of the rain-drenched Raurklor or the simmering growing smell of a hot forest day— had dashed aside all others and been all she really recognized. Now, though...

Abruptly Amteira became aware that her bare skin was now adorned with many patches of moss, and they felt a part of her, not something distasteful she should claw off as swiftly as she could.

More than that; she could *feel* the air around her through them. Feel it moving far more sensitively than before, every eddy and gust, subtle shifts in warmth and moments of chill.

She stood up, and abruptly knew something else. Turning her head, she nodded, certain of it. There was running water over *there*, though she couldn't see it—and yonder, too, though much farther off.

She felt part of the woods, now, rather than an intruder in the endless green vastnesses.

What had happened to her? This moss, her smelling and feeling... could this be the Forestmother, answering her prayer?

Amteira, will you serve me, or die?

The great, boomingly-soft voice in her head seemed as dark, tall, and terrible of power as a Stormar wave, about to crash over her and carry her away.

"F-forestmother?" she blurted out, more than a little afraid.

I am more than that, and less, but you may call me that.

"Call you—? Uh, I... I will serve you. If you'll have me."

Good. Welcome. Your first service will be to slay the traitor Cauldreth Jaklar for me. I demand his blood.

Relief flooded through her. "I'll slay him right gladly. Where is he?"

Gone back to Ironthorn. Having called on me to slay you with the wolves of the forest.

"The wolves?"

Abruptly a smoky-gray shadow loomed up over the scattered shards of the rock to regard her with blood-red, unblinking eyes. Its fangs were long, sharp, and many. There was a second shadow, moving sleekly behind it, and a third.

The wolves you shall lead into Hammerhold to rend Jaklar—and bid Hammerhold farewell. Ironthorn is your world no longer. You belong to me now.

Amteira Hammerhand drew in a deep, shuddering breath, bade her dead father a silent farewell, and replied, "Y-yes. Yes, I do. Command me."

Hunt now, and hunt well. Slay for Burrim Hammerhand—and for yourself.

Before Amteira could reply, the snout of a wolf was nuzzling her, its tongue rasping on her hand and thigh.

She looked down into its eyes, and smiled.

They smiled back, turning—just for an instant— leaf-green before they faded again to blood-red. She turned, naked and weaponless, and started running through the forest, heading for where she thought Ironthorn was.

The wolves howled once, eerily, then ran with her, one of them edging ahead to turn her firmly.

She followed, then as a test turned back in the direction she'd first headed, still running hard. All the wolves pressed close in around her, bounding along to nudge her with their noses and flanks, all of them working to turn her this time.

She ran where they led her, barehanded and bareskinned, hunger for the blood of Cauldreth Jaklor growing in her again.

For some reason, she felt very happy.

RUSTY CARROLL WAS gasping for breath. When had so many God damned *steps* been added, between the gleaming glass ground floor of Holdoncorp headquarters and Rear Second, where the Security Office was?

It sure as blazes hadn't felt like this many the last time he'd run up them.

Huh, and when exactly had *that* been?

Long ago, was all he could recall just now, with a freaking *sword* in his hand, twenty-some frightened secretaries and managers hurrying up the stairs at his heels—and *six lunatic murderers* on the loose in the building!

Dark Helms, mind you, who'd come striding in here with a *lorn* flying backup for them!

He didn't know what he'd do about them, but he did know he had to get back to the office before they went up the stairs—or, bejesus, took the elevators!—and got there first.

To where they could watch every corner of the building, turn off the lights and heat and air in any zone with the flick of switch and a spin of a dial—and lock or unlock any doors they pleased, too.

And Pete Sollars would be sitting there with his coffee cold and forgotten in his hand, staring at the forest of monitors and flickering alarm telltales and doing effing *nothing*. Except maybe shifting from camera to camera to watch them better, as they came to kill him.

Sollars was a nice guy, but he'd never had a swift and original thought in his life. Thinking on his feet was something he just didn't do. He was the other sort of security guy; the stolid, too-dull-to-get-bored watcher at his post.

Rusty topped the last step—at last!—stabbed his fingers at the codepad, and flung the heavy metal door open. "Pete! *Where are they?*"

Sollars swung around in the high-backed swivel chair—the Chief's chair, Rusty's chair—and stared at his boss, looking guilty. "Uh, I—ah—*No!*"

Rusty saw where Pete's stare was aimed, and flung himself at the floor and toward whatever Sollars was staring at.

Which meant the head of the fire axe came crashing down not through Rusty's skull, but over his diving body—to chip the concrete floor, right through the No-Slip tread coating. Secretaries screamed, and Hank staggered back, face going pale.

"M-mister Carroll?"

"I'm fine. No harm done, Hank!"

Rusty didn't have time for all the apologies; he was up on his feet and running to the monitors, sword in hand. He used it to point to the corridor running west. "Pete, take Hank and get all these ladies into Brain Central! Lockdown drill! Lockdown drill!"

Brain Central was the vault-like computer room not far behind him and one office to the west. It had walls like a battleship, a secure air supply, and its own power generator. It was a safe bet none of those oh-so-haughty managers had ever used such a primitive chemical toilet before, but... it beat having their throats sliced open or a sword thrust through their lovely midriffs, that was for sure.

Sollars was staring at him. "Lockdown? Brain Central?"

"Yes!" Randy roared into Pete's face. "*Move!*"

A frightened hubbub was rising, behind him—and amid it he could hear the President's unmistakable spluttering. Hank, at least, must be following Lockdown procedures as fast as he could.

He turned, seeing the tall custodian shooing well-dressed women ahead of him like a farmer herding chickens. "Hank?" he called. "Leave me the axe. Get another from the station inside there."

Hank turned his head and nodded, grinning apologetically. He leaned the axe carefully against the wall, then started moving toward the west corridor, spreading his arms wide and murmuring, "Let's go, people. Let's go."

He was sweeping the women—and a few bewildered-looking men in shirtsleeves and bedraggled ties, too, the angrily bewildered President of Holdoncorp among them, his golf putter still clutched in his hands—before him. Good. The fewer people screaming and rushing around to where they could be sliced open or taken as hostages, the better.

Where *were* those Dark Helms? By the looks of things, Sollars had been enjoying watching Holdoncorp vice presidents get chopped apart—and Rusty couldn't find it in himself to blame him for that—but had been so intent on watching tall, handsome, blustering Executive Vice President Jackman Quillroque plead for his life and loudly try to call various Holdoncorp designers to their dooms via the intercom from desk after desk, that he hadn't kept close watch over the grim Dark Helms to make sure all six of them were still together.

They weren't.

Rusty dialled most of the long row of doors shut before he even started checking monitors. Lock them in little boxes first and foremost, then worry about what to do to them.

Four of them were bullying Quillroque, slicing away clothing as the man blubbered and pleaded. Jack the Mouth was bleeding from somewhere, but Rusty didn't think he was missing any fingers or ears yet.

The other two...

He caught sight of one of them almost immediately, skulking along a corridor that would take him right to the stairs up. Up to this floor, of course.

All that was delaying him was the time it was taking to peer into every cubicle, to make sure no Holdoncorp employee still lived, cowering in hiding. Sword drawn, helmed head thrust forward, the Dark Helm was the very picture of confident menace.

Damn. Rusty looked wildly around, at monitor after monitor. He couldn't see the last of the six at all.

Had Mase or Sam or one of their men actually managed to take out one of the intruders, before getting killed?

Rusty doubted it. "All in," Hank called from behind him, and Rusty heard the heavy Brain Central door clank shut before he could even reply.

He looked around. "Pete?"

"Y-yessir?"

Rusty pointed at the monitors. "Find me the sixth one. Fast."

Two strides took him to the phone, and he found himself ridiculously relieved to hear a dial tone when he slammed it against his ear.

There was no way these Dark Helms could get to the underground fiber optic bundle, to cut it, but he'd been beginning to fear they could do bloody *anything*.

He pushed the panic button, that got him straight to the police.

"Yo, Rusty! What's up?" The sergeant's voice sounded bored. "Someone steal your corporate headquarters while everyone was on coffee break?"

Rusty sighed. "Derek, this is *serious*. We're under attack. We have dozens dead. Repeat: dozens of fatalities. Six—"

"Under attack by *what*? A friggin' army?"

"Uh—" Rusty caught himself on the verge of saying "hijackers." How do you "hijack" a computer company? An office building?

Right. Terrorists, then.

"Terrorists, six of them, and—"

Rusty paused again, deciding he wouldn't mention the lorn just now. The disbelief was strong and clear in the sergeant's voice; this wasn't the time to give the man any stronger ideas of introducing overworked security chiefs to looney bins.

"Like World War Two commandos," he said instead. "Only with swords."

"Oh, *ninjas*. Why didn't you just say so? Ninjas. *Right*."

"I'm *serious*, damn it!" Rusty found he was gripping the phone in both hands as though trying to strangle it. "Mase is dead, Sam's dead, most or all of their men are dead too, and—"

The line went dead at the same time as the lights flickered, sparks burst from a nearby wall-panel as its door banged open, and Sollars quavered, his voice rising almost into a scream, "S-sir? Mister Carroll, sir? I've found the last one!"

Rusty looked up from the security desk to see two spark-spewing ends of a power lead swinging back and forth. The Dark Helm who'd just severed that cable turned from them, shuddering only a little, to stalk slowly across the room toward Rusty, sword raised and ready.

For the first time in nineteen years at Holdoncorp, its Head of Security reached for a holster that held only a billyclub flashlight, and cursed the company's "No handguns outside of our computer screens" policy.

LORD IRRANCE TESMER came awake slowly. He was vaguely aware of a chill—the bedclothes were gone, leaving him bared to the night air—and knew with more pressing certainty that his head hurt.

Clara had snarled something in the night and stormed out of bed—she had, hadn't she?—and…

"Clara?" he mumbled, rolling over. No warm spot, and no heap of covers. His wife was gone.

He got himself hastily upright in bed, rubbing his eyes and trying to quell the prompt, severe blossoming of the ache in his head. "Clara?"

"I'm here, Rance." Her voice was coming from the doorway, and it was sharp with anger.

Lord Tesmer came hastily all the way awake. Something had happened. Something that mattered. Something bad.

"What?" he blurted, looking wildly around for his sword while trying to keep an eye on his wife's face.

She was quivering like a hunting-hound straining to be let off the leash. Barefoot, in a dark gown, black hair loose around her shoulders in a flood, eyes two coals beneath scowling brows as they glared at him. She was furious, all right.

"What's happened?"

Lady Telclara Tesmer folded her arms across her chest. "Our gems are gone. All three coffers. The sack of coins, too. No alarm raised in the night, and the guards swear no one even approached the gates."

Tesmer blinked at his wife. "All the gems? Not the—the tunnel! They must have taken the tunnel!"

She nodded grimly. "Which means the thief is one of us—or one or more of the children. My crossthreads haven't been disturbed."

"Clara, I swear *I* didn't—"

His clumsy protest stumbled into silence under the slicing edge of her look of scorn. "I'm *aware* of that, dolt. I sleep with you, remember?"

Irrance winced. "What about the vaults?"

She lifted one shapely shoulder in a shrug. "Undisturbed. The guardian snake still asleep, the sprinkled line I left there unmarked. No one's been in there. So, yes, Rance, we still have coins to our name." She took a long, slow step forward. "That's not the point."

Lord Tesmer winced. "Which of our children has betrayed us?"

She smiled, a tight grimace that held not the slightest trace of amusement. "All of them, and often. Neither the servants nor our warcaptains can be certain where any of them are just now, but last reports—"

He nodded wearily. His wife's spies were nothing if not energetic.

"—have Ghorsyn and Ellark still off hunting, some days away; Kalathgar still in that Stormar port busily buying and selling dockside hovels with our coins to make a fortune he can hide before he comes back to tell us how poorly coins fare in Stormar these days; Delmark and Feldrar stealing everything from our loyal citizens that isn't nailed down, including the virtue of their daughters—and wives, too—and Maera still spurning every suitor but seeing how much they'll gift her with, before she turns away."

"Delmark and Feldrar a-wenching? I thought it was Belard the women all swooned after!"

"That, husband mine, is the *real* news. It seems much magic was hurled in the forest last night. In the little dell nigh the Imrush headwaters—or rather, what used to be a little dell. Trees in plenty blazed like a brace of feast-torches, I'm told, and the deer are all fled three hills away or more. The result of a little disagreement between our Belard, and our Nareyera, and our little Talyss, too."

"What? They have that much magic?"

"Irrance, you'd be surprised at what our children have up their sleeves, in their back pouches—and under their codpieces, too. The fire's down to just smoke, now. That's not what matters."

Lady Tesmer took another step forward. "What matters, Rance, is that Bel and Talyss now trust each other enough to rut together."

Lord Tesmer's jaw dropped. "*What?* As husband and wife? Coupling?"

His wife sighed. "Yes, coupling, but you persist in missing the point. A night of sheathing the flesh-dagger is neither here nor there, even if they are brother and sister. Rance, they're *working together*. Scheming. When all of us thought their seething hatred for each other would keep them from ever even imagining such a thing."

Shaking his head rather dazedly, Irrance Tesmer stumbled out of bed and started to pace. "Bel and Talyss... Talyss and Bel..."

"Oh, dolt of a lord, will you *stop* trying to picture them together and leering over it! Try not to think with your night-horn for once, and use your brains!"

Lord Tesmer stopped his striding, gave his wife a glare, and barked, "So they're scheming together. What of it? That's all our offspring ever seem to do, aye? You've said it yourself, many a time! Why's this pairing so much a cause for alarm? Hey?"

"Irrance," his wife said gently, "you've heard all the talk—I know you have—that the Master may have sired some of our children, rather than you."

Lord Tesmer stiffened. "You've always told me those rumors were utter lies."

"So I have, though you've never quite believed me. Well, now it's time for you to hear the truth. Two of our children *were* sired by the wizard Narmarkoun, and may very well have his power to hurl magic. He may even have secretly trained them to become wizards."

Lord Tesmer went white. His voice, when he found it, was almost a whisper. "Their names?"

"Belard. And Talyss."

ROD EVERLAR FOUND sleep again at last, or thought he did. Were these not dreams, these scenes of him trotting down from a crumbling rampart in an afternoon mist, into a keep full of snarling, snapping dragons? Or no, narrow-snouted and baleful-eyed dragon heads, all at the end of impossibly-long scaled necks, that writhed and undulated and curved through archway after archway, across a vast and empty-echoing, many-shadowed castle interior, all to meet in some one unseen lower chamber...

Abruptly, Rod was somewhere else. Somewhere he'd seen only once, a sneeringly bold black marble and glass brick of a building, set amid the rolling green hillocks and neat sandtraps of a private golf course. The headquarters of Holdoncorp, gleaming and massive.

He was flying toward it, gliding low over the greens and fairways, and something was flying ahead of him. A lorn, alone and flapping along purposefully, as if on a mission.

Rod sheered quickly away, before it could turn its head and see him. He felt suddenly afraid, a deepening terror he could not explain that left him gasping, and thinking of that black building behind him become a huge abyss, a black maw that was sliding through the parting green hills and fairways to follow him... seeking to devour him, jaws widening into a gulf he could never escape if he foolishly looked back...

He dodged, around he knew not what, finding himself in thickening mists again. Then ducked, hearing the clash of swords and seeing a brief glimpse of grinning skeletons rushing down gloomy castle corridors with unsheathed swords in their bony grips. Then dodged again, in a place of thunderous crashes and tall stone castle towers falling ponderously down to earth, deep groaning rumble after deep groaning rumble, each of them ending in a thunderous, bone-shaking crash...

He was lying on a heap of clothes in a dark room in Malragard, and it was falling, too, leaning toward its gardens and the grass-girt slope outside the garden wall... leaning... leaning...

The bone-shaking crash rattled his teeth this time, and flung him up off the clothes an instant before huge stone blocks crashed down on them.

Rod joined the spreading, blinding dust, falling through it almost gently to slam bruisingly down onto the flood of fallen stone blocks.

He was awake now, and coughing hard, fingers of bright morning reaching out around and past him, and Harlhoh spread out below him, its far-off folk shouting in alarm and fleeing through the streets.

The crashing and shuddering went on, long-unseen spells flaring into sudden visibility in the air as the foundations they'd girded so long cracked, and walls and pillars fell. Rod saw gigantic spider legs writhing and curling in agony, and a falling wall flatten a purple-black hulk in a great spray of purple gore and quivering, convulsing tentacles.

Stone blocks tumbled, a wolf-head shook back and forth and bit at the air in helpless pain ere it sagged from view, and then there was nothing moving but the dust.

"So my plan worked," Rod croaked aloud, standing on the still-shuddering stones and clutching at his bruises, "but almost too well. I dreamed of Malragard falling, and…"

Behind him, another wall fell, hurling him into the air just far enough for his legs to go out from under him, and the landing—on his side and behind—to be wincingly bruising.

He groaned aloud, then rolled over, sat up, and tried to peer around through the dust. There wasn't much to see; there wasn't much left of Malraun's tower.

Thoroughly awake now, Rod Everlar wondered how long it would take the wizard to show up.

After all, that was probably just how long a certain fantasy writer had left to live.

Chapter Thirty-Two

"YOUR MAJESTY, I am no Doom of Falconfar," the black-bearded man in the robe protested, spreading his hands like a merchant proclaiming his innocence in a market-stall. "I can work small magics, honest magics, spells no velduke nor knight nor drover need fear save some hidden power, some dark secondary effect. When I am hired to blast down a hanging rock or enlarge a storage cavern, I do so with all the care I can, and—"

He shrieked, threw up his spread hands as all the color fled from his face in an instant—and toppled forward to fall flat on his face on the floor.

"Falcon-cursed hedge-wizards," one of the king's bodyguard growled, striding forward from beside King Melander Brorsavar's throne to nudge the sprawled and silent man with one gleaming-booted toe. "Get up, man. Your dramatics impress His Majesty *not*. Get *up*."

"Thalden," the King of Galath murmured gently, "stand clear from yon mage. Touching him may be neither safe nor prudent."

His knight obeyed in some haste, turning a puzzled frown to his king. "Majesty?"

"He was not indulging in dramatics," Brorsavar murmured. "Look; is his nose not broken?"

A thin thread of blood was running out from under the motionless head, to flow its unhurried way across the tiled floor of the court.

"Falcon," the knight muttered, drawing back. "What struck him down so, d'ye think?"

In reply, King Melander silently spread his hands just as the fallen wizard had done, to signify he knew not. The knight barely had time to see the gesture, and no time at all to catch any courtiers' eyes and decide if a polite chuckle was appropriate, when there came a stir from beyond the nearest entry arch, and the guards barring entrance there.

"Let me *through!*" someone snarled angrily. "*Majesty!* Urgent news!"

The King of Galath made a brief, beckoning gesture to signal the archway guards to let the new arrival through.

It was one of the court scribes, a man neither young nor humble. He had never before been known to appear before the throne sweating and wild-eyed with fear, but he was in such a state now. Melander wordlessly extended his hand toward the man, palm out, signifying that the scribe should speak.

The scribe bowed low, almost falling in his nervous haste, then went down on one knee, and then blurted out in a rush, "Great King, all the wizards you hired to scry the realm and map it have collapsed! All of them, at once, dashed senseless to the floor as if by some giant hand!"

"Dead?" Brorsavar asked calmly.

"N-no, though some of them bleed from mouth or nose or eyes, M-majesty," the scribe stammered. "One of them was clutching his head and mumbling, and we tried to question him. We shook him and spake loudly in his ear, but he fell dumb and dreaming like the rest. We heard him say just this: 'a great Shaping, and it begins.' Majesty, I thought you should know."

Then the scribe's gaze fell upon the man lying not far from where he was kneeling, and a little shriek of fear burst from him.

"Easy, Nollard," the King of Galath said soothingly. "Rise, and go take wine from our stewards yonder, and drink."

He stood, and added in a dry voice, looking out across the court, "I begin to fear that many of us, as this day unfolds, may have cause to join you."

Through another archway came the muted thunder of running booted feet, and the cry, "Majesty! Grave news!"

King Melander Brorsavar smiled wryly. "And so, as they say, it begins."

MALRAUN THE MATCHLESS sat up in bed, awake in an instant, alarmed. Though Darswords was quiet around him, something was very much awry.

In distant Harlhoh, something had shattered the very foundation-spells he'd cast when strengthening and warding his tower.

Which meant a wizard more powerful than any he knew of, anywhere in Falconfar, was at work with destroying spells—or something else had caused the tower to shatter and fall.

Either way...

He bent and kissed the bound and helpless Taeauna. Not out of any great affection, but so as to most swiftly and efficiently strengthen his mind-link with her, so it could be used to snap back to her body if he needed to flee in haste from trouble. Surrounded by all of the greatfangs bred by that idiot Narmarkoun, for instance, or—

Shrugging away such useless speculation, he closed his eyes and said the word that would take him in an instant to Malragard.

So it was that he never saw the flash of triumph in the eyes of the bound Aumrarr behind him.

Lorontar had been waiting a long time for Malraun to do this.

THE WIZARD NARMARKOUN stood alone in a large and gloomy hall in Yintaerghast, staring at a glowing sphere of his own conjuring that floated in the air before him.

He'd laughed aloud when Malragard had fallen. Oh, would Malraun be furious! The man of Earth, wandering alone and half-witted, somehow avoiding all the traps that had claimed the lives of veteran warriors, high-priced thieves, and the most daring of Stormar wizards-for-hire. Only to do *this*.

Nicely Shaped, indeed!

The dolt Everlar was still alive! He'd somehow brought the tower down around his ears—crushing most of Malraun's prized beasts, mind!—yet not been himself crushed in its fall! There he was, coughing in the dust, staggering away from the heap of gowns he'd snored on and—

But hold!

As the dust eddied and drifted, and Rod Everlar came stumbling out into a relatively clear area of floor, another figure appeared in midair just above him, literally standing over him.

It was Malraun, here by his own teleportation magic.

Narmarkoun snarled out wordless hatred, watching the Matchless One start to step down from the invisible, momentary platform of force his magic had created. Once Malraun set boot on the tiles of Malragard, the teleport spell would end and he'd be free of its force-echoes, free to work magic. Magic that would undoubtedly slay the meddling Shaper.

Malraun's foot came down, his other leg started forward—and Narmarkoun astonished himself.

Although he'd intended to bide here, watching all and awaiting his best time to strike, Narmarkoun found himself crying out an incantation he did not know, words and runes he'd never seen before.

It was if a door had opened in his mind to shine forth bright amber radiance through his head, a light he couldn't turn to look at however desperately he strove to... the spell he did not know was done and unfolding, more power than he'd ever felt before was flooding through him—and where had it all come from?—and he was trembling like a leaf in a storm wind, mouth open in slack-jawed amazement.

As the lambent sphere of his spying-spell showed Narmarkoun scenes of distant Earth, of his six servitor Dark Helms snatched bodily out of the strange glass castle they were scouring out there, bloody swords in their hands—and the lorn with them, a limp and dripping corpse in their wake.

As the blue-skinned Doom watched in mute wonder, the six warriors and the lorn hurtled at him and then flashed past him, hurtled along through a whirling tunnel of translocation, howling flows of magic Narmarkoun had called into being without knowing how. Flows that whispered a name as they whisked the six and the one to Malragard, and literally flung them at Malraun, dashing that wizard headlong across the tiles.

That name was "Lorontar."

MALRAUN RAISED HIS right hand, too angry to keep this Shaper as a useful captive. He would lash the man to death, lash him with lightnings, burn off his hands and feet yet use spells to keep this Rod Everlar awake in screaming suffering!

Malragard had been beautiful, and it had been his, and no one, *no one*, would take it from him and not pay the priii—

Lightning crawled up his fingers and spat sparks into the air, and he snarled and brought his hand down to hurl them at Everlar.

Who ducked, dodged, and fell hard, spinning and scissoring his feet around to sweep Malraun's ankles out from under him.

He crashed to the tiles, shouting in anger, and scrambled up to—

Do nothing to Everlar at all, as dark and heavy armored bodies slammed into Malraun in a tide out of nowhere, a tide that hacked and sliced and spat curses as it crashed into him.

His breath was gone, all thoughts of his spell with it, and Malraun numbed an elbow on hard tiles, then cracked the side of his head on tile hard enough for tears to come unbidden, and—something large and wet that stank very much of lorn blood slammed down on him and slid with him ere it bounced off and was gone.

Laughter, and running feet, and dark swords swinging down at him—

He rolled desperately, yet felt wet fire through his shoulder as a sword sliced deep. Falcon *shit!*

Malraun felt for the mind-link, desperate to take himself back to Darswords and away from these Dark Helms, to win time enough to *breathe*, Falcon spit, then high time enough to work a blasting spell that would—

Amber light flared along the link from Taeauna, light that became a smile and two dark, gimlet eyes that stabbed through Malraun like Dark Helm blades. Silently laughing at him as it came.

Yes, Malraun the Matchless, I am who you fear I am. Lorontar of Falconfar, THE Doom of Falconfar—and your Doom.

Those words were soft, yet thundered like fire through Malraun's head. Before he could do anything, the power just behind them struck.

And all Falconfar dissolved in amber fire.

RUSTY HELD UP the flashlight. It was heavy, of stout metal encased in rubber—and might manage him one parry.

Then he would die.

This Dark Helm was no overconfident, reckless fool, but a veteran, patiently herding Rusty and Sollars back across Holdoncorp's Security Office, away from any way out of here.

Slowly and patiently cutting off all escape, knowing he could slay at will. Pete Sollars stumbled to his knees in fear, and burst into tears—but the Dark Helm stepped back and gestured curtly with his sword until the crying "eyes" scrambled up again. A veteran, avoiding any chance of a "trip me by rolling at my ankles" ploy.

The Dark Helm advanced again.

Rusty Carroll drew in a deep breath, stepped forward with flashlight in hand, and prepared to die.

The sword swept back, the Dark Helm sidestepped faster than any dancer Rusty had ever seen, that sword came in at him so fast that he almost fell getting the flashlight into the right spot to parry, and—

The Dark Helm was suddenly gone. Vanished into thin air in a silent instant, one step away from carving Rusty Carroll in two.

SUDDENLY, IN SILENCE and without warning, his spying spell winked out. Narmarkoun stared in disbelief at the dark and empty air where the glowing sphere of his magic had been a moment ago, showing him Malraun being hacked at by Dark Helms in the ruins of Malragard.

Then there came a flash, light that cloaked him, whirled him around, and spun him—elsewhere.

Leaving the great castle of Yintaerghast dark and deserted once more.

ROD EVERLAR ROLLED desperately across cracked and rubble-littered tiles, trying to get away from Malraun.

Who was stiffening and shrieking out sudden wild cackles of laughter, gibberings of maniacal glee that made even the Dark Helms flinch back from him. Foaming at the mouth, his eyes gouting sparks, the wizard spread his hands and fed them lightnings that sent them flying, broken and burning, swords clanging down far away across the rubble of Malragard.

Rod ran out of space to roll to, fetching up against a great heap of fallen stone in time to see the wizard throw back his head, his face a bright mass of sputtering, leaping lightnings, and roar in triumph.

Malraun spread his hands again. Wands and scepters and small things of bright metal burst from here and there amid the rubble, racing through the air to his waiting grasp.

He flung most of them down as they arrived, in a great bouncing and clanging at his feet, but kept two of the longest, deadliest-looking things: scepters with heads like horned orbs. These he promptly aimed at a certain spot far across the tiles.

An empty spot, so far as Rod could tell.

Then there was a flash, and a tall wizard with blue and scaly skin stood there, looking bewildered.

"Narmarkoun!" Malraun crooned, in a voice deeper and older than the Matchless One had ever sounded before—and unleashed the scepters in his hands.

Narmarkoun had time to scream. Just once.

Once, before a whirling, tightening sphere of deadly clawing magics from the scepters drew in tight around him, rending and tearing. He was a sobbing cloud of red mist by the time his smashed and broken body was driven back across the tiles to what was left of a wall and through it, leaving a gaping hole and a flickering glow beyond. By then, a great smear of gore spattered across a more distant wall was all that was left of Narmarkoun.

The scepters failed, belching out puffs of sparks, and what had been Malraun let them fall. They struck the tiles without clangor, bursting into spattered ashes.

Then the wizard turned to Rod Everlar. His face raged with lightnings no longer, and wore a calm smile. Above it were two burnt-out pits where his eyes should have been.

"Rod Everlar," he said almost gently, "I am the true Archwizard of Falconfar."

"Lorontar," Rod whispered, getting up slowly, and looking around without much hope for rubble substantial enough to hide behind.

"Lorontar," the ravaged wizard agreed, strolling slowly across the tiles. "I've been hiding in the mind of the one called Taeauna for a long time, now. Now this body is mine, though I'm afraid the mind of Malraun is... broken."

He smiled a wide and crooked smile. "So I believe I'll have *your* body, now. Worry not; I have no intention of smashing your mind as I did Malraun's. It's far too valuable to me. I'll just enslave it instead."

"Oh?" Rod asked, backing away. "You want to write crappy fantasy novels?"

Lorontar's smile was almost pitying. "Once I have your dream-powers," he explained gently, as if addressing a small child, "*two* worlds will be mine to rule."

Then there was a sudden weight in Rod's head, a merciless surge of power that smashed into Rod Everlar.

He gasped, or thought he did, as amber fire raced over him and through him and—

The fire wavered and split, Rod felt pain and confusion that was not his own swirling over him... and—

Lorontar's mind was hurt, mentally staggering. Rod fought not to be buried under sudden floods of memories not his and emotions that threatened to drench him in darkness.

Taeauna had thrust at Lorontar from behind with all her fury and hatred, through the still-open link, and had struck deep.

The body that had belonged to Malraun fell on its face, clawing feebly at the tiles and working its legs as if still upright and running. Through its open mouth came a strange, incoherent sound.

Rod could run again, and he turned and did so, slipping and sliding in rubble and crying out, "Taeauna? Taeauna?"

There was no reply.

He found himself at the head of a staircase, now open to the sky and half-choked with a shattered roof that until quite recently had sheltered it. Looking back, he saw that Malraun—Lorontar—was on his feet and staggering blindly after him, arms outthrust like some sort of mindless walking corpse.

He could hardly help but see something else, too.

In the sky overhead, almost blotting out the bright morning light with their great bulk, were six greatfangs. Three of them were larger than the rest, and the two biggest were...

Holy Falcon!

. . . twice as large as Malragard had been.

They looked angry, their wings beating with furious haste and their jaws snapping often, biting at the air as they circled over the ruins, eyes glaring down at Rod Everlar.

Then the largest of them all rolled its great shoulders, tucked in its wings, and plunged down out of the skies in a long, terrible dive, great jaws parting.

The fire was back in Rod's mind again, faint but furious, roiling up to make his arms and legs tremble.

He fought to step forward, to hurl himself down that staircase. His head was turning, despite himself, to look back and see the staggering thing that had been Malraun come lumbering closer, reaching for him...

With an angry shriek of his own he fought off Lorontar's will long enough to turn his head the other way.

The jaws rushing down to engulf him looked as large and dark as the night sky, now.

Closer... closer...

Rod Everlar wrestled for control of his own body, trying to fling himself down the stair, and wondering if he'd get to safety in time.

Here ends Book 2 of the Falconfar Saga.
The adventures of Rod Everlar, Taeauna, and the other folk of Falconfar will continue in
FALCONFAR

DRAMATIS PERSONAE
[named characters only]

"See" references occur where only partial character names appear in the novel text (such as when a surname is omitted). Not all folk in Falconfar have family names; Aumrarr, for example, never have surnames.

Some lore has been omitted here so as not to spoil readers' enjoyment of later events in the Falconfar saga. These entries contain some "spoilers" for Archwizard, and for maximum enjoyment of this book, should be referred to when three-quarters or more of the text has been read.

(Alander: see Thaetult, Alander)

(Amaddar: see Yelrya, Amaddar)

Ambrelle: an Aumrarr; the eldest and most severe of "the Four Aumrarr" who fly together, seeking to avenge the slaughter at Highcrag that occurred in DARK LORD.

Arlaghaun: "the Doom of Galath," a deceased wizard who was widely considered the most powerful of the three Dooms (Falconfar's wizards of peerless power), and for some years the real ruler of Galath. Arlaghaun inhabited Ult Tower, the black stone keep of the long-dead wizard Ult, in Galath, and with his spells commanded armies of Iorn and Dark Helms, as well as every utterance of King Devaer of Galath. Some judged his power so great they called him "the Doom of Falconfar." He was slain at the end of DARK LORD.

Aumrarr, the: a race of winged warrior-women who fight for "good." They seem human except for their large snow-white wings, and fly about taking messages from one hold to another, battling wolves and monsters, and working against oppressive rulers. They are dedicated to making the lives of common folk (farmers, woodcutters, and crafters, not the wealthy or rulers) better, and laws and law-enforcement just. Their home, in the hills north of Arvale, is the fortress of Highcrag, where most of them were slaughtered, early in DARK LORD.

Baernel, Helkor: nondescript, burly veteran knight of Lyrose, sworn to Lord Magrandar Lyrose (and both utterly loyal to, and eager to serve, him).

Bramlar, Urbren: warrior sworn to Hammerhand, in Ironthorn; part of the garrison of the castle of Hammerhold.

Briszyk, Almbaert: veteran warrior sworn to Hammerhand, in Ironthorn; head of a patrol that finds Rod Everlar in the forest.

Brorsavar, Melander: Former Velduke of Galath, a stern, just, "steady" and therefore popular Galathan noble, well-respected by most of his fellow nobles. Large and impressive-looking, having shoulders as broad as two slender men standing side by side, he was crowned King of Galath by several fellow nobles at the end of DARK LORD. Some Galathan nobility were slow to accept his authority; although civil strife is still raging in his kingdom, he is slowly gaining wider acceptance.

Burroughs, E.R. (Edgar Rice): a real person; a deceased writer of pulp adventure fantasy, best known for his stories of Tarzan of the Apes, but also famous for his sword-and-planet tales of John Carter of Mars.

Carroll, Rusty: the grayhaired, honest, follow-the-rules Head of Security at the headquarters of Holdoncorp, on Earth. Note: a fictional character.

Chainamund, Glusk: deceased noble, the last (thus far) Baron of Galath, this fat, unhappy man was widely disliked among his fellow Galathan nobles for his dishonesty and his unpleasant, haughty, and aggressive manner. He was slain near the end of DARK LORD, and his barony, in southwesternmost Galath, remains vacant (held by King Melander Brorsavar, and administered by three knights in his name).

Cordryn, Fethel: the lazy, fussy, and pompous Master Steward of Lyraunt Castle, head of the household servants of Lyraunt, sworn to the service of Lord Magrandar Lyrose.

Corey, Corlin: an award-winning Earth writer of fantasy fiction known for his mastery of prose style and smart-mouthed first person narrators. Note: this is a fictional character.

Danonder, Thalden: zealous, swift-tempered knight of Galath, one of the trusted (and trustworthy) personal bodyguards of King Melander Brorsavar.

Dark Helms, the: warriors, aptly described as "ruthless slayers in black armor." Living men and (increasingly, as their losses mount over time) undead warriors, these enspelled-to-loyalty soldiers are the creations of Holdoncorp.

Darlok, Darlen: one of Lord Burrim Hammerhand's three loyal veteran warcaptains, in Ironthorn. A swift and capable warrior, of middling height, nondescript looks, and alert manner.

Dauntra: an Aumrarr; the youngest, most beautiful, and most saucy of "the Four Aumrarr" who fly together, seeking to avenge the slaughter at Highcrag.

Deldragon, Darendarr: Velduke of Galath (noble), who dwells in the fortified town of Bowrock on the southern edge of Galath, which surrounds his soaring castle, Bowrock Keep. A handsome, dashing battle hero, of a family considered "great" in Galath, who defied King Devaer and the wizard Arlaghaun, and was besieged because of it. Near the end of DARK LORD he was brought back from the verge of death by the wizard Narmarkoun, who (unbeknownst to Deldragon and everyone else in Falconfar) cast magics into Deldragon's mind, to make him Narmarkoun's slave henceforth.

(Devaer: see Rothryn, Devaer)

Devouring Worm, the: legendary monster of long-ago Falconfar, subject of many legends and still mentioned in the oaths of amazed persons. So many contradictory tales are told of its powers, deeds, and death that aside from the fact that it was a gigantic, wingless and limbless slithering worm with a maw large enough to engulf a man on horseback, that devoured everything edible in its path when it was awake, and that it was smart or at least cunning, nothing else about it can be said with certainty.

Dooms, the: wizards so much more powerful than most mages that they are feared all across Falconfar as nigh-unstoppable forces. For decades there were three Dooms: Arlaghaun (widely considered the most powerful); Malraun; and Narmarkoun. During the events recounted in DARK LORD, Rod Everlar came to be considered the fourth Doom, and Arlaghaun perished.

Drake, Mario: a short, bearded and mustachioed, constantly chain-smoking Earth anthologist and prolific fantasy writer. Note: this is a fictional character.

Dyune: a swift-tempered, agile Aumrarr usually active in Ironthorn and the nearby Raurklor holds, who makes Stormcrag Castle her usual home.

(**Empress of the Emaeraun Empire, the**: see Zaervedel, Aumra)

Enfeld, Hank: honest and a trifle slow-witted, but the largest and strongest of the custodians (janitors) at the headquarters of Holdoncorp, on Earth. Note: a fictional character.

Everlar, Rod: hack writer of novels, who believed himself the creator of Falconfar. During DARK LORD, he discovered he was one of its creators; in Falconfar, he is a "Shaper" (one whose writings can change reality), though non-wizards tend to think he is one of the Dooms (powerful wizards). He was referred to as "the Dark Lord" (the most evil and most powerful of all wizards, a bogeyman of legend) by the other Dooms, to blame him for their misdeeds. Considered to be the Lord Archwizard of Falconfar by the Aumrarr (the first Lord Archwizard since Lorontar). The Aumrarr Taeauna brought Rod into Falconfar and was his guide until the wizard Malraun captured her at the end of DARK LORD; as Archwizard begins, he sets out to regain her.

Falcon, the: *The* deity of Falconfar, the embodiment of all things, and fount of inspiration, wisdom, daring, and splendid achievement. All-seeing and enigmatic. Also known as "the Great Falcon," to distinguish it from lesser, mortal birds that share its shape.

Featherstone, Mike: a young, balding, mild-mannered, day-dreaming Earth reader of fantasy fiction. A fan of the works of Geoffrey Halsted,

Mario Drake, Sugarman Tombs, and Corlin Corey. Note: this is a fictional character.

Forestmother, the: recently-risen deity of Falconfar, gaining swift and wide popularity, and standing for wild ways and the unspoiled forests, against excessive woodcutting, land clearances, and despoiling overhunting and farming.

Fynkle, Penelope: the highest-ranked (and the only "Senior") among the many Executive Graphics Facilitators employed by Holdoncorp. An aging but still bottle-beautiful woman of slender build, immaculate tailored suits (she always wears a jacket and pants, never anything that shows her long legs, spurring many office rumors that they are deformed or tattooed), and wears an everchanging selection of striking—some say strikingly *odd*—designer eyeglasses. She works at the Corporate Headquarters of Holdoncorp, on Earth. Note: a fictional character.

(Gold Duke, the: see Yuskel, Irraunt)

Goldman, Mase: a burly, good-natured former football star who is now head of Ground Floor Security at the headquarters of Holdoncorp, on Earth. Note: a fictional character.

(Great Falcon, the: see Falcon, the)

Gulkoun, Garfist: Often referred to as "Old Ox" or "Old Blundering Ox" by his partner Iskarra Taeravund, this coarse, burly and aging onetime pirate, former forger, and then panderer later became a hiresword (mercenary warrior), and these days wanders Falconfar with Iskarra, making a living as a thief and swindler. "Garfist" is actually a childhood nickname he took as his everyday name, vastly preferring it to "Norbryn," the name his parents gave him.

Halsted, Geoffrey: a tall, scholarly, bearded and mustachioed Earth historian and award-winning writer of fantasy fiction, seldom seen in anything less formal than a business suit, or without a walking stick. Note: this is a fictional character.

Hammerhand, Amteira: daughter of Burrim Hammerhand, she fiercely insists on riding on hunts and taking war-training like any man. She has shoulders as broad as many men, long brown hair, startlingly dark eyebrows, and snapping blue-black eyes.

Hammerhand, Burrim: Lord of Ironthorn, a large, prosperous, militarily-strong hold in the forests north of Tauren and northeast of Sardray, that for years has had three rival lords, ruling from three separate keeps. Gruff and shrewd, Hammerhand is the strongest of the three, a large, hardy, capable warrior and battle-leader. He rules the northernmost part of Ironthorn, a small demesne that includes the market town of Irontarl and the north bank of the Thorn River, from his crag-top castle of Hammerhold. His badge is an iron gauntlet (a left-handed gage, upright and open-fingered, on a scarlet field).

Hammerhand, Dravvan: fearless and grave eldest son and heir of Burrim Hammerhand, foremost of the three rival lords of Ironthorn.

Hammerhand, Glaren: deceased third son of Burrim Hammerhand, foremost of the three rival lords of Ironthorn. Strong, slow-witted, ugly, but a good warrior and a just man.

Hammerhand, Jarvel: deceased second son of Burrim Hammerhand, foremost of the three rival lords of Ironthorn. Sly, handsome, swindling, and a merry prankster.

Hammerhand, Venyarla: deceased Lady of Ironthorn, wife of Burrim and mother of Dravvan and Amteira. Venyarla was raped and then dismembered by Lord Melvarl Lyrose, who was in turn slain by Lord Burrim Hammerhand for doing so.

Heldohraun: reclusive and scholarly deceased wizard of Galath, whose tower the Aumrarr pillaged decades ago, after he died of a fever.

Heldrake, Saul: a fat, talkative editor of an Earth publishing firm that has offices in the Hardy Building, who customarily handles the novels of the writer Mario Drake. Note: this is a fictional character.

Herkimer, Morton Morton ("the Third" or III; the third successive generation of his family to bear the same name): the Vice President Legal of Holdoncorp. Herkimer is a brisk, efficient man. He is also pompous, jowly, and wears eyeglasses that he is constantly pushing back up the bridge of his nose. He works at the Corporate Headquarters of Holdoncorp, on Earth. Note: a fictional character.

Holdoncorp: a large computer gaming company that licenses the electronic media games rights to the world of Falconfar from Rod Everlar, and develops a series of computer games that increasingly diverge from Everlar's own vision of his world. (Holdoncorp is NOT based on any real-world corporation or group of people. The Falconfar tales are fantasies, not satires of, or swipes at, anything or anyone real.)

Hollinshed, Sheldon Daumark: the Vice President Finance of Holdoncorp. Hollinshed has a booming voice and a florid face. He frequently "windmills" his arms wildly about and throws red-faced "towering rages" to get his own way. He works at the Corporate Headquarters of Holdoncorp, on Earth. Note: a fictional character.

Hooldan, Sam: burly, experienced, unflappable head of Loading Dock Security at the headquarters of Holdoncorp, on Earth. Note: a fictional character.

Horgul, Amaxas: warlord, leader of an "Army of Liberation" marching north from the Sea of Storms to conquer Raurklor hold after Raurklor hold. Said to hate and fear all who wield magic, and to execute all hedge-wizards and altar-priests he finds. Described as "more boar than man, a brawling, rutting lout governed by his lusts and rages," but a great warrior who dominates battlefields and warriors, inspiring and commanding swift and unquestioning obedience.

Howard, Robert E. (Ervin): real person; a deceased Earth writer of pulp adventure and heroic fantasy stories, best known for his tales of Conan the Barbarian.

Imvaer, Chanszel: man of Ironthorn, a household servant ("scullery cellarer," or traveling buyer of foodstuffs and drinkables) in the castle of Hammerhold, but also secretly a paid spy upon that household for House Tesmer.

Inglestock, Tony: the Senior Brand Overmanager of Strategic Marketing Initiatives for Holdoncorp. A sly, handsome, glib breaker-and-bender-of-rules who is not well-liked in the corporation, yet is a "survivor" to whom no blame ever seems to stick. He works at the Corporate Headquarters of Holdoncorp, on Earth. Note: a fictional character.

(Iskarra: see Taeravund, Iskarra)

Jaklar, Cauldreth: the Lord Leaf of Hammerhold, in Ironthorn. Priest of the Forestmother, a cruel, nasty, and ambitious young man, vigorous and judgmental by nature.

(Jelgar: see Thusk, Jelgar)

Juskra: Aumrarr; the most battle-scarred, hot-tempered, and aggressive of the "Four Aumrarr" who fly together, seeking to avenge the slaughter at Highcrag.

Klammert: deceased wizard, one of the youngest and least accomplished apprentices of the wizard Arlaghaun; a pudgy, less than brave man. He was slain at the end of DARK LORD, but Rod Everlar gained some of his "how to work magic" notes.

Korlhund, Rauldro: a cook in the Army of Liberation led by Horgul. A large, ugly, hairy man; a veteran warrior, but less than skilled in any kitchen.

(Lord Leaf, the: see Jaklar, Cauldreth)

Lorlarra: an Aumrarr; the calmest and quietest of the "Four Aumrarr" who fly together, seeking to avenge the slaughter at Highcrag.

lorn, the: race of winged, flying horned and taloned predatory creatures that dwell in rocky heights such as castle towers and the Falconspires mountain range. Often described as mouthless by humans because their skull-like faces have no visible jaws, they typically swarm prey, raking with their talons and even tearing limbs, bodies, or heads off or apart. They have bat-like, featherless wings, barbed tails, and slate-gray skin. Arlaghaun, Malraun, and many lesser wizards discovered or developed spells for compelling lorn into servitude.

Lorontar: the still-feared-in-legend first Lord Archwizard of Falconfar, once the fell and tyrannical ruler of all Falconfar, and the first spell-tamer of the lorn. Long believed dead but secretly surviving in spectral unlife, seeking a living body to mind-guide, "ride," and ultimately possess. So greatly is his memory feared that no one, not even a powerful wizard, has dared to try to dwell in his great black tower, Yintaerghast, since his disappearance and presumed death.

(Loroth the Highest: see Xundaer, Loroth)

Lovecraft, H.P. (Howard Phillips): real person; a deceased Earth writer of many horror (and other) stories, best known today as the creator of what is now called the Cthulhu Mythos.

Lyrose, Eldred: eldest son and heir of House Lyrose, one of the three rival ruling families of Ironthorn. Cruel and treacherous, he fancies himself to be "sophisticated."

Lyrose, Horondeir: second son of House Lyrose of Ironthorn, a burly, cruel, loud and fair-haired giant of a man. Masterful in the hunt and a good warrior, if a trifle slow-witted.

Lyrose, Maerelle: Lady of Ironthorn, and wife of Lord Magrandar Lyrose. Tall, slender, and raven-haired, possessed of a hard-edged, cruel beauty. She is as hotheaded and as cruel as her husband.

Lyrose, Magrandar: Lord of Ironthorn, head of one of three rival houses that claim lordship over Ironthorn. Father of Eldred, Mrythra, Horondeir, and Pelmard, and husband of Maerelle, Lord Magrandar Lyrose rules the southwestern three valleys of Ironthorn, south from the ford of the Thorn River. He is wantonly cruel and hotheaded, where his father was more sly, patient, and scheming. His home is Lyraunt Castle, and his badge is a caltrop-like pinwheel of three steel-gray thorns, joined at the base, on a yellow field. For some years, House Lyrose has quietly been aided by the wizard Malraun.

Lyrose, Melvarl: deceased Lord of Ironthorn, father of the current lord, Magrandar. He raped and murdered Lady Venyarla Hammerhand, and for doing so was swiftly caught and killed by her husband, Lord Burrim Hammerhand. A sly, cruel, darkly-handsome villain of a man.

Lyrose, Mrythra: daughter of Lord Magrandar and Lady Maerelle Lyrose, she inherited her mother's dark good looks and build, and her father's cruel, scheming ways, being far smarter and more subtle than her brothers (and so, a better successor to the lordship than any of them).

Lyrose, Pelmard: the youngest son of House Lyrose of Ironthorn; quieter, more sly, and far more cowardly than his brothers.

Malraun: "the Matchless," wizard, one of the Dooms of Falconfar. A short, sleek, darkly handsome man who dwells in Malragard, a tower in Harlhoh, a hold (settlement) in the green depths of Raurklor, the Great Forest. Malraun is served by lorn and spell-subverted traders, and after the death of his chief rival Arlaghaun, increasing numbers of Dark Helms he's magically bound to himself. At the end of DARK LORD he captured the Aumrarr Taeauna and, with Arlaghaun dead, set in motion bold plans to conquer all Falconfar north of the Sea of Storms.

Narmarkoun: wizard, one of the Dooms of Falconfar; a tall, blue-skinned, scaly man who dwells alone in a hidden subterranean wilderland stronghold, Darthoun, a long-abandoned city of the dwarves—alone, that is, except for dead, skull-headed wenches animated by his spells. He breeds greatfangs (huge dragon-like scaly flying jawed lizards he uses as steeds) in the hollowed-out mountain of Closecandle, and maintains several other strongholds (notably his first tower, Helnkrist), where "false Narmarkouns" (doubles of himself) dwell, that he has fashioned from his undead servitors so that Malraun and other foes will attack them, and not him. Most mysterious of the Dooms, and always popularly regarded as the least of them in magical might, Narmarkoun is an accomplished, patient magical spy.

Nelgarth, Rheos ("Ree-ose"): Chief Archer of Hammerhold, tutor and leader of Lord Hammerhand's yeomen archers. A loyal, capable man, always level-headed and calm.

Nelthraun, Jeszkur: Lord of Stelgond, in Tauren; a tall, patrician ruler of a small but prosperous hold, coerced into serving the wizard Malraun on pain of death.

(Norbryn: see Gulkoun, Garfist)

(Nornautha: see Quilnurr, Nornautha)

Onthras, Laerynd: knight of Hammerhold, in Ironthorn, pledged to the service of Lord Burrim Hammerhand.

Orthaunt, Illynd: long-deceased wizard of Ironthorn (where he once ruled), who now exists as a talking skull. He once made war on Lorontar, then Lord Archwizard of Falconfar, who presumably killed him and forced him into undeath, returning him to Ironthorn as a disembodied talking skull. This relic retains Orthaunt's sentience—though the wizard is widely rumored to now be mad—and wields some magical powers.

Osturr, Raeryk: long-deceased warrior hero remembered across Falconfar from an old fireside tale, "Osturr and the Three Maidens." The real man wasn't nearly as good, noble of intentions, and handsome as the tale paints him, but did carve out a now-vanished kingdom and give it firm and fair justice that made its folk prosperous and happy. In the tale, Osturr uses magical gates to journey to far places, and romance three maidens. In reality, he did just that, taking all three of them as his wives; they lived long and happily together.

Pendarlgrast, Melman: the President of Holdoncorp, a small, sharp-featured, lazy, do-little, pettish and very wealthy man given to firing employees at a whim, snapping arbitrary commands, and spending the better part of most working days playing golf on his expansive office carpet (which has been fitted with below-floor-level cups so he can actually "hole" balls). He works at (and seldom leaves, though he has a personal helicopter for the purposes of grand arrivals and departures) the Corporate Headquarters of Holdoncorp, on Earth. Note: a fictional character.

Perthus, Darlt: young knight of Hammerhold, in Ironthorn, pledged to the service of Lord Burrim Hammerhand.

Quillroque, Jackman: the Executive Vice President of Holdoncorp. "Jack the Rock" is in charge of the company's day to day operations, and is tall, loud, decisive, blustering, fearless, and ruthless. He loves a fight and eagerly confronts trouble. He works at the Corporate Headquarters of Holdoncorp, on Earth. Note: a fictional character.

Quilnurr, Nornautha: deceased yet still famous prostitute and "dancer of desire" (exotic dancer) of the Stormar ports, famous for her large and (thanks to enchanted ointments, applied before performances) glowing nipples. Swearing by them passed into common usage among coarse men inhabiting the ports, such as Garfist Gulkoun.

Reld, Mauksel: knight of Hammerhold, in Ironthorn, pledged to the service of Lord Burrim Hammerhand. Laconic, quick-witted, and possessed of a large, broken beak of a nose.

Rothryn, Devaer: deceased King of Galath, a young, handsome, and haughty wastrel youngest prince who became the puppet of the wizard Arlaghaun (after the Doom of Galath slew all of Devaer's kin, to put him on the throne of Galath). Utterly controlled by Arlaghaun, he became widely known as "the Mad King" because of his apparently nonsensical decrees, pitting noble against noble. He was slain during DARK LORD; Velduke Melander Brorsavar succeeded him on the throne of Galath.

Sollars, Pete: a pleasant, stolid, and a trifle slow-witted security "eyes" (monitor watcher) at the Corporate Headquarters of Holdoncorp, on Earth. Note: a fictional character.

Sorn, Malagusk: long-deceased wizard of Galath, who hollowed out his abode, Sornspire, from the heart of the southwesternmost mountain in Galath (now nominally part of the barony of Chainamund), centuries ago.

Striding Thunderstaff, the: Rod Everlar's private nickname for the Chamberlain of Hammerhold, the elderly retired merchant Ermeir Ahlowhand.

Syregorn, Qalant: a laconic, scarred man who has long served Lord Hammerhand as his most trusted warcaptain. Balding, weapon-scarred, and senior among the three warcaptains of Hammerhold.

Taeauna ("TAY-awna"): Aumrarr, who in desperation "called on" Rod Everlar and managed to bring him to Falconfar to use his powers as a Shaper to deliver her world from the depredations of the Dark Helms and the Dooms (wizards) who control them. A determined, worldly, experienced Aumrarr who harbors secrets yet to be revealed, she was captured by the wizard Arlaghaun, and then, at the end of DARK LORD, by the wizard Malraun.

Taeravund, Iskarra: best known as "Viper" from her thieving days in the southern port of Hrathlar (her longtime partner-in-crime, Garfist Gulkoun, prefers to call her "Vipersides"), this profane, homely woman has been a swindler all her life, and has used many false names (including "Rosera"). Possessed of driving determination and very swift wits, she is as "skinny as a lance" (in the words of Garfist Gulkoun), but usually wears a false magical "crawlskin" (the magically-preserved, semi-alive skin of a long-dead sorceress), that she stole from a wizard in far eastern Sarmandar, and can by will mold over herself to make herself look fat, lush, or spectacularly bosomed (and cover leather bladders in which she can hide stolen items). She now makes her living as a thief and swindler, wandering Falconfar with Gulkoun.

Tarlkond, Morld: one of Lord Burrim Hammerhand's three loyal and veteran warcaptains, in Ironthorn. A darkly handsome, stolid, patient man, who speaks only when he must, and sees much.

Tarth, Usker: knight of Hammerhold, in Ironthorn, pledged to the service of Lord Burrim Hammerhand.
(Telrorna: see Zrendel, Telrorna)

Tesmer, Belard: eldest of the sons of Lord Irrance Tesmer and Lady Telclara Tesmer, but won't inherit the lordship unless his three elder daughters predecease him. Darkly handsome, sardonic and "sophisticated" (dabbling in all the latest fashions, and cultivating a mastery of the arts, finance, and "knowing all that it's important to know"), Belard is deadly with both his sword and a cutting insult, and has discreetly sampled many of the women of Ironthorn, of high station and low.

Tesmer, Delmark: fourth son of Lord Irrance Tesmer and Lady Telclara Tesmer. Nondescript of appearance and quiet in his movements and speech, he's quick-witted, sharp-tongued, deceitful, lazy, resentful of his kin's successes, sadistic, and a "sneak" and tattletale.

Tesmer, Ellark: fifth son of Lord Irrance Tesmer and Lady Telclara Tesmer. Large and very strong, he has great endurance, even in the face of pain, but is ugly, clumsy, and much sneered-at by his brothers. The most kindly and understanding of others, of all the Tesmers.

Tesmer, Feldrar: sixth and youngest son of Lord Irrance Tesmer and Lady Telclara Tesmer. A handsome wastrel, prankster, liar, and dashing wencher and swindler.

Tesmer, Ghorsyn: second son of Lord Irrance Tesmer and Lady Telclara Tesmer. Large, strong, fair-haired, and ruggedly handsome, he is coarse and bullying, yet a successful and persistent scourge of Ironthar females.

Tesmer, Irrance: Lord of Ironthorn, one of three rival lords of that isolated Raurklar hold. Tesmer is the husband of Telclara and the father of (in order of precedence, eldest to youngest): Maera, Nareyera, Talyss, Belard, Ghorsyn, Kalathgar, Delmark, Ellark, and Feldrar (however, see Tesmer, Telclara). He rules the southeastern Ironthar valley of Imrush, from his keep of Imtowers. (The valley takes its name from the River Imrush, that flows down its heart to join the Thorn River where the Tesmer lands end and those of Lyrose begin.) Formerly owner of all the gem-mines in Ironthorn, and a buyer of many slaves. His badge is a purple diamond on a gray field.

Tesmer, Kalathgar: third son of Lord Irrance Tesmer and Lady Telclara Tesmer. Of middling size and nondescript appearance, he is often forgotten and overlooked, and resents it. Taciturn and farsighted, capable with his hands and in matters of war and trade-tactics. Scornful of his kin and restless to depart Ironthorn for a better life elsewhere—almost anywhere elsewhere.

Tesmer, Maera: eldest daughter and heiress of Lord Irrance Tesmer and Lady Telclara Tesmer. Of haughty manner and coldly-cutting speech, she has raven-black hair, sharp but beautiful features, and brains almost as sharp as her mother. She never lets anyone forget for a moment that she is first in standing among the risen generation of Tesmers.

Tesmer, Nareyera ("Nar-RARE-ah"): second daughter of Lord Irrance Tesmer and Lady Telclara Tesmer. Even more darkly beautiful than her sister Maera, she has long, glossy raven-black hair, flashing eyes (black pupils flecked with gold that seem to flash when she's excited or angry), and is sharp-tongued.

She devotes her every waking moment to scheming to gain wealth, power, holds over people, and greater influence in the Tesmer lands and beyond. She thinks herself the smartest of all the Tesmers, who will (she believes) one day rise to attain far more power than even lordship over all Ironthorn.

Tesmer, Talyss: third and youngest daughter of Lord Irrance Tesmer and Lady Telclara Tesmer. Tall, quiet, long-haired, and graceful, her movements always seeming languid, she resents being overlooked, pushed aside, and thought "feminine" and so brainless and subservient. She is vicious to others whenever she dares to be.

Tesmer, Telclara: Lady of Ironthorn, one of two living women to use that title (the other being Maerelle Lyrose). Many Ironthar rightly say Lady Tesmer rules her husband, and has the keenest wits in all Ironthorn. Two of her children weren't sired by her husband; although this has long been rumored around the Tesmer lands, she doesn't admit it, or identify which two, until near the end of Archwizard.

Thaetult, Alander: hedge-wizard of Tauren, coerced into serving the wizard Malraun upon pain of death.

Thalden, Evran: elderly, kindly knight of Hammerhold, in Ironthorn, pledged to the service of Lord Burrim Hammerhand.

Three, the: see "Dooms, the." Specifically, the three paramount wizards of Falconfar before the arrival of Rod Everlar.

Three Maidens, the: long-deceased women remembered across Falconfar from an old fireside tale, "Osturr and the Three Maidens." They were the three wives of Osturr, Raeryk (q.v.).

Thusk, Jelgar: knight of Hammerhold, in Ironthorn, pledged to the service of Lord Burrim Hammerhand.

Tombs, Sugarman: a debonair, whimsical, darkly handsome Earth writer of fantasies, rumored to have a lucrative and very shady career as a lone, "buccaneering" swindler. Note: this is a fictional character.

Ult: deceased wizard of Galath, who built Ult Tower, a black stone keep in the heart of the realm that he magically linked to himself, stone by stone, so the tower was like his skin; he could feel what was done to it and see out of it. Before the events recounted in DARK LORD, the wizard Arlaghaun took over Ult's body and conquered his mind, inhabiting both, and so gained control of Ult Tower.

Urlaun, Narl: a warrior sworn to Hammerhand, in Ironthorn; the younger member of a patrol that finds Rod Everlar in the forest.

Vanderthand, Marie: the calmly professional and pleasant front desk receptionist at the Corporate Headquarters of Holdoncorp, on Earth. She is elegantly beautiful and has a warm, buttery sensual voice. Note: a fictional character.

Verlen, Greth: a young, grumbling household

servant of Lyraunt Castle, in Ironthorn, with the title of "manjack" (footman).

Waerend, Larl: guard of Lyraunt Castle, Ironthar warrior sworn to serve Lord Magrandar Lyrose.

Welver, Derek: a sarcastic but sensible veteran policeman of Earth, desk sergeant at the local precinct in which the Holdoncorp Corporate Headquarters is located. Note: a fictional character.

Xarrental, Nollard: Royal Scribe of the Court, of Galath. A scholarly, well-spoken, sheltered man, one of the senior "younger pens" among the court scribes.

Xundaer, Loroth: the highest-ranking priest of the Forestmother, a lone forester mighty in magic who constantly roves the wildest depths of the Raurklor. Known as "the Highest" because of his rank, and often assumed to be the personal champion of the goddess. A tall, gaunt man who says little and wears ragged brown robes, or less.

Yelrya, Amaddar: a young, darkly handsome Stormar trader about to embark on his first foray north into the Raurklor holds, notably Ironthorn. His father, who had earlier traded in the holds, is now too elderly and ill to do so.

Yuskel, Irraunt: Duke of Yuskellar, a valley in the land of Tauren. So rich and miserly that he's known across Falconfar as "the Gold Duke." Inherited a pauper's title but built a fabulous fortune through shrewd mercantile dealings; is widely known to hate the nobles of Galath (for their protectionist ways and arrogance toward outlanders and outland titles, such as his own).

Zaervedel, Aumra: Empress of the Emaeraun Empire, a string of coastal city-states almost as far from Galath and the Raurklor as it is possible to get, and still be in Falconfar. "Impossibly tall" (over seven feet in height), sleek, and long-limbed, the Empress is the Overpriestess of the Seven Cults of the Empire, its Supreme Sorcerer, and said to be the most learned—and bored—woman in all Falconfar. She is also reputed (correctly) to be cruel, sophisticated, and masterful at intrigues and the spreading of rumors, purely for her own entertainment. She murmurs almost all of her utterances in a soft, unhurried voice.

Zrendel, Telrorna: undead sorceress of the Stormar cities, defeated and slain in spell-battle by the wizard Malraun decades ago, drained of life and spells but animated in undeath and bound by him into his service forever, to be "his slave beyond death." Largely forgotten, and left in Malraun's fortress of Malragard, in the Raurklor hold of Harlhoh.

Zundarl, Mallatar: wizard of Turentarn, in Falconfar, served by lorn he spell-disguises as humans. Zundarl is a cruel, ambitious mage seeking to expand the lands he rules; they are distant indeed from Galath and the Raurklor, but something—the magical backlash of a spell cast by Zundarl, perhaps—makes Rod Everlar dream of him.

UK ISBN: 978 1 844166 17 6 • US ISBN: 978 1 844165 84 1 • £7.99/$7.99

When he mysteriously finds himself drawn into a world of his own devising, bumbling writer Rod Everlar is confronted by a shocking truth - he has lost control of his creation to a brooding cabal of evil. In order to save his creation, he must seize control of Falconfar and halt the spread of corruption before it is too late.

 WWW.SOLARISBOOKS.COM

Follow us on Twitter! www.twitter.com/solarisbooks

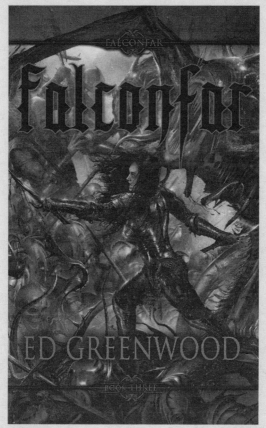

GAIL Z. MARTIN
DARK HAVEN
Book Three of the
CHRONICLES OF THE NECROMANCER

"A fast-paced tale laced with plenty of action."
— SF Site on *The Summoner*

UK ISBN: 978 1 844167 08 1 • US ISBN: 978 1 844165 98 8 • £7.99/$7.99

The kingdom of Margolan lies in ruin. Martris Drayke, the new king, must rebuild his country in the aftermath of battle, while a new war looms on the horizon. Meanwhile Jonmarc Vahanian is now the Lord of Dark Haven, and there is defiance from the vampires of the Vayash Moru at the prospect of a mortal leader. But can he earn their trust, and at what cost?

 WWW.SOLARISBOOKS.COM

Follow us on Twitter! www.twitter.com/solarisbooks

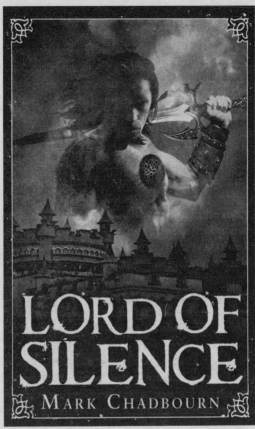

UK ISBN: 978 1 844167 52 4 • US ISBN: 978 1 844167 53 1 • £7.99/$7.99

When the great hero of Idriss is murdered, Vidar, the Lord of Silence, must take his place as chief defender against the terrors lurking in the forest beyond the walls. But Vidar is a man tormented — by his lost memories and by a life-draining jewel. With a killer loose within the city and a threat mounting without, he must solve an ancient mystery to unlock the secrets of his own past.

 WWW.SOLARISBOOKS.COM

Follow us on Twitter! www.twitter.com/solarisbooks